DEAD IS DEAD

Also by John Lansing

THE DEVIL'S NECKTIE

BLOND CARGO

DEAD IS DEAD

John Lansing

GALLERY BOOKS / KAREN HUNTER PUBLISHING

New York London Toronto Sydney New Delhi

Gallery Books
An Imprint of Simon & Schuster, Inc.
1230 Avenue of the Americas
New York, NY 10020

Karen Hunter Publishing,
A Division of Suitt-Hunter Enterprises, LLC
P. O. Box 632
South Orange, NJ 07079

First Karen Hunter Publishing/Gallery Books trade paperback edition May 2016

GALLERY BOOKS and colophon are registered trademarks of Simon & Schuster, Inc.

For information about special discounts for bulk purchases, please contact Simon & Schuster Special Sales at 1-866-506-1949 or business@simonandschuster.com.

The Simon & Schuster Speakers Bureau can bring authors to your live event. For more information or to book an event, contact the Simon & Schuster Speakers Bureau at 1-866-248-3049 or visit our website at www.simonspeakers.com.

Manufactured in the United States of America

10 9 8 7 6 5 4 3 2 1

Library of Congress Cataloging-in-Publication Data is available.

ISBN 978-1-5011-4756-2
ISBN 978-1-5011-4356-4 (ebook)

For Vida

Dirk: A short dagger of a kind formerly carried by Scottish Highlanders. Origin mid-sixteenth century.

One

Toby Dirk snugged the smooth wooden stock of his Ruger .22 semiautomatic rifle tight against his shoulder. He sighted in on the small Mediterranean stucco house directly across the street. It was one of many vacation bungalows built in the 1950s on narrow lots. Faded pink paint, overgrown shrubs, and tufts of green grass littering the burnt lawn shouted neglect, or poverty, or renters.

In this case it was poverty. The house was clean, but the home's decline had outpaced the Sanchezes' bank account. Toby had known the family for years—solid people, Hispanic, struggling to put food on the table. He had no issues with their youngest boy, Juan, dealing dope.

Juan wasn't his target.

Venice Beach these days was an eclectic mix of million-dollar designer digs and old-school bungalows from a time when rents were low and the neighborhoods were inhabited by immigrants, blue-collar workers, street gangs, and artists. Gentrification was crowding out many of the longtime residents, but the gangs were ingrained. Their members would have to be jailed or hauled out in pine boxes to make way for the upscale clientele looking for a "teardown."

Toby listened for signs of life in the house he was using as cover, but the precaution was just reflexive. He knew Mrs. Montenegro wouldn't return home from her deli until after dark. Through her rangy bamboo hedge he had a clear shot of Juan's driveway and front door.

Now all he needed was a target.

Tomas Vegas would be dropping off a bag of dope to his newest dealer in less than five minutes. Vegas ran his drug business with precision, just like his iron fist. You could set a clock by his daily rounds.

Unfortunately for Vegas, he'd set up Toby's girlfriend, Eva Perez, for a nine-month stretch on trumped-up drug and weapons charges. She'd been out on parole for three months now, but she was changed. Damaged. Not the same free spirit. It broke Toby's heart, and it fueled his rage.

Two men in love with the same woman. She had chosen Toby. Gotten his name tattooed on her shoulder in neat calligraphy. Had been pregnant with his child. Toby was head over heels, crazy in love.

Jealousy's a bitch, he thought, and Vegas was about to pay the ultimate price. Three shots max, to make sure Vegas wouldn't get up again. If all went according to plan, Toby would soon be paddling out into the Pacific, catching the late-afternoon swells at Sunset Beach.

Toby, twenty-three, had thick, unruly strands of shoulder-length sandy hair held off his face with a black watch cap. A faint shadow of freckles dusted his high cheekbones, set in a chiseled, angular face. His lean body was sinewy with the long ropy muscles of a surfer. His blue eyes were steady and intelligent. He had tested in the top two percentile in the standardized IQ tests at Venice High, and he had been offered a scholastic scholarship to UC Berkeley. He turned it down. All he was interested in was smoking righteous bud and being an outlaw.

He and his two brothers were doing just fine in that regard. If you played by the rules, you were a sucker. It had killed his father, and he wasn't going down that dusty trail. He didn't buy into the old saw that life was a bitch and then you die. Toby was sure of one thing and it guided his life choices.

Dead is dead. There was nothing else. No great beyond. No nothing. You created your own heaven and hell in the only lifetime you'd ever know, so grab life with two fists while you were young enough to enjoy it, fuck it, eat it, drink it, or smoke it.

Juan Sanchez peered out of his bedroom door and then silently closed and locked it. He could hear his mother working at the kitchen stove, banging her long wooden spoon against the aluminum pot, filled with enough black beans, garlic, onions, and rice to feed the family for three days.

Juan stooped down beside the only piece of furniture in his room besides his bed, a scarred wooden four-drawer dresser. He pulled out the tall bottom drawer and set it aside on his threadbare rug. On his hands and knees he strained reaching in, and pulled out a tightly banded roll of greenbacks he had taped to the back panel of the dresser. He slid the money into his pocket, then pushed the drawer back onto its chipped plastic runners until it closed.

Juan glanced nervously toward the door, averting his gaze

from the wooden crucifix nailed to the wall over his neatly made bed. He stood sentry at his window, waiting for the pounding of his heart to settle and his dealer to arrive.

The sound of Tomas Vegas's baffled mufflers preceded his arrival in front of the house.

Juan hurried quietly down the hallway, unnoticed by his mother in the kitchen, and into the living room, where his six-year-old sister, Maria, was struggling to pull a sweater over her Barbie's head. The bright-eyed girl looked up at her brother with such love and admiration, it washed over Juan like a bucket of guilt. He grabbed the doll from his baby sister, yanked the sweater's hole over the mop of long blonde hair, and handed it back to Maria. "*Gracias*, Juan," she said with an angelic smile. Juan returned a tight grin, nervously tapped the roll of bills in his pocket, and steeled his nerve.

"C'mon, be a man," he mumbled as he headed out the door.

———

Toby adjusted the rifle's sight, mindful of the half-inch play in the gun's trajectory. He had chosen his .22 because it was quiet and, from this distance, deadly as a viper. The bullets would rattle around in his target's chest, kill him dead, but he wouldn't have to worry about collateral damage.

Toby started a silent mantra . . . and slowed his breathing.

As he visualized a tight cluster tearing into Tomas Vegas, an antique electric-blue Ford Fairlane glided to a stop across the street.

Young Juan Sanchez ran out of the house and reached the curb before the screen door slammed behind him.

Vegas slid out of his car with a studied cool and sauntered

up to his newest recruit. With icy cool he checked out the houses behind Juan, up and then down Fourth Street toward Rose. He was preening like a fucking peacock, Toby thought.

The young men fist-bumped, exchanged a few words, and Vegas popped the trunk and pulled out a fat brown grocery bag.

Juan nervously dug in his pocket for the roll of cash, and as Vegas thrust the high-grade weed toward his newest dealer, Toby let out an even breath. *Now.* Yet just as he squeezed off a round, a car sped by, blocking the play.

He jerked the gun at the last second. The high-velocity .22 LR load flew wide, shattering a front window. Toby instantly readjusted, fired, and then again.

Vegas's face registered surprise as he dropped the bag, ripped open his shirt, stared down at two tight holes in his chest.

Screaming, Juan dove behind the safety of the Ford.

Loose buds of marijuana spilled onto the street.

Tomas Vegas fell to his knees and keeled forward face-first, stone-dead, in the gutter.

Toby Dirk madly grabbed for the spent shells, palming two from the thick grass. Where was the third one? A primal wail drifted from the target house and chilled him for a beat. Why the hell would anyone shed tears for Tomas Vegas? he wondered as he army-crawled toward the back of the Montenegro house. He had to get out of there before the shit hit the fan. When he was hidden from view, he jumped to his feet and leapt the chain-link fence.

Toby dropped the butt of the rifle into a Whole Foods bag he had stationed in the rear for that purpose. He held the warm barrel discreetly under his arm, close to his body, looking like he'd just gone shopping. He walked swiftly up the hill, being careful not to run, but flying with adrenaline. He tossed the bagged rifle into the rear compartment of his matte-black ragtop Jeep, covered it with a spare wetsuit, jumped in and fired up the engine. The sound of a distant siren could be heard, along with the plaintive screams of a woman. Still puzzled by this reaction—who would cry for a drug dealer?—Toby Dirk sucked in a lungful of air, clicked on Bob Marley, cranked up the volume, and powered away from the scene of his crime.

Two

Jack Bertolino stood behind a large hedge, trying for inconspicuous, and watched a team of heavily armed LAPD narcotics detectives pound toward the front door of a modest California ranch protected with security bars on all the exposed windows.

Jack tensed, despite himself. An ex-NYPD inspector, standing down, not invited to the party. In his twenty-five-year career as a narcotics detective Jack had personally served hundreds of warrants on drug and money-laundering cells. And now he was a casual observer.

The first detective carried an electronic battering ram that he wedged in the front door jamb and splintered the door frame.

The second officer ran past him, smashed in the door, and edged inside the house with his bulletproof shield leading the way, shouting "Police! Down on the ground!"

The operation was textbook perfect, until it went dangerously wrong.

The third detective, a young male, got to the front door, weapon raised, and froze in his tracks like a deer in the headlights.

A female detective right on his heels, concerned for her exposed men, shoved him to one side and entered the house, cocked and loaded, shouting for the occupants to get down on the ground! Now! Now!

The young officer shook off his fear, and as he was about to enter the fray, two LAPD black-and-whites came screaming up the street, sirens wailing, horns blaring, light bars flashing.

The cars blew past their location—and a man on a loud-speaker yelled, "CUT!"

"What the fuck, Kenny?" the female actress said to the first AD, who followed her out of the house. Susan Blake glanced at Jack with raised eyebrows and he gave an imperceptible nod of approval, careful not to overstep his bounds with the director.

Susan stripped off her vest, shook her shoulder-length chestnut-brown hair with an angry toss of her head, and strode across the crabgrass toward the director.

Jack stepped out from behind the hedge and started walking toward the camera crew, who were set up across the street. They were shooting a master for *Done Deal*, a new movie starring the next big female star.

Susan Blake had flawless skin, gray-blue eyes, zero body fat, the musculature of a gymnast and moved with the fluid grace of a dancer. Not yet a household name, she was enjoying strong buzz in the industry, and with two films in the can, she had the full weight of the studio behind her.

Jack kept his eyes on the star as he approached one of the off-duty motorcycle cops hired for security and crowd control while the crew was filming on a public street. The man clicked his phone off as Jack approached.

"A shooting couple of blocks over," he said to Jack. "They think it's gang-related, drive-by, possible drug deal gone bad, whatever.

Killed a banger and a six-year-old girl. Fuckin' Venice. Hell, we'll probably get a meal penalty this way. Make some overtime."

Jack didn't like the cop's attitude but didn't push it. He understood cops could get inured to violence if they were in long enough. He said "thanks" to the veteran and walked toward the female star, who was huddled with the director, Henry Lee.

Jack didn't hire out as a glorified bodyguard/technical advisor as a habit. In fact, he still wasn't comfortable with the title of private investigator. *Jack Bertolino & Associates, Private Investigation* looked fine on a business card, but didn't come trippingly off his tongue.

If not for his bum back, caused by an accidental fall doing cleanup at Ground Zero, he'd still be on the force. Simple as that. As it was, the accident left him eating Vicodin-Excedrin cocktails to stay off an operating table. Jack's doctor promised him that the third operation would be the charm, but after two failed attempts and months of painful rehab, Jack Bertolino was a nonbeliever.

George Litton, the head of Epoch Studios, had just paid Jack an embarrassingly large sum of money to sign off on the film rights to the kidnapping and sex trafficking case Jack had broken wide open a few months earlier.

Jack loved to negotiate with Hollywood types. On the force, if he had said no to the dollar amount of a pay raise, they'd say fine and pass him over. Every time he said no to the studio's offer, they upped the ante.

Finally, Tommy Aronsohn, Jack's good friend and lawyer, advised him to accept before they rescinded what he coined "the deal of a lifetime." Jack didn't argue the point.

Litton phoned Jack at home before the ink was dry and

explained his dilemma. The studio wanted Susan Blake to play the lead in the movie.

Susan Blake, the new "It Girl," grew up in NYC with a brother and a "stage father." A child actress who became an overnight success after fifteen years of small parts, commercials, and knocking on doors. Her father, a frustrated actor himself, pushed his kids into the business and managed their careers.

A renowned New York theatrical agent discovered Susan in a Broadway production of *Rent* and signed her on the spot. The man used his formidable power to open doors for her in New York City and Los Angeles, and Susan delivered. After winning critical accolades playing Juliet at Shakespeare in the Park, and then Kate in *Taming of the Shrew* at the Longacre, she started to land small roles in important films. The powers that be decided she was ready for prime time and threw the full weight of the agency behind her, grooming her for stardom.

Her meteoric success in show business also brought out the crazies. An Internet stalker had been harassing Susan Blake. Since the studio already knew Jack, they suggested he sign on as her bodyguard, and technical advisor, while she was in Los Angeles.

———

Jack approached Susan and Henry Lee, a diminutive man who wore a perpetual self-satisfied look on his face.

"How did we do?" Henry asked Jack, confident in the answer.

"She was all in. I wouldn't want to be the cop that screwed the pooch on her watch."

"I agree."

Susan took the compliment in stride. Jack hammered home the notion that even with all the prep in the world, every time you went through the door, you didn't know what was on the other side, you didn't know if you'd get shot in the face. That's one hell of a motivator.

"Glad you're on the team, Jack. Great work, Susan. Take twenty, we'll reset and go in for your close-up."

"Thanks, Henry." Susan raised her eyebrows and nodded for Jack to follow her. Their not-so-subtle movement together tracked by the crew.

"Something about a man wearing a gun," Susan said to Jack.

"If I didn't know better, I'd think that was a come-on line," Jack deadpanned.

"You wear the gun, I'll bring the cuffs. Now, that's a come-on line."

She got no argument from Jack.

"You told me you cooked Italian," Susan challenged, enjoying herself. "Are you ready to put your money where your mouth is?"

Jack was about to fire off a clever response when Susan stepped back awkwardly. Her smile faltered and the color drained from her face.

"What's wrong?"

"He's here," she said, deadly serious.

"Who's here, Susan?"

Susan paused before speaking, the silence filled by a passing car accelerating. "The man who's been stalking me."

Jack spun in place, spotted the black SUV already reaching the end of the block, about to turn. Jack pounded the pavement after it, but by the time he reached the corner, the side street was empty. Jack's breath was ragged, his back was tight, and he was pissed off as he walked back to Susan. This was the first time the stalker had made an appearance on his watch.

The off-duty motorcycle cop had pulled up beside the star to check things out, and Jack addressed him, "Keep your eyes open for a black Ford Explorer. Couple of years old. The driver could be trouble. Too far away to ID the plate."

"I'll check out the neighborhood." The motorcycle cop powered down the street and made the right-hand turn.

Jack turned to Susan. "Was it him?"

"I'm fine, Jack," she said, evading the question. "I'm sorry, I'm probably wrong, it could've been anyone." She was acting strangely, no longer scared. "No, Jack, I'm not sure it was him."

"I want you to sit down with a sketch artist."

"Really, Jack. There's no need to overreact."

"Overreact?" Jack said tightly. "I was hired to protect you, but I need some help here."

"Okay, Jack," Susan said, lowering her voice but unable to hide a flash of anger. "Please, I've got a scene to shoot. We'll talk later," and she strode away.

What was that all about? Jack watched Henry raise his hands in a question that went unanswered. Susan Blake stormed past her director, banged up the metal steps of her mobile home, and slammed the door behind her.

Three

Sean Dirk stood at the sink in the kitchen of the family home, wiping down a bamboo cutting board. His gray eyes darkened and his brow furrowed in concern as his brother's Jeep pulled into the driveway and glided past the leaded-glass kitchen window. Sean's reddish-brown hair was cut in a tight crew, and one tattooed arm was a solid sleeve of color. No jailhouse ink, but a rain forest motif.

The twelve months he had spent at Lompoc Federal Correctional Institution, housing low-security male prisoners, destroyed his sense of humor, hammered home the need for discipline, and kicked his violent proclivities up a notch. It also served as a master class in breaking and entering, and expanded his connections for offloading stolen property.

Once a month, on the full moon, he'd launch his one-man kayak for a midnight run from Marina del Rey to Shark Harbor, on the backside of Catalina Island, just to keep his anger in check and his head screwed on straight.

Toby hit the remote control and pulled his car into the two-car detached garage that was the same design and age as the family's

Craftsman house. The siding was gray-green with dark-brown wooden trim.

Jumping out, he grabbed the .22 and stashed it in a hidden compartment he had made behind a loose wooden board on the rear wall. When he rehung the rake, shovel, and clippers over the secret panel, it disappeared. He slid his surfboard up on one of the rafters next to a vintage longboard and a pair of kayaks. He shook out his wetsuit and hung it on the backyard clothesline to dry.

Gazing at the back of the house he and his brothers had occupied since the death of their parents, he gathered his thoughts. Toby knew questions would be raised with the murder of Tomas Vegas, but decided he could handle anything thrown his way. With his emotions firmly in check he jogged into the house through the rear door. Just another perfect day in the sun and the surf.

Toby Dirk idolized his oldest brother, Terrence, who was a nihilist and didn't believe morality was worth a crap. He had all but raised Toby after their father dropped dead of a massive coronary in their men's clothing store on Main Street in Santa Monica.

But Terrence didn't have to inculcate his young brother. He discovered, while fucked up on eighteen-year-old Macallan, expounding his theories on life, death, and beating the odds, that he was preaching to the choir.

Sean, the middle brother at age twenty-six, was an unapologetic hellion who had dropped out of Venice High soon after his father's death. He used his intelligence to live off the fat of the land and developed into a prolific second-story burglar and break-in artist. Why waste a brilliant mind? He was a good earner, but he got sloppy and was busted for selling a roll of stolen gold coins and a platinum Rolex to an undercover cop posing as a fence.

Mrs. Dirk, widowed and confronted with a mountain of undisclosed debt, never recovered from the shock of having to give up her membership at Wilshire Country Club. She turned to the comfort of Dr. Jim Beam, rarely leaving the sunroom in the rear of the family's bungalow, just east of the canals in Venice. The empties stacked up outside her door as she exponentially shrank in size. The boys knew it was just a matter of time before she disappeared altogether. The more they tried to help, the more ornery she became, until they finally threw in the towel. His mother had chosen to march inexorably toward her own prepaid burial site next to her philandering husband in the family plot.

All the while Terrence had constructed a well-defined business model for the family's criminal enterprises: five more years of pinpoint assaults, continue to launder their dirty money through the family store, keep a low profile, make conservative investments, and then cash out and buy a compound in Costa Rica and a summer home on the Scottish coast. They would all retire young enough to enjoy the fruits of their discipline and labor.

Nothing wrong with that plan, Toby thought. Live for the pump, and then live like gentry. He was all in.

"How was the surf?" Sean asked as he slid the cutting board onto an upper shelf, flipped the cabinet door shut, and turned to face his brother. At six-foot-three, he stood two inches taller than Toby, as wiry as the rest of the family. The main difference, though, was that Sean's time in the slammer had rendered his face unreadable.

"Two-foot swells, but nice curls," Toby answered as he swept the watch cap off of his head, shook out his hair, and tossed the cap onto the kitchen table. He avoided Sean's probing gaze as he opened up the fridge, grabbed a bottle of water, and sucked it down in one tilt of the head.

"You there all day?"

Toby didn't like his tone but played dumb. "Yeah."

"With your buds?"

"Yeah, why?" he said with attitude.

Sean opened the dishwasher, banged a plate in, and closed the door with more force than intended. "Friend of yours met his maker today. You didn't hear?"

Toby had already rehearsed the right face. "What the fuck, Sean? What're you talking about?"

"Tomas Vegas," he said, devoid of emotion. "Shot dead."

"No shit?"

Sean focused his stony eyes on his brother. "You didn't know?" It wasn't a question.

Keep the face. "No."

"You had nothing to do with it?"

"Fuck you, Sean!"

Sean took in a deep breath and let it out with a labored sigh. "Good to hear," but he wasn't letting his brother off the hook just yet. "'Cause a little girl took a bullet to the back of the brain pan. She's dead, too."

Sean's eyes lasered into his brother. Toby didn't blink, but his mind was whirling. That's what the lady was crying about. He knew it couldn't be Tomas Vegas. The pause that stretched out between them developed an uncomfortable life of its own.

"That sucks," he finally said, tossing the accusation along with the empty bottle into the recycling bin. His shot banged slightly off the 1950s red Chambers stove that dominated the large kitchen.

"Yeah," Sean said. "You know we don't need any heat, of any kind. We've got a lot going on."

"I know." Toby was loose again, in control.

"There're a lot of people who are aware of the threats you made against the scumbag."

The older Dirk brothers, overly protective of Toby by long habit, didn't sanction his relationship with Eva Perez. The beautiful blonde had the good looks of a Valley Girl, but her roots were gangland. Eva's mother was an exbanger who eked out a better life for her daughter. She'd cut off ties with her set and raised Eva as a single mom. Terrence and Sean didn't buy the conversion. They thought Eva was trouble in spades.

"Hey, I'm not the only one," Toby said. "I'm cool. If it happened today, I was on the water. It couldn't have been me." He kept his voice casual as he dug for more information. "So how did the girl get shot?"

"Stray bullet. Drive-by. They said on the news it went through a window."

He felt his heart sink. "Huh. Where?"

"Across the street from Mrs. Montenegro's house. That Guatemalan family."

"That's the shits," Toby said almost to himself.

Sean's voice grew hard again. "Nobody cares about a drug-dealing banger, but a six-year-old girl, they'll be lighting candles and sitting vigil until they find their shooter. It's a good thing you were surfing today, Toby, because your name's gonna come up, sooner or later. You'll be on a list, and the cops will be asking some hard questions."

"Fuck Vegas. Fuck that scumbag. I wish I had pulled the trigger," Toby said, not having to fake his anger. "But, hey, that's terrible about the girl."

"And your homies? They will vouch for you?"

"Sean, seriously, go fuck yourself. You're fuckin' up my mellow."

"Okay, brother."

But he didn't sound convinced, and Toby quickly changed the subject.

"Terrence?"

"At the shop."

"I'll jump in the shower and head over," Toby said as he sauntered out of the kitchen.

He was well aware that Sean continued to watch him move down the hallway. To escape his gaze, Toby took the stairs two at a time.

———

Jack Bertolino was staring up at the ceiling of his loft with a satisfied grin. A duvet cover was draped haphazardly over his nether regions and his hands were laced behind his head. His arms were heavily muscled, his body scarred, a roadmap of battles fought. A pale crescent scar under his left eye straightened when he grimaced or smiled. A man-made barometer of his mercurial moods.

Diana Krall's live Paris recording of "The Look of Love" played softly in the background. The loft smelled of garlic, onions, and sex. A perfect trifecta, Jack mused contentedly as the door to the bathroom opened and out stepped Susan Blake. One towel wrapped around her head, the other around her supple body.

"Not sure if that was a good idea," Jack said, smiling.

Susan matched his smile. "That's not what you shouted ten minutes ago. Were you taking God's name in vain or testifying?"

"The latter," he said, hand-raking long strands of damp dark hair off his forehead. The silver-gray that feathered his temples gave him an air of solidity; his intense brown eyes, danger.

"You can put the blame squarely on the tomato sauce," Susan said. "I take full responsibility. There's something about a man taking command of a kitchen that makes me weak in the knees."

"My good fortune. Still."

"You mean you don't like to shit where you eat?"

"Lord," he said, shaking his head.

"Oh really," she said quickly. "You should hang out backstage some time. Theater people are notorious potty mouths."

Susan took a look around Jack's loft. It was fifteen hundred square feet of concrete and glass. Two bedrooms, two bath, open floor plan. The front bedroom served as Jack's office, along with a galley kitchen, and a sliding wall of glass that opened onto a balcony that was reminiscent of a NYC fire escape. It had just enough room for a top-of-the-line Weber grill, a bench, and a handful of wooden stakes that were populated with green tomatoes.

"I like it," Susan said. "It's got a New Yorky feel."

Jack hadn't been looking to change his life when he stopped in Marina del Rey after dropping his son at his first semester at Stanford. But he fell in love with the area, decided to take a flyer and reinvent himself. He picked up the unit in a fire sale after the real estate bubble burst and the building went into foreclosure. He packed up his life on the East Coast, and the fourth-floor unit now served as his home and his office.

"You should get another boat," she said, "living this close to the marina."

"It's in the works. Hey, I'm gonna rinse off," Jack said, stepping out of the bed, "and we can finish what we started."

"Really, Jack," she said, coquettish.

"The pasta."

"Hah!" Susan barked in a friendly, astonishingly unlady-like way.

Jack loved the unpretentious outburst and said, "I'll save the rest for dessert."

Susan gave him a swat on his bare ass as he walked past. She headed over to the wall of glass and gazed past the FedEx lot next door toward the landing lights on the jumbo jets, strung haphazardly like constellations, making their final descent into LAX. The sky was midnight blue threatening black. The full moon on the rise just above the horizon was a startling pumpkin orange.

Her cell phone chimed. Susan ran for her bag, grabbed the phone, checked the caller ID, and with a groan let the call go to voice mail.

Jack was drying off in the bathroom when Susan's cell phone chimed a second time. Able to see her reflection in the mirror, he watched her walk out onto the balcony, quietly closing the sliding glass door. Jack didn't want to interfere, but he couldn't help but observe Susan getting worked up and then, red-faced-angry, abruptly terminate the conversation.

Jack stepped into his jeans and shrugged into his black T-shirt as Susan walked back into the loft avoiding eye contact.

The tension in the room was thicker than the marine layer threatening to envelop the FedEx lot.

"You get some bad news?" Jack asked, trying to tread lightly.

Susan spun toward him, ready to attack. "What are you talking about?"

"Easy with the attitude," he said, still relaxed. "I could see you on the balcony, the phone call. You didn't look too happy, and you look a damn mess now. You want to tell me what's going on?"

"It's none of your business," she snapped.

"Now, that's where you're wrong," Jack said. "I was hired to protect you. It's not your call."

"Stop pushing, Jack. You don't know me well enough. Don't overstep your boundaries."

He gave a slight laugh. "Our boundaries became a moot point tonight."

"Bullshit. We had sex, Jack. Sex. You only know what I want you to know. Stop talking or you'll get hurt. I don't want to hurt you. It's the last thing I want. To hurt you." And the fight seemed to drain out of her. For a split second she seemed a lot older, worn out with strain. "Please take me home, Jack. I've got an early call and I'm not feeling very well."

Jack didn't have to be asked twice, but as they prepared to go, he couldn't help but wonder what the call was all about. He had thought this assignment was going to be easy, but he recognized the tingle he felt on the back of his neck. Trouble was brewing on the other end of that phone call.

———

A lanky blond man with a hawkish nose and dark, close-set eyes, wearing a yellow and black bandanna, was hiding out in his black Ford Explorer. He was parked across the street from Jack's building on Glencoe Avenue. His telephoto lens was so powerful, Susan and Jack's images so sharply defined, that he felt as if he were part of the conversation. And then they stepped out of view. They didn't look very happy, the man thought. He laughed for the first time in days, knowing he was the cause of their discomfort.

The man's reverie was cut short by the arrival of a rusted Winnebago that rattled to a halt at the curb, blocking his view, and settled in for the night. The blond man cursed and was about to pull away when he saw Jack's Mustang roll out of the building's underground parking garage and speed down Glencoe with Susan in the passenger seat.

The blond man thanked the gods for this piece of good fortune and followed their car at a safe distance. The arrival of this ex-cop on the scene wasn't going to stop the gravy train. He had the star right where he wanted her.

Four wireless phones echoing in the empty loft announced that Cruz Feinberg was on the line. Cruz was a millennial computer genius who handled everything technical in Jack's company. Jack tossed his keys into a wooden bowl next to the door and hoofed it over to the kitchen extension. He picked up a millisecond before the call was directed to voice mail.

"Turn on channel two," Cruz said with enough urgency to spark Jack's curiosity. He picked up the remote from the couch, hit Power, and his flat screen pinged to life.

The onscreen tableau showed a scene of mourning: lit candles, a small shrine of flowers, stuffed animals, and cards penned in childlike scrawl.

And a framed picture of a little girl.

A loose group of grieving family members stood behind a microphone that was set up in front of their house. A female reporter introduced Mrs. Sanchez, the victim's mother, who was inconsolable, but spoke bravely in broken English through her tears.

"My Maria, she is only six. My angel. Gone. Who did this to my angel? Why you do this?"

The woman's eyes rolled back in her head, her knees buckled, and she reeled. Her husband grabbed her before she hit the sidewalk. Still, she dissolved in a flurry of choking sobs and stark grief only a parent could fully understand.

Jack knew this was the shooting that had occurred while he was on the movie set.

"Do you know the family?" he asked Cruz.

"Yeah, the Sanchezes. They live a few houses down from my place."

Cruz had moved into a garden guesthouse in Venice, near the Rose Café, as soon as he started working for Jack on a regular basis. The hours were ungodly when they were on a case, and living at home had led to hassles. His parents were sad to see him go, but glad not to be woken up in the middle of the night.

"Their son Juan is at the police station," Cruz said. "It looks like he was involved in a drug deal with the male victim and lucky to be alive. The word on the street is the deal was just pot. The police think it was a gang-related drive-by."

"Is Juan a banger?"

"No, just a kid, a worker bee. Still in high school."

The female reporter, caught up in the emotion, reiterated Cruz's story in hushed tones and drew Jack's attention to the screen. He'd seen too many of these reports and attended too many of these scenarios when he was a detective working undercover in narcotics. They always left him feeling empty and angry. Frustrated at the waste of human life.

"They're good people," Cruz went on. "Father's an illegal, afraid of the police, afraid of being deported, afraid for his family, and doesn't know who to talk to. His son needs help. I thought . . . ?"

Cruz had proven himself in the heat of battle, but you couldn't teach compassion and Jack was impressed.

"Why don't you and I meet for breakfast at Three Squares, and then take a drive over? When the emotion settles down some."

"That would be great, Jack. It's a heartbreak."

"I'll see you at nine."

Jack clicked off and listened to the reporter implore the television audience that if anyone had seen, heard, or knew anything about the shooter, they should call the Pacific Division of the LAPD. The phone number and address on Culver Boulevard flashed by on a crawl at the bottom of the screen, obscuring the dead girl's photograph and the makeshift shrine.

Jack wasn't optimistic. In his experience, if the shooting was gang-related, the community would be tight-lipped, afraid of retribution.

Their fear was reasonable, but Jack had ways of making people talk. If it was possible, someone would soon be held accountable for that little girl.

Four

Terrence Dirk was framed by the three-way-mirror in the Dirk Brothers shop, checking out the shoulder fit on a new black motorcycle jacket he'd ordered from Burberry. It was British, leather like butter, and had the retro look of a sixties Carnaby Street rocker. He wore black peg-legged pants, a classic English boot with a discreet silver buckle on the side, and one-inch heels that needlessly accentuated his height.

Six-foot-three, rail thin, with his rangy orange-red hair and gaunt face, he looked like the front man he was. Startling hazel eyes had the luminosity of a cat and showed no humor unless they were tempered by a fifth of highland scotch, and even then he looked mean.

Terrence stepped off the six-inch wooden platform where his father had died pinning the cuffs on a pair of Sansabelt slacks.

At twenty-eight, Terrence was now the reluctant family patriarch. He had dropped out of his freshman year at Duke, taken over the foundering family business, and found new ways to direct his own anger at the unfairness of life.

Retail was a mind-numbingly bore, but he learned all the tricks of the trade and discovered it provided a perfect outlet to launder money. Two sets of books. Doctored inventory. Inflated sales. Terrence vowed never to spend his time comparing the day's receipts to the previous years, while tossing back Mylanta on every downtick, like his father had wasted his life doing.

Within a year, he had expanded the store and branched out into custom-made furnishings along with handmade suits. He discovered that with interior designer pieces, couches, mirrors, lighting, and art, he could gain entry to his clients' homes to install the items. It was relatively easy to inflate the cost of materials and his own fees as a design consultant. A couch that was commissioned for two thousand could be sold for five, and on paper reported as ten. Five thousand dollars of dirty money could be cleansed on one transaction.

As long as he paid his estimated quarterly taxes on time and ran the numbers through a respected accounting firm, the family's fat profit margin didn't raise any red flags with the IRS. Everyone was happy as long as everyone got paid. The more money banked, the larger the commission.

Willful blindness.

This new line of work also put him in contact with a wide array of vendors, some who had a penchant for cutting corners, doing dirty deals, and fencing the occasional stolen object. Drugs—their specialty was stealing product and cash from other dealers—and high-end theft from the million-dollar properties that were interspersed among the older local denizens, guaranteed a consistent income stream.

The Dirk brothers, by selling to the yachting and country club set, knew when their marks were taking that dream cruise, the size of their art collection, and the number of carats in their wives' engagement rings. They were making inroads into the Malibu colony and had photographs of a number of show business clients on the wall behind their bronze antique cash register.

People loved to brag when they were getting their inseams measured or their living rooms redecorated. Retail hadn't worked out too well for Terrence senior, but he had left behind a loyal patronage and a perfect front for the Dirk brothers' gang.

Terrence, suitably impressed by his new look, turned his attention to his younger brothers. Toby was slouched in a gray Barcelona chair, mildly distracted, drinking a long-neck Pacifico. Sean poured highland scotch into two glasses, neat, handed one to Terrence before giving him the floor.

Security bars were accordioned across the front door, the CLOSED sign hung in place, and the gray mesh shades had been pulled down, obscuring the two front windows. The shadows of late-night Main Street revelers walking past the shop played across the translucent window coverings like apparitions while the Kinks' "Lola" drifted softly from hidden speakers.

Terrence took center stage. "The Diskins are leaving on the eighteenth for two months. They've got three Monet hand-signed color lithographs that we can switch out with copies and an original Basquiat from the eighties conservatively appraised at three hundred. Jerry has a client in Japan willing to go two hundred and a collector in Germany who'll guarantee two seventy-five. He also has a client who's Monet crazed and will toss in another fifty for the trio. He takes sixty percent and that nets us a little over—"

"They have a regular house sitter," Sean said, cutting him off. "She's a professional."

"And she takes the dogs to the Airport Dog Park every day at three thirty for an hour and a half," Terrence countered, clearly unhappy at being cut off.

"Why are we trading out the Monets?" Sean pressed. "They're going to see that the Basquiat is missing. It's a fool's game and diminishes our bottom line."

Terrence couldn't argue that point. "So we take as much as we can carry, in and out in ten."

"I don't like it. We're too close to Diskin. He generates enough income without stealing from the man. We'd be at the top of the list with the cops and the fine arts adjuster."

"He makes a good point," Toby said.

"And, we're basically working for Jerry. It's bullshit. We find the job, take the risk, and a sixty percent hit? The math's all wrong," Sean said, angrily tossing back some single malt.

"We still pocket a hundred-seventy-five K give or take," Toby said, thinking purely about the bottom line.

"Right?" Terrence air-jabbed Sean. Met with dead eyes and deaf ears, he upped the volume a notch. "We spend twenty minutes inside the fucking house and walk away with a nice chunk of change."

"Back the fuck off," Sean said. "We're just talking here. What about the grass? The deep-sea drop-off I pitched last month. We take the risk, but could walk away with as much as three-fifty. Cash dollars."

"And we risk having the Sinaloa cartel up our ass."

"How the fuck are they gonna know who scooped 'em? It's a random act, a one-off. And I can unload it out of the area. Toby and I'll drive the Mercedes to Sacramento as soon as we hit dry land. Ricky J's got five medical marijuana pharmacies in operation and is always willing to take discounted product."

"Toby?" Terrence asked, fishing for an ally.

"Day after Sean stumbled onto that tuna boat dropping bales

off Catalina, everyone in my crew showed up with a bag full of dope and shit-eating grins. Same story two weeks ago."

"They only had two guys on the ski boat running the product to shore," Sean said, adding to his pitch. "There was a half hour lag time between drop-off and pickup. The bales were floating out in the middle of nowhere, shouting: take me, take me."

Toby was sold. "And I like the pirate aspect. With two of us in kayaks, and you covering us in the Zodiac, we should be able to disable the GPS, hook up the bales, and make a run to the backside of Catalina before anyone's the wiser. Even if the Mexicans overlap our play, three against two, we could probably get away clean without firing a shot."

Terrence walked over to Sean, grabbed the bottle, and gave himself a generous pour. Stopped short of corking the bottle and tipped some into Sean's glass. He looked around the shop, at the midcentury modern furniture, the Italian blown-glass lighting fixtures, and the fine local art and photography. Imported woolen suits hung in neat rows against a wood-paneled wall. He wasn't happy.

"If they stay on schedule, we're looking good for the end of the week," Sean said, trying to close the deal.

The vote had to be unanimous.

Toby added, "My guys get a heads-up the day before the drop-off, gives them time to pool their money."

"I heard Tomas Vegas ate a bullet," Terrence said, taking a left turn, trying to catch Toby off guard, looking closely at his reaction.

Toby didn't blink an eye. "One Lenox scumbag down, there's always someone ready to take his place. Shouldn't slow down commerce. I ain't crying."

"So we're cool?" Terrence hammered the point, making the question a statement. "We don't need the blowback."

"Good to go. No worries," Toby said with his studied cool.

Terrence wanted to believe his little brother. He understood that a successful criminal enterprise was only as strong as its weakest link.

"So we vote," Terrence finally said. "All in favor of the art scam?" He was the only man to lift his arm. And then, "Pirates it is," and he cracked a wicked grin. "But we've got to do this right or everything we've worked for comes tumbling down around our ankles."

Toby growled, "Arghhh." And that set Sean to cackling.

The three brothers lifted their drinks in a silent toast to a successful venture and the wealth that would follow. After all, those bales of marijuana would be just floating out there for the taking.

Five

The summer rain canted toward the house and drummed against the picture window in the Sanchez family's living room. Within the dark, damp room itself the overwhelming sense of heartache was palpable. A small side window was boarded up from the gunshot, leaking, the water dripping down the faded yellow wall like tears.

It wasn't bad enough that their six-year-old daughter had taken a bullet to the head and their youngest boy was sitting in a jail cell for intent to sell marijuana, it's gotta rain, Jack thought. The dampness inflamed his back, which was throbbing as he sat uncomfortably on the edge of the brightly upholstered couch, listening to the father's lament, heavy with grief, while Cruz interpreted.

Mr. Sanchez hadn't slept, shaved, or fully come to grips with the nightmare that had enveloped his family. His wife was in the bedroom, medicated, unable to cope. Extended family and neighbors milled through the house, preparing it for the friends who would be stopping by later in the day to pay their respects.

Jack's gaze drifted to the blown-up photograph of Maria, bright-eyed with a toothy grin. He could tell she felt secure in the knowledge she was loved, and now she was dead.

"Tell Mr. Sanchez," Jack said, "that I'll find out who's handling the case and do everything I can to help. I've already put in a call to my lawyer. His name is Tommy Aronsohn. He's a good man who will try to get your son released on his own recognizance. If that doesn't work, he'll move for an immediate bail hearing on the drug charges. I'll need to talk to your son myself as soon as possible." Jack lowered his voice. "Plus, he'll do everything in his power to gain the early release of your daughter's body."

In cases like this, Jack was certain there would be an autopsy. The bullet that killed the young girl could be an important piece of evidence, and it had been reported that the shot wasn't a through-and-through.

Tommy Aronsohn had flown into L.A. that morning, checked himself into the Marina Ritz-Carlton, and hit the ground running. Being an ex-DA still carried enough weight to have a few favors granted. And Tommy wasn't troubled by pro bono work or afraid to throw his weight around when needed. He had put in a call to DDA Leslie Sager, who immediately agreed to look into the matter. A thoughtful move not lost on Jack. He had been in a committed relationship with Leslie, but career choices and political aspirations created a wedge that was their undoing. They were on a trial separation that was pushing toward permanent.

Jack turned to Cruz, who had finished the translation. "Also, ask Mr. Sanchez if he'd be willing to use his house as collateral for his son's bail, if needed."

Mr. Sanchez nodded his head before Jack had finished speaking.

Platters and trays filled with cold cuts and foil-wrapped casse-roles were being arranged on the dining room table. The doorbell rang and the sound of the rain became more pronounced as the door was pulled open by one of the family's young cousins.

"Jesus Christ. Bertolino," were the first irreverent words out of Lieutenant Gallina's mouth as he stood in the doorway, drip-ping water onto the living room rug. Gallina, with a jowly face, soft build, and receding hairline, looked older than his thirty-five years. His partner, Detective Tompkins, cleared his throat and was finally allowed entry, generating his own puddle as he wiped the raindrops off his nose and wire-rimmed glasses. Six feet, lean, and African American, he stood a head taller than Gallina. As Jack had learned by now, he was the more reasonable half of their partnership.

"Jack," he said.

Jack nodded his greeting to Tompkins, handed a business card to the father, and stood, ready to vacate the premises and let the good lieutenant go about his police business.

Mr. Sanchez pulled his wallet from his back pocket, but Jack put his hand over the grieving man's hand. "It's not necessary. You can call me, anytime, 24/7."

Mr. Sanchez tried for a smile as he slid Jack's card into the top pocket of his work shirt, but it never reached his tear-stained eyes.

As Jack moved toward the door, he was stopped by Gallina's voice.

"What should I know?" he asked, not pleased Jack had gotten the first shot at interviewing the family.

Their relationship was better of late, but there was no love lost between the two men. At best they shared a begrudging pro-fessional respect. Of course, in Jack's case, it was hard to warm up to the man who'd once arrested him for a murder he hadn't committed.

"What's the word?" Jack said, answering the question with a question.

"Drive-by. Drug deal. Internecine gang rivalry. The male victim was a Lenox Road banger. The gang squad's rousting the usual suspects."

"Who phoned it in?"

"A neighbor up the block in that white two-story modern job dialed 911 at the same time that Mrs. Sanchez called."

"Did he see the shooter?"

"That's a negative," Tompkins piped in. "Heard the shots and saw a car drive by. Late-model Japanese sedan. Coulda been silver, coulda been white, dark windows, didn't see the occupants or catch the license number. Wasn't really sure what had happened until he saw the male hit the pavement face first and dialed it in.

"We had two uniforms canvassing the neighborhood, but this guy's the only one who caught any of the action."

Gallina and Tompkins were robbery-homicide and would be sharing intel, coordinating the investigation with the gang unit. Jack didn't expect to be kept in the loop, but he could always put in a call to Detective Nick Aprea, his one good friend on the force, if he wanted the inside scoop.

"Need I ask why you are here?" Gallina asked as if the effort pained him. "But more important, whadda ya got?" he said, flicking the fingers on his right hand like he was playing standup bass.

"That there's a big hole in the family's heart and they're afraid justice might not be served," answered both of Gallina's questions, Jack thought.

It didn't satisfy the lieutenant, but he didn't press. "The mayor, being elected on the promise to lower violent crime," he said, "keep the streets safe and what-not, saw the little girl's face on the tube last night, woke up the captain, who shared the joy and dragged us out."

Gallina glanced over at Mr. Sanchez, who was huddled with Cruz. "The family will get all the justice politics can buy. You did not hear that from me." And then, "Let the man know that his immigration status is not on the table. If he plays ball, we'll do all we can to arrest the shit-heel who pulled the trigger."

Jack walked back to the couch and spoke in hushed tones to Cruz, who relayed the information to Mr. Sanchez. The broken man looked warily at the lieutenant and then nodded in agreement. He let out a sigh that caught in his throat and caused Cruz to turn away, not wanting to intrude on the man's grief. There was no relief to be had in the Sanchez house that day.

———

The storm cell rolled through Venice by midafternoon as it made its way north toward Ventura County, as predicted by Dallas Raines, the local weatherman on Channel 7.

Toby leaned back in his Tommy Bahama beach chair, placed in the wet sand directly beneath the takeoff path from LAX. He snapped a picture of a wide-body Lufthansa jet as it broke through the dense cloud cover, darkened the sky, and then roared out over the Pacific, the vibration thrumming in the pit of his stomach.

It was damp with a light breeze at Dockweiler beach; the blue sky radiated the kind of brilliance used on travel posters to entice out-of-towners to visit Southern California.

Toby checked his latest photo on his iPhone, posted it on Instagram, and then looked over at his girlfriend. Eva Perez sat in an identical chair, a lime-green scarf pulled up tight to her chin, framing her beautiful face, eyes closed.

A single tear appeared in the corner of her eye and streaked down the curve of her cheek. And then a second. Toby's heart caught in his throat. He felt a burning rage that he tamped down. He started to speak, to ease her pain, but had to wait for the next jumbo jet to pass. He wished he were on that flight to anywhere.

The air was thick, clean, and salty; the dark waves were white capped and broke on the shoreline in rapid hypnotic succession. The wide beach was all but empty, two lone lovers on a vast stretch of white sand.

"Why're you crying?" Toby asked as he wiped the tear from her cheek.

"Would you tell me—if you did it?" she asked, referring to the murder of Tomas Vegas, the gangbanger who had destroyed her life.

Toby gave her his most sincere gaze, which challenged anyone to doubt his word. He'd been perfecting it since he was old enough to speak. "I'd never lie to you, baby. And as far as the scumbag goes, bad things happen to bad people. Fuckin' karma."

Eva gave that some thought and her brow furrowed. "But . . . the little girl?"

Eva had lustrous blonde hair that was cut at a sharp angle just above her shoulders, and her wide brown eyes were ringed with gold. Her skin was what poets called honey and cream, Toby thought, or was that shampoo commercials? He didn't really care. He could spend days lost in her gaze and the rest of his life between her thighs.

Toby had no answer for the death of little Maria. He was thankful another jet lumbered overhead and filled the painful silence with its prolonged roar. Finally, "You were at your aunt's yesterday?"

Eva wiped her eyes with the back of her delicate hands, pulled out a Kleenex, and blew her nose. The trumpeting sound so belied her beauty that it made Toby laugh.

Eva fought the smile that was trying to form and shook her head yes.

"So you're in the clear," he said lightly.

"You know I was at Mona's. You told me to go," she said with attitude.

"And when did you start listening to me?" he snapped back.

Eva gave him a firm poke in the arm.

"So you're good," Toby said. "'Cause the cops might come around and ask questions. So, no sweat. Nothing to worry about."

Eva's eyes betrayed her fear of what might happen if she had another run-in with the law. She had told Toby that she'd lost a piece of herself, of her heart; she knew it was gone forever.

"I love you," he said roughly. "We're strong."

"Forever?" she asked tentatively.

"Forever. Believe it. Our love is . . . damn, perfect."

"Even now?"

"More than ever. I'll never leave you. We are all the way good."

But Toby knew there was one more target that needed to be run through with the karmic sword of retribution before he could move on and truly be free.

"Here, with me." He pulled his chair tight against Eva's, wrapped a comforting arm around her shoulder, and snapped a cheek-to-cheek selfie as a massive American Airliner sliced through the clouds and enveloped the lovers in shadow.

———

The Pacific Division Police Station on Culver was a modern, utilitarian rectangular box, with clean brick siding topped by a band of smooth beige concrete that ran the entire length of the building. A waterlogged American flag hung limply on a tapered brass pole in front of the building's entrance. It was as nondescript as the beige detention room where Juan Sanchez was seated next to his court-appointed attorney.

Jack said, "I just want you to know that there are a lot of people working very hard on your behalf."

Juan looked smaller, frail, and younger than his seventeen years. He hadn't slept and the death of his sister was tearing him up. He was wired, on edge, and the only thing keeping him upright was the electrical charge surging through his veins.

"Now, DDA Sager is willing to let you go home to your family on your own recognizance, you understand?"

Juan nodded his head, his foot tapped nervously under the table.

"To help you all deal with this tragedy," Jack went on. "But the story you're telling, what you're confessing to, doesn't jive with what we understand to be the facts of the case. We need you to man-up, Juan, and tell the truth."

"I was selling the weed to Vegas," he said, tight but losing control, "not the other way around." His resolve faltered and his voice cracked.

Jack gave him a moment to pull himself together. "And who did you buy it from, again?"

"A guy on the street, don't know his name. He hung around sometimes."

Jack squeezed the bridge of his nose and continued. "Tell me how it went down again, with Vegas. Maybe we can clear this up and get you on your way."

Juan took a sip of warm Coke out of an aluminum can. "We talked some trash for a bit," he said, "me and Vegas, and then I handed him the grass, and he handed me the money. And then a car drove by."

"What kind of a car?"

"A Nissan, a Toyota, could've been a Sentra. White, silver, not new. Windows had a tint, I think."

"Was one of the windows rolled down?"

"Must've been. I didn't see, 'cause I was looking at Vegas. Then I heard a *pop*, and the window in my house exploded behind me. I turned to look and heard *pop, pop*, and saw that Tomas got shot and so I dove. I dove behind his car."

Juan showed Jack the scrapes on his hands and elbows and the knees of his jeans to prove his point.

"And then Mama screamed. I didn't know what happened. I didn't know what. I'm so sorry."

Juan broke, his face contorted, and the tears started streaming down his cheeks.

"I never would've done nothing like this if I knew what was gonna happen. Little Maria, oh my God. I'm so sorry, my sweet sister."

"I believe that, son. I believe you."

Jack pushed a box of Kleenex across the table and let Juan gather himself.

"Did Vegas have any enemies you were aware of?" Jack asked.

"He was Lenox Road. Any set not on Lenox." Like duh.

"Not the SM18's, or the Culver City 12's?"

Juan sat mute. He knew the rules.

Jack had cheated death a few months earlier. A contract had been taken out on his life, and the young banger who was hell-bent on earning his first teardrop tattoo and full membership into the gang had missed his mark. Jack walked away from the scene happy to be alive. In between court appearances he had re-searched the gang activity that was simmering just below the sur-face in the Venice, Culver City, and Santa Monica areas.

"Juan, let's go back to the drug deal, okay?"

Juan looked at his lawyer who prodded him with a nod of his head. Juan followed suit, sucking in his runny nose and wiping his eyes with the tissue.

Jack continued, "There were five pounds of marijuana in the trunk of the Fairlane, Juan, besides the one with your name on it. You see my problem here? With you being the seller? Now, I already checked and I know you're not ganged up. Not yet, and this wasn't commercial weed, this was high-grade bud. What are we talking, fifteen grand for the lot? That's a major stash for an unconnected kid. And it's also a mandatory prison sentence. Work with me, Juan, and maybe I can send you home."

Jack was also having trouble for another reason. "If it was an-other gang who targeted Vegas, a known dealer, why didn't they grab the dope before driving away?"

"Because I was selling to *him*," Juan said, adamant.

Juan might have been seventeen, but he looked fifteen and was altar boy pretty. Jack knew he was more afraid of retribution against his family than he was of spending time in lockup, but he wasn't thinking straight. He didn't understand real fear.

Juan said, "He just paid me, that's why the money was in my pocket."

"I hate to tell you this, but yours were the only prints on the money, not Tomas's, no way," Jack said, lying, but knowing it was probably the case and willing to stretch the truth to get Juan to do the right thing. "And Tomas wasn't wearing gloves. You see what I'm saying here?"

Jack gave Juan time to process the new information, looked at the court-appointed attorney, and shook his head in frustration, but didn't allow his emotion into his voice.

"And one more thing, Juan, your fingerprints were not on the bag of dope, nowhere to be found. Now, you're a smart kid. You can see the problem we're having with your story."

The kid stared at Jack, holding on to his lie, but he couldn't control the hot tears that turned on like a faucet and streamed from his red-rimmed doe-eyes.

"I tell you what," Jack said. "Why don't you talk this over with Jeff here, man to man, and try to work something out so I can do right by you and your family? Your parents love you, Juan. They don't blame you for what happened to your sister. They're hurting and they need you." Jack was watching him carefully, trying to see if he was getting through. "You're their only son, and they want you home."

"Don't tell me you slept with Susan Blake. Don't tell me. I mean, even you don't deserve that," Tommy Aronsohn said with youthful exuberance.

Jack was getting caught up with Tommy in the hallway outside the interrogation room. A few uniformed officers ambled past, not paying the two any mind.

Tommy Aronsohn was forty-five with broad shoulders, a ruddy complexion, and an easy smile that could darken in a heartbeat. He had short-cropped hair that he covered with a baseball cap to keep it from severely curling in the rain. A light East Coast accent, but a heavy New York attitude.

The two men were like brothers. They'd been in the trenches together when Jack was a rookie undercover narcotics detective and Tommy, a baby DDA. He went on to become Manhattan's district attorney, a constant thorn in the Castellano family's side in the nineties, responsible for taking down twenty-nine made men. He now owned a high-end private practice with an office on Park Avenue and a grand home on Long Island.

Tommy was also responsible for Jack becoming a PI and had delivered a few lucrative contracts as promised.

"I didn't sleep with her," Jack said, poker-faced.

"Oh shit, so you did sleep with her. And she's beautiful."

"What did I just say?"

"Bertolino, it's me. And you looked down, you son of a bitch, when you denied it. What do you call that?"

"A tell."

"A tell! You are damn right, my friend. And you are one lucky son of a bitch."

"Are you finished?" Jack said.

The door to the interrogation room opened a crack and Jeff, the public defender, stuck his head out.

"Juan's ready to recant. He'll sign off on buying the drugs. First-time offense, extenuating personal circumstances, as Ms. Sager couched it, so he should get a pass. I personally want to thank you for this, Jack. And thank you, Mr. Aronsohn, you did a good thing. Oh, and send my regards to DDA Sager."

Jack gave that last notion some thought, and then turned to Tommy. "Do you still have juice with the Feds in Manhattan?"

"I could reach out. What do you need?"

"A conversation with the agent who handled Susan's stalking case in the city. I'm getting a bad feeling and something's not adding up."

Six

Toby straddled his surfboard a hundred yards off Sunset Beach. The waves were nonexistent and Toby sat calmly with a thousand-yard stare. He was digging the water lapping against his board, the warmth of the late-afternoon breeze, and the bright orange sun that was trending toward the horizon, painting the shoreline with a golden brush.

His friend Dean paddled alongside, muscled to an easy sitting position, and gave Toby an appraising look. "You look bummed, man."

"Nah, just a few things on my mind. I'm mellow."

"Not buying it, but I can help your disposition, bro. Wanna kick something into the kitty?" he asked with a wide grin. Dean had a short crew cut with an oversized blue bar code tattooed on the back of his neck and blue eyes that were bloodshot from the saltwater.

"Oh yeah?" Toby said, snapping out of his reverie. "Put me down for two hundred."

"Done. It's coming in tomorrow night. I'll have your taste on Thursday."

"For sure?"

"Guaranteed."

"Sweet. Meet me up at the Jeep. I'll slide you the cash." Now that Toby was back to himself, he realized he didn't need a friend like Dean being his pal, asking him questions that Toby didn't want to answer. "Later." Toby paddled for shore, no longer interested in the setting sun.

Jack decided to stop by the scene of the shooting and interview the only known witness of record. He wasn't due on the film set for another few days. Susan Blake was shooting interiors, scenes dealing with her character's family life and personal relationships. With Jack's contentious divorce still a nagging wound, he didn't think he was the right man to give advice on marriage. The director, Henry Lee, would be glad to have Susan's technical adviser off the set.

Jack pulled his sterling gray Mustang convertible to the curb a few houses beyond the Sanchez residence. The shrine that had been set up to honor six-year-old Maria had grown in scope: rows of lit prayer candles, wilted flowers that had been battered by the rain covered with fresh bouquets along with a grouping of soggy stuffed animals. He'd decided to give the family some privacy. He'd let Jeff give the family the good news about Juan's release.

There was only one white house on the block, so referenced by Lieutenant Gallina, and Jack was taking a flyer and stopping in unannounced. A six-foot varnished redwood fence obscured the property, exposing only the second floor of the dwelling. He was about to press the intercom at the front gate when he heard, "Son of a bitch!"

The entrance to the driveway was open, and Jack walked

toward the voice. A man who appeared to be the owner of the house was balanced precariously on an upper rung of a fifteen-foot ladder that had been propped against the side of the house.

Leaves, mud, and water were running down the front of his Hawaiian shirt, dark green khaki shorts, and thin bare legs. His orange Crocs were filled with the runoff. The copper gutter was stuffed with debris and the muddy water was now overflowing the blockage and staining the white stucco side of his house.

"I just had the fucking house painted," he said to himself as he threw a glob of detritus on the cobblestone driveway with a muddy thwack.

After one more handful of gunk the water started running properly and the man shuffled carefully down the ladder.

"What can I do you for?" the man said with a thick Brooklyn accent as he picked up a hose and trained it on the side of his now less-than-pristine house.

"Jack Bertolino," Jack said by way of introduction.

"Oh, okay, sorry, I hate doing things twice," he said, referring to the paint job. "And uh . . . my name's Mike Triola. Give me a second, will ya?"

Jack nodded and looked back toward the shrine. The Sanchez house was five doors down.

Mike finished spraying the house, sprayed down his own legs, his Crocs, and turned off the spigot satisfied that the sun once again reflected off white paint.

"You're probably here to ask about the incident?"

Mike clearly thought Jack was a cop, and Jack would not dissuade him of that notion if it would get the man talking.

"I know you spoke to one of my colleagues, but if I could hear your story firsthand, it might help my investigation."

"Happy to. Damn shame. Nice family. The little girl used to ride her tricycle on the sidewalk and come to my house on Halloween."

"Anything you can recount would be a help," Jack said, wanting to keep the man on point.

"Not much to say. I was doing a little gardening on the side of the garage, and I head a *Bap!* Or a *Pop!* It sounded like a motor scooter backfiring. Nothing more. It was glass shattering that got my attention. I started up the driveway toward the street, and heard *bap, bap,* as a Toyota drove by. Gray or white, older. I glanced down the block as the young man fell onto the pavement and I saw Juan crawling behind an old car that was parked there with the trunk open. When I realized what had happened, I jumped back behind the fence in case there was any more shooting. I pulled out my cell and dialed 911."

"So you heard, *pop, pop,* and saw the car."

Mike nodded his head.

"Were the windows rolled down?"

"No."

"Did you see a weapon?"

"No, like I told the other cops, I think the windows were tinted, gray or black. I couldn't see inside. I thought it was just a car driving up the street, a coincidence. I didn't put two and two together until I saw the kid fall to the ground. I heard his head smack against the asphalt. It was sick."

The order of events bothered Jack and he couldn't put his finger on why. Sometimes the mind completes a picture and misreads what really happened. It's why eyewitness accounts could be misleading and innocent men ended up in prison.

"I want you to do me a favor, Mike. Could you re-create

exactly where you were on the property, and what you heard and saw as the shooting occurred?"

"You want me to walk through it?" he said irritably, fighting his natural urge to say no.

Jack knew the right tenor of voice to persuade him. "Just take a second."

"Yeah, sure," Mike said, audibly sighing. He walked across the driveway next to a narrow bed filled with blue fescue and dark-green Mondo grass. He gazed skyward for a moment, trying to mentally re-create the scene.

"This is where I heard the first shot, and the sound of glass breaking." He confirmed his position as he spoke. "I started toward the sidewalk," Mike went that way, walking as he talked. "My view was still blocked by the fence, and then I saw the hood of a car, I think it was a Corolla, and I heard, *bap, bap.*"

Mike was standing on the sidewalk now. "The car drove past and I looked up at the Sanchez place and saw the kid fall forward, and Juan crawling. I was in shock for a second, not sure what I was seeing, and when it hit me I pulled back behind the fence. I heard Mrs. Sanchez scream—it was awful—and dialed 911."

"Just to be clear, you saw the hood of the car and then you heard the second two shots?"

"Yeah, I'm pretty sure. Oh yeah," he said, raising his eyebrows in question. "If I saw the car and then heard the shots fired, how could they have come from the car?"

"Thank you, Mr. Triola. You've been a big help."

"Like I said, anything I can do."

Jack handed Mike his card. "If you think of anything else, give me a ring? Sometimes things pop up in your mind after the fact that have bearing on the case."

"Oh, you're a PI, huh? I thought you were a cop," Mike said, not happy about being deceived.

"Retired, trying to help the family."

Mike nodded uncertainly and watched Jack cross the street. He walked slowly back in the direction of the shooting, measuring all the way. The only house that had a clear shot of the Sanchez house seemed to be directly across the street from the shrine. It was a fifties gray-clapboard two-story dwelling with a wrap-around porch.

Jack knocked on the front door, got no response, and tried again.

"She's at work," Mike shouted from his driveway. "It's the Montenegro woman, owns the deli down on Venice. She'd be okay with you looking around. She's devastated."

Jack waved his thanks and stepped off the porch into the side yard. A rangy stand of bamboo partially obscured the view toward the Sanchez house, but if Jack crouched next to the house, it made a perfect sniper's nest.

He continued into the backyard and sized up the chain-link fence to the street beyond. An easy up and over protected from neighbors' eyes. Jack made a mental note to canvass the street one over, see if anyone had seen or heard anything unusual the day of the shooting.

Jack walked back along the side of the house, inspecting the tidy bed. He was looking for footprints or markings, but knew the rain had probably destroyed any evidence left behind.

And then he saw it.

A shiny brass object shone from beneath a wet tuft of grass.

He squatted down and carefully pulled back the grass without disturbing the object.

It was a spent .22 shell casing.

Jack had a momentary thought to call Gallina, but vetoed the notion. If the information was made public, the shooter would be put on notice, making the hunt for him or her that much more difficult. Returning to his car, Jack popped the trunk and pulled out a small brown paper bag he stored with his evidence kit.

He snapped on a pair of rubber gloves as he jogged back. First, he pulled out his cell phone and snapped shots of the side of the house, the view toward the Sanchez property, the view over the back fence, the location of the spent shell casing, and then the shell itself. Then Jack carefully bagged the evidence. As a final precaution he crisscrossed the area to see if he could spot anything else of interest. He came up empty.

Jack heard a car pull to the curb across the street. He went back to the sniper position and watched as Juan Sanchez and Jeff jumped out of the lawyer's Camaro. The young man ran toward the front door and into the arms of his father, who came out onto the porch and lifted his son in a bear hug. Both men started wailing, and Jack flashed on Chris and the powerful love he felt for his own son.

Mrs. Sanchez ran out and wrapped her arms around her men. The distraught family disappeared back inside the house.

Jeff followed slowly in the family's wake. Jack was sure he saw the young lawyer swipe away a few tears of his own before closing the door behind him.

———

Jack slid behind the wheel of his Mustang, and as he drove away from the curb, he replayed the logistics of the double homicide, as he now understood it.

Someone had killed Tomas Vegas from a sniper's nest. A lying-in-wait charge, added to the murder beef, meant the shooter would be eligible for the death penalty. It didn't feel like a straight-up gang execution. Not their MO. Jack needed everything he could find on Tomas Vegas. He'd have Cruz compile a list of anyone who had a grudge against the Lenox Road banger and see where it led.

All in all, Jack thought, a fruitful visit to the scene of the crime. When he had amassed enough evidence, he might even inform Lieutenant Gallina.

In the meantime he phoned Molloy, the medical examiner who was handling the autopsies. He would be in a position to check the shell casing for prints—on the QT—and answer a few of Jack's questions about the lead slug he had pulled out of the skull of six-year-old Maria Sanchez.

Seven

Chris had always been the perfect son, Jack thought as he booted up his iMac and clicked on Chris's number. Jack's stomach clenched as he waited for him to pick up.

Chris had weathered his parents' brutal divorce while maintaining a 4.0 grade average at Saint Johns Prep, and won a full baseball scholarship to Stanford. No small feat. One of the reasons Jack moved to the West Coast was the proximity to his son. Father and son Skyped two or three times a week, just shooting the breeze, and Jack felt at peace for the first time in many years.

But happiness in his new home in California was short-lived as his past came roaring back with a vengeance. Arturo Delgado, a high-ranking Colombian drug lord whom Jack had outmaneuvered in a major narcotics bust years earlier, was hell-bent on revenge. His plan was to destroy Jack by killing his only son.

Delgado came very close to succeeding when he ran Chris down crossing the street in front of Jack's loft building in a seven-thousand-pound Cadillac Escalade. A murder attempt witnessed by Jack. Chris had been thrown headfirst under a transient's parked van, into a concrete curb. The catastrophic injuries sidelined Chris from the baseball squad and turned him to prescription drugs to assuage the psychological and physical pain brought on by the severe concussion and broken radius. The bone had snapped in half and jutted through the young man's perfect skin, an image that continued to haunt Jack. His pitching arm was now held together with titanium pins.

Chris had suffered no permanent brain damage, but his recovery was rocky. He suffered from PTSD, posttraumatic stress syndrome. He couldn't sleep through the night—afraid he'd be cut from the team, or never throw a fastball again, or get killed walking across the street. The orthopedic surgeon promised that his young arm would heal stronger than before, but Chris wasn't convinced and it was a constant source of guilt for Jack.

And twenty-five years in narcotics did nothing to prepare Jack for the gut punch he felt discovering his son's theft of Vicodin out of his Dopp kit on a recent visit.

Chris's arm was healing as promised. He'd been given the stamp of approval from the team's orthopedist and was doing light workouts. He was still seeing an off-campus psychiatrist and promised Jack he was clean, but Jack found himself holding his breath, and his tongue, whenever they Skyped or talked on the phone.

After five unanswered rings, Jack was about to sign off when his son's anxious face filled the computer screen.

"Dad . . . I know I'm not supposed to take sides, and I know that you've taken the high road, even though Mom, who I love, divorced *you* . . ."

"Yes, son?"

"But Jeremy is a dick."

"Chris."

"A dick, Dad. End of story."

Jack, of course, didn't know the beginning or middle of the story. "All right, take a deep breath, think before you speak, and continue."

"Jeremy thinks I should quit the team. Give up baseball. Concentrate on my studies and use Stanford as my calling card."

Jack felt a slight burn. He wasn't comfortable Jeremy had stepped into the dad role. "It seems he has it half right. That was half of the plan," he allowed.

"Right, but not until I gave it my all. If he wasn't a dick, he would understand that simple formula."

"What's his reasoning?"

"He kept talking percentages. Said only ten percent of NCAA players make it to the majors."

Any fool knew that. "Okay, so what?"

"As opposed to the number of Stanford grads with four-point-oh averages who get drafted by companies in the Silicon Valley. He thinks I'm jeopardizing my future. And now with the injury . . ."

"How did it come up?"

"He saw my report card."

"What's your grade-point average?"

"Dad!"

"Just asking, son."

"Three point five. My grades took a hit when I took a hit."

Jack understood the last jab was meant for him, and he rolled with it. That was part of being the real father. At least he was glad he could count on the loyalty of his son.

"Understand one thing, Chris. Your mom and I both understand how hard you worked to achieve your place on the team. Remind me, how many kids from your high school won full athletic scholarships?"

"Three."

"Did you deserve that honor?"

"Hell, yes."

"So, there's only one thing I'm getting from this conversation."

"What?"

"Jeremy's a dick."

Chris coughed a laugh and his young face relaxed some, but Jack had a feeling there was more to the story.

Jack sighed, trying to push aside his personal feelings. "He makes your mother happy, Chris. Leave it at that. Your life plan won't be derailed by Jeremy. So, try not to engage the man on that topic."

"Well, that's not going to be a problem."

"Okay . . ." Jack said, waiting for the other shoe to drop.

"Mom kicked him out of the house."

"Huh." Jack had to assimilate this unexpected turn of events. He had never been a fan of Jeremy's. Thought he was pretentious, but understood the man served a useful purpose. Namely, keeping his ex-wife in check at times of emotional stress. Jack didn't get the hysterical calls anymore.

"And now Mom's doubling down on phone calls," Chris said, almost in an echo. "I've got a new girlfriend at UCLA, and I don't want to share the guilt, but . . ."

"Point well taken, son. Let's give it a couple of days and see how it shakes out. You keep doing your thing, and let me worry about the rest."

Chris was clearly relieved by this offer. "Okay. Uh, thanks, Dad. Later."

Chris clicked off, leaving Jack staring at his own reflection in the computer screen. He was not thrilled at learning his wife was at loose ends. No good could come of it.

———

"Are you decent?" Susan Blake asked over the phone.

"I am," Jack answered, smiling despite his gloomy mood.

"Too bad."

"What'd you have in mind?"

"You have a sports coat? Grab it and meet me downstairs. I'm going to kidnap you."

"Best offer I've had all day."

Susan Blake might act a bit crazy, but she was talented, sexy, and a breath of fresh air after the emotional politics of Jack's family.

Jack brushed his teeth, hand combed his hair, stepped into some Cole Haan shoes, grabbed his black Armani sports jacket that dressed up his black T-shirt and jeans, and headed out the door in under five.

Susan Blake sat in the back seat of a stretch limo idling in front of Jack's building. The driver opened the door for Jack, who ducked and stepped in.

The cabin looked like the inside of the private jet Jack had confiscated from a Colombian drug lord in the early 2000s. Ostentatious, a bit decadent, sexy but inviting, with light jazz emanating from hidden speakers. It was all burl wood, gold appointments, and plush rugs. There was seating for eight and a fully stocked wet bar. Jack would discover later that George Litton, the head of Epoch Studios, had provided it for their traveling pleasure.

"Perfect," Susan said, giving him the once-over.

Jack said, "Back at you."

Susan could dress up a diamond, he thought. She was a knock-out, framed in the plush honey-colored leather seat. The amber lights in the compartment were dimmed except for one spot that lit her face and those killer eyes. Jack had learned on the movie set that actresses always found their key light. Jack brushed her lips and sat back in the seat across from her, letting the tension of the past twenty-four hours drain away.

The blacked-out privacy partition between the driver and the rear of the car was securely in the up position. The limo glided silently away from the curb, and Jack saw an opened bottle of Dom Pérignon chilling in a silver ice bucket next to two crystal champagne flutes.

Jack picked up the thick green bottle as Susan began to rhyth-mically drag her silk dress up over her milky thighs, swaying to the funky jazz bass guitar line. He put the bottle back on ice, never breaking eye contact, but knew from the increased beating of his heart that the only thing Susan was wearing under the her dress was her abundant gifts from God.

"You make me wet," she whispered, her eyes crinkling into a sly smile.

Jack never broke eye contact, but couldn't hide his physical reaction. Susan leaned forward, reached across the aisle, and grabbed Jack's belt as the limo made a right onto Admiralty Way and took a gentle curve past the moored yachts.

Jack said, "This show business is okay," and closed the dis-tance in a heartbeat, their bodies melding, his lips moving from her lips to her ear, down the sculpted arch of her neck, and then dropping lower. A man on a mission.

Susan sucked in a ragged breath and let out a moan that could have suggested pain, but was the opposite.

She clicked off the overhead lights.

Jack was the first to exit the limousine, not comfortable having someone open a car door for him. He had wild bedroom hair, blinking eyes, and a crazy grin as the paparazzi's flashes strobed. Outside, a crowd waited for a glimpse of the new "It" girl.

One of the photographers thrust his camera inches from Jack's face and snapped a series of photos, temporarily blinding him with the flashes. When his vision cleared, the man had disappeared into the crowd, leaving Jack pissed off he'd let his guard down. He turned back toward the limo and reached his large hand into the car.

Susan, powdered and perfect, demurely exited the stretch, held on to Jack's arm while he parted the seas, and nodded to security as they entered the art gallery on Abbot Kinney.

The gallery echoed with muted excitement. Thirty-foot ceilings, white plaster walls, concrete floors, and oversized canvasses. Their dramatic primary colors seemed to take on a life of their own glowing in the pin spotlights.

The crowd was as colorful as the oil paintings, populated with every sex, color, ethnicity, and age: actors, artists, agents, lawyers, writers, wannabes, and the press. The glue that bound the group together was having enough money or political cache to get an invite to the opening. A very self-satisfied group, Jack thought.

An agent from CAA stepped rudely in front of Jack and corralled Susan, immediately joined by a small group just waiting to pounce. Everyone wanted a piece of Susan Blake, as if her success might rub off on them and change their lives. It was fine with Jack. No biggy. He winked at Susan, grabbed a surprisingly good glass of red, and walked the perimeter of the room, casually taking in the art.

Each canvass featured groupings of elongated abstract figures, their bodies alien, Jack thought. One particular painting caught his eye and held it. In it two figures were standing shoulder to shoulder, looking beyond a picket fence at a lonely grouping of gravestones next to a red barn and stylized trees. Like father and son, he thought. No faces on the figures, but they gave Jack a sudden jolt of emotion.

Across the room, he found Susan glancing his way, while listening to a man with striking red hair. He was so tall and thin, he could have been the model for the painting. He was dressed in a tight-fitting black sports jacket, similar to Jack's, pointed black boots, but his black and purple silk button-down shirt probably ran him five hundred bucks. Business must be good, Jack thought. Susan smiled and gestured for Jack to join them.

Jack was more than comfortable letting Susan do her own thing—these were her people, after all. He knew there might be blowback coming his way just escorting the star, but he felt great, light on his feet, and a little buzzed. What the hell, he thought as he crossed the room and sidled up to Susan.

"Jack, I want you to meet Terrence Dirk. He owns one of the most forward-thinking shops in Santa Monica. He has offered to take a look at my living room and help me out with a few design ideas I had. If I'm going to be staying longer than originally planned," she said, raising her eyebrows, "I want to make the house my own. And he did such a great job with Henry Lee's beach home."

If Terrence Dirk was good enough for Henry . . .

Jack proffered his hand. Terrence shook with more pressure then expected. That was accompanied by the steely look in the man's eyes that Jack recognized from years in the field.

"Are you the artist?" Jack asked.

"Don't I wish," Terrence said with an easy smile. "That's him over in the corner."

A middle-aged man with a furrowed brow and flyaway hair, five o'clock shadow, multicolored paint-splattered jeans and sneakers, and a rumpled navy-blue blazer was being interviewed on camera. He looked perplexed at the questions being thrown his way by the reporter.

Terrence said, holding his thumb and index finger together, "John Piccard is on the verge of greatness. His work is under-priced at the moment. Buying him now, well, it's an annuity. In five years' time you'll triple your investment."

"I'll keep that in mind," Jack said. That painting he'd been studying had a price tag of eighteen thousand dollars. It had never occurred to Jack that he might spend that kind of money on art.

"He already has a piece hanging in MoMA, and I've been fortunate enough to place a few of his paintings with discerning families. Does he speak to you?" Terrence asked.

"Yeah, there's something about them. Not sure what the artist's trying to say, but yeah, he does." Jack sounded surprised at his own reaction, eliciting a comfortable smile from Susan and Terrence.

Susan looked over Jack's shoulder at the painting that had stopped him. She told Terrence she'd call and set up an appointment early next week to talk design. She slid her arm through Jack's and they were off.

"How'd you do that?" Jack asked. "I would've been stuck talking to the guy all night."

"It's a necessary skill set. No one takes offense." She gave him an appraising look, but not the kind used for a painting. "So, Mr. Bertolino, why don't we take a shower and then get dirty?"

"I like the way you think." He escorted Susan out onto Abbot Kinney, past the sea of paparazzi, excited voices shouting her name, flashing strobes playing off their faces, into the waiting limo.

Mercury vapor security lights cast a green pallor over the exposed parking lot at St. Joseph's Hospital in Burbank. The treacly sweet smell of night-blooming jasmine wafted in from the garden that fronted the parking lot and left Toby Dirk feeling slightly nauseous. Or maybe his Venti house blend had set his teeth on edge. Or the accidental death of the Sanchez girl.

Visiting hours were almost over, and the lot was three-quarters empty. He had plenty of cover, he thought as a group of nurses finishing their shift all but ran to their cars and headed home.

Toby knew what Dr. Paul Brimley looked like; he was just doing his homework. Is that him? Toby wondered as he slid down in his black Jeep, his pulse accelerating a notch. No, shit, he thought, and then, yes, the revolving door spun again and, okay, there he is. The man himself.

Toby waited until the doors on the elevator closed, taking the doctor to the underground parking. He did a U-turn and waited curbside with a clear view back toward the pay booth, ready to pick up the doctor as he exited the lot.

The fucker drove up in his silver Lexus LS. Pretentious prick, Toby thought. Enjoy the ride, asshole. While you can.

The doctor exchanged a few pleasantries with the man in the booth, pulled out without signaling, and made a right-hand turn. Toby let the car take the lead by a half block before following in his wake onto the 134 freeway heading north. He knew where he was headed.

He liked the hunt more than the killing. The killing was a product of circumstance, of necessity, but the hunt, that was the sport. And he was good at it.

His mentor, Dewey, was an old surfer mystic who held on to his longboard as tightly as the belief system that he proselytized, but nobody seemed to mind. He was also a deer hunter and taught Toby how to shoot. When the sage man went on a hunt, he walked into the wild with a single bullet. Evened the playing field, he would say.

Dewey would field-dress the deer and hump out the carcass using winches and ropes no matter how far down country he drifted.

He taught Toby about patience, stillness, and meditation. About discovering the ancient trails the deer had followed for generations, understanding the pattern of behavior that had controlled the animal's destiny for centuries. It was hardwired into their DNA.

As a result Toby was never surprised to see a buck with a full rack grazing next to the San Diego Freeway off Mulholland. Small herds still thrived in the middle of one of the largest cities on the planet.

Toby applied the same skill set he had learned at Dewey's side to his own hunt. Men lived in patterns, close to home, in their comfort zone, and then ventured out in concentric circles. Once you understood a man's patterns, hunting them and then killing them became a matter of course. As long as you didn't set patterns yourself, and leave clues that the police could follow. The hunter becoming the hunted.

Toby never killed a man who didn't need killing. His first was a drug rip-off gone bad. The dealer drew down on the Dirk brothers instead of handing over the dope and cash as instructed. Toby had to kill or be killed. Cost of doing business, outlaw business, and Toby didn't lose any sleep over it.

The Sanchez girl had been an accident. She could also be his undoing if he wasn't careful. It weighed heavily on him. Collateral damage he had planned to avoid. In time, the guilt would fade, Toby knew. But for now, it was a living hell.

Toby spaced out and almost missed the doctor's Lexus as it merged left from the 134 onto 101 north. He knew the doctor was heading for the hills on top of Reseda Boulevard. This wasn't the first time he'd followed the man home.

The prick never used his fucking signals, Toby thought as he pulled hard on the steering wheel, skidding across two lanes of traffic. He'd check the doctor's pattern one last time. Tomorrow night he'd end the butcher's life with as much mercy as the doc had shown his unborn son.

Eight

"No prints on the cartridge," Jack said as he snapped off his cell phone and stepped up to his regular booth at Hal's Bar and Grill. Detective Nick Aprea was already seated across from Tommy Aronsohn, who was picking at the fries on his plate, having decimated his bloody cheeseburger.

Nick was as tall as Jack, but thicker, solidly muscled with a faded Marine tattoo on his beefy forearm, thick salt-and-pepper hair he wore brushed back, and a trace of childhood acne that rendered him more attractive to the feminine set. He had dark eyes that made bad men tell their secrets, and a smile that cut both ways.

Two cops and a lawyer who had spent most of his career working with cops. There was no question that the three men having lunch were law dogs.

Jack slid in next to Tommy, took a sip of his diet Coke, and chased it with a few of his own fries before continuing with Nick.

"A fragmented .22 entered the back of the kid's skull. Two .22's in Vegas's chest. It was a tight grouping. One ended up in his heart, one banged off his spine and tore up his lung. The spine slug is too damaged for comparison, but the one to the heart is intact."

"FYI, here's the vic—I mean, scumbag's résumé," Nick said, sliding a folder containing Tomas Vegas's mug shots, criminal history, and formidable rap sheet across the table to Jack. "Shred it when you're done."

"That was some solid shooting," Tommy observed.

"Tell that to the Sanchez family," Nick said tightly.

"From that distance . . ." Tommy said, finishing his thought undeterred.

It was a point well taken and not overlooked by the table.

"We'll give him a medal when we run him to ground," Jack added, needling his friend. He couldn't help himself.

Nick looked at his tuna sandwich as if he was going to ask it a question and took a bite instead. "So, you're not feeling the gang connection?" he asked Jack with his mouth full.

"It might be connected," Jack said, "but how many bangers you heard of that fired from a sniper's nest? They like to get up close and personal. It's that machismo thing."

No argument from Nick, who had butted heads with more than his share of street gangsters in Los Angeles, working narcotics with twenty-three years in.

"Why didn't they take the dope?" Tommy asked.

"Good question," Jack said. "Thoughts?"

"They didn't know the drugs were there?" Tommy continued, spinning. "They were afraid of being ID'd?"

"The shooter knew enough to set up an ambush on Vegas's delivery route," Jack pointed out. "And you were right about the shooting being solid. No question that Vegas was the intended target."

"It wasn't about the drugs," Nick said and emptied his second shot of Herradura Silver. "It was retribution. Some fuckin' slight. He might have looked at someone sideways. Who knows with these jamokes?" But the question left him feeling uncomfortable. "Give the information to Gallina, let him run with it."

"Man won't change his colors," Jack said. "He's comfortable with the drive-by. Path of least resistance. He wants to put the case to bed and get a pat on the ass from the mayor."

"The mayor's that persuasion?" Tommy asked, eyes crinkling into a smile.

"Ask his wife."

Nick barked a laugh.

"Do we know their supplier?" Jack asked.

"I'm thinking Sinaloa," Nick said. "The Lenox gang has ties to the Mexican mafia who have ties to the cartel."

"We know they're not averse to sending a shooter if someone's double-dipping," Jack said, knowing he wasn't educating Nick to the cartel's behavior.

"Or on the payroll," Tommy said, referring to a drug dealer turned informant being managed by the Feds.

"The shooting feels too clean," Jack said. "They would've shredded him to make a statement. But it's something to think about. I'll put in a call to Kenny Ortega and see if the DEA had Vegas in their database, or on their radar screen."

Kenny Ortega was an old friend and DEA agent Jack had a major history with. Jack, Kenny, and a CI named Mia had shut down a Colombian drug lord and put a ton of cocaine on the table.

Nick shot a glance through a six-foot-tall metal sculpture that divided the dining room from the bar, checked out a score on the wall-mounted television behind the bar. "Fuckin' Lakers," he said under his breath, and then with a wolf grin, "So, Jack, you nailed her, right?"

Jack played it straight, ignoring Nick's knowing gaze and Tommy's chuckle.

"Who?"

"Who, my ass. Come on, bro. . . . You made the eleven o'clock news, for crissakes. You were all over TMZ. Looked like a kid on prom night with the limo and that crazy hair and goofy grin. My wife replayed it for me in slo-mo three times. We had a good laugh. No doubt about it, my friend, you nailed her."

"You were laughing with me, right?" he said, not smiling but not upset.

"You made my night."

"I think your detecting skills are getting rusty." He took a bite of another fry, letting the male camaraderie die down before he deflected their attention. "We should get a car on the Sanchez house. Get someone to watch young Juan."

Nick waved his hand. "Call Gallina; it's his case. Bring him up to speed, he can get it done."

Jack glanced over at Tommy, who stifled a shit-eating grin and nodded his head in agreement.

"Fuck." But Jack knew it was the best course of action. He couldn't roam for too long. In the end, Gallina had to take credit for the case.

"Yah know, Bertolino, I see you, I get an instant pain in my gut," Gallina said from a crouched position as he eyeballed the view of the Sanchez house from the alleged sniper's nest. Gallina grunted, and his knees cracked as he stood up. The oldest young man Jack knew.

"It's a gift," Jack said.

"Don't get your tighties in a wad, it's not personal anymore. I see you, I know a clear-cut case is going to get complicated. My life's complicated enough."

Jack couldn't argue the point.

"It's a clean shot," Gallina conceded. "No footprints?"

"If there were, with the rain and all, there was nothing left."

"And you didn't call me why?"

"You're here now. I saved you a few steps."

"I don't even know what that means," Gallina said as he walked to the chain-link fence that spanned the rear of the property. He checked out the quiet of the suburban street beyond. "Anybody see anything?"

"Cruz knocked on all the doors . . . nothing unusual. The shooter had perfect cover."

"If it *was* the shooter and not some neighborhood kid gunning for squirrel."

Jack handed over the envelope with the shell casing and the photos documenting the exact location and time the evidence was discovered.

Gallina let out a labored sigh, too frustrated by the potential legal ramifications to go into it. "Prints?"

"Clean as far as I can tell."

"I'll get Malloy on it."

"Can you run the slug through IBIS?" Jack asked, knowing the police were keeping a computer database of bullets used in crimes. The Integrated Ballistic Identification System. Every slug has an identifier, a personal mark created by the spin of the lead as it travels down the gun barrel. If there was a match with a bullet used in another crime, the case could be cracked wide open.

Gallina didn't deem the request worthy of a response. An aggravated nod was all he could muster. "And I'll have some of my men recanvass the block. Sometimes having a badge loosens lips," he said pointedly.

"You'd think the mayor's fifty grand would help." But both men knew potential retribution from the Lenox Road gang would keep mouths cemented shut. Dead men couldn't spend reward money, and the dollar amount wasn't enough to bankroll a new life, in a different town, with a new identity.

Jack made a mental note to give Malloy a heads-up on the shell casing. "Can we get a black-and-white on the Sanchez house? Juan was pissing himself. Willing to take the fall rather than implicate Vegas. He's got a plateful of reasons to be concerned."

Both men paused as their attention was grabbed by a neighborhood girl struggling to light a votive candle with her mother's Bic lighter. At last she added it to the growing shrine in front of the Sanchez residence. Mother and daughter genuflected, made the sign of the cross, clasped hands, and continued down the street.

"I'll talk to Burns," Gallina said. "Should be able to get it done." Burns was the newly elected mayor's city attorney and main fixer. "The last thing the mayor needs is having to explain to his constituency why he allowed more grief for the Sanchez family that he could've prevented."

"Thanks."

"And you buy Triola's story about the time line of shots fired?"

"I walked him through it. It's solid."

"I'll have Tompkins bring him in and take a statement."

"Just a thought," Jack said, trying to be politic, "but we should keep this on the QT."

Gallina bristled at the implied team play. "Am I losing my mind here? There is no *we* in this equation, Jack. And if we don't have anything else for the mayor's press conference this afternoon, this is gonna lead the local news. Not to mention, a thank-you is in order, fuck you very much. I should run you in for evidence tampering in a murder investigation. Or have you forgotten in your retirement how the law operates?"

"No sense warning the shooter," Jack said, reiterating this point.

"Yeah, whatever. Find me something else or all bets are off."

Gallina started for his gray unmarked Crown Vic that every punk in the country could make as a police vehicle. He turned after keying the door open. "You know there are 175,000 white and gray late-model Sentras and Toyotas registered in L.A. County?"

Jack knew where Gallina was going. "Even if it wasn't a drive-by, the occupants might have seen something." If the driver had been ID'd, Jack knew, the cops could have whittled down the numbers.

"Shit out of luck for us," Gallina said as he slid behind the wheel of the car, "but I'll keep my guys on it. The mayor wants a resolution posthaste." He slammed the door. End of conversation. Gallina's tires squealed as he pulled away from the curb and powered past the crime scene.

That went worse than expected, Jack thought, praying he hadn't made a big mistake. And Jack wasn't a religious man.

———

"Jack Bertolino, isn't she too young for you?" Jeannine said in a melodic, teasing voice that sounded like nails on a blackboard.

Jack fought the urge to hang up on his ex-wife, knowing he would just delay the inevitable. "What're you talking about?" he asked, feigning ignorance, struggling to hide his irritation. It didn't work and just egged Jeannine on.

"Really, Jack, my phone was ringing off the hook this morning. Susan Blake . . . ? She's young enough to be your daughter."

"I was on the job," he said, not taking the bait, but knowing he'd already been filleted.

"Is that what they call it these days?" Droll.

"What can I do for you, Jeannine?"

"Like father, like son."

"Will you please get to the point?"

"Don't bully me, Jack. I won't put up with your condescension."

"You called me, for the love of Christ, Jeannine, what can I help you with?"

"Your son has a girlfriend."

Jack let out a sigh that couldn't be taken back. "I'll remember to congratulate him the next time we speak."

"How long has it been?"

"I spoke with him yesterday."

"Well, at least he answered your call."

"How's Jeremy?" Jack asked, taking a high dive into a dry pool.

"He told you, didn't he?"

Jack didn't want to throw Chris under the bus, but desperate times. . . . "He was upset. Didn't want you caught in the middle of a misunderstanding."

"Is that what it was? Well . . . your son won't talk to me about baseball anymore." She sounded truly aggrieved, and Jack could sympathize with her there. She had attended countless ball games through the years. "Really, the person who has been behind him all along. Remember how proud he was playing t-ball, Jack? He was only five and so determined. And then Little League. This has been his dream since forever, Jack."

"So, what does he talk about?"

"That's just it. He doesn't. He doesn't really engage at all. Not since Jeremy, the meddling fool, opened his big mouth. Chris has cut me out of his life." Jeannine's voice broke, and her pain was palpable. It stopped Jack in his tracks. The love they had shared in twenty years of marriage was a distant memory, only sparked on occasion by the love they both shared for their son.

"I think he's afraid, Jack."

That was a gut punch. Jack was the cause of his son's pain.

"You're right, with good cause," he admitted. "But he's working on it, his arm's healed, and he'll work it out. We raised a good kid, strong kid . . ." Jack's voice trailed off.

"He won't let me help," she cried. A silent weeping that had the power to chisel through Jack's armor.

"I know, it hurts," he said quietly. "But he's a young man, and I believe he'll come out the other end stronger."

Jack was met with an excruciating silence while Jeannine gathered herself.

"I've gotta go, Jeannine, I'm on a job."

"But you've got enough time for Susan Blake."

"I'm hanging up," Jack said gently.

"Call your son and call me back after."

"Okay."

"You're not going to call me back, are you, Jack?"

"I'll call," he lied, and disconnected.

———

Courtroom 2B at the Los Angeles Superior Airport Courthouse was filling in fits and starts. Lunch break was over in five, and nervous laughter and strident tones echoed off the burnished wood-paneled walls. The mayor had drawn a line in the sand with this heartless shooting, and the public was clamoring for a suspect. Jack stood in the back of the room, with a perfect vantage point of the entire proceedings.

Jeff, Juan Sanchez's court-appointed attorney, sat in the second row of benches, shuffling computer printouts and studying his handwritten notes scrawled on a yellow pad. It was the area, not unlike a bullpen, where attorneys waited for their client's name to be called on the docket before taking center stage and entering a plea. Juan sat one row back, reading over his lawyer's shoulder, his leg drumming to a silent adrenaline-fueled beat.

The preliminary hearing would determine if there was enough evidence to try a suspect, assign bail, or remand back to prison if the court deemed the suspect a flight risk, or in the case of a capital crime, deny bail as a matter of course.

Juan and his lawyer had already struck a deal with the DA's office under the tutelage of DDA Leslie Sager, and Jack's heart raced a beat as she entered the courtroom.

A court of law was Leslie's bailiwick. She was strong, intelligent, and knew how to control a jury. And with her shoulder-length blonde hair, athletic body, classic features, and magnetic personality, she sucked the air out of the courtroom as she strode past family and friends of the accused, the odd news reporters, defense attorneys, and court flies, toward the bench set aside for the state.

They'd been in a committed relationship. Jack met her after being falsely arrested for the murder of a beautiful Colombian informant Jack had been intimate with. After they sorted out the State's mistake, and Jack had run the killer to ground, the two started dating.

But the inherent dangers involved in Jack's line of work, and Leslie's political ambitions, created a schism. They decided to take some time off to reassess their future together. The separation couldn't have been called amicable, but a strong attraction remained and reconciliation wasn't out of the question.

Yet that wasn't why Jack was in the courtroom. He wanted to view the members of the gallery, people who might have a grudge to bear, or an intimidating message of fear to dole out. Jack had promised to have Juan's back.

The carnival atmosphere was silenced with the drop of Judge Irma Solerno's gavel. No nonsense, of the street, an even-handed jurist. Her proceedings took all of forty-five minutes for seventeen defendants. Court dates assigned, plea deals accepted, and extenuating circumstances adjudicated.

Jack hit pay dirt when a skinny tweaker struggled with his plea. Juan was next on the docket and had turned to his father for reassurance—and Jack saw the young man jolt upright as if he'd been zapped by 120 volts of electricity.

Three young Hispanic men slouched in the last row of the gallery sporting major attitudes and florid ink. Their dark eyes lasered onto Juan, their intentions clear, and their smirks deadly. They flashed a subtle gang sign that panicked Juan and spun him back toward the judge, wild eyes looking for an escape route that wasn't there.

———

Jack was already standing in the hallway when the court was adjourned for the day. The entire process would begin again at 9:00 a.m. with a new cast of jokers, actors, and criminals. Not that Jack had any disdain for lawyers in general. That would be over Tommy's dead body. Although Tommy—and Leslie, for that matter—were exceptions to the rule. The courtroom spilled out past Jack, down the hallway, and out the glass front doors toward the parking lot. Jack stood ready to run interference for Juan and his father if needed.

His intense brown eyes crinkled into a warm smile when Leslie arrived at his side and buzzed a light kiss on his cheek.

"I saw you on TMZ last night," she said.

"So much for anonymity."

"You only fade into the background when necessary, Jack. You looked good." Her eyes were smiling now. "But watch yourself. You're playing with fire. You think life on the streets was tough."

"Nothing like politicos," Jack answered without rancor.

"Very much the same. Their nails are sharp, and their wallets corrupt."

"I didn't know you cared."

"I'll always care, Jack." And she hit him with those killer eyes. "I just couldn't take the heat."

Leslie's honesty caught him off guard. Yet his attention suddenly turned to Juan and his father exiting the building, followed—a few groups back—by the three young gangbangers walking with swagger, wearing baggy white tee's, baggy pants that mocked gravity, and gang tattoos on their necks and arms that advertised their affiliation.

"Thanks for the heads-up," Jack said. "And, Leslie, you look good, too. I mean great."

"I'm getting too much sleep," she said. Dry, but resonant.

Jack questioned her implied meaning, but he didn't have time to sort it out. "Huh . . . I've gotta run. Thanks for this. With Juan, I mean. I think it's the right move."

———

Jack jetted out the lobby door—a little thrown by the encounter—and jogged into the parking structure just in time to see the three gang members slide into their ride and a puff of white smoke belch out of the custom exhaust pipes.

Jack approached the green Chevy Biscayne from the driver's blind spot and thundered a solid fist against the blacked-out window.

The window powered down.

"What the fuck, ese?" yelled the angry voice, rising an octave.

"Smile."

Jack stepped into view, raised his cell phone, and snapped a few quick shots of the car's inhabitants before they had time to react. If looks could kill, Jack would've been spitting dirt.

Juan Sanchez and his father drove past the opening of the parking structure, unaware of the clash. Jack tapped a few commands into his phone.

"Your faces were just sent to the gang squad, the district attorney's office, and the detectives working the Vegas case, assholes. Intimidation of a defendant is against the law, and I know a whole bunch of people who'd be happy to take you off the street."

"You're barking up the wrong tree, homeboy," the driver said with a studied, breathless hiss. "We was just slumming. It's a better show than Judge Judy. Now step away from the ride, you know what's good for you."

Jack took a step closer and lowered his voice. "And you'll want to drive with one eye on your rearview mirror."

The driver's eyes narrowed. "Why's that, ese?"

"To see the train wreck coming your way if you cross paths with Juan Sanchez again."

"Do we have a problem?" a uniformed officer asked, walking briskly toward the confrontation.

"No problem, officer, these boys were just exiting the premises."

The uniform gave the bangers the evil eye as they rolled their car out of the parking structure, trying to save face, and drove off.

Jack thanked the officer and headed for his Mustang, parked on Level 2. He'd left Cruz at his loft with Nick's paperwork on Tomas Vegas, and he was anxious to see if the dead man's file had revealed any secrets.

Nine

Jack stepped into his loft and fist-bumped Cruz, whose work was spread out on the dining room table.

Cruz was dark skinned, twenty-four, short, wiry, with an engaging smile, intelligent brown eyes, and could still pull off the spikey black hair. His mother was Guatemalan, his father a Brooklyn Jew who founded Bundy Lock and Key and taught the kid everything he knew.

The Vegas files were strewn, the laptop was opened, and a yellow pad had fresh scribbling. Two crushed cans of Coke and an empty Subway wrapper littered the glass top.

"How'd it go?" Cruz asked.

Something caught Jack's eye and he walked deeper into the loft, past the kitchen island, into the living room area without answering. He stopped dead in his tracks, doing a slow burn. A large canvas now adorned what had been an empty space on his wall when he'd left his loft that morning. It was the oil painting by John Piccard he had admired at the gallery opening.

"What the hell is this?" he said quietly.

"Uh, rhetorical question?" Cruz said fearfully, more statement than query.

"How the hell did it get here?"

"Easy on the attitude, Jack. I didn't paint it, I didn't buy it, I didn't deliver it."

Jack did a slow turn, eyes bored into Cruz, not amused. "You didn't think to call me? Text me?"

"Uh, it was a surprise," he said, pulling a note card out of his pile. "Surprise!" he delivered with mock conviction as if Jack had just walked into a party. Dead eyes from Jack. "I'm sure Susan will be pleased with your reaction."

Jack stood waiting. Cruz continued.

"She came in with *Red*. Tall, thin man, red hair. Terrence Dirk. He left his number in case you wanted it hung on another wall."

"You know how much this painting cost?"

Cruz was still trying to make light of the situation, like getting an expensive painting happened every day. "Being as it's a gift, my guess is, nothing. Maybe you owe someone a thank-you—and I'm not talking about me. A simple apology would work where I'm concerned."

That finally penetrated Jack's haze of anger. He cracked a small smile. "I pay you too well. You were more deferential when you were hungry."

"Not much of an apology but accepted. Oh"—Cruz handed Jack the card—"Susan left this for you. Damn, you know, she's even more beautiful in person."

The note was handwritten in beautiful cursive.

Dear Jack,

I hope you don't take offense. I know how bullheaded you Italians can be. The painting was perfect, you loved it, you needed color in the loft, and I bought it with the pay-or-play

contract my agent just negotiated to star in your film, thank you
very much. We took Georgie boy for a small fortune. This is just
a small token of my appreciation.
  XO, Susan

He had to smile at her moxie. Susan had taken George Litton
all the way to the bank. He stared at the bold colors and abstract
figures in the painting, and damn, if it didn't strike a chord. Finally, he realized it reminded him of an adult figure in his past.

Jack's Uncle Litz, in his not uncommon buzzed state, loved to
share his hard-earned experience about men and women with an
eager twelve-year-old. He'd pour some handcrafted wine from a
jug he kept within easy reach under his chair, pour a thimbleful
for Jack, take a long pull on his jelly jar of red, savoring the earthy
taste, and let loose with his pearls of wisdom. He spoke in hushed
tones when the subject drifted to the opposite sex, and Jack, re-
membering, lost his smile.

In one of their conversations Uncle Litz had counseled Jack
never to accept expensive gifts from a woman, unless it was his
mother or his wife. And in both cases, he said, his eyes narrowing
with import, payback was still a bitch and would come due. But
in general, a man accepting an expensive gift from any woman
could upset the delicate balance of sexual power. And oh, by the
way, he added, it was in bad taste.

"I can't keep it," Jack said with the full knowledge that the
rejection wouldn't go down well with Susan. He placed her card
on the kitchen island and grabbed a bottle of water out of the
fridge.

"I don't have a wall big enough," Cruz said, trying for humor.

"Thin ice," Jack shot back as he one-hand popped the cap on

the Excedrin bottle, tapped two bitter pills into his mouth, and took a swallow of water.

"Duly noted, boss." He waited until Jack had come to stand by his side before he continued, all business now. "So, I don't think anyone will be crying at Tomas Vegas's funeral except his mother. And that's not a definite. He's been on the wrong side of the law since the nineties. Spent more time in courtrooms than high school. His juvie record is sealed, but he was arrested for assault, robbery, and drug dealing by the time he turned seventeen, dropped out of school, and never looked back. Two murder charges and one attempted. The case was dismissed in the attempted for lack of evidence, and the murder charges ended in hung juries. Busted for strong-arming local retailers who were too afraid to press charges, and did a thirty-six-month stretch for battery. His victim is paralyzed from the waist down, has to be fed through a tube, and still doesn't recognize his own family.

"Vegas had been operating under the radar since his time in Corcoran, his drug trade keeping him healthy. He only dealt with people he could control and handled them more like a pimp than your typical dealer. He showered his young retailers with gifts and then controlled them with violence. This all came from one of his dealers who was on the Fed's payroll."

"Was?"

"Kid was found buried in a landfill up near Lancaster. Teeth pulled, fingers cut off. Face battered so badly they could only ID the body by the shape of his left ear and his DNA. Murder's still unsolved. Vegas had a solid alibi."

"We've got to keep our eyes on Juan," Jack said, worried. This was truly an animal, and he would have violent friends. "So, when's the funeral?"

"He's being laid out at Kolinsky's tomorrow night from seven to nine. The burial's the next day, eleven, at Woodlawn Cemetery."

He gave Cruz a light tap on the shoulder. "We should take a ride over to Kolinsky's and see who's paying their respects and who's gloating. Bangers are like old ladies from Staten Island. They can't pass up a good wake."

———

Toby and Eva were lying naked on the pink sheets in the guesthouse behind her mother's modest California ranch house in Van Nuys. The rough wooden siding of the finished garage was painted white, as were the crossbeams in the 450-square-foot structure. A glass sliding door opened onto a small well-tended garden. The low-slung platform bed rested on a flea market oriental, which was woven in shades of pink, red, and gray. The small structure reminded Toby of a music box. There wasn't a male touch to be found, and if Toby hadn't been madly in love with the woman, he wouldn't have battled through his discomfort. He hated music boxes.

As it was, the fragrance of sex, the allure of Eva's devastating eyes, and the shape of her neck drove him mad. And that wasn't metaphoric, he mused. He was crazy in love.

Eva sensed Toby's growing excitement and rolled on top, grabbing his erection and placing it smoothly into her wet sex. She stared into his smoldering eyes and started rocking and lifting, tightening, and lowering herself, taking her lover to just this side of excruciating pleasure. Yet suddenly she emitted a tortured moan. Her shoulders shuddered and her face turned into a mask of emotional pain. A stream of tears welled out, slapping against Toby's abdomen.

"Hey, it's okay." He carefully slid out of his lover, rolled onto his side, and gently pulled Eva down onto the pink sheets beside him. He drew her close, furious, dreaming of the revenge he would exact on the man who had reduced his beautiful woman to a fragile shell.

Sleep enveloped them both for a while until Toby's eyes snapped open. He checked his phone for the time, leapt out of bed, and dressed in a heartbeat. He memorized Eva's face and used the passion it inflamed to steel his resolve. Toby silently locked the door behind him.

It was a perfect summer evening as he powered his Jeep up a steep section of Reseda Boulevard, past golf courses and million-dollar homes all but obscured behind stone walls and armed-guard gates. Protected from evil and prying eyes. The air was thick with the scent of dry scrub and night-blooming jasmine.

Toby passed Braemar Country Club on his right, his long brown hair whipping in the breeze as he made the final ascent toward Mulholland Gateway Park. A white owl, talons locked in strike mode, rocketed silently past the Jeep's windshield like an apparition—and gave Toby the willies. He pulled curbside at the end of the road. Readying himself for what was to come, he squeezed the steering wheel for strength. Twinkling lights in the San Fernando Valley undulated on waves of heat escaping the valley floor. The shrill screech of summer insects and the white noise rising from the Ventura freeway obscured the beating of his heart.

A few minutes early—which was his way—Toby jumped out and started stretching his quads. Just another jock about to work out on the concrete incline. He uncovered the package tucked between the bucket seats and did a few jumping jacks to unlimber and slow his heart rate.

At 9:15 p.m. on the dot, Dr. Paul Brimley appeared from his jog and started his own stretches, using the metal gate that separated the road from the dirt paths that crisscrossed the Santa Monica Mountains. The wiry man was meticulous as he worked each muscle group, but Toby knew it was a waste of the last few moments the man would spend on earth. Dust to dust for all those muscles.

Toby checked for activity back down the hill. Everything remained quiet. During daylight hours the area was filled with hikers, joggers, and dog walkers. But this time of night the place was desolate.

He grabbed his .22, keeping it low, and easily chambered a round. As the doctor approached on his way down the hill and the safety of his home, Toby pushed away from the Jeep and stopped the man with the barrel of his rifle.

"Dr. Brimley?" Toby asked, knowing the answer.

"Look, I-I don't have my wallet," the doctor sputtered, hoping it was a robbery. And then, "Do I know you? You look familiar."

"That's not important right now. It's my girlfriend that's important, Brimley. She's the reason I'm here. Eva Perez, my girlfriend, said I should forgive you."

"Who? I don't know who you're talking about." The doctor had put on his officious attitude now, fighting to control the situation. Yet Toby could see he was on the verge of hysteria.

"The baby she was carrying was mine, Doc. My blood. And you took such good care of her, she'll never have another. You played God, judge, and jury. You put your hands on her, you cut her, and you made sure of that."

The doctor's eyes betrayed a dawning recognition; he knew what this beef was about, even if he didn't remember the particular woman. His hand moved slowly into his red training jacket, reaching for his cell phone.

The first bullet punched a tight hole in the center of Dr. Brimley's forehead. As it filled with blood, it looked like a dark red Buddhist marking. A third eye.

But this was no holy man, Toby knew. He watched dispassionately as the doctor's eyes went gray, his skin turned ashen, and he crumbled to the pavement, rolling onto his back, his mouth twitching his last garbled words.

Toby stood over the doctor's body. "Forgiveness isn't in my lexicon, scumbag. I only wish I could kill you twice!" He fired another round into the doctor's heart and then a third into his groin. The lithe man's body bucked with the muzzle blasts, then went still.

Toby, well aware of the noise he'd made, moved quickly. He tossed the rifle into the back of his Jeep. Grabbed the doctor by his Reebok cross trainers, pulled him, skull thumping, over the curb, and rolled his lifeless body down the hillside into the scrub bushes below and out of sight. Let the vultures have their way with him.

Toby picked up the three shell casings, jumped into the Jeep, and executed a smooth U-turn, being mindful not to leave identifiable tread marks. His grim smile widened as he glided down the macadam road, gaining speed with the sharp angle of descent that finally matched his racing pulse.

Ten

Susan Blake's face was as tight as a porcelain doll's. Tommy sat across from her in Jack's booth at Hal's, disconnected, while Jack sat next to Susan, staring straight ahead, fighting for calm.

"That's crap, Jack," she said.

"I'm keeping the painting, Susan," he said in measured tones. "It was a beautiful gesture, greatly appreciated. I'm just paying for it, that's all." But Jack was sure the issue wasn't over. "It's the thought that counts on this one," he said, and knew he sounded lame.

"Oh bullshit!" she said a bit too loud. If not for the volume in Hal's Bar and Grill that night, heads would have turned. "It's bad luck, you know. Returning a gift. I thought all you Italians knew that."

"All you Italians?" The blush on Jack's neck burned his ears and rose to his face. "I'm not returning it, in any case. It's . . ." Jack realized he should stop talking. He didn't do well verbally when he was put on the spot.

Stone-faced, Tommy sipped the dregs of his Gray Goose martini and twirled the olive with the toothpick in the empty glass. He wasn't drawing any fire.

"Oh hell, Susan," Jack plowed on. "It's beautiful, but too damn expensive. C'mon now, I'll straighten it out with Terrence. It's too soon."

"It wasn't too soon . . ." she snapped and then wisely chose not to finish the sentence. The low blow had landed, and Jack was now officially pissed off.

And then Susan switched emotional gears on a dime. Jack had never seen anything like it. "We're not always so disagreeable, Tommy."

"I'm fine," he said, taking a long sip of the empty glass. A move not lost on Jack, who controlled his impulse to laugh at his friend's discomfort.

Jack motioned for Arsinio, his favorite waiter, and hand ordered Tommy another drink.

"Who's hungry?" he finally asked.

"You know what," Susan said, "I'm going to call it a night." So, Jack wasn't off the hook, after all. She took a light sip of her chardonnay and pushed the nearly full glass away. Tommy was mesmerized by her every move. "I had a five a.m. call and I'm really wiped out. Are you coming by the set with Jack tomorrow, Tommy? I'll introduce you around. You can't say no," she said as if the emotional outburst had never occurred.

"If it's not too much bother," he grinned, a big kid.

"Oh, Lord no, it'll break up the day," Susan said, already on the move toward the exit. Jack grabbed her wrap and caught up, escorting her through the dining room, past discreet turning heads, diners pleased to have a star in their midst.

Everyone was pleased but Jack. He wanted to toss the damn painting out the window, but then again, it did speak to him. And he could afford it. His problem right now was that he trusted her taste in art more than her mercurial emotional crap that left him cold and confused.

The limo was parked in front of Hal's, but Susan turned left, and when she got to the corner made another left up the street, away from the early-evening crowds on Abbot Kinney.

Jack stayed at her side, vowing to remain silent but losing control.

"You know, I find this whole situation a little bit crazy," he said.

Susan flinched on "crazy" as if Jack had slapped her.

He soldiered on. "Who in God's name spends eighteen thousand dollars on a gift for someone they hardly know?"

"You said we had crossed boundaries." Punch.

"And you said we just had sex. Sex! Your words." Counterpunch.

Susan took a swing at Jack, who caught her wrist in midflight.

"Calm down," Jack said through clenched teeth. Wondering how he'd let this encounter spin out of control.

"Let go of me," she said as if Jack was the perpetrator of the violence.

"Take a deep breath." By degrees he loosened the grip on Susan's wrist, trying to defuse the moment.

"You've got quick reflexes, Mr. Bertolino." Her stone-cold face crinkled into a sly smile that dazzled, but Jack didn't trust for one moment. "By the way, I talked Terrence down to fifteen. Don't you dare let him charge you full price."

They walked back to Hal's in silence. Jack got Susan squared away in the limo, took a few deep breaths to slow his heart rate, and reentered the restaurant.

Angry but hungry as hell.

———

"Where the fuck is he?" Terrence tossed over his shoulder. He was sitting at a workbench in the family garage, wearing rubber surgical gloves and concentrating on loading his two spare clips.

The two Hobie kayaks were already loaded onto a trailer, hitched to the rear of his Ford F-350, which had been backed into the garage to be protected from view. Sean walked over with a lithium-manganese battery that powered the German-made electric motor on the craft and stowed it easily into its custom compartment next to another battery that was already locked down in the trailer. "I'm not his mother," he said, low.

"His mother wasn't his mother."

"Probably getting a full dose of Eva," Sean said without attitude, nonjudgmental.

"Let's hope that's all he gets from her."

Sean was always the calm one before a crime. He had the most practice. "Cut him some slack. He'll be at the launch site with the Mercedes, gassed up, food in the cooler, and ready to roll up north, all things being equal. Plus, he's better on a job when he's relaxed."

"If he doesn't show, I'm calling it off," Terrence said, hitting the release in the heel of his HK P7. He checked the rounds in the magazine of his 9mm to make double sure the eight bullets were ready for work. Measure twice, cut once. Terrence was fastidious to a fault.

"He'll be there," Sean said, elongating the words.

"Did you put fresh batteries in the walkie-talkies?"

"Done."

"You armed for bear?"

Sean pulled a sawed-off Mossberg 590a1 shotgun with a nine-shot magazine out of the storage compartment of his Hobie by way of answer. It carried four reloads in the stock of the weatherproofed black synthetic stock. Perfect for sharks on his long trips to Catalina, and a workhorse if needed in a life-and-death experience out on the open sea.

"I have my ankle rig on too," Sean said. "But we won't need it if I timed it right. I've got the coordinates programmed into all three GPS systems. And we'll work a grid in the general area in case they changed the play. If they dump the pot, we'll find it."

"Whoever spots the tuna boat calls it in but lays low, and the two men out will swarm," Terrence said, pulling off the white protective gloves with a snap and tossing them into a trash bin.

"Hell, we're stealth," Sean said, referring to the black paint on the kayaks that rendered them nearly invisible on the open sea. Both brothers were dressed entirely in black.

A black watch cap would keep Terrence's distinctive red hair obscured. "The full moon isn't our friend tonight," he observed.

"You fucking worry too much."

"Somebody has to," he said pointedly. "I'll be on my cell. Did you charge your phone?"

"Yes." And then, "Ten o'clock. Straight up."

"Straight up, brother."

Sean started for his truck and then turned, his mood darkening. "You think Toby killed Vegas?"

"I would've," Terrence said without blinking an eye.

"Why'd he lie?"

"To protect us."

Sean rolled that notion around. "Given any thought to our move if it goes south on him?"

"We'll worry about that at the appropriate time."

Pure bullshit. Sean knew for a fact that his brother was always thinking three moves ahead of the field. He chose to let the lie pass. He had more pressing issues on his mind, like the Sinaloa cartel. He walked out of the garage and jumped into his truck.

Terrence stepped out behind Sean and watched the F-350,

towing the kayaks, rumble down the driveway, make a wide turn onto the street until the edge of their Craftsman house snuffed out the red taillights. He glanced skyward, worried about the full moon again. He checked his cell phone, looking for the text from Toby that hadn't been sent. Frustrated, he hit the remote button sending the custom doors rolling down and headed into the house.

———

Jack's desk was littered with the Tomas Vegas files. The Hollywood Hills sparkled in the distance, but Jack hardly noticed. A half-empty bottle of Cab and a half-full yellow pad with a list of Tomas Vegas's potential killers kept him occupied. Jack scoured the files for people or groups who had clear motivation for wanting the gangster dead. A grudge shooting thoughtfully planned, expertly executed.

Except for the one errant shot.

On a clean page Jack made a second list, pulled from court records of Vegas's arrests, his court appearances, and his victims, dead and alive. He then added their family members who had testified for or against him.

The page looked like a dysfunctional family tree, but it would help Jack get an overall feel for the scope of the case.

He also flagged one particular court case where Vegas had been called as a witness for the prosecution and added the female defendant to the list.

One of the local rags had called the murder of Vegas an assassination. It chaffed Jack. Presidents and heads of state were assassinated . . . gangsters got murdered.

The shooting had a military feel, he thought. Surveillance, scheduling, precision shooting.

Jack still wondered why the gunman's first bullet flew high and wide.

He'd check fathers, brothers, and sisters for military background, law enforcement, and anybody with a personal grudge.

He agreed with Nick: a revenge killing felt right.

———————

Sean Dirk pulled his watch cap low on his forehead to keep any light from reflecting off his face and putting the mission in jeopardy.

It had taken close to three hours to arrive at the previous cartel drop-off point, two miles east of Catalina, and now it was a waiting game. The temperature on the water was a comfortable sixty degrees; the night sky was brilliant with planets, constellations, and the Milky Way, a reminder to Sean of his insignificance in the grand scheme of things.

The only illumination on the black surface of the sea was the full moon, and at one o'clock it perched far over the horizon and shone like a beacon across the ocean surface, splitting north from south.

Sean had cut off all communication with his brothers until the drop-off was completed. Sound traveled great distances on the water, and as long as he stayed low, and silent, tucked neatly into his Hobie kayak as it bobbed with the light chop of the waves, he was all but invisible.

After an hour of nothing but a container ship crossing between his position and the twinkling lights of Los Angeles behind him, Sean started to doubt. The plan was his, and he'd never hear the end of it if the brothers came up empty.

Then he saw them.

A quarter mile west, with the island of Catalina looming

beyond, a fifty-foot fishing boat cut sharply through the reflected moonlight, raising wild ripples of silver. The boat circled once, and then without pause dumped a large parcel off the stern of the boat and powered away, due south, at a high rate of speed.

Sean's heart pounded as he keyed his walkie-talkie and alerted the troops, shouting out coordinates. He clicked on the kayak's motor, checked for all-clear behind him, and throttled silently ahead toward the bales of drugs floating in the water beyond.

They were engaged in a race against time. The first job would be to find the GPS beacon on the packages and disable it. Then Terrence would drag the floating bales of drugs to Shark Harbor, on the backside of Catalina, where they would be broken down, stowed in the body of the kayaks, and returned to a protected cove on the mainland, where the F-350 and the Mercedes van were parked.

Terrence would power back to Marina del Rey. If he were stopped and searched by the Coast Guard entering the marina, he'd be just another hapless fisherman with an empty hold who got skunked by the fickle sea. He'd pick up the F-350 in the morning. In the meantime his brothers—driving the drug-laden van—would head to Sacramento and a major payday.

Eleven

The Dirk brothers heard the boat before they saw it. The loud thrumming engine of a high-powered ski-boat. It was closing the distance fast, running without lights.

Terrence had discovered and dismantled the GPS beacon imbedded in one of the waterproofed bales, but that discovery came too late, as the volume of the throaty engine grew nearer.

Sean had already tied off the marijuana to the rear of Terrence's Zodiac, ready to roll, while Toby drifted off to the side, lying in wait.

A twenty-eight-foot Scarab traveling at thirty miles an hour was in danger of plowing into the brothers as it entered the drop-off area. The two men aboard didn't see the Dirks at first, because their eyes were trained on the onboard GPS screen. At the last moment, the passenger looked up and yelled, "Fuck!"

The pilot throttled back and cranked the wheel hard to the left, generating a huge wake that threatened to scuttle Sean's kayak as it pulled alongside the two smaller crafts.

"It's about fucking time!" Terrence shouted angrily over the sound of their engines as the two men on the boat eyed them with surprise, then suspicion. Terrence stayed on the offensive, "Let me get this offloaded so we can get the hell out of Dodge."

"Who the fuck're you?" the pilot of the Scarab shouted, his eyes black as ball bearings.

"Who the fuck am I?" Terrence shot back. "I'm your fucking meal ticket, fucking thirty-minutes-late assholes."

The pilot of the Scarab pulled a Glock 9mm and the stocky man in the passenger seat leveled an AK-47 at Terrence in response.

"I'm gonna ask you only one more time," the pilot said, "and then I'm done talking. Who the fuck're you?"

"You didn't get the memo, scumbag," Sean jumped in, not reacting to the hardware pointed at his brother but letting his kayak drift away from the Zodiac, splitting the focus of the men on the boat. Two targets were harder to hit than one.

Terrence picked up his brother's thread. "There was Coast Guard up and down the coast. We met the captain five miles out and busted our humps to get here on time."

"Here's how it's going to play," the Scarab's pilot said, not buying it. "You two are going to load the bales onto the back of our craft, and if you do it quick enough, we'll give you a lift back to shore and you can do your explaining to the Sinaloa boys. They're good at getting to the meat of a story."

The passenger with the AK snorted at the implication.

"Do it yourself," Sean hissed, not backing down, still drifting wider.

The pilot growled, "And did you call me a scumbag?"

Toby's first bullet ripped into the pilot's cheek, shattering his teeth. He screamed in searing pain and blind-fired his 9mm in the direction of the shot.

Terrance drew his P7 and rapid-fired, hitting the pilot in the neck, and then the shoulder, and then the abdomen. The pilot grabbed for his throat with one hand, his belly with the other, and flopped onto the windshield, bleeding out over the glass before slipping to the deck.

As Sean fired his Mossberg at the passenger, the kayak rolled dangerously. The first shot flew wide.

The man with the AK held on to the rocking boat with one hand and arced a spray of high-powered rounds in Sean's direction with the other. A round punctured the skin of his kayak above the water level.

The AK-47 drifted toward Terrence and one round connected with the stainless steel tubing that secured the steering wheel housing, sending a shard of metal ripping into Terrence's shoulder.

Sean's shotgun spit flame once again.

The man's thick forearm exploded. Body part and automatic weapon pinwheeled into the ocean. Blood spray fountained from his ragged stump as the man roared in pain.

Sean's third shot punched a hole in the man's barrel chest, knocking him off his feet into the passenger seat, dead.

Frenzied, like a starving wolf pack, the Dirk brothers circled the Scarab, firing their weapons into the dead men, riddling their bodies and boat with bullets. Pouring in lead in a fury of sound, blood, viscera, and shattered glass and bones.

Then they stopped. Like a single organism. The only sound they heard was their heavy breathing, the ringing in their ears, and the pounding of their hearts.

The three brothers stared wild-eyed, crazed, panting, at the bloody carnage and then from one craft to the next, checking for personal damage.

Sean's kayak had taken a hit, but nothing that would scuttle the mission.

A trail of blood leaked from Terrence's sleeve. He'd deal with his injury in due time.

The brothers surveyed the water in all directions, on the lookout for pursuers. Finally it dawned on them that all was quiet, they were clear for the moment, and damn lucky to be alive.

Terrence signaled Sean, who blew four gaping holes into the stern of the Scarab's fiberglass body. Nobody would find evidence at the bottom of the ocean.

———

The Scarab was listing toward the stern, taking on heavy water by the time the Zodiac and the two kayaks cleared the massacred men and their disabled craft.

The three bothers had witnessed a hell of their own design. Terrence and Sean had the jacked-up, haunted look of soldiers returning from a sortie, not sure how they ended up with so much blood on their hands. Toby stared straight ahead, his placid face and calm demeanor troubling, a coldness not lost on his brothers.

The Dirk brothers' small armada headed for Shark Harbor to stow the drugs. They turned as one as the bow of the Scarab breached skyward like a painted whale, and then knifed backward, silently disappearing beneath the dark surface of the Pacific.

Twelve

Susan was enveloped by the white down comforter and overstuffed white pillows in the center of her king-sized bed. The room was ice cold, the way she liked it, and she was soundly asleep in a white silk teddy and red fleece blackout mask she was never without.

Her digital alarm clock read 2:30 in glowing amber numbers. Susan had to be on set at 7:00. The house was silent, the only sound a soft purring from Susan who suffered from allergies but was loath to admit it.

Her cell phone ring tone echoed in the empty house. The volume had been set on high to wake Susan in the morning, and it was obnoxiously insistent. Just before it rang for the fifth time, Susan shot upright and angrily ripped off the sleep mask. Checking the caller ID, she answered the call, going on the attack.

"Fuck you. Fuck you! Stop calling me. I'm going to cut you off, I swear to God." She listened for a moment, her face tight with rage. "Did you blow through the twenty grand? . . . No! No! I'm warning you, I want you out of L.A. Stay the fuck out of my life."

Susan's plea was answered by a loud banging on her front door, while her caller informed her that he was standing outside her house and demanded to be let in.

Susan clicked off her cell. She fumbled for the alarm fob that was next to her bottled water on the nightstand, and with a shaking hand, engaged the alarm as she leapt out of bed. With alarm bells shrieking, Susan stood at the doorway for a heartbeat and then went into action. She ran down the stairs, grabbed the remote, clicked on the flat-screen television, and set the channel to a triple-X–rated porn station. Then she punched up the volume.

Sexual breathing and cheap jazz joined the alarm as she ran back up the stairs, slammed the bedroom door shut, and secured the lock.

The heavy panting seemed to get louder, and Susan realized the sound was emanating from her. She was hyperventilating; the piercing alarm fueled the pounding of her heart.

Susan welcomed the panic as she grabbed the phone and speed-dialed Jack's number.

––––––

Jack was out the door and flying down Lincoln Avenue in his Mustang four minutes later. He skidded a left across the empty boulevard and powered down Palms, where Susan's rental house was located. Having advised Susan to dial 911, he was sure the cops were on their way, but Jack arrived first.

He jammed on the brakes as he turned into the driveway, skidding to a stop. He left the driver's door open as he pulled out his weapon and checked the front yard. Seeing that was secure, he punched in the alarm code, quieting the shrill wail, and keyed the front door open.

His Glock 9mm led the way into the expansive living room. Right away he saw a tawdry X-rated film playing on the big screen, its volume unbearable. He hit the light switch and the entire house was bathed in soft light.

Jack took the steps two at a time, shouting Susan's name as he ran. "I'm here, it's Jack. Are you okay?"

"Yes."

"I want you to stay put while I check the house."

"Hurry."

Jack advanced quickly through the second floor of the designer home: bathrooms, closets, and two spare bedrooms. He looked out through the window to the backyard below, but it all looked secure. As he made his way back to the top of the stairs: "Police! Drop your weapon! Get down on the ground. Down on the ground now! Now!"

Jack knew better than to flirt with disaster. He'd been in enough high-octane situations to know when to submit.

He carefully placed his automatic on the hardwood floor and assumed the position.

Two uniformed officers pounded up the stairs, guns trained on Jack.

"I work for Susan Blake," Jack said evenly. "My license to carry is in my wallet in my left back pocket."

Jack could hear an *all-clear* being called from the front of the house while the second team leader cleared the main floor.

"Where's the occupant of the home?" the lead officer asked while securing Jack's weapon. His partner's gun remained trained on Jack's kill zone.

"She locked herself in the bedroom at the end of the hallway. She said she was fine."

"Jack?" Susan peered from behind the heavy bedroom door, which was cracked open a few inches now.

"LAPD, ma'am. Are you okay?"

"I think so. Jack Bertolino is with me. I called him before I dialed 911."

Jack could hear the squeal of more brakes out on the street as the armed security guards joined the fray.

"Can I get up now, officer?" Jack asked without any animus. He knew the guys were just playing it by the book.

The lead officer nodded his head, which was a miracle because the man was built like a refrigerator and had no neck. "Let him up," he said to his partner, who lowered his weapon. "I know him. Know of him. You're that guy outta New York. Nice work on that kidnapping case, by the way. You made the department look good. Not a glory hound," the cop said, no nonsense but ratcheting down the intensity.

Jack stood stiffly and Susan stepped into his arms, struggling to stay in control.

"First floor's all clear," shouted a wire-thin cop standing in the living room. His partner, who had checked the perimeter of the house, joined him. He had the lean, green look of a rookie. "No forced entry," he said. "Back gate's secure, no broken windows, no nothing." His attention was drawn to the two busty naked women cavorting on the big screen before staring up with embarrassed recognition at Susan.

"Who set off the alarm?" the lead cop asked.

"I did. I'm sorry, I got scared. I've had issues with a stalker in New York. The FBI are on the case. I guess I may have overreacted."

"Let's go downstairs and see what we've got going here. Are you okay?" Jack asked Susan gently.

"Been better."

"You did good."

The big man nodded and they filed down the stairs.

"Was the front door unlocked?" he asked Jack.

"No, I shut off the alarm and used my key." By way of explanation, he went on: "Susan Blake's an actress in town working on a film project. She's renting this place. We had it set up for security, and nothing was tripped on our system. I don't know if the owner had his television programmed on a timer, but we should get him on the wire and check out his story."

The lead officer said, "We can get that done.

"I was sound asleep and then I heard that." Susan glanced toward the television set.

The rookie blushed and reached to turn off the set.

"Don't touch anything until we've dusted for prints," Jack said. The young officer instantly complied, knowing he'd been in the wrong.

"Just to be safe," Jack said, putting the young man and Susan at ease. He went around the back of the set and pushed the power button on the surge protector. The lurid picture and sound thankfully blinked off.

The lead officer said, "Seems like a false alarm, Ms. Blake. Everything's tight as a drum."

"I feel like such a fool."

"Better safe than sorry," he said, showing some compassion. "Your line of work and all."

A van pulled up in front of the house, and a TMZ cameraman jumped out and started for the front door, digital camera rolling.

The 911 call must have gone out on a scanner because two more vans were pulling up out front. The news choppers would follow.

"Can we keep the media off the premises?" Jack asked. "I think Miss Blake's been through enough."

The tall, thin cop took the lead and walked out, carefully closing the front door without touching the knob. That blocked the TMZ camera operator's view into the home.

A few neighbors had congregated across the street and were peering up the driveway, trying to catch a glimpse of the star. The man wearing the yellow and black bandanna stood amid the crowd. With his blond hair pulled behind one ear, he focused his telephoto lens and snapped a few shots into the house before the cop's maneuver shut him out. His eyes narrowed and he muttered a curse under his breath, but on the whole seemed pleased with the proceedings.

He flashed a cruel smile and an exaggerated wink at a birdlike octogenarian wearing a pink housecoat and matching slippers.

"Susan Blake," he said, sharing a pearl. "She's gonna be big."

He turned on his heel and walked blithely down Palms Boulevard.

Thirteen

A flash of orange broke through the gash of salmon brushed across the horizon. The star fields were still visible but would disappear within the hour in a wash of California blue.

Toby was behind the wheel, having traded driving duties with his brother Sean at a 24/7 McDonald's. The van was on cruise control, the GPS system guiding the way, and the brothers were motoring at a highway-patrol-safe sixty-eight miles per hour. Toby was frustrated at the slow pace, felt like he was standing still.

Sean had a handful of fries in one hand and a double cheeseburger in the other that he eyed lustfully. The slate-gray Mercedes Sprinter van powered up a rise and suddenly, on their right, the brown hills became eerily alive.

"What the hell's that?" Sean asked, lowering the burger.

"Stockyard."

As far as the eye could see, acres and acres of cattle, undulating, bellowing, and waiting for slaughter. The windows were up, the AC was on high, and he could still taste the stench of death.

Sean looked from the scene of impending carnage to his cheeseburger.

Toby threw him the most judgmental, sarcastic mug a brother could muster. "You have got to be fucking kidding me."

"Fuck 'em," and Sean bit through a satisfying mouthful of two fried patties of beef, cheese, pickles, and onions on a sesame seed bun. "You know, cows are so stupid, if they're standing in a ditch and get caught in a downpour, they'll drown before walking to higher ground."

"Bullshit."

"Google it."

"Under what, urban legend?"

"No, little-known facts, dickwad."

"Every burger you eat has the DNA of a million cows in it. Tasty?" Toby fired back.

"You got that off NPR. Big fucking deal. I heard the story and ran down to Ruth's Chris for dinner." Sean pointed toward him with the bit-off edge of his burger. "I don't hear you swearing off shoes, and belts, and your leather jackets."

"Enjoy," Toby said, cranking up the music. His eyes creased into a smile, hoping he had ruined his brother's meal. He turned toward a grove of black walnut trees on the left and fallow, dry-cracked fields on the right. Victims of the California drought.

"You smoke too much weed," Sean said.

"Then I'm in the right van."

No argument from Sean. They were both flying from the thick smell of high-grade bud.

"If we get stopped, we get popped," Toby said without any tension.

"We're cool. I'll spell you on the way back."

"Gimme a bite."

"Fuck you. Enjoy your fillet o' fish. Eighty percent cardboard."

"Hah, I forgot I had it. I could eat anything with tartar sauce on it."

Sean's cell rang like an old rotary phone, and he answered.

"Yeah? Hey, Ricky J, what're you doing up so early?"

———

Ricky J, coffee mug in hand, stood in the kitchen of his mid-century California ranch, located on a secluded half-acre outside Sacramento. A long macadam driveway led up to the front of his neatly appointed cedar-shingled house, set back on the lot hidden from nosy neighbors. The drug business wasn't for pussies or fools, and Ricky J had vowed that his nine-month stretch in the joint was going to be his last.

A lit cigarette smoldered in an overflowing ashtray. He wore baby-blue Calvin Klein boxers and nothing else. His back was an ink canvas of an orange, black, and red tiger, teeth bared. His dark hair was cut like a banker's. In fact, put Ricky J in a button-down shirt and he could pass for a bank manager. Very conservative, very smart. His thick eyebrows were knitted in concern as he searched for the right words.

"Something's come up," Ricky J said, taking a careful sip of hot coffee to stave off his dry mouth. He knew Sean Dirk was nobody to fuck with.

"Yeah?" Sean said suspiciously. Their agreed-upon verbal contract was that Ricky J would buy the drugs at a steep discount and unload the shit through his five medical marijuana shops. "We should be rolling in early afternoon," Sean went on. "You have time for lunch before we transact and hit the road?"

"Many apologies, Sean, but it's not going to happen."

"You don't have time to break bread with your old cell mate?" Sean said, knowing it wasn't the message being sent.

Ricky J set down his coffee, pushed his food-hound black-and-white Boston terrier away with his bare foot, and continued.

"The Sinaloa cartel sent out a 911 on Silk Road."

"For what?" Sean said.

"One of their shipments got hijacked. Boat, men, drugs, gone missing. They sent out word to all of us . . . independent contractors to keep an eye out."

The Silk Road was a black-market website, the eBay of narcotics. The alternative Deep Web, fancied by thieves of all color and creed. In the market for hot credit cards? Have a scud missile to unload, or AK-47s, illegal computer programs, bulk ammunition, this was where the connection was made. One-stop shopping for drugs and contraband.

"They threatened to cut off the heads of anyone involved in the theft of their product and the lives of their men. Posted a reward for information."

"Our shit's out of Chicago. I told you it was coming a week ago. It's been in transit for three days. What the fuck?" Sean said feigning outrage, trying to remain civil. "I'm majorly out of pocket here."

"That may be, but I can't take the risk. It's bad timing, Sean. And for that I'm very sorry."

"That may be? Don't fucking . . ." He wisely dialed it down a notch. "You have got to be fucking kidding me. This is not right, Ricky."

"Point well taken and I'll make it up to you in the future. But I don't need the heat. What can I say? I've got the feds all over my shops as it is. Any more scrutiny and they'll shut me down. The cartel will have my head on a stake if they even smell complicity."

He heard Sean let out a ragged breath. "Okay, Ricky, I can appreciate your concern. Don't say another word. I mean really, don't say another word. We never had this discussion, or business pending. Correct?" Sean wasn't asking. "I know. It's all about trust, Ricky. I have your back too. Always, brother. Okay, later."

———

Toby and Sean drove on in silence. His little brother knew to keep his trap shut until the red drained from Sean's face and he stopped hyperventilating.

"There's two hundred grand on our heads," Sean stated, rattlesnake deadly.

"That didn't take long."

The sun was on the rise and the I-5 was filling with eighteen-wheelers, farm trucks, and 4Xs. A heat mirage was rising off the black macadam in the distance, matched by the heat emanating from Sean's slow burn and the sweat trickling down his back.

"Is Ricky J cool?" Toby asked.

"He apologized for ruining our day. Said to keep him in mind if anything else comes down the pike at a much later date."

"He couldn't really cash in without risking his own life. The cartel would torture him to find out how he knew it was us. See if he was telling the truth. Is he cool?"

Sean gave that some serious thought. They'd been thick as thieves at Lompoc, and had done some substantial business through the years, but honor among thieves was as fallacious as his own story about cows.

"Not two hundred grand cool."

"Who's gonna tell Terrence?"

"It was my call. I'll take the heat."

Sean weighed their options, absently nodding his head as he heard Toby say: "We've got some cleanup to do."

———

Jack was dead on his feet. His back was in spasm and he belted down two aspirin from the craft service table, but knew a heavier drug was in order when he got back to the loft. He glanced over his shoulder at the behemoth Stage D at Sony Studios in Culver City, where *Done Deal* was filming. The studio, steeped in history, had been MGM back in the golden age of Hollywood, turning out some of the classic black-and-white noir films Jack favored.

Jack walked Cruz into Susan's mobile home and set him up with his computer.

"You are now officially Susan Blake's bodyguard. She okayed you, thinks you're cute. I told her I had other business to attend to."

"She has to be on her phone."

"Not a problem. She gets off set and makes calls to unwind. I need phone numbers. She was arguing with someone the other night and is being tight lipped. I can't do my job unless I'm in the loop. Do your best."

"I feel a little uncomfortable."

"It's impossible to protect her without knowing who, or what, she's afraid of."

That seemed to appease his young associate.

Tommy was set up at video village, where he could watch Hollywood magic being made. True to his word, he had reached out to the FBI agent in New York City who had been assigned to

Susan Blake's stalking case. The agent agreed to help in any way he could. Jack was waiting on a return call.

Jack exited the building seconds before an alarm bell rang and a red light flashed, alerting all that the set was alive and cameras would begin to roll, or whatever digital cameras did these days to capture a moving image.

Jack grabbed a breakfast burrito from the catering truck, and as he headed for the parking lot his cell phone rang. It was a New York area code.

"Agent Jameson, thanks for returning my call."

"How can I help you?" Jameson asked.

Jack could hear horns blaring in the background and thought the agent was probably out on the city streets.

"Here's what I'm dealing with. It appears that Susan Blake's stalker has followed her to L.A. I believe she's legitimately frightened. He did a drive-by when we were shooting on location, but I have the suspicion that she waited until he couldn't be ID'd before alerting me. And when I requested she sit down with a sketch artist, she refused. We had another incident last night at two a.m. Susan sounded the alarm, I ran over, the police responded, and she claimed there had been an attempted break-in at her home."

"What was the upshot?" Jameson asked.

"Again, she was honestly rattled, but the police couldn't find anything on scene to corroborate the allegation. Called it an honest mistake."

"And you're not sure?"

"You got it," Jack said.

"All I can say is my experience was similar," Jameson said. "Something about her story never rang true. And unless I caught her stalker in the act of harassment, I had nothing substantive to go on. If you come up with anything of interest, I'd be happy to run the leads from my end, but personally, I hit a dead end and had to move on. Send my best to Tommy."

Jack thanked the agent for his time, belted down the burrito, mounted up, and drove west toward the marina.

———

Ricky J pulled an olive-drab canvas rucksack out of his closet, heaved it onto his bed, and checked the contents. Neatly freeze-wrapped bundles of cash. Three hundred fifty thousand dollars, to be exact. He would have made a killing on the Dirk deal, but it wasn't worth his life. Felt bad screwing his friend, but what the hell? As he dragged the bag down the hallway and opened the rear door, his cell phone trilled.

"Shit," he said, running back to the bedroom. He didn't see his phone, so he followed the sound into the kitchen, where he grabbed the cell phone off of his counter and clicked On before it went to voicemail. He checked the caller and grimaced, "Yeah?"

"Where's the love, Ricky J? Look, I've been driving all night. I'm totally fried. Throw some burgers on the grill and we'll get caught up before I head back."

"I thought you were already turned around," Ricky J said, alarmed by this change in plans. "Listen, it's not a good idea. I'm not even at the house."

His Boston terrier appeared and started whimpering for food. "Shut the fuck up." Ricky pushed him away with his foot.

"What'd you say?"

"Somebody's dog, sorry."

"I thought we had the day carved out. How'd you get so busy?"

At least this lie was in his hip pocket. "You know the business. Have to jump through hoops to make a buck."

"You want me to drive into a ditch? I've got no one to spell me. And I don't trust leaving the van in some no-tell motel parking lot."

"You know I love you like a brother, but—"

"Cut the shit, Ricky. I can see you standing in your kitchen. Put on a fuckin' shirt and crack open a couple of beers."

"What?" Ricky J spun around and tweaked open the louver blinds. Sean's van was parked in the driveway. He gave a quick wave.

"You prick," Ricky said, trying for lite. "Why didn't you tell me you were here? Gimme two seconds to put on some shorts and turn the alarm off. I thought you were down in Salinas by now."

"Make it quick, I've gotta take a wiz."

Sean's unexpected appearance was setting off all sorts of trip wires. Ricky clicked off the phone, grabbed his pistol out of a drawer, and slid it under his belt in the small of his back. He hurried into the bedroom and pulled on a T-shirt, making sure it covered the weapon. All the while his dog remained underfoot and barking.

"Shut the fuck up!" he hissed. Ricky started back and remembered the bag of cash. "Mother fucker." He spun and hoofed it down the hallway, bent down to grab the bag of cash out of the open doorway.

When he straightened, he was staring down the barrel of Toby Dirk's .22.

The tight bore of the .22 looked massive, was Ricky J's last thought. He saw the flash before he could react. Two small holes painted his forehead. His eyes widened in surprise and then were extinguished. Ricky J was dead before his knees buckled.

Toby pulled him out of the house and onto the grass before he could bleed out on the hardwood floor. The only witness to the crime, Ricky J's Boston terrier, appeared unfazed.

———

Sean and Toby did a systematic search of the backyard. The large evergreen shrubs and old-growth trees that surrounded the perimeter of the property offered total privacy from the road and houses beyond. They had left Ricky J propped against the detached garage next to a four-by-six green-and-gray Rubbermaid garden shed. At first glance he looked like he was sleeping.

Sean had been sitting in the van with the windows rolled down when he heard the *pop pop*. Could've been anything, but Sean recognized it as the sound of sudden death. When he was sure all was quiet in the 'hood, he walked around to the back of the house.

"He said he'd never risk being arrested again without having a bag of cash in the ground somewhere for bail," Sean said. "It would have to be close, don't you think? Where was he dragging the bag?"

"Maybe to his car?"

"Wells Fargo didn't dry-wrap the cash. And he's in a cash-and-carry business. Where the fuck is it?" Sean directed to the very dead Ricky J.

And that's when he saw it.

A line of dead grass, two inches wide, ran the width of the shed. Sean put his shoulder to the six-foot-tall plastic structure. It slid smoothly away from Ricky J, revealing more dead grass and then the top of a steamer trunk buried in a neat hole, flush with the grass. Toby sprang toward it and pulled open the hinged metal top.

The trunk was filled with cash.

Neat parcels of money. Lots of them. Dry wrapped and theirs for the taking. Sean stooped down and rubbed the back of the dog's head as it stood by his side peering into the hole. He waited for his heart to stop pounding before getting to work.

The brothers found rubber cleaning gloves in the pantry and put them on. They went through the house taking cell phones, iPads, and computers. They grabbed Ricky's phone book, anything that could tie them to the dead man.

Toby discovered the hidden security system in a closet. He shut off the power and pulled out the disk. In its place he inserted a blank.

They worked silently and efficiently. Sean bagged the money and stowed it in the back of the van. Both brothers were needed to bend Ricky J at the waist and slide him into the steamer trunk. The lid closed with a click, and the realigned shed served as his makeshift headstone.

The dog whimpered when the brothers stepped into the kitchen for one last look around.

"What do we do with the dog?" Toby asked, picking him up and cradling him in the crux of his arm. The dog nuzzled in the warmth of Toby's black hoodie and gave him a soulful stare. "Should we take him with us?"

Sean pulled a large bag of dry food from the pantry. He liked dogs too but he pointed out, "He's probably chipped. First visit to the vet and they can trace us back to Ricky." He emptied the kibble in a mound on the floor.

Toby saw the sense of that. He lifted the dog, face level, looked at him eye-to-eye, and set him down. He grabbed a large bowl, filled it with fresh water, and placed it next to the pile of food.

Sean and Toby walked out the back door, made sure the doggy door was unhinged before locking up behind them. Sean grabbed the hose and washed the blood spatters off the grass and dirt on the edge of the garden bed. After pulling off the rubber cleaning gloves and tossing them into the bag along with the electronics, Toby picked up the .22 shell casings from the grass and the two men hit the road.

Toby pulled the Mercedes van out of the driveway, heading toward I-5 South and what was sure to be a hellish drive back to L.A. He'd been tired enough when they arrived. Sean pulled the battery and memory card out of the phone and iPad, tossed them out the window before hitting the freeway entrance.

"That's it. We were never here."

Fourteen

An athletic man dressed in black jeans and a tight black T-shirt sauntered into Susan's modest office overlooking the police department's bullpen and stood in front of her desk. He was the detective who had frozen in the doorway during the location shoot in Venice. Susan didn't offer the chair.

"Do you know why I called you in, Steve?"

"I've got a pretty good idea," he said wryly, with a grin that turned into a smirk.

"Do tell," Susan said, smoldering now.

"Uh, to apologize?" And the grin was back.

Susan's brow furrowed and she fought for control.

Steve was on a roll. "You stepped on my effin heel outside the door, Lieutenant. I almost took a header."

Susan's voice got so quiet, Steve had to lean in to hear. "Are you living in an alternate universe? You compromised the warrant. Endangered my men."

"Two sides to every story, babe."

Susan's hands tightened into fists, but she stayed seated. "Here's your choice, Steve. You put in for a transfer to something less strenuous or I write you up and your career stalls."

"We all know why you were promoted out of turn. Your skirt. Listen to me, babe—"

Susan shot out of her chair, muscled Steve against her office wall, her forearm pressed against his throat. A picture of George W crashed to the floor; the glass frame shattered. Steve's eye started bugging, his face turned beet red.

"You call me babe again, I'll twist your balls until you're singing soprano in the Chiefs choir. You got that?"

Steve's cool dissolved as he fought for breath and nodded his head.

Susan pushed a little harder and then: "Cut!"

She backed off, breathing heavily.

"What the fuck, Susan?" the actor said, rubbing his throat, out of character now. "Uh, what we were doing? It's called acting."

"It's called growing a pair," she snapped.

"Okay, people," Henry Lee shouted from behind the monitor, trying to defuse the tension. To the script supervisor he said, "Print that. Good work, you two."

Susan turned off the anger like a light switch being thrown. "Shit! I am so sorry, Matt. No sleep. You're right, sorry. Won't happen again."

"No harm no foul . . . babe."

Susan's eyes flashed with anger, but she covered it by turning away.

"That's a wrap, ladies and gents. Moving on," the first AD intoned.

———

Susan strutted along the wide aisle of her million-dollar mobile home, sipping Perrier and talking on her cell phone. She was playing to an audience of one, and she knew she was killing, enjoying Cruz's discomfort.

"Cruz Feinberg," she said, flirty. "A man protecting me from danger."

The pink blush on Cruz's neck worked its way up to his ears that turned bright red.

Susan stifled a laugh, not wanting to embarrass Cruz any more than she already had. She'd never seen him this jumpy. "No," Susan went on, flying high on adrenaline from the success of her on-camera scene. "They're rigging the lights for the next shot. Matt's pissed off because he had to do a little acting . . . no, he'll recover."

All the while Susan was talking, Cruz's fingers flew across his laptop. He looked up after hitting Send and blushed a second time when he realized Susan was trying to get a look at his screen. He quickly opened his dashboard to hide the evidence.

Susan's makeup artist came and went, and while Susan nursed a latte and did a little online bill paying, Cruz kept digging. She had no idea they were visiting the same site as he surreptitiously retrieved her bank statements for the past six months.

———————

"Old man Diskin was cool?" Sean asked as he passed an eighteen-wheeler on the highway and pulled back into the right lane. Above all, he wanted to blend with the flow of traffic. The van was now filled with drugs and cash, more than enough for a long stretch in the big house. Not a scenario Sean was eager to relive. The brothers were traveling just outside Sacramento talking to Terrence over the van's Bluetooth system.

"He's leaving for Italy next week. Said to enjoy the view.

Thinks you boys deserve a rest. Called us the hardest-working young men in L.A. He doesn't know the half of it."

The three brothers chuckled. Gallows humor.

"Head down the five and take 152 West," Terrence went on.

"No worries, I'll plug into the GPS," Sean said.

"If you get to Esalen, you passed the driveway. The key's hidden at the base of the third fence post on the right as you drive toward the gate."

"Cool," Toby said.

"I promised to reupholster that sectional in his yacht we installed last year for being so supportive of the family," Terrence went on. "Again, he doesn't know the half of it. The man didn't say no, left me the keys. And Toby, dump all of it, I'm not kidding. No trace, nothing that can lead back to us."

"Neighbors?" Sean asked.

"No direct sight lines onto the property. You're a hundred feet above the deck."

"It's a lot of product," Toby said wistfully.

"No time to get greedy. You did good, my brothers. Stay light on your feet and we'll come out the other end of this rich men. Have yourselves a nice dinner at the Post Ranch Inn when business is completed. Use the store credit card—the story is you had a furniture pickup in San Francisco. I'll create an invoice and send it up to Rob. Tell him you stopped by and missed him. He won't remember, but he'll cash the check.

"Buy a piece of art at the Hawthorne Gallery in Big Sur. Spend a few thousand. You know the room we're doing for Daphne? I'll send the color palette. Pick out a few things that work with our design, text me your choices, and we'll make a decision before you pay.

"And, Toby, you had a visit from the LAPD. A Lieutenant Gallina and a Detective Tompkins. We knew they were going to show up sooner or later. Nothing to sweat. You've got Dean to cover you on the Vegas hit, and I told them you've spent the last two days picking up furniture and art for one of our clients. He left a card. I told him you'd call when you got into town. He seemed okay with that."

"Sounds good," Toby said, then added, chuckling, "Your head's gonna spin when you see the cash."

"Just stay focused until the job's done. I'm proud of you both."

Sean and Toby took the compliment to heart. The feeling of being in a gang, an organization founded on blood, made them greater, more powerful, than the sum of their parts.

"Air out the van before you head south," Terrence went on. "Diskin said to strip the beds and leave the linens in the laundry room."

"Roger that," Sean said. "Can't piss off the gravy train."

Terrence's voice changed as the electronic bell over the door chimed and the men knew someone had entered the store.

"Later, Susan Blake's man just stepped in. Gotta run," and Terrence hung up.

———

Jack walked into the Dirk Brothers Clothing Store looking worse for the wear. His back was blazing, his eyes were burning, but he wanted to take care of personal business before heading home.

"Jack, wow, you look worse than I feel," Terrance said, all smiles.

"Thanks, I needed that."

"You made the news. Is our girl okay?"

Jack didn't like the tone of the question and the familiarity it implied, but he chalked it up to his own fatigue.

"Susan's fine. Just a scare. Seems to go with the territory."

"The painting looked terrific on your wall. I hope it was okay. I'm not keen on surprises myself. But Susan . . . is very willful, and you have to admit, she has great taste."

"That's why I'm here." Jack pulled out his credit card and handed it to Terrence. "I'd like you to credit her card, and put the charges on mine."

"I understand. I'll take care of it right away."

Terrence slipped behind the register while Jack looked at the pictures that adorned the wall behind him. Terrence had already mounted a framed picture of him with Susan at the art opening, some actors he recognized, and what appeared to be a family portrait. Terrence and his two younger brothers in their teens. They looked like hell on wheels.

"Good-looking crew," Jack commented, with a cop's instinct to dig for more.

"Couldn't run the business without them." Terrence abruptly changed the subject: "In the market for a suit? I liked the Hugo Boss jacket you wore over your jeans, it's a good casual look on you, but you might want something more upscale, forward-thinking."

Jack laughed, too tired to take offense. "No, I'm good. But I'll keep it in mind."

Terrence hoped he'd just move on and vacate the premises. The last thing he needed was an ex-cop snooping around. "I spent the night doing inventory. The new fall line is coming in next week."

"No help from your brothers?"

"They're up north on a buying trip."

"So that's why *you* look as bad as I feel."

"What?" said Terrence with a spark of anger.

"The inventory."

"Oh, right," he said, covering lightning fast. A move not lost on Jack. "Dead on my feet."

Jack checked his credit card receipt, signed on the dotted line, and accepted his card back. Fifteen thousand, even. Terrence led the way to the door. "You just bought your first major piece of art, Jack. Enjoy it."

"Thanks," he said, surprised he felt no buyer's remorse.

"Totally my pleasure." Terrence closed the door so quickly, Jack felt he'd just gotten the bum's rush.

A strange duck, Jack thought as he walked up Main Street and headed for the Mustang. At least he'd taken care of the issue of the painting. Until the end of the month, when the credit card bill arrived.

Fifteen

Jack spent twenty minutes in a scalding shower, trying to cleanse himself of the past twenty-four hours. He was unhappy about the emotional tug-of-war with Susan and regretted their sexual involvement. He had never crossed that line when he was on the force, and now it had complicated his life in ways he couldn't readily articulate. The Vicodin had kicked in but offered little relief. He chased it with a couple more Excedrin and sat down at the computer with wet hair and a snarky attitude.

Four long days had passed since little Marie Sanchez was gunned down, and he was making little to no progress on the case. He had a list of people who wanted Vegas dead, shell casings found at a distance that proved the shooter was a sniper and changed the killer's profile, but not much else.

The four phones in the loft rang as one. Jack picked up the receiver and hoped he wouldn't live to regret extending an olive branch to his ex-wife.

"Jeannine," he said.

"You sound tired, Jack."

"It was a long night. What can I help you with?"

"Oh, do I sound that needy?"

"A figure of speech, you sound fine."

"Well, thank you."

Jack waited for Jeannine to get to the reason for the call.

"It's so quiet here. In the house."

Not what Jack was expecting.

"At first I thought, what a relief, to have that pompous ass out of my hair," she went on. "And now it's just quiet."

"No call from Jeremy?"

"No, nothing."

Jack was a little confused. "Let me get this straight. You did throw him out?"

"He didn't fight to stay, Jack. At least you fought for your family. I think he was relieved. I think he was looking for an out."

"Doesn't sound like Jeremy to me. I don't think he can survive without having someone to listen to his worldly views." Jack said "worldly views" like the put-down it was meant to be. But he knew taking sides in a breakup was a fool's game. Because when they got back together, Jeannine would use his own words to nail him.

"You're so bad, Jack Bertolino."

Now Jack was totally confused. She made it sound like bad was good. Jeannine hadn't used that coquettish tone of voice in recent memory. Jack was avoiding those complications like an IED.

"So, I was thinking . . ."

"Yeah?"

"There's nothing keeping me here, so I was thinking about taking a road trip. Like you did, Jack."

"That sounds like a plan. Where to?"

"I was thinking California. I'll rent a car and drive up the Pacific Coast Highway. You've been so kind the past few days, would you mind terribly if I spent a few nights at your loft? To save the expense of a hotel. I wouldn't be a bother."

Jack understood that there was no correct answer to be had.

"I don't know," he said, scrambling for excuses. "I'm working two cases simultaneously, and the loft is also my office."

"You won't even know I'm there."

Jack's next pause verged on toxic. "All right, Jeannine. Let's see how it plays out. But if I'm up to my neck in alligators, well, we'll have to work something out."

"I'm pleased, Jack." He nearly groaned at the note of triumph in her voice. "I know you're busy, so I'll let you get back to it." And she hung up.

Jack walked over to the sink and popped a second Vicodin. Was his memory going bad, or was she the one who had demanded that he move out, out, out of his own house?

———

The waning sun loomed over the Pacific, and then dipped below the horizon sending shards of orange capping the midnight-blue waves that pounded the rocky shoreline.

Toby and Sean sat cliffside, legs dangling a hundred feet above the water, smoking a fatty, and watched as the churning waves pulled $350,000 worth of high-end marijuana out to sea. Toby took a long drag off the joint, grabbed the bottle of Dom Pérignon Sean was bogarting, and tipped some into his mouth, spilling more down his chin. He handed it back to his brother and got up to dispatch the last bale of pot. They had seven thirty reservations at Post Ranch Inn and he had worked up an appetite.

Toby ducked into the back of the van, checked to make sure

he was alone, and pulled three five-pound waterproof parcels out of the green plastic-wrapped bale. He opened one of the custom-built side panels in the rear of the van and secreted the drugs. He'd heard Terrence's warning, but he had plans that didn't include his brothers. He'd take the fall, if necessary, but he didn't feel like he was standing on a precipice. Just being careful. Thinking three moves ahead, like his older brother had tutored.

Toby dropped the bale next to Sean and in a sleight of hand cut the wrapping off the bale before his brother could see the weight differential.

Sean looked over at Toby and passed him the joint. "You okay?"

Toby raised his eyebrows in a question and exhaled a thick cloud of blue smoke.

Sean said, "You look . . ."

"We should've taken the dog," Toby announced.

"Huh. That's what's got a hold of you?"

"Why?" he said with more attitude than intended.

Sean took a long pull of the Dom Pérignon. "You've killed a lot of men in the past few days."

If you only knew, Toby thought.

"It was a blood bath out in the water," Sean went on.

"You protect blood with blood," Toby said. "The dog didn't do shit to us." And then, "Why? It's fucking with you?"

"It'll pass," Sean said.

Toby knew that fact to be true.

"Besides, Ricky J was on me," Sean said. "I should've pulled the trigger."

"It was a good play. The only play. No worries, bro."

Toby and Sean got back to work. They knifed the last of the keys and scattered the drugs over the cliff's edge like ashes of the dead, where they were sucked into the rough sea below.

———

Kolinsky's Funeral Home was a twenties Victorian, white clapboards and subtle blue trim. The lawn was so green it looked like AstroTurf. To add to the charm, the cloying smell turned Jack's stomach as he entered the vestibule with Cruz at his side.

"How many more days do you want me to track her?" Cruz asked.

"Until we get some answers. And it'll give me time to knock on doors. Are you holding your own there?"

"Oh yeah. Caterer's great, Susan's easy on the eyes, and one of the makeup girls seems to be interested in *moi*."

Jack smiled. Cruz never had to worry in that department. "Don't forget you're on the job. Stay focused."

"No worries. Hey, BTW, Susan sure spends a ton of money. I mean, she's rich. So, she's got it to spend, but spend she does. Wait till you check out her bank statements."

Jack was wearing a black blazer and black jeans; Cruz, a black T-shirt and jeans. Jack looked like a cop, and Cruz, a neighborhood friend of the deceased.

They staggered their entrance, walking separately into viewing room B in the middle of the service. The neighborhood priest was straining to relate the positive history of the dearly departed. The wails emanating from the deceased's mother could've curdled milk.

It was an open casket, and Tomas Vegas, dressed in a green sharkskin jacket and lounge lizard shirt, looked younger than his years, waxy, and, well, dead. He was overly made up, too much red in the lips, Jack thought. He would've been pissed off.

Cruz was clearly uncomfortable with the proceedings, but moved to the far side of the room within listening distance of a group of young gangsters.

Jack, who had experienced far too many of these events, was all business as he eyeballed the room from the rear.

Heavenly viewing room B was filled with an equal number of cops, gangbangers, and relatives. The young bangers, members of Vegas's set, Lenox Road, who Jack had tussled with at Juan Sanchez's court appearance, stood in a tight knot giving Jack the stink eye. Jack looked through them as if they were invisible, adding insult to their bruised egos.

A few members of SM18 and Culver City 12's had showed, keeping an eye on the proceedings, but Heavenly viewing room was Switzerland, for one night only.

Gallina and Tompkins stood in the back of the room, trying to blend in and failing. Gallina scowled when he saw Jack step inside. Tompkins, who was eating a cookie he'd grabbed from the tray in the vestibule, gave him a welcoming nod as he wiped crumbs off his mouth.

The priest, who finished his service with the Lord's Prayer, invited the friends and family of Tomas Vegas to pay their respects to the dearly departed. The procession started calmly enough with some kids running up to the casket to see their first dead body.

Yet the proceedings quickly turned into a Spanish telenovela. Tomas's grandmother, a slight woman shrouded in black lace, stumbled down the aisle, weeping, pushed past the priest, and nearly toppled her grandson as she tried to crawl into the casket with her boy shouting, "Take me, take me, Lord!"

Family members ran up and grabbed the distraught woman. As she regained her equilibrium, she broke away, bolted back up the aisle, and lashed out at a blonde woman in a red dress standing alone behind the last row of folding chairs.

"*Puta!*" the distraught woman shrieked as her bony hand slashed out, raking the young woman's cheek below the eye.

One of Vegas's cousins ran up and lifted the slight woman off her feet before she could strike again. He carried her kicking and screaming out of the Heavenly viewing room.

Some of the gangsters had their cell phones out, snapping photos and videos of the high drama, posting on Instagram and Facebook before the funeral director could close the doors to the room. The sound of the wailing was muffled and then died away. Jack remembered a time when the only thing people came to wakes armed with were rosary beads. The photo feasting made him feel tired.

The young blonde knockout looked like she was crying blood, but no tears were being shed. The buzz in the room went silent as she parted the seas, walking past Vegas's gang members who showed no pity, family members who blamed her for Tomas's death, and the cops who didn't understand what the hell had just transpired.

She looked beautiful, Jack thought, but cold as ice, and a little unhinged. He snapped his own photo as she strode past, grabbed Kleenex from a box near the door, and exited the room.

Jack hand-signaled Cruz to stay put and followed in her wake. He was delayed by a crowd of mourners exiting viewing room A and spilling into the lobby, beelining for the table filled with gratis cookies, cakes, and coffee.

A baby-blue late-model Volkswagen bug was just pulling away from the curb as Jack hit the front porch. He muttered a curse as he jotted down her license plate number. Jack caught a glimpse of her dabbing the bloody cut in her rearview mirror as she stepped on the gas and cold vapor poured out of her exhaust pipes.

Cruz walked up next to him, checked his watch like he was waiting for a ride, and gave his report. "Vegas got dumped by our lady in red for some white dude."

"No name?"

"White dude was all Vegas's cousin knew. The family blames Eva—that's the girl's name—for all of his troubles."

"Love's a bitch," Jack said dryly. "No last name on the girl?"

Cruz shook his head. "His cousin got suspicious with all my questions. Asked if I was a cop. I laughed, and he laughed, and I played it off, saying I was thinking to hook up with her," he said, enjoying the challenge.

"You did good, but be careful. You live in their neighborhood and don't need the heat."

"I hear you."

"My guess is Eva's last name is sitting in Vegas's criminal history file back in the loft. The deceased was a witness for the prosecution in a trial about a year ago, which is why it caught my eye. I think Eva was the defendant. We need a list of all the witnesses for the prosecution and the defense. That might be a trail worth pursuing."

"She's hot," Cruz said admiringly.

"And she wasn't there to mourn. Wearing red to a wake is provocative."

"Why was she there?" Cruz asked.

"To make sure Tomas Vegas was really dead."

———

Jesus Arcaro, with one fishing line already running off the Redondo Beach Pier, was carefully cutting a strip of calamari and attaching it to the hook of his second weighted rig. His son was wrapped comfortably in a blanket, sitting on his wife's lap in a folding lawn chair, sucking on a pacifier, and enjoying the swirl of activity around him.

The bell on Jesus's first line dinged and the tip of his pole dipped slightly, making the baby laugh. Jesus handed the rod he was working on to his wife, grabbed his live pole, set the hook, and started to reel in. Big smile on his youthful face.

His good mood was short-lived as he realized his catch wasn't fighting back. It was probably seaweed or garbage, he thought as he reeled it in, being careful not to break the line and lose his pricey rig. He pulled a clump of seaweed close to the cement pylons, where it was illuminated by one of the pier's spotlights.

Jesus wasn't sure what he was looking at. In the center of the mass of dark green was a white bloated . . . fish, maybe? No, it wasn't a fish.

A man's severed forearm bobbed in the chop, a gold pinky ring glinting between swollen, nibbled fingers.

Jesus stood paralyzed. His wife, concerned, walked over to the rail, looked over the edge, and cried out. Their baby picked up on his mother's distress and started to wail.

Sixteen

Day Five

Jack hit the gas, and his Mustang's eight cylinders responded effortlessly. He powered up to seventy-five and shot over the rise on the 405 in anticipation of a stomach-churning roller-coaster ride down the far side.

Instead Jack had to stomp on the brakes. The tires chirped, and he was thankful for the car's antilock system. The freeway had turned into a parking lot, backed up all the way to the 5. Welcome to the San Diego Freeway.

Jack considered lowering the convertible top and then vetoed his naïve New York optimism. He made his descent, heel to toe, 3 mph, into the San Fernando Valley, a suburban sprawl veiled in a thick ribbon of yellowish-brown that shrouded the endless neighborhoods below.

Jack had lived here long enough to understand that Van Nuys scoffed at Reseda, and Encino thumbed its nose at Van Nuys, and wouldn't be caught dead shopping in Reseda. It was zip-code snobbery. And to everyone on the West Side where Jack lived, it was all *the Valley*.

As he made a right off Sherman Way a few blocks past Balboa, he felt like he'd been transported back to the sixties. California ranch houses, well maintained, large lots, no sidewalks, lawns toasting in the 101-degree heat. Mandated water rationing generated brown lawns and cracked soil, evoking images of the Dust Bowl. The people who thumbed their noses at the water restrictions had lively border gardens with colorful annuals that thrived despite the unrelenting heat.

Something about the Valley always left Jack feeling a little depressed. He couldn't put his finger on it. Jack rolled to a smooth stop when the voice on the Mustang's GPS system alerted him that he had arrived at his destination on the right.

Good-looking home, Jack thought as he walked up the path toward the front door. Modest but well kept, showing pride of ownership. Light-blue stucco, white shutters, and a white gravel roof to reflect the unforgiving sun and mitigate some of the valley heat.

Jack reached for the doorbell, but was stopped by a neighbor walking a reddish-brown dachshund whose belly threatened to scrape the hot sidewalk.

"Not at home," the spry octogenarian shared. "Erica's at work, Eva's been gone since nine."

"And you know this how?"

"Live across the street. Keep my eyes open."

A man who took his neighborhood watch seriously, Jack thought.

"Any idea when they're coming back?" he asked.

"You a cop? You're not driving a cop car."

"I was a cop."

"You look like a cop."

Jack didn't want to be rude, but wanted to get off this wheel of conversation. "Any ideas? I need to talk to Eva."

"What's your interest?"

"A six-year-old girl was killed in her living room, playing with her Barbie doll. The intended target was a gangbanger who testified against Eva in her trial last year. I've been hired by the grieving family to track down the shooter."

The gentleman gave that some thought while his dog pissed on the sidewalk. Not far to go, Jack noted idly.

"Eva's a free spirit. A good girl. She was set up. The gangster you're referring to was scum."

"You'll get no argument from me, sir. I've seen his rap sheet."

"He's got blood on his hands and deserved to die."

"I'm not a judge and jury."

The neighbor lightened up a little. "Eva comes and goes. Like I said, she's a free spirit. Erica works the seven-to-five shift at Costco over on Sepulveda. She'll know. Mother and daughter, they're very close. Tight-knit family."

"Is there a Mr. Perez in the equation?"

"Not my place to say."

A man who could keep secrets. "Good enough. I'll reach out to her mother. Thank you for your help."

"It's my pleasure to be of service to law enforcement."

Jack fought the urge to smile. "You have yourself a good day, Mr. . . ."

"Marks. Ralph Marks."

"Have a good day, Mr. Marks."

"I'll do just that. And you're not the first cop to come calling."

"Really?"

"A Mutt and Jeff team. Salt-and-pepper. Came an hour ago and left empty-handed."

"Thanks."

At least Gallina and Tompkins were on the case, he thought. Jack slid behind the wheel and cranked up the engine as Mr. Marks walked across the street and pushed through his black wrought-iron gate. Jack couldn't be sure, but he had the distinct feeling Mr. Marks was making note of his license plate number. Jack respected that. He understood one could never be too careful.

———

Jack followed on the heels of Erica Perez as she stormed through the cavernous box store. "I've got a thirty-minute break and I'm giving you ten. Don't waste them," she said over her shoulder as Jack dodged zombie-eyed shoppers pushing ankle-crushing pushcarts filled with massive quantities of paper products, produce, meat, crates of fruit, cleaning supplies, electronic equipment, and booze.

Outside Costco's main entrance he waited for Erica to pick up a stuffed chicken roll and Coke at the food court. He fought the urge to grab a hot dog, and then followed her to a red metal table with a red umbrella that shaded only half of the table. Erica sat in the shade, forcing Jack to squint directly into the sun. He didn't think it was an accident.

Erica was a stocky woman, hard but feminine, thick in the waist and shoulders. Deep lines in her face defined a life of hardship; her smoky brown eyes were guarded, but Jack felt an innate compassion. Shadows of florid gang ink on her cleavage and the world-weary visage told the story of a woman who had been to hell and back and lived to raise a daughter outside the 'hood.

"When are you people going to give my Eva a break?"

"I'm not here to jam up your daughter. From the looks of her, she can take care of herself."

"You were at the wake?" she said, clucking and shaking her head.

"She caused quite a stir."

"She gets the stubborn from her father."

"Are you still married?"

"The hell that's supposed to mean?"

"The shooter feels like a man, but not necessarily. Retribution is on the list of possibilities." Jack raised his hands in supplication. "But it's a long list."

"Fair enough," she said, relenting. "That one's got an airtight alibi. Died in Corcoran ten years ago. My father died in Compton," she added sourly, "shot down on the street like a dog."

"And you moved out of the neighborhood to give your daughter a better life. I can see you're a hardworking woman."

"Yeah, I work," she said without bitterness, just a statement of fact. "I can't change my past. It's written in blood and ink. My grandfather, my father, my husband, but not my daughter. I refused to let that happen."

"You broke the chain."

"But I couldn't save her. You and your kind took care of that. You set her up and beat her down. Hurt my baby good."

Jack didn't argue the point, not having looked over the court transcripts yet. He'd reach out to Leslie for those. "I just want to find the shooter. Not for Tomas Vegas, believe me. There's no love lost between me and the bangers."

"Why don't you leave well enough alone then?"

"Tell that to the family of a six-year-old girl named Maria, who also got shot down like a dog in her own living room," Jack said, using her own words to make the point. "Mr. and Mrs. Sanchez are suffering the kind of pain I think you can relate to."

Erica didn't respond to that. She ate politely and drank some of her soda, checking her watch.

Jack let the silence grow before he broke it.

"What was your take on the trial? How did Eva get on the wrong side of Vegas?"

"My daughter is a beautiful woman. A lot of men wanted a piece of her." She sighed. "Vegas wanted to own her. When she shut him down, he repaid the favor. If he couldn't have her, he was going to guarantee nobody would."

"Was there another suitor? Someone else she was in love with?"

She took another bite instead of answering.

"One of Vegas's cousins seemed to think there was a love triangle at play."

"And you'd take the word of a snake?" Erica checked her watch again and stood to leave. "Like I said, lots of boys wanted to date her. But no one in particular. She had a lot of friends but liked her freedom. She didn't deserve what she got."

Jack could sense a lie, but he wasn't going to get any more, he could tell. Instead he handed Erica his card. "Tell her I just need a few minutes of her time. Tell her it's for the little girl. If she's anything like you, she'll call."

Erica looked at the card; her eyes went dark. She sized him up again, and started to turn without responding.

"Oh, Erica," Jack said, stopping her, "you have protection at the house?"

"You don't wanna walk through my door without knockin'."

Jack's face creased into a grin as Erica marched back into Costco. He wasn't surprised her house was heavy. His guess was she inherited her husband's personal armory. He wanted to ask if there was a long-barrel .22 in the group, but he didn't want her shutting down or destroying the weapon. He'd save that for another day.

He watched as Erica pulled out her cell and one-hand dialed before he lost sight of her beyond the aisle of sixty-inch, flat-screen TVs.

————

Jack was always amazed how much food Nick Aprea could consume without gaining weight. Nick chalked it up to having a two-year-old running around the house. That, and an incredibly active sex life with a woman who was eleven years his junior. Who could argue the point?

Nick was concentrating on his churrasco ribeye steak with chimichurri sauce at Oscar's Cerveteca Venice, on Rose. One eye drifted across the street watching the comings and goings of the local denizens.

Rose used to be a ganged-up neighborhood, but was now giving Abbot Kinney Boulevard a run for its money with all the new high-end real estate and trendy eateries.

Jack's stomach finally stopped growling as he destroyed a plate of chicken enchiladas with a green tomatillo sauce, black beans, and rice. He washed down the hearty food with a diet Coke, fully aware of the caloric irony.

Nick took a long pull of Dos Equis. "So, here's the skinny," he said, wiping the hot sauce off his mouth with the back of his hand, and then rubbing his eye with the hand with the hot sauce on it, making his eye water, which he finally cleared with his clean napkin. "Duggy, one of my street connections," Nick went on without blinking, "was waiting on his bimonthly shipment of pot. He buys a half, three-quarters of a pound, sells enough to stay in weed for a couple weeks . . . doesn't mind talking about it because it's pot. And if he wanted to pay boutique prices, he could walk down to the corner and buy it legal, like."

"Yeah?" Jack said.

"Here's the linkage," Nick said, knowing the story was getting away from him. "Duggy, up until five days ago, was being supplied by Tomas Vegas."

That got Jack's attention.

"Duggy was contacted the day after Vegas was killed by another Lenox Road banger, name's"—Nick pulled out his pad and flipped a few pages—"Joey Ramirez, who was sliding into Vegas's spot and assured him that business would go on like normal. They were just experiencing a personnel shift. No worries.

"Only, two days ago, Duggy is standing in his usual spot with a roll of greenbacks, holding his dick because there was no drop-off."

"Who's supplying Lenox Road?"

"Has to be the Sinaloa boys. They're like Wal-Mart's. They've got deep inventory to keep prices low. That, and they struck a deal with the Mexican Mafia to retail their product in L.A. The Mexican Mafia controls the local sets, so Tomas Vegas and his ilk became part of their distribution chain."

Jack knew there was more to the story and let Nick shovel in a few more mouthfuls before interrupting his flow.

"And here's the kicker, last night a fisherman off the pier in Redondo—night out with the wife and kid—gets a hit and starts to reel it in, thinking he caught the big one. But it ain't no fish."

Nick was about to fork another piece of meat, but Jack prodded him on with, "What was it?"

Big grin from Nick. "It was a forearm with the hand still attached. Fingers swollen like Oscar Mayers. Some fishy had been snacking on them, but he was still sporting a gold pinky ring."

"Any missing persons reported?" Jack asked.

"Nada. Even put in a call to your Coast Guard buddy Captain Deak, said there'd been no maydays, no bodies, nothing. I ran a missing per through our system, but no hits on a beefy male."

He noticed Jack's look: "The arm coulda come off a bear. But Deak did add that there's been increased activity in drug drops off the coast, from Orange County up to Santa Barbara."

"Prints?"

"Talked to the Feebs, they're running them through IAFIS and VICAP now. If the guy has a criminal history, we'll know later today."

"Any identifiers on the ring?" Jack asked.

"Couple initials. We're on it. The ME said the arm had only been in the water twenty-four hours give or take."

"So, a panga, a single prop, or helicopter, whatever, makes a run across the border and a drop off shore. It's typically picked up by a local and run back to terra firma. Only this time they're not the only one with an eye on the prize. So where's the boat? Where's the body, the drugs?"

"Captain Deak's on the case. He's checking the digital tapes of every boat leaving the marina on Wednesday and not returning. It'll take some time, but might prove interesting. And his men are eyeballing the waters from here to San Diego. Looking for a floater minus a forearm, a scuttled boat, an oil slick, life vests, any fucking thing."

"So Vegas's crew was pushing Sinaloa weed. You think they went outlaw on their supplier. Cut out the middleman?" But Jack didn't like the sound of that play the moment it left his mouth.

"Doesn't make good business sense," he went on. "You could only get away with it once. El Eme wouldn't put up with it."

"Only way it plays is if there's a rogue group within Lenox." Nick didn't sound convinced. "But they're probably scared shitless as it is," he said.

Jack nodded in agreement. "First Vegas, now this. The cartel will put a few heads on stakes to get the natives talking."

"It's already in play. My man Duggy was knocking back a few long necks at The Cantina, trying to stay mellow, looking to score, when he was braced by two middle-aged, dead-eye, Indians, Mexicans, he don't know, but he was definitely chilled. Said they looked like stone-cold killers. The gist of the conversation was if anyone hears about a new source appearing on the scene, said information could be quite valuable. Two hundred grand worth of value."

"How is Duggy supposed to get the information back to the guys?"

"The Cantina's bartender."

"Can we sit them both down with your sketch artist, get a computer-generated photo of the cartel operatives?"

"Never gonna happen," Nick said. "They're too afraid of having to testify. Can't blame 'em. Their lives wouldn't be worth spit." Jack was sure that was right.

"My boy Duggy's hitting the road. The Indians put the fear of God in him. He don't know how they located him, he don't know nothing, but he's heading back to Minneapolis until the temperature in the room changes.

"He did say the short one of the two had a radical scar—his words—on his neck. Ear to ear."

Jack gave that some thought. "If these cartel guys are going down their list of buyers and sellers, they're going to have Juan Sanchez in their sights. I'm going to run by the house and make sure the family has the police protection Gallina promised."

Jack pulled out his wallet, but Nick waved him off. "Later pard, I'll keep you in the loop," he said and signaled for another Dos Equis from the waitress as Jack hustled out of the restaurant.

Seventeen

Eva sat on a bench in Balboa Park, cell phone to her ear. She watched a blue heron streak across the lake, circle once, and come in for a heavy touchdown, leaving a wake behind and scattering a noisy raft of mallards, feathers ruffling at the imposition. The sun was low on the horizon, the shadows growing longer. She waited for a trio of bikers to pedal past before continuing.

"Not just the cops showed up. A guy named Jack Bertolino talked to Mr. Marks and my mother today. He wants me to call him about Vegas."

Toby was sitting in bumper-to-bumper on I-5, drumming his fingers nervously on his knee. Sean was driving. They'd been making good time until Magic Mountain appeared on the right and traffic all but came to a standstill. In fact, all the optimism Toby had been feeling about the trip and his future turned into a gut clench when he heard Jack Bertolino's name.

Toby was well aware of the Susan Blake connection, heard about the painting, and knew Bertolino had been inside the family shop. He was also very aware of the ex-cop's track record and the reason he was connected to Susan. The last thing he needed was some supersleuth on his case.

"Why the hell's he involved?"

"He's working for the family of the little girl that got killed."

Toby shuddered at this news. Karmic payback. The only murder he'd take back if he could. Little Maria could be his ultimate undoing. The only mistake that replayed in his mind and kept him awake till the wee hours, until he was sufficiently anesthetized on pot and beer to pass out.

"Terrence said the cops stopped by the shop today. I'll call them tomorrow and be done with it. Babe, you have got nothing to worry about. You can talk to Bertolino, or not. It's your call."

"It's not that simple anymore."

"How so?"

"You really don't know?"

Toby fought to keep the edge out of his voice. "What? Eva, what's going on?"

Eva audibly sighed. "Someone shot Dr. Brimley."

"Brimley?" Toby said, feigning ignorance. The lies just kept coming.

"*The* doctor . . . Toby."

"Oh. Holy shit. Is he okay?"

"Shot dead. Police dragged him out of a ditch near his home. He lived up in Reseda Hills. The news said the coyotes made a mess of his face."

"Fuckin' prick deserved whatever he got."

Sean's head jerked in Toby's direction and they almost rearended the Chevy Volt that had come to a dead stop in front of them. Toby gave him a placating wave of the hand and dug the phone deeper into his ear, staring out at the monster roller coaster at Magic Mountain.

"Listen, stay with your aunt tonight. I've got unloading to do and inventory when we get back to the shop, and we're parked on the 5. It's a nightmare. It'll be a late night. I'll pick you up first thing in the morning. We'll go to IHOP and figure things out, take it one step at a time. No one can blame you for being leery of the police. It's a normal response after what you've been through. We don't even know if they've made the connection."

"Is there a connection to be made?"

Toby hastily corrected himself. "Not from our point of view. Just a coincidence, but you know the cops, they're always looking for an angle."

"Jack Bertolino asked Mom if I was seeing someone special when Tomas set me up. He heard it was jealousy, a lover's triangle. He's gonna be knocking on your door."

"How did he find that out? What did your mother say?"

"That there were a lot of guys interested, and I didn't want to get tied down."

Eva's mother was sly, he'd give her that. She didn't even like him. "That's the answer, then. I'll call you late, okay?"

"You know it is."

"Love you . . ."

"Call me later."

———

Jack discovered a black-and-white police car parked in front of the Sanchez house. Gallina had delivered as promised, and with Jack's concern appeased, he headed back to the loft, where he planned on going through Susan Blake's phone and bank records.

Jack soon had all of Cruz's files laid out on his desk. He color-coded certain repeated numbers and started to see a pattern developing. One particular New York number came up randomly, but frequently enough to be of interest.

Cruz let himself into the loft and dropped his gear on the dining room table. "Susan wrapped early today."

"How did she do?"

Cruz clicked his tongue rapidly a few times. "Woman's got talent."

"Check this out." Cruz walked into Jack's office and stopped just behind him. "There's a thirty-minute phone call an hour before Susan made a twenty-thousand-dollar withdrawal from her personal checking account, not her corporate account. Then a two-minute call was placed to that same number after her withdrawal."

"And get this," Cruz added, "her number was called and messaged seven times in the past twelve hours. Same number."

"And the same person phoned Susan at two thirty in the morning, the night of the alleged stalking attack at her rental home."

"That is so awesome. We've got our person of interest." Cruz always got jazzed when the puzzle pieces started to fall into place. His enthusiasm was infectious, and reminded Jack why he got into the game.

"It looks like Susan Blake knows her stalker. And said stalker might be bracing her for cash. Let's see if we can identify the caller."

Jack typed a number into his computer and Skyped Kenny Ortega in Miami.

"*Mi hermano!* Kenny shouted. "You have put the first legitimate smile on my face today."

"Hey, Kenny, you remember Cruz?"

"I may be overworked, but I'm not brain-addled, my friend. How's life in the fast lane?"

"Hollywood isn't what it's cracked up to be," Jack said.

"He's lying," Cruz shouted. "It's very cool."

"Hah!" Kenny barked a laugh. "Who have they cast to play me in your movie, Jack? I'm still thinking George Clooney."

"I'll get back to you on that, Kenny. Look, I need some help," Jack said, cutting to the chase. "Susan Blake is being stalked. It started in New York and followed her to Los Angeles. But we discovered that she may know her stalker, and refuses to share that intel. I'm trying to do an end-run. Cruz worked some of his magic and we have a series of phone numbers that coincide with specific events. I'd like to get the location of the calls in L.A., and a name to go with the number would be greatly appreciated."

"Hmmm, I've got a drug task force in play, so it might take a few days, but I'll try and fast-track it. Sit tight, my friends, I'll get back to you ASAP."

"Thanks, Kenny." Jack clicked off and turned to Cruz. "Why don't you take the afternoon off? You had an early call, and you've earned your keep for the day."

"Okay, boss, what're you up to?"

"I've got a few leads I want to follow up on. I may pay a visit to Leslie Sager, and then try and get a line on Eva Perez."

"Happy hunting, Jack. You need me, I'm on my cell." And Cruz vamoosed out the door.

Jack splashed some water on his face, pulled his cell from the charger, and grabbed his keys. Before he reached the door, it resounded with a light knock. Jack opened the door and was stopped dead in his tracks. Speechless.

"Are you going to invite me in?" she said, smiling shyly.

"What are you doing here, Jeannine?" Though flustered, Jack

grabbed her suitcase and stepped back so his ex-wife could enter the loft. "Why didn't you call? I would've picked you up."

"I didn't want to be a bother, Jack. I Ubered," she said with a youthful grin. "I'm posting my trip on social media, I'll have you know. I'm on Facebook now. I had my Uber driver stop at Gelson's. Do you still drink Cabernet?" she said, handing him a bottle. "I didn't get you a housewarming gift and I thought you might need a drink. You were never too fond of surprises."

Jeannine looked the loft over with a wife's discerning eye. "Very nice, very spacious."

"What are you doing here?" Jack asked again. Not accusatory, just perplexed.

"I'm not getting any younger, Jack."

"You should have called. We agreed to give it some thought."

"Oh Jack, twenty years. You think I don't know how you operate? You would have talked me out of coming. So, I stepped outside my comfort zone, booked a flight, and here I am. What an adventure."

"It's a surprise, all right, Jeannine. Just an FYI, not being insensitive here, but I'm working two cases. I was on my way out the door. I'm already running late."

"Oh?"

Jeannine had a gift for packing a lot of pain into one word.

Jack tried to soften the blow, though more in the line of how he'd treat any unexpected guest. "There's food in the fridge, a bookstore, coffee shop and movie theater up the block. I'll be back by the end of the day."

Jack rifled through his junk drawer and handed Jeannine his extra set of keys. "The gray fob opens the front door to the building, and this is the house key. Make yourself comfortable. Say, you can sleep in my bed tonight, and I'll bunk in the office. Clean towels are in the master bath."

Her voice was chilly, but she did show a smile of appreciation for his efforts. "Okay, Jack. I might just lay down for a bit. It's been a whirlwind. Thank you for not being mad. It means something to me."

Jack wasn't sure what that meant. In fact, he wasn't sure of anything at the moment, except he wanted to get the hell out of there. He mustered a half smile, locked the door, and took the stairs down, two at a time.

Eighteen

The CLOSED sign was hung early at the Dirk Brothers store on Main Street. A few hapless customers knocked on the door to no avail. Their cell phone calls went unanswered and then directly to voice mail. If customers tried to peer through the translucent shades, all they could make out were ghostlike images of carefully hung suits, framed photographs, designer furniture, and lighting fixtures.

Terrence stood in the storage room with a calculator in his hands, surrounded by stacks of Hugo Boss dress shirts and a fortune in vacuum-wrapped packages of banded hundreds and twenty-dollar bills.

Toby was on his laptop, reading from a Google search. "U.S. currency weighs exactly one gram per note. There are four hundred fifty-four grams in a pound. Therefore, one pound of U.S. one-hundred-dollar bills would be worth, drum roll please, forty-five thousand, four hundred dollars. A pound of twenties gives us nine thousand, eighty."

Sean was sipping from a crystal glass of eighteen-year-old Macallan, his eyes blood red from eight hours behind the wheel of the company van driving in rush hour gridlock.

"Holy fuck," Toby went on. "Twenty-two point oh five pounds equals a million, and we've got what?"

Sean glanced down at the yellow pad on his lap. "We've got eighty-three pounds of hundreds, and eighteen pounds of twenties."

Terrence notated the numbers on a tall cardboard carton filled with English suits. He hand-combed his long red hair behind one ear as his fingers flew over his calculator. "We've got three million, seven hundred sixty eight thousand, two hundred, in hundreds." He scratched the number on the carton and then inputted the number of twenties. "And a hundred thousand sixty-three, four-hundred-forty in twenties. For a grand total . . . of"—he tapped the add key and turned to his brothers for maximum effect—"three million, nine hundred thirty-one thousand, six hundred and forty. We're just shy of four million dollars."

The three brothers looked at the bundled cash with awe. Terrence stood tall with his calculator. Toby, slouched, grinning, in a chair holding his iPad. And Sean, intense, leaned forward with his single malt. They were gazing at more money, in one place, in their own storeroom, than they'd ever imagined seeing in their lifetimes.

They were looking at early retirement, freedom, dreams fulfilled, if they didn't fuck up. If they didn't get greedy. If they didn't let personal problems get in the way of family. If they stayed alive.

And Toby had a plan to keep it real, protect his family, and keep everybody on track.

Terrence was the first to speak. He walked past the mountain of cash, picked up a perfectly sized scotch glass he had bought from an antiques shop, and poured two fingers of Macallan for himself. Tipped the bottle to top off Sean's glass, walked over to the minifridge, grabbed a chilled long neck of Dos Equis, popped the top, and handed it to his little brother. Sean and Toby waited in deference for the family elder to speak.

The brothers tipped their glasses and let out their collective breaths.

"So, we went after three-fifty and walked away with close to four-mil."

He looked into each of his brother's eyes before continuing.

"But here's the rub. An arm floated up onshore last night off Redondo. My guess is that it belonged to the pilot of the boat we scuttled. I've got Sean to thank for saving my life with a clean shot. But the cartel, per *your* information, is already looking for retribution with a heavy reward attached. That's per Ricky J's account and also the man we should thank for enriching our family at great personal expense."

"To Ricky J," the brothers intoned in unison.

"And now with the errant body part," Terrence went on, "the cops are involved. We know that Toby will be questioned in regards to the killing of Tomas Vegas and the little girl. It's just a matter of time before they tie Eva to our family and come knocking on our door.

"We also have to factor in the connection to the doctor who got snuffed up in Reseda. Toby's sure there's no traction between the two cases, but we have to remain mindful of the possibility. After all, Eva was butchered by the prick. That gives Toby probable cause and me a bad feeling in my gut."

He had more than a bad feeling. Terrence would keep a sharp eye on the proceedings. Toby had proved himself in the field, but was he willing to let the entire enterprise self-destruct because Toby worked outside the family? Terrence wouldn't entertain that notion. Keep thinking positive thoughts, but make contingency plans.

Terrence went on, "Plus, now Jack Bertolino's on the fucking case and he's nobody's fool. I would've let the bitch pay for the painting if it were me, but what the hell."

"So, how do we launder the cash?" Sean asked.

"Slowly, carefully. We stagger the deposits, nothing over eight thousand dollars to be safe, stay under the radar screen, and continue to dollar-cost average into our retirement accounts. We'll be making money while we clean the cash. Nothing has changed except for the fact that by the time the money is untraceable, clean, and solidly invested, a couple years at the most, we, my brothers, will be rich men."

Nobody balked at the time frame, which made Terrence feel confident about getting into business with family. With blood. Most criminals were mindless and greedy. They would've immediately demanded their cut of the profits, guaranteeing that the only thing that would end up cut would be their throats at the hands of the Sinaloa cartel. He was concerned about Toby's possible extracurricular activities, but he had saved the family's bacon out in the Pacific, taken care of business up north, and Terrence would give him a pass at this point in time.

"Toby, did Dean call you regarding the order that couldn't be filled?"

"No, I texted him from Big Sur, asked him to hold the product, that I was up north working a rush contract. I'll connect with him tomorrow, catch a few waves, be a little pissed there's no dope, and see what's up."

"Good man."

Sean took a sip of scotch. "I hate to bring it up, but we've gotta dump all of the weapons we used out on the water. Everything. We buy again, but we hold nothing that can be traced back to us. That's ammunition too."

"Fuck," Toby said.

"Absolutely," Terrence said, proud that his brothers were smarter than the herd. Better than that, they had made him rich.

———

Jack pushed the food tray across the simple gray cafeteria tabletop and took a seat. He tried not to be drawn in by the shadowed blue eyes of DDA Leslie Sager. The two of them had political differences, but politics were lost in the bedroom, and even though Leslie had chosen the wrong side in Jack's last case, he couldn't deny their chemistry. And he'd been around the block enough times to know that when the body talked, the mind listened, for better or for worse.

Leslie grabbed one of two hot black coffees off the proffered tray with her right hand and slid a manila envelope toward Jack with her left. Even as he kept his eyes averted, he knew she was enjoying his discomfort. She could play him like a fiddle whether he liked the music or not.

"It's the witness list from both sides of the case," she said. "If it helps catch the scumbag who killed that little girl, I'm happy to bend the rules." Sharp as ever, she noticed that he was on edge. "What's going on, Jack? You seem preoccupied."

"My ex-wife showed up on my doorstep with a full suitcase."

"Jeannine? What does she want?"

"Don't really know. I ran out the door five minutes after she arrived." He saw the rebuke on Leslie's lips and held up his hand in innocence. "Not my proudest moment. I didn't intend to hurt her feelings. Still, I wouldn't be disappointed if she were gone when I get back."

The slightest hint of jealousy entered her voice. "You've got to simplify your life, Jack."

"Thank you, Obi-Wan."

Leslie laughed. "Point taken. So . . . Laureth Curran was the prosecuting attorney. She'd be happy to talk to you if you think it will help, but be warned she's up to her neck in alligators. She remembered the case because the defendant was such a beautiful woman. Eva's conviction was a slam-dunk: overwhelming physical evidence and no sign that her car had been tampered with.

"The defense claimed the drugs and gun were planted. Eva had two priors, one for possession, just a few joints, and one for shoplifting makeup at a Walgreens when she was seventeen. Lightweight, high school hijinks. She'd also been cited for resisting arrest when she was pulled over and the car legally searched. It was enough for the jury to find for the prosecution, and Judge Annatto to send her away."

Listening to Leslie talk about a case, that glint in her eye even if it wasn't her case, was a total turn-on for Jack, what had attracted him in the first place.

Jack had been falsely arrested for murder and was fortunate enough to see Leslie decimate the arresting detective's case, eliciting a rare apology from the LAPD, freeing Jack and taking Lieutenant Gallina down a few pegs. It was a thing of prosecutorial beauty.

"I could see Eva resisting arrest," Jack said. "She put on quite a show at the wake last night. Her mother's an ex-banger who made it out of the 'hood to raise her daughter on the straight and narrow. Broke the chain, but there's a lot of history. Grew up with guns in the house."

"Could she be the shooter?"

"Doesn't feel right, but I'll know more when I speak with her." He nodded in thanks for her info. "I might reach out to Laureth if I hit a dead end. Find out if anybody in the courtroom had a vested interest in her *not* going away, besides family."

"I'll e-mail you her number if you need it. I want you to get whoever killed that little girl, Jack. If anybody can do it, you can."

A compliment from Leslie felt good, Jack thought. Like putting on his favorite pair of jeans straight from the dryer. All warm and soft.

"Gotta run, Jack," Leslie said as she checked the time on her cell, grabbed her briefcase, buzzed Jack on the cheek. She raced out the door to Court 3A, where she was sticking it to a hit-and-run driver who killed a mother of three, knocking her off a bicycle while he was texting.

———

"Was it something I said?" Jack asked as he pulled his Mustang convertible up tight next to Eva's Beetle, parked in front of her mother's house in Van Nuys, blocking the young woman's escape.

Eva, caught tossing an overnight bag into the trunk of her car, indignantly slammed the hood shut but failed to diminish his grin.

"I spoke with your mother earlier today," he went on. "I'm glad I caught you. Obviously, you know who I am; I just need to know a little about you. Ten minutes max, and I'm out of your life."

Eva gave that some thought and answered Jack by waving off Ralph Marks, her protective neighbor, who was moving stiffly but resolutely in their direction.

"You're lucky she didn't take out an eye," Jack said, trying to diffuse some of the heat, referring to the aftermath of Tomas Vegas's grieving grandmother's attack. Eva's right eye was black and green; angry nail cuts extended below the Band-Aid–sutured wounds onto her cheeks.

Eva deflated. "Look, I'm on my way to my aunt's. What can I

help you with? Mom said you were working for the family whose little girl was killed. I feel terrible, but I didn't know the family. And I don't know anything about the shooting."

"I'm looking at anybody who had a grudge against Tomas Vegas. Any ideas?"

"I could've shot him. I hated him that much."

Jack's eyebrows raised in an unspoken question.

"I didn't, but I could've."

"One of Vegas's cousins seemed to think you had someone special in your life before your arrest."

"No one in particular. I tried to keep myself free. I dated, but nothing serious."

Jack thought he might've hit a dead end. Eva seemed sincere, believable. Jack wasn't feeling a lie.

"Would you mind giving me the names of who you were spending time with? All I want to do is to cross them off my list. The deaths are probably tied to a rival gang, but I have to ask the questions."

Eva's face went tight. "No. No, Jack. I've been through enough already. I don't want to relive the experience. Now, if you'd please move your car, I'm running late."

"Eva, take my card. If you think of anything that might help, call me. This isn't about Vegas, it's about Maria Sanchez."

That rocked Eva's stride.

"Can I have your number in case I have a question? I won't abuse it," Jack said.

Eva snapped Jack's card out of his hand and gave an angry recital of her cell number. Jack inputted it in his phone, said his thanks, and hopped back in his car. As he was about to pull away, he called out the open window, "Your mother said she had weapons in the house. It's a good idea to have some protection. If I knew enough to pay you a visit, and Vegas's homeboys blame you for his death, directly or indirectly, well, I'd be careful."

"I will, thank you. Now move."

"What does she have? What kind of gun?"

Eva's eyes darkened. She reverted to her prison stare; her voice became steely. "An old police-issue .45. It was my father's. He said it was solid protection, never jammed. He didn't trust 9 millimeters."

"Shotguns are the best for personal protection," Jack said. "Usually just the sound of the gun ratcheting does the trick without firing a shot."

"No rifles in the house. Just the one pistol."

Jack wasn't sure he believed her. "Do you shoot?" he asked.

"I can take care of myself."

Jack didn't doubt her. "Where were you the afternoon Vegas was killed?"

"With my aunt Mona. She'll corroborate my story."

"Thanks, Eva. I had to ask. You can call me anytime."

She looked like she was going to say something, and then made a grand gesture of looking at her wrist, minus a watch, but making the point.

"Okay, later."

Jack didn't believe Eva was the shooter, but had a strong suspicion she knew who it was. If Jack were going to crack the case open, he'd have to find another way in, because he also believed Eva would go to the grave without giving up Maria Sanchez's killer.

He executed a U-turn on the wide street and watched Eva in his rearview mirror jump behind the wheel of her car and power away. Jack needed some answers—and suddenly realized that he needed to make an unscheduled stop.

Nineteen

Mrs. Montenegro stood behind the well-worn gray and pink Formica countertop at her Venice Deli, a place she'd been running for the past thirty years. A refrigerated meat case hummed on her left and on her right, a glass case filled with potato, macaroni, and Greek salads, coleslaw, olives, pickles, and cheese.

Her thick white hair had woven slashes of silver and was pulled back into a studied bun. She looked to Jack to be in her early eighties. Her gaze was focused on a cell phone as she pecked out a text, unresponsive to the entrance bell that dinged announcing Jack's arrival.

"I hate these damn phones," she playfully scolded, concentrating on her iPhone. "My fingers are arthritic, my eyes too weak, and I can't remember what in God's name I tried to say by the time I hit the Send button." Her trim forefinger tapped Send, and as she looked up from her cell, her face crinkled into a warm smile that was mirrored by Jack's. "Do I know you?" she asked with youthful curiosity.

"Don't take this the wrong way," Jack said, "because it's meant as a compliment. But you remind me of my grandmother. That's why I was staring." He proffered his hand, "Jack Bertolino."

"Liz," she said as she pointed at the painted sign that domi-

nated the white wall behind her and proudly presented the Montenegro Deli's name, and then shook Jack's hand. Mrs. Montenegro's
hand was smooth and dry and Jack was surprised by the strength
of her grip.

"I'm not concerned with age, young man," she said, letting
Jack off the hook. "My body is a constant reminder, but I've made
peace with the process. What can I do for you . . . you don't look
like you came here to shop?"

"You know, I didn't," Jack said, liking this woman instantly. His
eyes swept the cold cuts display. "But I'll take a roast beef and Swiss
with lettuce, tomato, salt, pepper, and mayo on a French roll."

"A man who knows what he wants. Do you want me to wrap
a pickle?"

"You bet." He watched Mrs. Montenegro pull a demi-French
loaf out of a brown bag and slit it down the center. "And I'll take
a quart of that potato salad. Looks good. You use olive oil instead
of mayo?"

"And roasted garlic and fresh oregano with a pinch of red
pepper, squeeze of lemon, chopped onion, chopped parsley, and
a sprinkle of Romano. My grandfather's recipe. An Italian take on
a German salad. It's been in the family for thirty years. What else
can I help you with, young man?"

"Hopefully the answer to a few questions. I'm working for
your neighbor, the Sanchez family, trying to find out who was
responsible for the death of their young daughter."

Mrs. Montenegro straightened and her eyes filled with tears,
startling Jack, and Jack didn't startle easily.

"I am so sorry," he said. "That was really insensitive."

Mrs. Montenegro shushed Jack with a flick of her hand while
she regained her composure. "Maria was a perfect little angel. She

could be polite in one moment and then precocious and full of the devil the next. She was a joy to be around. It broke my heart."

"I can understand that. And just know, I'm going to do everything in my power to bring the killer to justice."

"Are you the man who was looking around my yard?"

Jack nodded.

"My neighbor Mike Triola spoke of you, said the killer hid on my property. I should have trimmed those bushes years ago. Maybe if I had . . ." And her voice trailed off.

Mrs. Montenegro grabbed a Kleenex and dabbed beneath her eyes, damming a thin flow of blue mascara before getting back to the task at hand.

"Now, Tomas Vegas, the man shot in front of your house, he was no angel."

"I knew Tomas since he was knee high. He was bad news"— her voice brittle now.

"There's a long list of people he hurt through the years, and if I can figure out who held a grudge, or who wanted to take over his drug territory, or who wanted retribution for a perceived slight, I might get closer to Maria's killer. Since you have lived in the neighborhood for so long, my guess is you know the local players."

Mrs. Montenegro gave that some thought as she pulled a side of rare roast beef out of the refrigerated glass case next to rows of salami, Sopressata, Mortadella, pancetta, pepperoni, ham, prosciutto, turkey, and fresh sausage. She slapped the heavy piece of beef onto the deli slicer with astounding ease.

The woman was a machine, shearing off thin slices of meat and cheese, assembling Jack's order.

"And you can add a pepperoni, please, six hot sausages, and a quarter-pound piece of the imported provolone to my order. And know, you've got a client for as long as I live on this coast," Jack said like a kid in a candy shop.

"We've operated unmolested for all these years because this was a safe place for families and their kids."

"Even when their kids grew up and joined gangs," Jack said without judgment.

"Even when the kids became fathers and their kids joined gangs. A tight-knit, tight-lipped society is what we've got working here. But now, with this . . ." Mrs. Montenegro looked up from her work. "Light or heavy on the mayo?"

"Light."

"Go ahead," she said as she slathered the crusty French roll with mayo and then salt and pepper. "Ask."

"I'm looking for motive here. Murder's usually precipitated by anger, greed, or jealousy. A young woman, Eva Perez, showed up at the wake. She went to Venice High before her mother yanked her out and moved her to the Valley."

Mrs. Montenegro's eyes registered recognition as she cut the hero in half and expertly wrapped it in waxed butcher paper.

"There's a story floating that Vegas was in love with Eva, but she wasn't feeling him. She was supposed to be in love with someone else, and I'm interested in talking to that someone else."

The old woman didn't hesitate a moment. "That happened more than a year ago, almost two summers," she said. "Tomas Vegas was madly in love with Eva, and Eva was smitten with one of the Dirk boys."

"One of the Dirk brothers?" Jack asked, hiding his surprise, but feeling that first jolt of electricity.

"Toby, the youngest of the three. Their father owned a clothing store over on Main Street. They're locals. I've seen them on and off through the years. I think the family still runs the shop."

Jack went over all the possible implications of this bit of news and felt a wash of dread, knowing if he leaned on the Dirks, it would complicate his already complicated relationship with Susan Blake. "The story I heard was there were lines of suitors who were interested in Eva."

"There were. But Tomas kept them at bay. Until Toby stepped into the picture. Then Tomas was pushed out in the cold." Mrs. Montenegro was growing more sure as she remembered. "Eva and Toby, they were in love. Madly so. You could see it the way they walked down the street and looked into each other's eyes. They couldn't hide it, and I don't think they cared to."

"And that created bad blood between the Lenox boys and the Dirks," Jack said.

"It was like the Montagues and the Capulets. Very steamy," she said like an ingénue, "and extremely dangerous."

"And how did it play out?"

"Eva went away, didn't she? She was a good girl, as far as I could see. Her mother made sure of that by moving them to the Valley somewhere before graduation."

"Was there any blowback, scenes that played out after she went away?"

"If there were, I never heard. Time passes. People move on and new families replace the old," she said as she weighed the sausage, wrapped it in butcher's paper, and repeated with the pepperoni. She filled a plastic container of the potato salad and packed a paper bag with Jack's order. "The neighborhood gossip was Tomas was the one who set her up for her arrest."

"To make sure if he couldn't have her," Jack said, "no one else would."

Mrs. Montenegro nodded, but the truth saddened her. "The courts ruled against her. No one really knows the truth, and the secret probably died with Tomas."

"And you're not aware of anybody else who might have held a grudge?"

"I wasn't aware of his business dealings," she said archly, "and made a choice not to get involved. It's been better for me in the neighborhood, to be a safe haven, to stay neutral."

Jack totally understood her philosophy. His neighborhood on Staten Island was rife with Mafia families, made men, soldiers, and button men. Kids he went to school with, played baseball with, graduated from high school or college and drifted into the family business. But Jack's parents lived there and Jack had been careful not to bring his work home with him. Asking questions would have made life too dangerous for his family. The mobsters knew Jack's reputation as a cop, and everyone went along to get along in the neighborhood.

Jack slid his credit card over the counter to Mrs. Montenegro, who tallied the bill, and Jack signed off.

"You've been a real help, ma'am. I appreciate your time. And you have my word this won't come back on you."

"Visit again, Jack. I may remind you of your grandmother, but you remind my of my husband when he was your age."

"Thank you," Jack said, his eyes crinkled into a smile as he grabbed the bag of food and headed out the door. The dinging bell echoed in his wake.

———

Jack jumped into his Mustang and dialed his son's number. After the third ring, "Answer the phone . . . answer the . . . Chris! I'm glad I caught you. Something I have to run by you. No, son, you're not in trouble, no, you didn't do anything wrong."

Chris informed his father that he was sitting in one of the nosebleed seats at Sunken Diamond Stadium at Stanford. He had finished his physical therapy and was watching his baseball team do their own workout on the field below.

"What do you need, Dad?"

"Who do you think is staying at my place?" Jack said like a game show host, trying for light.

"Susan Blake?"

"No.

"DDA Sager?"

"No.

"Dad . . ."

"Jeannine Bertolino."

"What?"

"Your mother, son, your mother. And don't get any wild ideas, that ship has sailed. But here's the deal. She claims she wants to take a road trip. I'm letting her stay overnight and then I'm checking her into a hotel. That should piss her off royally. Where do you think she'll head next?"

"Oh no," Chris said.

"Oh yes."

"Dad, my life's just getting back to normal. I have a new girlfriend."

Jack nodded his head, preparing to sink the hook. "Your only option is to talk to Jeremy. Give him dispensation. He was trying to do the right thing, and all that. He just didn't know how important baseball played into your past. How could he?"

"I can do that," Chris said with youthful resolve.

Jack felt like a skunk putting words into his son's mouth, but he added, "The clock's ticking, son, and you're the only man who can make this right."

"I'll get on it. I'll get on it now. Thanks, Dad."

Jack still had minor pangs of Catholic guilt. But he might have just dodged a bullet. Hell, if Chris didn't end up making the call to Jeremy, he'd call the bonehead himself.

———

Jack was motoring up Washington Boulevard when his cell phone trilled. His heart skipped a beat, not prepared for a confrontation with Jeannine. Not sure how he'd handle it. Knowing there was no winning in a situation like this. He let out his breath when he heard Nick's voice.

"Good catch, Jack," Nick Aprea said over the Sync system in the Mustang. "The driver of the green Chevy you braced outside the courtroom? *The* Joey Ramirez. Duggy said he's definitely Tomas Vegas's replacement. The big man sitting shots is called Playa. And the skinny dude in the back's named Tito."

That piece of information thrust Ramirez into first position, Jack thought. "So, he had financial motive to take out Vegas, and personal motive to put the fear of God into Juan at the courthouse. If Juan testified, the heat would fall on the Lenox gang and affect Ramirez's expanding bottom line."

Jack brought Nick up to speed on Toby Dirk's relationship with Eva Perez and found it left a sour taste in his mouth. He didn't know if it was his initial impression of his brother Terrence setting off his cop radar when he first met him at the art gallery, or just an inbred prejudice against kids raised with silver spoons, but he felt a little let down moving Toby into second position.

The news about Ramirez wasn't going to stop him from having a conversation with the youngest Dirk. But if it was Toby, Jack wondered, why did he wait until Eva's release to exact his revenge?

———

Jack stepped off the elevator just as Susan Blake walked up to his front door. "Susan!" he all but shouted before she knocked. Jack wondered what kind of karmic debt he was paying. All he could do was take the high road.

"How are you?"

Susan stepped up to him, her blue-gray eyes bright with anticipation, and she hit Jack with a sly smile that rendered him weak in the knees. "Can you forgive me for being such an ass? I'm a little too sensitive sometimes. My bad."

Jack stood his ground, hugged his bag of groceries, but couldn't stop the smile from creasing his eyes. "Yes I can," he said. "You tried to do something nice, Susan—no, not nice, for chrissake, extravagant, and I get it. You were disappointed."

"I should have known better. Can we let it go and move on?"

"Gone and done."

"Are you going to invite me in?"

Jack hated emotional complications. "Here's the thing, my ex-wife flew in from Staten Island and she's spending the night. Big surprise."

"Oh God, Jack. I scared you right into the arms of your ex-wife." Susan was grinning. "This is a new low, even for me."

Jack felt better about taking the high road. "Long story," he said, adding humor to his own voice. "How about I come over and throw on a pot of sauce?"

"Sounds like a plan. Well, come on. Let me meet your surprise guest."

Jack wasn't sure that was a good idea, but he keyed the door. As he set the bag of food from Montenegro's deli on the kitchen island, he could hear water running from the master bathroom. He tossed the potato salad, pepperoni, sausages, and cheese into the fridge, and when he tried to straighten to his full six-foot-two stature, his back screamed at him. Too many hours sitting behind the wheel.

"Jeannine?" Jack called.

Susan was studying the unmade bed. A confused expression creased her brow. And then Jeannine walked out of the bathroom wrapped in nothing but an oversized navy-blue bath towel.

"Oh," Jeannine said, surprised, but not put out.

Susan, on the other hand, turned dark on the instant.

Jack stifled his groan, and said simply, "Susan, this is my . . . ex . . . Jeannine."

"Hi, I don't want to intrude," Susan said with a tight smile, trying for pleasant but failing. "Enjoy your trip, Mrs. Bertolino." She turned to Jack: "I think I'll pass on dinner tonight. You seem to have your hands full." And Susan flew out the door before Jack could mount a reasonable defense.

Jack finally looked back at his towel-wrapped ex-wife. "Who is this woman standing in front of me? And what has she done with Jeannine?"

And as if Jack had never spoken . . . "She looks older in person," Jeannine said and walked promptly back into the bathroom.

"Okay, there's the woman I know," Jack mumbled as his cell phone trilled.

"Mr. Aprea," he said and listened. The news galvanized him. "I'll be there in five. I know where it is."

He slid his phone into his pocket, grabbed his sandwich and car keys. With a certain joy to be escaping with a good excuse, he called out, "Taking a boat ride. Coast Guard found a floater off Catalina missing an arm." Jack was out the door before the bathroom door opened.

Twenty

United States Coast Guard Captain Deak Montrose, Captain Deak to his men, stood at the helm of the twenty-eight-foot, armor-plated gunboat. The boat was ripping through the rough chop at forty knots. Thirty-two, trim, with a square jaw, straight white teeth, sandy brush-cut hair, and lively, intelligent eyes, he was a man in his element.

Jack stood by his side, hair pinned back, Ray-Bans firmly in place, a contented look on his face.

Captain Deak, piloting this very vessel, had saved Jack's life and the life of Jack's client, Angelica Maria Cardona, in a boat-to-boat gun battle Jack waged in the waters off the Terranea Resort in Orange County. The captain had promised Jack a joy ride when things settled down, and this was his first opportunity to show off the Coast Guard's newest toy, enlisted for the United States war on drugs.

Nick was sitting on a padded bench in the stern of the boat, eyes trained intently on the horizon. From the grim look on his face, Jack knew he was fighting to keep bile from winning the tug-of-war being fought in the back of his throat.

Catalina Island loomed over the starboard side of the craft, and the growing figure of a Coast Guard salvage barge appeared off the bow, surrounded by two large red buoys, a weathered green buoy off to one side, and a derrick poised to pluck something from the dark waters of the Pacific.

Two men in underwater scuba gear surfaced from the waves and were instantly helped on board the barge by the young crew.

As Captain Deak throttled back, the men could hear a diesel engine straining to winch a thick cable upward until a Scarab powerboat broke the surface. Seawater gushed from four gaping holes in the fiberglass stern. The crew on the barge made short work of tying the scuttled boat to the red buoys as they waited for Captain Deak to pull alongside and tie off on the barge.

"I didn't want to retrieve the first body until the medical examiner arrived," the officer in charge said to Captain Deak.

"You did the right thing. What's their ETA?" he asked.

"Running a little bit behind. Should be here within the hour. We'll set up lights. They don't have a slick ride like yours, Captain," he said with a grin.

"Good work," Captain Deak said as he strode across the barge with Jack and Nick to do a visual inspection of the floater and the destroyed Scarab.

The sun loomed large over the horizon, casting an attractive orange glow on the proceedings, and reflected off the oil slick created by the downed craft. No one saw the beauty as they took in the one-armed floater whose swollen body had been ensnared in the weeds and chains of the permanent green buoy.

A second dead body, a male, revealed itself as seawater drained from the wreck. It appeared to be the boat's pilot, whose crumpled shape looked to have lodged up beneath the dashboard of the luxury craft by the pressure of the water as the boat sank. His head hung at an unnatural angle, his cheek ripped from his septum to his jaw. A flap of pale skin pulled back revealed a mangled mess of shattered teeth, blackened gums, and exposed jawbone, giving the macabre impression of a tortured smile. He'd also taken several bullets to the neck. This man's body would also remain in place until the ME had made an appearance.

"It was a blood bath," were the first words out of Nick's mouth since their arrival. Some of his natural color had returned to his cheeks, or maybe that came from the pastel glint of the setting sun.

"There's going to be hell to pay," Jack said.

Nick nodded in sage agreement. "Sinaloa boys don't take kindly to being dissed like this."

"And you're sure that's your man?" Captain Deak asked, referring to the floater.

"Be a hell of a coincidence if there were another one-armed cartel douchebag gone missing," Nick said. "I guess it could happen, but I'm doubling down on that being one Dominic Cabrera."

The three men looked over at the green buoy and the bloated body of Cabrera bobbing in the water.

Nick went on to explain, "D.C. was engraved on his pinky ring, and his prints were in the system. A Colombian national, he was the midlevel exec who ran the cartel's stateside distribution chain. Whoever was the perpetrator of our crime scene stepped into some deep shit."

"Gotta be a few shooters," Jack said. "Look at the size of the holes in the stern. Looks to be shotgun blasts. But the windshield spiders, the holes could be 9mm, .38's, whatever. Smaller-caliber rounds. And look at how the seats and the instrument panel are torn up. Different angles, different trajectories. Speaks to a sub-stantial vessel blocking their egress or more than one boat."

"It was a blood bath," Nick reiterated.

No one argued the point. The three grim men turned as a Coast Guard Boston Whaler's roar grew in intensity. It was carry-ing the medical examiner, who Jack recognized as Malloy, toward his next appointed duty.

It was unusually hot. The scent of honeysuckle vine hung as thick as five-and-dime perfume. The shrill sound of cicadas enveloped the night air like high-tension wires. Two o'clock in Venice, Cal-ifornia, and all but the incredibly high, or incredibly depressed, were tucked in bed until daybreak.

Sweat trickled down Toby's neck from under the watch cap he wore. Dressed entirely in black again, he moved silently from shadow to protective shadow, listening for any sound that might alert the unsuspecting to what was in store.

He strode across the street like a Navy Seal carrying two bundles, past the green Chevy Biscayne, quickly down a cracked concrete path that fronted a grouping of four decrepit Spanish bungalows. Ramirez and his girlfriend lived in the last one-bed-room unit on the left. The houses were dark.

Toby, lowering himself to his stomach, pulled out the garden trowel he'd brought along for the job and eased open a shallow trench in the soil beneath the kitchen window. His beloved .22 had been wrapped in a plastic dropcloth, all fingerprints scrubbed clean with bleach. He said a silent prayer of gratitude to a trusted friend as he carefully laid the .22 in the trench, covered the rifle with loose dirt, and continued his work.

The cartel's drugs demanded a deeper hole but ended up lightly buried underground in the rucksack he had purchased for cash at the Big Five earlier that day. He pulled some overgrown ivy over the recognizable lump and declared the job done.

Toby froze at a sound, making his blood pressure spike, but it was merely a clucking mockingbird.

He duckwalked back up the pathway, crossed the street, hid behind the protective comfort of a hedge with a view of the four bungalows, and exhaled, stilling his heart.

Toby pulled out his Ruger .38 special, sucked in a breath, and sprinted down the road, rapid-firing the pistol.

It was like the fourth of July. *Bam, bam, bam, bam, bam!*

His rounds penetrated the metal skin of the burnished green Chevy Biscayne. The passenger-side window exploded, the rear whitewall tire sagged. Toby got to the end of the block and turned the corner before any lights winked on.

He jumped into his Jeep and powered away from the curb. He was three blocks away before he snapped on the headlights. The 911 operator picked up his cell call: "There's been a shooting at 2748 Trumble Avenue," he croaked, his tone throaty to mask his voice. "One man down. Lenox Road banger. Name's Ramirez. No! Place is full of drugs and weapons," he said, elongating the words *drugs* and *weapons* like he was talking to a six-year-old. "Last house on the left . . . because that's where he tried to rip me off. No, no fucking way. I want to live to see the sunrise."

Toby clicked off and headed west, pleased with the surge of adrenaline he felt. Time to relax and enjoy a little R&R, he thought. Spend some quality time with Eva. Maybe surprise her with a well-deserved vacation.

He pulled the Jeep into the lot next to the Venice pier and

walked calmly out to the farthest point—hidden from view by the structure at the end of the pier—and tossed his safe phone, Ruger, and nine boxes of ammunition into the black waters of the Pacific.

Now the Sinaloa cartel had a target for their anger.

———

At three thirty in the morning, Jack bolted upright at the sound of his cell phone trilling. A cop was never happy when the phone rang in the middle of the night because it was invariably bad news.

"Nick, what the fuck?" Jack croaked, and then he listened. And then he swung his legs off the pullout sofa. "I'll be there in ten."

———

Jack found Nick standing in the courtyard in front of a rundown bungalow. "The responding officer tried to calm Ramirez down," Nick said. "He was pissed off someone shot up his car. Not as pissed off as he is now, being under arrest and what-not."

"So, what's the story?" Jack asked, trying to keep the conversation on track.

Nick wasn't done yet, though. "So, his old lady jumped on the uniform's back and that slippery fucker Ramirez jackrabbits. He didn't get too far. Sustained a few bruises in the scuffle."

"Never make a cop run in the middle of the night," Jack said.

A tight grin from Nick. "Yeah, it's a real shame. But the upshot is . . . we found two midnight specials and uh, a rifle. A .22. Buried in one of the dead flowerbeds," Nick said, teasing Jack with the pertinent information like a runway stripper.

"Any drugs on scene?" Jack asked, his blood circulating a bit faster.

"Yeah, about fifteen pounds of high-class weed. Buried near the gun. Ramirez's eyes bugged out when we confronted him. Started losing it. Thought he was gonna have a heart attack. Shouting that he never hid drugs at his crib, how stupid did we think he was, and then he called me a *pendejo*. I ignored the slur and explained that everything he said could be used against him in a court of law, and he had just admitted to being a drug dealer."

"So you're thinking you've got the murder weapon?"

"If I was a betting man, I'd bet the farm."

"If you were a farmer . . ."

"Right, whatever. We should have our answer by midmorning. Check the rifling in the barrel against the marks on the slug they pulled out of the girl and Vegas's heart. I'll keep you in the loop."

"Where's Gallina?"

"Picking up Tompkins and on his way over. Woke him out of a dead sleep. Never heard the guy so happy. I had to talk him down from phoning the mayor. He saw the wisdom of waiting until it was a done deal." Nick clasped him on the shoulder. "This goes to you, Jack. You brought Ramirez into play. Good for you, my friend."

"Hmmmm," was all Jack could say.

Somehow it all seemed too convenient. The gun buried next to the house, along with the drugs. Why bury a small quantity of marijuana? And who was the guy who shot up the car?

Jack keyed the lock and stepped quietly into the loft. He all but collapsed onto the pullout sofa in his office, fully clothed, trying not to wake Jeannine. A wave of fatigue washed over him.

"Did you get your man, Jack?" Jeannine called out from the other room.

Jack found Jeannine's voice oddly comforting. A throwback to the old days when he was a rookie undercover narcotics detective working a case. It didn't matter what time of day or night he returned home. Jeannine always asked if he'd gotten his man.

"We took down a bad guy," he said. "The jury's still out whether he's the main man."

Jack rolled over onto his back, the only way he could sleep without pain. He lay there listening to the white noise rising off the occasional vehicle passing below, his troubled eyes opened wide.

Twenty-one

"There's no winning in this kind of situation. No high-fives," the mayor said with seemingly genuine respect. He stood rigidly at a makeshift podium that had been erected in front of the Sanchez house. The shrine's candles had been replenished and lit to honor young Maria Sanchez. He was flanked by the chief of police, Lieutenant Gallina, and Detective Tompkins, who looked uncomfortable in front of the camera. "But I'm here to announce the apprehension and arrest of a suspect, one Joey Ramirez, who is now in custody, charged with the shooting death of Tomas Vegas and Maria Sanchez.

"Young Maria Sanchez, a six-year-old innocent"—the mayor glanced over at the framed photograph of the girl to good effect—"who was gunned down playing in what was believed to be the safety of her own living room.

"I would like to thank Lieutenant Gallina and Detective Tompkins for their uncompromising investigation, and the team of talented police officers who worked around the clock to bring this criminal to justice."

The mayor went on, using the airtime to cement his bid for reelection. He wisely gave more praise than he appropriated for himself, a smooth, studied politician.

"You don't get to be the mayor of the second-largest city in the country without political acumen," Jack shouted toward the bathroom as he drained his coffee mug and poured a second cup.

Jack looked back toward the flat screen just as one of the mayor's aids stepped up to the mayor, whispered in his ear, and quickly departed.

"We've just received news that the weapon found buried at the suspect's home was the same weapon used to gun down both of our victims. The weapon was recovered along with fifteen pounds of high-grade marijuana."

The reporters started peppering the mayor with questions as Jack poured coffee into a second cup and handed it to Jeannine, who was wearing an exotic, semitranslucent floral bathrobe, hopefully not on his behalf. He was having enough trouble with a movie starlet.

"I guess congratulations are in order," she said, taking the proffered mug. She blew over the scalding liquid, taking a careful sip. "Strong," she said. She knew Jack wasn't pleased with the outcome of the press conference.

"Nick Aprea told me a 911 call came in reporting shots fired, giving a name, an address, the particular location of the house, and the possible whereabouts of drugs and weapons on the property. Pretty fucking neat," he said with understated sarcasm. "And as far as I know, no one has come forward to claim the fifty-thousand-dollar reward for information leading to the arrest of the killer."

Jeannine reached over to pat Jack's forearm, common enough

during their years of marriage. But he found himself bracing and fought the instinct to pull away. The awkward moment was cut short by a loud banging on the front door. Jack put down his coffee, strode to the door, and yanked it open.

Jeremy stood there, with wild hair, bloodshot eyes—in need of a shave and an attitude adjustment. He glared at Jack as he rushed past, shot daggers at Jeannine in her provocative bathrobe, discovered the unmade bed, and started to shake uncontrollably.

And then, totally out of character, Jeremy threw a wild roundhouse punch in the general direction of Jack's face.

Jack stepped to the side, grabbed Jeremy's wrist, and spun him around, twisting his arm behind his back, and subduing his wife's heartbroken lover.

"Really, Jeremy?" Jack asked incredulously.

"Owww. I have tendonitis, Jack."

"Jack, you're hurting him," Jeannine screamed. "Stop!"

"Are you going to calm down?" Jack asked, his words measured.

"Me calm down?" Jeremy cried, his voice quavering. "Can't a man get into a fight with the woman he loves without you trying to horn in?" And with that said, Jeremy's aggression left the building. Jack lowered the man's arm and went for his coffee cup, wondering what else the gods had in store for him today.

Jeannine, tears in her eyes, walked toward her shaken boyfriend. "You said you loved me."

Jeremy grimaced as he rubbed his shoulder and moved closer to Jeannine. "I stepped over that unwritten law," he confessed. "I never should have insinuated myself into your son's life or tried to kill his dreams. I'm ashamed of myself. I let my ego get the better of me and projected my own fears onto Chris. Who accepted my apology, by the way."

"You spoke with Chris?"

"He called. We had a good talk."

Jeannine caught Jack's eye, knowing who had orchestrated this reconciliation. "You're a horse's ass, you know that?" Jeannine said to Jeremy with more love than rancor.

"I do."

"Then I accept your apology," she said. And then, "You look terrible."

"You two enjoy yourselves," Jack said, wanting to move this right along. "I booked a room for Jeannine at the Beverly Hilton for tonight. I'll drive you over, and then I have to get to work."

"Oh Jack, we can Uber."

"I'm sure you can. You pack, I'll drive."

———

Toby and Dean sat on their boards, bobbing in the light surf. Toby's mind drifted from their conversation to Eva, sitting in her Tommy Bahama chair on shore. A green and white umbrella protected her skin. She wore a pale blue blouse with cutoff sleeves and a pair of white short-shorts. Her bare, elegant legs were crossed casually at the ankles. She was reading a Sue Grafton paperback. She hadn't been much of a reader until her incarceration, he thought moodily, then snapped out of it. Look on the bright side. Life should finally start getting better for them. No more obstacles to their happiness.

"So, I couldn't really remember the exact day the cop was going on about, and I told him that yeah, you were here. He seemed satisfied. Were you here?"

"Yeah, for chrissake, Dean, you're smoking too much weed."

"Don't I wish. And I spent part of your two hundred," he informed Toby. "I'm a little light with no product to sell. I'll get it back to you next week if that's all right."

Toby nodded his okay. He was rich now. He checked for a wave, but the ocean was still.

"And where the fuck were you?"

"I texted you. Didn't you read the text?"

"Oh yeah, yeah, your deal in Frisco."

"It's all a moot point anyway," Toby said.

"What is?"

"You don't watch the news? They picked up Joey Ramirez for the shooting of Vegas and that little girl. Tied a gun in his possession to the murders."

"Fucking square?"

"For real."

Dean reared back on his board. "That's low, man. Killing one of your own. And killing a child. Fuckin' low, man. Hate to be that fucker in the joint."

"Man must've been looking to move up the ladder. So, when are you going to score?" Toby asked, changing the subject. "I'm bone dry."

"Hard to say. If I could figure out who ripped off the shipment, I could retire."

"You don't work."

"Figure of speech," Dean said, annoyed, not happy to be tapped out. "Those fuckin' Mexicans I was talking about, the short dude had his throat cut at one time in his life. Gnarly scar, dude. Ear to ear." Dean let that hang in the air for dramatic effect before going on.

"They offered me two hundred large for any information about the missing drugs. Didn't seem to give a shit about the two men the Coast Guard pulled out of the water. I told them I couldn't help 'em. Didn't know Jack squat. They wanted to know who Jack was. I didn't laugh, those were two scary dudes. Dead eyes. Bad news."

"No one's gonna collect if Ramirez turns out to be the one who hijacked the pot."

"Right," and then, "Hell, I would've sold my mother for two hundred thou and moved to the north shore of Oahu if I had the information."

Not comfortable with the direction the conversation was taking, Toby kept steering toward the information he wanted to plant. "It said on the news that he was busted with fifteen pounds. Where'd he score that if the neighborhood was dry?"

"It's a definite quandary."

Toby glanced over his shoulder, slid down on his board, and started paddling hard, Dean following suit. The swell grew in size, Dean went down, Toby was up. His callused feet stuck fast to the board. He inched toward the front, crouched low, and cut left across the four-foot face, then cut right, ripping across the apex of the swell, into the edge of the curl. With the muted sound in the pipe, the opaque baby-blue water, Toby felt like he was in church. One with the gods. When it started to peter out he muscled down, spun a one-eighty, and paddled back out to where Dean was sitting.

He was hoping Eva had seen his ride. She said it made her hot to see him in action, and Toby aimed to please when it came to his woman.

———

Jack stepped into his loft, nodded to Cruz as he passed his work space, and tossed a quarter pounder with cheese onto the dining room table. Cruz pushed aside his computer, iPad, and yellow pad, wasting no time unfurling his burger.

"Beautiful," Cruz said, taking a big bite. "I forgot to eat lunch."

Jack set up shop on the kitchen island and pulled out the paperwork provided by Leslie. It was the list of all the witnesses called to testify from both sides of the isle in Eva Perez's trial.

Jack skimmed the list. In twenty-seventh place out of thirty witnesses called to testify for the defense was Toby Dirk's name.

Both Tomas Vegas and Joey Ramirez had testified for the prosecution. That had to have been a first for the gang members.

He filled Cruz in on yesterday's events while he ate some burger and pulled the tab on a diet Coke, took a big swig, and downed it with a Vicodin. He was behind the pain curve again and would have to eat standing up until the drugs kicked in.

"So this is what I'm thinking. I want a full workup on Toby Dirk. The whole nine yards. In fact, all three brothers. They all went to Venice High, and so I want you to look at yearbooks, friends, background checks, website for the Main Street store, social media, police reports, anything and everything."

"I thought Ramirez was in first position."

"He is, and Nick and the mayor, and the police chief, all think he's good for the shooting. I prefer to keep an open mind. Best-case scenario, we clear Toby's name. But if Mrs. Montenegro is to be believed, and she feels straight arrow to me, then Eva's mother was covering for Toby, and Eva should be nominated for the best bald-faced liar in a drama. The question remains, why would they yank my chain if there were nothing to hide?"

Cruz cocked his finger at Jack. "That logic works for me."

"You start on the Dirks, and I'll do a full-court press on Ramirez and see where that takes us."

———

As Jack pulled to a stop a few doors down from the modest bungalow that Ramirez called home, his green Chevy Biscayne was being winched onto the flatbed of a tow truck. The diesel engine strained and thick black smoke bellowed out of two stacks bookending the truck's cab. A young woman who looked older than her years because of the severity of her makeup and her unbridled fury observed the proceedings and wiped the acrid smoke out of her eyes with the back of her hand. She seemed to be having a conversation with herself, for her silent lips moved with an unconscious shake of her head. Harsh, penciled eyebrows, tight blood-red lips, and elaborate gang ink under the torn collar of her chocolate-brown sweatshirt's scooped neck.

"Damn shame," Jack said as he approached her and surveyed the high-velocity damage to the vintage vehicle.

"He loved the damned car more that me. Fuck him."

Jack saw an opening in her anger. "Did you get picked up, too?"

"Would I be standing here?"

"No, I guess not." Jack had done better with opening gambits.

"And who the fuck are you, white boy? You undercover? You look like a cop."

"No, not a cop. Not anymore. I'm working for the Sanchez family, trying to get a handle on who fired the shot that killed their young girl."

That gave the woman momentary pause. "The cops have already convicted Joey. He's as good as gone. Why don't you get gone, too?" It wasn't a question.

Ramirez's girlfriend turned on her heel and started back up the broken concrete path toward home. She was solid muscle, and wore tight-fitting jeans that screamed storm warning.

"Five minutes of your time," Jack said, hot on her heels. "Your life's in danger."

That slowed her some. She turned back, suspicious, flat-eyed and dangerous.

"What's your name?" Jack asked.

"Angel."

The name didn't fit the face and she read it in Jack's eyes. "I may not be an angel, but you sure as shit ain't no saint."

"Can't fight you there." Jack handed her a card.

"You'd lose. So what's your angle, Jackie?" she said, reading his name off the card.

"I'm trying to get to the bottom of this case, help a family out, and even though I'm no fan of your old man, I don't think he killed the girl."

That gave Angel something to think about.

"If you don't help me, help yourself," Jack went on. "My guess is he's going down for the murder and you'll end up dead. Tortured and dead. Ugly dead, Angel. The cartel is gonna want to know where he got the drugs in a dry town, and they've got a lethal way of getting answers. My guess, it's part of their shipment that disappeared along with two of their men who were killed out on the Pacific. Their boat sank. It's been on the news. I'm sure the Lenox boys are all looking over their shoulders."

Angel didn't say no. She stood frozen in place. And then she made an interesting comment: "Joey gets seasick, man. He couldn't have done those guys."

This was a smart woman, Jack thought. There was a chance

to break through. What she left out was that the drugs weren't the cartel's. That was a guaranteed death sentence.

"Tell me how it played out last night with the shoot-up and arrest. Tell me what your old man was doing two nights ago, when the boat and drugs were hijacked, everything you know. And we've gotta find you some place to hide out until this blows over."

Angel's eyes flickered back toward the street and she got in Jack's face, spitting fury, "Get the fuck outta my face, *puto*! We got nothing to talk about. *Maricon*."

Jack could see Ramirez's buddies walking up the path at a high rate of speed.

He shot Angel a look, accepting her unspoken message. He wouldn't bust her in front of her friends, but he hoped she'd be smart enough to call. He spun and the two men slowed to a stop, making room for Jack but forcing him to walk through their gauntlet. Angel slammed into her house.

Jack stood his ground. "How does it feel to be next in line?"

Playa was the melon-headed mouth who'd sat shotgun in the green Chevy outside the courthouse. Built like a bull, with tattooed biceps the size of ham hocks, and an ego to match. "You talking to us, ese?"

"First Vegas, then Ramirez steps up to the plate," Jack said. "He lasts forty-eight hours, and now up from the minors, it's you two jamokes. It's gonna be a rocky ride, boys."

"You talking shit, save it for someone who's listening," Playa said. "We'll finish this somewhere else, ese; we don't need no more civilian casualties. They all swim in our pond. But you ain't a civilian. You, we'll take outta the game."

"At least your momma will have something to remember you by," Jack said.

"Don't force my hand, homeboy, start talking shit about my mamma."

"Sinaloa boys'll strip the skin off your body until you admit to stealing the drugs Ramirez was busted with. They'll send your tattoos in an envelope to *su madre* as a warning to others and a keepsake for her. Something to remember her son by."

They seemed scared and Jack poured it on. "And then after you admit to killing their men, and stealing their drugs, you will tell them what they want to hear, they'll cut your head off and leave it curbside for your boys to play soccer with. And all the time you were just trying to be a good earner and get ahead in the world. Doesn't seem fair."

"Get the fuck outta here while you're still mobile, ese." But Playa's threat seemed weak and the heat was lost in translation.

"If you have an alibi for Tuesday night," Jack said quietly, "I'd give it up. Give me something to go on, anything to prove you weren't out on the water Tuesday night and I'll try to make it right."

"Fuck you, scumbag."

As the bull charged, Jack grabbed the big man's muscled forearm and, using his forward momentum and weight, yanked him past his own body like a matador, ankle-swept him, and sent him careening down onto the hardpack.

Tito's razor-thin body had muscles like twisted leather, severe enough to make an anorexic blink. He stood five-foot-five and Jack guessed his gunplay did most of his talking on the street. Tito flashed his most potent side-glancing stink eye and hissed, "You're a dead man. Not here, but soon. You better grow eyes in the back of your head, ese."

"Say good night, Gracie," said Jack as he walked past the seething Tito while his partner brushed the crabgrass off his knees and mumbled curses in Spanish.

Jack exited the depressing courtyard and headed for his ride just as the tow truck rumbled away from the curb. The diesel engine belched black smoke as the shot-up green Chevy Biscayne rolled past the crowd of onlookers like a homespun float at the Rose Parade.

Jack spun around just as a blond man with a camera snapped a photo of the green Chevy as it passed Jack's position. Hurriedly, he turned and walked off in the opposite direction. Jack had the strange sensation that he'd been the focus of the picture, and that he'd seen the man before. He just couldn't place him.

Twenty-two

Joey Ramirez was processed by noon and led to a holding cell in the 77th Street Jail, which would be his home until he was transported to the Airport Courthouse. He was scheduled for a meeting with his attorney, who would run down the state's case against him, talk strategy, and handle his bail hearing.

The prison guard turned and walked out of the cell, his leather boots echoing on the linoleum floor. Ramirez didn't remember hearing the metallic click of the door locking, but was so pissed off he was seeing double and not thinking straight.

He had to take a crap, but was damned if he'd freeze his ass off using the metal toilet in the claustrophobic cell. He'd wait and use the bathroom at the courthouse. It wasn't the first time he'd been arrested, and in his line of work, he was sure it wouldn't be the last. In this case, though, he had been framed.

The rifle wasn't his, but he was more concerned about the drugs. The wrong people could get the wrong idea, and that could be detrimental to his health. He'd send a message out to his boys through the lawyer who the Lenox gang had on retainer. Damned shyster was making more money than he was lately. That fucking pissed him off, too.

The cell door swung open and a trustee stepped in carrying an extra blanket. Ramirez wouldn't say no to a little warmth, and he reached for the blanket, nodding his thanks.

In a lightning strike the trustee punched through the skin beneath Ramirez's sternum. The honed needlepoint of the icepick penetrated his heart muscle and instantly paralyzed the life-giving organ. The state's newest prisoner was bewildered, but dead before the trustee could pocket the icepick. He wrapped Ramirez in the blanket and rearranged his body to look asleep.

Only hours later would anyone be the wiser.

With its deadly message sent, the cartel had exacted the first phase of its revenge. They would still brace every member of the Lenox Road crew until they discovered who the other traitors were. A single man couldn't have done the job alone. When business was completed, the two enforcers would take a flight back to the city of Culiacán, Sinaloa, where the cartel was based.

The prison guard already knew how he was going to spend the fifty grand that had been wired to his secret account by a Sinaloa CPA.

The trustee's family could now build that extra room his wife so dearly wanted for her mother on the family compound in Reseda.

———

Jack keyed the door to his loft just in time to be greeted with the sound of four ringing phones. Cruz, set up at his usual spot at the dining room table, grabbed the receiver. The flat-screen television was set to CNN, sound muted. Jack plugged his iPhone into the charger near the door as Cruz said, "He just walked in," and handed the phone to Jack, who mouthed, who is it? His eyes narrowed as Cruz raised his hands, palms up, in a . . . what could I do? gesture.

"Jeannine," Jack said as he walked the phone into his office.

"Hi Jack, we're leaving for Santa Barbara tomorrow, and going wine tasting in Santa Ynez." She sounded youthful and pleased and Jack was genuinely as happy for her as he was for himself. "Thank you for the wonderful hotel room. Jeremy and I made up. All is well. We plan on staying overnight at Big Sur, and then we'll spend a night in Carmel before going to visit Chris. Don't tell him, Jack," Jeannine scolded playfully. "We want it to be a fun surprise."

Good luck with that, Jack thought. "I won't," he assured her.

"I'm feeling so good; I wanted to share an observation, Jack. I can read the pain you live with every day, and it hurts my heart."

Jack let out a labored sigh that wasn't lost on Jeannine and wished he hadn't. "I'm not going under the knife again," he said. "If the operation went south, I could end up in a wheelchair. It's not worth the risk."

"I understand, Jack. I can't tell you what to do anymore. I'm not sure I ever could. You never listened to half of what I had to say when we were married; why should I expect anything different now?"

Jack was almost pleased Jeannine had spun the conversation around, making her the focus. He wisely chose not to get pulled into the rhetorical.

"But, you're not a stupid man," she soldiered on. "Stubborn as all getup, but not stupid. You can't take the pills forever. You're eventually going to have to . . . what did you call it . . . face the lion. That's what you're going to have to do, Jack, face the lion. You don't have to say anything. I know you. And I know you'll do the right thing, at the proper time. There's no quit in you, Jack Bertolino, and just know . . . know that your family is here for you," and Jeannine quietly hung up the receiver, leaving Jack speechless.

The silence enshrouded the open loft space and Cruz, who could read Jack's moods, wisely kept his face on his computer screen.

Jack walked into the kitchen, poured a glass of water, and grabbed two Excedrin and one Vicodin from the cupboard. He downed all three pills in a swallow and finished the glass of water in one sharp tilt of the head. He walked the length of the loft, stood at the sliding glass doors, and watched a few FedEx trucks exit the lot next door and blend with traffic on Glencoe. Then his gaze shifted to the planes that were stacked up in the distance waiting to land at LAX.

"It was posted in the Venice High Facebook page that Sean Dirk took a year off after graduation to travel the world," Cruz said, breaking the silence.

"I'd like to take a slow boat to China right about now. What was he really doing?" Jack asked.

"Serving a twelve-month sentence at Lompoc. Busted for selling a roll of stolen gold coins and a platinum Rolex to an undercover cop posing as a fence. Sean was a second-story man. That takes some balls."

What about Terrence?

"Clean. A few tickets. One drunk and disorderly when he was nineteen. Dropped out of college when his father passed away, and it says on the Santa Monica Chamber of Commerce site that he's been a runaway success, growing the family business. And as a Rotarian, he gives back to the local community."

That didn't necessarily mean anything. "And Toby?"

"Graduated high school with honors. Won multiple scholarships, passed on them, opting to stay in the neighborhood. All three brothers work and take a salary from the store."

"Is their mother still alive?"

"No, I found an obit page. Membership at Wilshire Country Club lapsed after the death of her husband. Fall from grace. Sounds like it killed her."

"Terrence was here in the loft," Jack said, still musing about him.

"Yeah, to hang the painting."

"Selling high-end clothes, furnishings, art, lighting. Hobnobbing with the rich and famous. Not a bad way to gain entry into the homes of the well-heeled. Dirk Brothers store, not a bad way to launder money. Something to think about."

"How'd it go at Ramirez's?"

"Talked to his old lady, Angel, and got into a scrap-up with one of his guys. Tried to put the fear of God into them. Only hope I sowed some seeds of doubt. I left a few cards."

Alerted by a headline, Cruz shot out of his seat and walked to the television, grabbing for the remote. The printed crawl at the bottom of the screen announced the stabbing death of Joey Ramirez in a holding cell at the 77th Street Jail. A young reporter stood outside the prison walls fighting to keep her blonde hair out of her eyes while reporting on yet another death in the broken Los Angeles penal system. The screen abruptly cut to Iran, and Jack knew he'd get the rest of the story from Nick later in the day.

"Damn, the cartel believes they arrested the right man," Cruz said, awed. "That was some swift street justice."

"Angel said Ramirez got seasick. He couldn't have ripped off the cartel," Jack said, brow furrowed.

"They always lead with a lie," Cruz said.

That gave Jack pause. Simple truth.

"I hope your father's proud of you," he said, then walking toward the door, "I'm available on my cell. Good work today." Jack grabbed his cell from the charger, walked out, and locked up behind him.

Twenty-three

Jack felt his tension melt away as he opened the chain-link gate that led down a wooden ramp to the dock where his newest, used Cutwater 28 cabin cruiser was moored.

His last boat had been destroyed on the rocks off Terranea Resort during a boat-to-boat gun battle that saved a young woman's life.

The symmetrical rows of sailboats, the scent of saltwater, the clanging of lines against rolled steel masts, the echoed shrieks of seagulls riding the thermals, all made Jack's blood pressure tick down a few notches.

He stopped on the ramp to survey his new boat. It was the spitting image of his last, a year younger, loaded with high-end electronics. He'd invited Susan, who had accepted his invitation as well as his explanation of his wife's unexpected visit. He wasn't sure that she'd be as forthcoming if he broached the subject of her stalker. Jack decided to play it by ear.

Susan had been shopping again, Jack realized as he stepped onto the boat's transom. He wisely decided to dummy up and say nothing but thank you. He saw new wineglasses on the dining table in the cabin, towels and linens on the bunk beyond, a case of

Benziger cabernet in the galley. Tommy was sitting in a deck chair on the boat's open cockpit with an ostentatious captain's cap raked low, sunglasses in place, fast asleep and snoring mildly. Susan appeared from the cabin looking radiant, wrapped her arms around Jack's neck, and whispered, "I can see the change already. Good for you, Jack. I like it," she said, referring to the boat. "You deserve a little R&R."

"What's up with Captain Bligh?"

"He spent two hours playing hardball with the insurance company. They buckled and agreed to pay the full replacement cost for your new boat. He said having to negotiate with small-minded bureaucrats and money crunchers wore him out. I told him to stay out of show business or he'd lose his hair."

"Good advice."

"I don't think it took."

The sound of the champagne cork flying into the air was enough to rouse Tommy, who made a grand show of not really being asleep. "It's got all the bells and safety whistles," he said, rising to unsteady feet. "Bill Weller was happy to unload it."

"And I'm happy to take it off his hands," Jack said as he poured the champagne. "Thanks for doing this, Tommy." They all clinked and shared a celebratory drink.

Jack lowered his champagne glass and locked eyes with Susan. "Take a walk with me?"

"You sound so ominous, Jack."

Susan winked at Tommy as she followed Jack up the ramp. They strolled down the sidewalk, looking at the acres of high-end sailing yachts and motor craft. A slight ocean breeze buffeted Susan's hair.

Jack took a sip of champagne and Susan slid her arm through

Jack's, stepping in close. He could feel the warmth of her breast against his biceps and hated to break the mood.

"I was hired to protect you, Susan," he began.

"And you've done a marvelous job."

"So, it's time for you to get honest with me."

Susan wasn't sure where the conversation was going. "Meaning?"

"I think you know who your stalker is."

Susan let her arm drop away. "And what makes you think that?"

Jack read caution in her voice, stopped walking, and leaned against the chain-link fence. "You've had a series of phone calls that concern me."

"And you know that because?"

Jack continued, not wanting to get derailed. "When you were in New York, you had a thirty-minute conversation an hour before you withdrew twenty thousand dollars from your checking account, and then you spoke to the same party for two minutes directly afterward."

Susan's eyes darkened, her breathing quickened.

"You spoke to that same party, at two thirty a.m. the night of the stalking incident. Look, I can't help you if you're not honest with me."

"Honesty? How dare you?" she said indignantly. "Did Cruz hack my accounts? That little shit. Is that why he was in my trailer?" She was working herself into a fury. "Computer genius. Trust. That's a major violation of my, of my . . . personal . . . damn you, Jack!" She tossed her champagne, glass and all, into the dark marina water.

Jack wasn't buying the show. "Susan, I think your life is in danger, and I think you know that. It has to be frightening. I want to help; let me help you."

"That little shit."

"Cruz works for me, I'll take the hit. Give me a name. Give me an address. Something to go on. If you're being extorted, it will never stop. I can make it stop."

Susan looked Jack straight in the eye, and exposed her pain, her vulnerability, for the first time. "I can't, Jack. I'm not ready. Please."

Something very strange was going on here, but whatever it was, he could see that she was deeply affected. "Okay . . . Okay, Susan." He wrapped her in a protective hug. Jack knew if he pushed any harder, Susan would shut down and he'd lose her forever.

———

The patrons stood three deep at the bar at Hal's Bar and Grill, and the decibel level was as high as the clientele. The Lakers played silently on a flat screen above the bar, and the crowd roared on every worthy play. A knot of couples jostled for the attention of Rebecca, the maître d', blocking the entrance to the dining room. Yet Rebecca grabbed three menus, waved Jack and company forward, and started toward the back of the room and his regular table.

Susan was a terrific actress, but Jack could sense her guard was up and firmly in place. "You were smart to make reservations," she said, aloof. Her hair was windblown, her skin pink from the sun, and amid discreet murmurs of recognition, the seas parted as she trailed Rebecca, followed by Jack and Tommy, who was basking in his newfound show biz glory.

A jazz quintet, set up by the windows that fronted Hal's dining room, played a tight postbop piece Jack didn't recognize, but it was enjoyable.

They were halfway into the room when the color red caught

Jack's eye. It was unmistakably Terrence Dirk's striking hair. The tall, thin man, looking like a sartorial Mick Jagger, was pouring Dom Pérignon into three champagne flutes. Given that the other two men sitting in the booth shared similar knowing grins, body types, and attitudes, Jack suspected he was about to meet the rest of the Dirk clan.

Susan veered toward their table. "Terrence," she said, extending her hand. Terrence stood up, smiling in recognition, and shook her hand across the largest booth in the joint.

"I don't know if you've met my brothers, Sean"—who was seated next to Terrence—"and Toby," who sat at the end of the large rounded booth. "This is Susan Blake, Jack Bertolino, and . . . ?"

"Jack's dear friend, Tommy Aronsohn." Susan made a show of grabbing Tommy's arm and pulling him close. "If you ever need a good lawyer."

Sean was dressed in a crisp navy shirt, and his eyes seemed to probe more than socialize. Jack, now aware of his criminal background, wondered if Toby, who wore loose-fitting high-end surfer grunge, wasn't following in his brother's footsteps.

Jack flashed on Ramirez's girlfriend stating that Ramirez got seasick. He picked up the same hard edge from all three brothers and wondered if it was hard enough to hijack a shipment of drugs from the Sinaloa cartel. That would've taken some balls, he thought. He decided to check out their time line for the past few days when he spoke to Toby.

"Someone had a good day," Jack said to Terrence, referencing the pricey champagne, but wondering if they were celebrating Joey Ramirez's death.

While handshakes and introductions went on, Jack checked out Toby's reflection in the glass of an oversized black-framed photograph hanging on Hal's back wall. The youngest brother was harder to read than his criminal brother. Could he have sat in that sniper's nest next to Mrs. Montenegro's?

"We won't keep you," Susan said. "Enjoy your meal, boys, and call me next week, Terrence. I've got some ideas for the living room."

"My brothers brought some samples back from our vendor in San Francisco. I've given it some thought myself, and have a few ideas I want to run by you."

"Great," she said, sliding into their booth. Tommy said, "A pleasure," to the Dirks and followed Susan's lead, grabbing the seat opposite her.

Jack made a decision to linger. He turned his focus on Toby, whose instant change in demeanor was subtle but not lost on the retired inspector. "Say, Toby, I spoke with a good friend of yours yesterday."

"Really, who?" Toby asked, self-assured and comfortable.

Neat trick, he's good, Jack thought. "She didn't tell you? Eva Perez."

Toby took a sip of his champagne, his eyes crinkling into a questioning smile.

"You look surprised," Jack said. What the hell, he decided to push the point. "I'd heard you two were an item."

When Toby didn't immediately respond, he followed up, keeping his tone light. "Hey, this isn't the time or the place. Are you going to be in the shop tomorrow? I'd like to pick your brain for a few minutes, ten minutes max."

"I've got you down for the afternoon shift," Terrence said, accommodating, shifting Jack's focus to him. "Any time after two o'clock."

"Jack, leave the men alone and come sit down," Susan said playfully over her shoulder.

"We're not an item, Jack," Toby said, all charm now. "Eva's an old friend."

"Ten minutes?" Jack asked, flashing his most winning smile.

"Since you're a friend of my brother's—with great taste in art, I've been told—and one of the reasons we had a great week," Toby tipped the champagne flute slightly in Jack's direction, "I'll give you *eleven* minutes and sell you a suit."

Toby, Terrence, and Jack shared polite chuckles while Sean observed. The guy had a creepy vibe, Jack thought.

"Enjoy your meal, gentlemen."

As Jack slid in next to Susan, she jumped right on him. "What was that all about?"

Jack decided not to engage. "This town never ceases to amaze."

"You're telling me, I love it," Tommy said, still suffering from a major case of Hollywood fever.

"How so?" Susan asked.

"Small world is all," Jack said, interrupted by his favorite waiter, Arsinio, who took drink orders over the solid applause from the room for the fluid solo of the jazz group's trumpet player.

Jack took in Susan's beauty and smiled as he felt the heat of three sets of eyes boring into the back of his skull. If he wasn't mistaken, the Dom Pérignon had just lost some of its fizzle.

Jack had only begun to rattle their cage. His cop radar was flaring, and he had a strong feeling the Dirks were involved in more than selling designer suits and furnishings to the Malibu Colony set. Politics with Susan Blake aside, Jack wouldn't stop digging until he had an answer.

Twenty-four

Day Seven

"Got a call from Molloy," Aprea said to Jack as the two men walked past four black-and-whites, red and blue lights flashing, blocking the entrance to one of the small bridges that crisscrossed the Venice canals. An ME tech team in white coveralls hustled to hook a generator to their portable light.

It was 4:00 a.m. and Jack had been awakened after three hours in the sack and knew he'd pay for it later in the day. Jack and Nick stopped at a yellow nylon rope that was tied to a light pole and stretched taut over the side of the bridge's cement railing.

"Frag of a .22 was wedged in the cartilage that hinges the jawbone," Nick said, referring to one of the cartel drug runners killed on the high sea. "Tore his cheek and smashed a few molars on the way in. Not pretty."

"Enough for a match?" Jack asked.

Nick, whose eyes were red rimmed but still bright from his nightly Herradura fix, shook his head with mild derision. "On the other hand, not enough to discount it. It looks like our boys got greedy and the cartel is exacting its revenge."

They crossed the bridge and made a left onto the footpath that edged the canal.

The grating whine of the generator assaulted the early morning quiet, and then the light snapped on, revealing a grotesque tableau.

Playa, the bull, was hanging over the side of the bridge. The yellow nylon rope, his noose, cut so deeply into the heavy man's thick flesh that a light breeze threatened to force the issue and decapitate him.

His face was swollen and pulped. Eye sockets empty, bloody tears stained his purpled face. His knees, exposed by his bloodied white baggy athletic shorts, had been shot, both kneecaps shattered. One black high-top sneaker on, one foot bare, dangled in the water and swayed eerily with the light current.

A local news chopper circled overhead along with a police bird whose high-powered spot danced over the macabre scene below.

"So much for being able to corroborate Ramirez's time line," Jack said, gazing at the dead body dispassionately.

"If I were Tito, I'd be in the wind," Nick said.

"If he's still alive," Jack said. "There are a lot of bridges in the L.A. area."

Nick nodded, turning away from the carnage. "The gang squad's headed over to his mother's crib. It's his last known address."

"We should break the news to Angel before the cartel pays her a visit. See if she's got any relatives out of state she can visit."

"If she had been inclined to make a statement, I think it's safe to say, that ship has sailed."

Two cops wearing jeans and black T-shirts and jackets with LAPD stenciled on the back waded into the canal and tried to position a small zodiac inflatable next to Playa's bare foot, to catch the body as it was carefully lowered.

On the bridge, three cops gripped the taut nylon rope, as a fourth cut the line with heavy-duty bolt cutters.

The slick rope streaked through the men's hands, burning and cutting their palms. Playa's massive body dropped like a log onto the rounded edge of the inflatable, bounced once, and splashed facedown into the brackish water. Frustrated, angry voices from above and curses below as the two drenched cops in the water tried and failed on their first attempt to slide three hundred pounds of dead weight onto the Zodiac.

"So much for protecting the crime scene," Nick said sotto voce to Jack, wisely fighting the urge to put in his two cents and mess with the officer's already frayed nerves.

"Let's take a ride?" Jack said.

The men walked back up to the road and left the cops and ME's to sort out the sordid mess as news vans arrived en masse.

———

Jack and Nick walked up the broken concrete path past three dark one-bedrooms to bungalow number four. The yellow police tape barring the front door had been ripped off and hung loosely down the sides. The house was still. It felt empty, Jack thought, and the sound of a mockingbird riffing did little to change his opinion. It was early morning damp, and the air was thick with the smell of rotting leaves. They were an hour ahead of sunrise but thought they owed Angel a wakeup call.

The small exposed porch allowed room for only one. Jack knocked quietly while Nick peered into the living room through the blinds that covered the front window. He shook his head, while Jack tried the doorknob. It was locked.

After Jack knocked again, the men split up and started around opposite sides of the house. Jack stepped over the fallow garden beds the cops had dug up twenty-four hours earlier. It was an odd place to stash drugs, Jack thought as he looked through the kitchen window. It appeared empty, the cupboards left partially opened.

"Nothing," Jack said when they met up at the back entrance. "Looks like she cleaned house."

Nick used a penlight to peer into the dark bedroom. "Bed's stripped. Closet doors open. Looks like Angel hit the road when she heard her boyfriend wouldn't be making bail."

"Smart girl," Jack said as he tried the back door. It was unlocked. The men pulled out their weapons and followed them into the house, turning on harsh overhead lighting as they went. In less than thirty seconds they had cleared the small bungalow.

The bedroom closet had been emptied of all women's clothing. Ramirez's clothes hung neatly on wire hangers. Clean spots on top of the dusty drawer indicated where framed pictures probably sat, Jack thought. Two drawers were filled with men's underwear, socks, and T-shits; two drawers were empty.

The only thing Jack found in the bathroom was one frayed toothbrush, a flattened tube of paste, and some male hair products.

Jack walked into the living room. Nick tossed down an empty scratch pad, pulled out his phone, and snapped a few pictures of some phone numbers that had been scribbled on the wall next to a green Barco lounger. "She left the television and an Xbox and some video games," he reported. "Silverware's gone, plates, the usual. She's not planning on coming back anytime soon."

"Let's knock on the neighbor's door, see if they know where she went, what time she left, and if she left of her own accord," Jack said.

Nick nodded. "You get the lights, lock up, I'll catch you out front. You hungry?"

"I could eat," Jack said.

Once Nick had walked out the front door, Jack locked it behind him, gave the house a quick once-over. The only evidence of note was outside. He turned off lights as he made his way back through the small house and locked the door securely on his way out.

———

Jack fielded a call from DEA agent Kenny Ortega as he was parallel parking on Main Street in Santa Monica.

"I've got news for you, *mi hermano*."

"Lay it on me, Kenny. I need all the help I can get on this one. It's gotten personal and that's not helping the cause."

"I think this will put a smile on your face. My guys triangulated the phone calls, using pings off the local cell towers, and locked down two locations. One was Susan Blake's rental home, and the other, a garage apartment in Venice. I already sent the particulars to your computer and phone. The mug's name on the cell phone account is Frank Bigelow. I checked VICAP, no hits."

Jack loved technology. "That's great, Kenny. I owe you."

"I'll collect. Let me know how it plays. Gotta ring off."

"Thanks, Kenny." And Jack clicked off. Still, he was going to have to wait for the right time to share his new information with Susan. He couldn't forget that fragile, pleading look in her eyes. The crack in her psyche. Frank Bigelow would have to be handled carefully.

———

Jack walked along the alleyway that ran behind the Dirk Brothers store, staying close to the wall. He stopped behind a Dumpster so he could watch Sean Dirk offload large wardrobe boxes. He made note of the Mercedes step van's model. Jack assumed it came with a hefty price tag, and again flashed on the notion that business must be good for the three brothers. He hustled back down the alley after Sean disappeared inside the rear entrance.

Toby was waiting on a customer as the front doorbell rang, and Jack walked into the store. He waved a "give me five minutes" signal and Jack nodded his assent.

Toby was dressed to impress that afternoon, Jack thought. Black pegged slacks, black boots with heels that raised him an inch taller than Jack, along with a dark purple shirt and black snakeskin belt. He was showing a design book filled with sofas and chairs with multiple colored swatches of fabric and leather to a well-heeled brunette with a yoga body, a natural tan, and a flirty demeanor. She seemed to be as interested in Toby as the furniture.

Jack could hear boxes being stacked in the back room and the faint sound of the Rolling Stones emanating from hidden speakers. He grabbed a 41 long off the racks and shrugged into a Burberry camel-hair sports jacket. It dressed up his black T-shirt and jeans just fine. Plus, it fit Jack's six-foot-two frame like a second skin. The twenty-three-hundred-dollar price tag seemed only fair.

Sean stuck his head into the front room, waved hi to Jack without giving away any emotion, and disappeared into the back.

Toby ushered his client to the front door with promises to call when the work was ready. As the doorbell rang, Jack cruised by the design book, making note of the San Francisco vendor who would build the chosen designs.

An L.A. air kiss on both cheeks at the door and the woman was gone.

"It's like stealing money," Toby said with a winning grin.

"How so?" Jack asked.

"Her husband's a cinematographer. Does very well. We just finished her neighbor's house on Panay Way, and she wants everything we delivered there, and more. Keeping up with the Joneses. We're happy to oblige." His eye lit on the coat Jack was trying out, and he commented, "You're a clotheshorse, Jack. Fits you like a glove. Right off the rack. Unheard of."

Immune to the sales pitch, Jack shrugged out of the sports jacket and rehung it. "What's your take on Joey Ramirez?"

If the quick-punch question threw Toby, he didn't show it.

"I know he's dead. It was on the news. Karma. Killing that little girl."

"So, you think he was good for the crime?"

"He had a reputation for being Tomas Vegas's weak sister," Toby informed him. "Tried to act like him back at Venice High, but fell short. I only knew of him," he clarified. "Could pick him out in a crowd, but didn't *know* him."

"What's your theory?"

"Greed, pure and simple. Wanted what he couldn't have while Vegas was in the first position."

"I guess we'll never know," Jack said, staying casual. "By the way, where were you when Vegas got shot? That was a week ago today, about one o'clock in the afternoon."

"I thought it was case closed, with Ramirez dead and all."

Jack took note of the stone-cold gaze. "Just finishing up the paperwork for my files. And because of your relationship with Eva, there were questions that had to be asked to complete the picture. No pressure here, Toby, I just want to put this puppy to bed."

"I spent the day surfing with my crew at Sunset Beach. Some

cop already questioned my bud, Dean, and all was good from his point of view."

"Was that a Lieutenant Gallina?"

"I wasn't there, but it could've been. I know Gallina stopped by the shop when I was up north, wanted to speak with me. I phoned him as soon as I got into town and he said it was case closed. Cut me loose. He thanked me for getting back to him in a timely fashion."

Jack snapped his fingers, as though that reminded him of something. "And when did you go up north?"

"Tuesday. We left after dinner, around seven. Wanted to miss the traffic on I-5."

"Good. Okay, can you walk me through your relationship with Eva Perez?"

"I told you about Eva last night." His eyes had a bit of a charge now. A flash of defensiveness, and then gone.

"I know, and I appreciate that, Toby. I just, the word on the street is, well, you were a bit more involved than you're letting on. I spoke with Laureth Curran, the prosecuting attorney who handled Eva's case, and she remembered you. Said you were in the courtroom every day, even when you weren't testifying, and the tension between you and Vegas was palpable."

The young man seemed stunned. "You want a Coke, an Evian?"

"Diet Coke?"

"Done." Toby opened up a hidden mahogany panel revealing a small fridge.

Jack knew Toby was regrouping. He had to go easy on the kid, or this might be his last opportunity to question him. "I know Eva was busted for possession and illegal weapons charges, with intent to sell."

"It was bullshit. A trumped-up charge orchestrated by Tomas Vegas. And if Eva hadn't had a prior, she might not have served time."

Jack cracked open his soda and took a long sip.

Toby was rolling something around in his head, and Jack saw his resolve when he came to a decision. "I'm going to run this by you once, Jack. And then we're done here. Deal?"

"Fine."

"Vegas was in love with Eva, but I was fucking head over heels. Eva felt the same way. We had big plans for the future. A family, kids, travel. Tomas Vegas wouldn't let that happen. He'd lose face with his set if I won his girl. So he dropped a key of coke, and a gun with a pedigree, into the back of her car." Jack was listening with concern, and Toby went on.

"I visited her every week, until one Sunday she refused to see me. Stopped returning letters. Cut me off. It was harsh.

"Breaking up wasn't my choice. Eva changed after her arrest. She cleaned house. I still testified on her behalf. Hell, I would've taken a bullet for her. You've seen her. She's beautiful. But I have an ego. I don't want anybody who doesn't want me. Beautiful woman, her loss."

"And Tomas Vegas?"

"I wanted him dead. But I don't have the DNA for it. I love surfing, and ganja, and my brothers, and the store. I wouldn't jeopardize the life I have for any woman. I got over it, and got on."

Jack pretended to be duly informed, though he planned to check out his story. "Thanks, Toby, that couldn't have been easy."

His confession over, Toby brightened up. "How do you like living with the Piccard? It's a big, bold piece of art."

"Like I told Susan, it speaks to me, I'm just not sure what it's saying. But I like it, a lot."

"Good. That's good. Art is good for the soul. I hope I helped."

"You did. Thanks." Jack shook Toby's hand and started for the door, then pulled up short. "Say, did you know Playa, another Lenox Road banger, he ran with Ramirez?"

"Just around."

"Yeah? He's dead. It appears the Sinaloa cartel is cleaning house, too. They think the Lenox boys were good for stealing their drugs. Tortured Playa and hung him off a bridge in Venice."

Toby's face remained opaque. "That's rough, I hadn't heard."

"You don't know the half of it. I won't bore you with the gory details, you'll see it on the news. Do you by any chance know Ramirez's girlfriend, Angel?"

"No, never met."

"You know, she told me a funny thing. She said Ramirez couldn't have hijacked the cartel's stash. The man got seasick. Would puke on a blowup raft in a swimming pool."

"Huh?" Toby said.

"Go figure," Jack said, smiling at the mystery. "I took down my share of Colombian kingpins in my career. I know how the cartels operate. It looks like they didn't get the answers they wanted, or Playa might still be alive. Walking with crutches but alive." Jack kept on digging, seeing if he could open any cracks in that young façade.

"That's how they do business. If he had given up the drugs, they would've made Playa work like an indentured servant until he paid off his debt. But I think he couldn't tell them what they wanted to hear, because he didn't know."

Jack finally came to the point. "So, whoever went pirate on the Sinaloa cartel needs some serious help. Help I can provide. I've got friends in the DEA, FBI, and LAPD. They can provide protection, possibly immunity if the thieves come forward."

"Interesting story, Jack. But it means nothing to me," Toby said, sipping his Coke and checking the time on his cell. "Thanks for stopping—"

"But where I get hung up in this whole scenario," Jack said, cutting him off. "I mean, do you see the weak sister—your words—Ramirez, firing a rifle from a sniper's nest, killing Vegas and little Maria, and then firing out on the Pacific chop and hitting his target? Someone like you, maybe, you've got the balance, you surf right, but Ramirez? Puking his guts out all the way to the score? I'm just saying."

Jack handed Toby his empty can of Diet Coke and one of his cards. "Call me if anything or anyone comes to mind, or if there's anything I can do for you." The bell rang when Jack opened the door, and again when the door closed behind him.

———

Toby stood perfectly still, his face placid, until his heartbeat adjusted, and he was sure Jack was gone. The man was going to be a problem. He'd have to give that some serious thought. He checked himself out in the three-way mirror as he walked to the fridge and grabbed two beers.

Sean walked in from the back room, his face rigid, his eyes steely.

Twenty-five

Jack was talking to Cruz even before the gray metal door to his loft shut heavily behind him:

"I basically queered my relationship with the Dirks."

"It went that well?"

"Oh, it was good, it just shut off all lines of communication with the brothers. I gave Toby a full-court press, and he should have responded by throwing my ass out of their store. It's what I would've done."

"And?"

"He made nice. He fought what was reasonable emotion. He was protecting someone. Himself? His brothers? Eva? Somebody." Cruz was watching him carefully, knowing this was leading to something.

"So, this is what I need. Can you hack a Mercedes GPS system?"

"I think so. It's a bit more sophisticated than OnStar, but doable. All I need is the vehicle's VIN number. Then I can hack into the Mercedes global tracking system, and that, with the VIN number, gets me into the GPS system's records files."

"Good. I'm looking for the Dirks' itinerary and time line for the past week."

"What model Mercedes do they drive?"

"It's a high-end step van. A gray Sprinter. As far as I know, they leave it parked in the alleyway behind the shop at night. Terrence said he pulled an all-nighter doing inventory when the cartel was being robbed, but normally they close their doors at nine."

"I'll do a recon after dinner, and see if it's cool."

"I also need a phone number on Forward Thinking; it's the San Francisco design shop that fabricates the custom furniture the Dirks peddle. It was one of their stops up north," Jack said as he walked into his office and booted up his computer.

Cruz found it and sent it.

"Thanks. Oh, Kenny Ortega reached out. He delivered a name and an address on the potential stalker. I sent the particulars to your computer."

Jack was on a roll, and Cruz was bobbing his head, feeding off his energy. He snapped his laptop shut, straightened up his work space. "If I can access the van, I might have something for you in the a.m."

"Try to stay out of jail."

"Will do, boss," and Cruz banged out the door, locking up behind him.

If Jack was correct, his son, Chris, would have just completed his day's studies and the physical therapy for his pitching arm. There was a good chance he'd catch him in the dorm. Jack dialed the phone and felt himself tightening as it went to three rings. His son lived in a dorm room the size of a shoebox. Jack was about to click off when Chris's Skype line picked up.

"Hey, Dad. Did it work out?"

"Better than you know, son. Jeremy appeared on my doorstep and fought for your mother's honor."

"Wow, that's very unlike the man, and quite cool. Where are they now?"

Jack's dilemma. Throw his son under the bus or give him a fighting chance. "Probably wine tasting in Santa Ynez."

"Isn't that north of Los Angeles?" he spit out rapid-fire.

"About a third of the way to Palo Alto." Jack chose to err in favor of his son.

"Crap," he said, doing the math, unhappy with the results. "Weren't you going to tell me?"

"I'm calling you now, aren't I?"

Jack could sense Chris's wheels turning. "I'm glad they're back together. I felt guilty being the cause. Mom's not as good living alone as you are."

What a great attitude, Jack thought. "I love you, son. How's the arm?"

"Not bad, getting better."

"You're not throwing yet?"

"No, Dad. Not until I get the okay from the doc."

"Good, I'll stop worrying then."

"No, you won't. Love you, Dad."

Chris clicked off, leaving Jack feeling that either he was overly tired or turning into a sap, because his throat was thick with emotion.

———

Sean stood at the kitchen sink rinsing off dinner dishes and placing them in the dishwasher. His face was tighter than usual, his body language tense, his shoulders rounded, like a man at the starting block of a relay. Terrence stood behind him, leaning on the fridge, nursing a scotch on the rocks. Contemplative.

Both men raised their heads as Toby's Jeep fired up, and head-lights bled through the kitchen window. Toby flashed a peace sign as he rumbled down the driveway, knowing his brothers were standing by the window talking about him.

"I think he's in over his head," Terrence said, staring into his scotch glass as if it held the secret of life. He twirled the ice cubes and emptied his glass in one swig waiting for his brother to weigh in.

"So what should we do?" Sean said, closing the dishwasher, grabbing his own glass, and pouring two fingers of Macallan neat.

"Keep him from drowning."

"He's generating more than his share of heat. It could go bad. For all of us."

Terrence gave that some thought. "Might have to kill Berto-lino," he said. "Give us some breathing room. I've been working on a few ideas," Terrence said, refilling his glass, passing on the ice.

Sean wasn't surprised. He was confident his brother could fi-nesse the technical aspects of a workable plan if needed. Probably had it all mapped out in his head.

"I'm not ready to let him drown," Terrence said, matter of fact. "Ricky J was on you, Sean. Toby had your back. And I love you, bro, but the biggest issue we face was your idea. Your pitch."

"It was also our biggest score, so blow me."

"You can't spend money in hell."

"Fuck you."

"Fuck me? Fuck you!"

The two brothers knew they weren't going to let the conver-sation devolve into physical violence, so they both dialed it back.

"They got nothing to tie us to Ricky J," Sean said quietly.

"Did you read the *Times*?"

"I was swamped."

"They dug up a .22 rifle outside Ramirez's crib. Sounds like Toby's."

"Not a bad move," Sean said, mulling that over. "With Ramirez dead, there's no way to prove ownership."

"So, if Toby was the shooter, he's clear on Vegas, and the kid. No one ever accused him of being stupid," Terrence said with brotherly pride.

Sean raised his glass on a silent clink. "Impetuous, controlled by his dick, but not dumb."

"And the Sinaloa cartel seem to have bought the Ramirez connection because they're tearing through the Lenox boys."

"And the doctor?"

"The butcher," Terrence corrected, his eyes cold. "He doesn't seem to be making any noise from the grave."

Sean knocked back the rest of his drink. His eyes grew hard as he said, "Maybe Toby should take a vacation."

Terrence's head snapped toward Sean, eyes blazing.

"What?" Sean shouted. "A *vacation. Hawaii. Ireland. Whatever*. Just out of sight for a spell. Let everybody calm the fuck *down*," he said pointedly.

"Something to think about," Terrence said, composed again, seeing the sense. "Definitely something to think about."

Twenty-six

Day Eight

Jack knew it was eight thirty without checking the clock, because the honking horns, revving engines, radios blaring, and squealing brakes created by the procession of FedEx trucks leaving the lot next door was his daily wakeup call.

Susan was in the first shot of the day, and had been picked up by her driver at six. Today was another series of interiors, and she wasn't scheduled to work again for the next five days. Jack, focused on the case, knew exactly how he was going to use this window of opportunity.

He showered, shaved, poured some coffee, pulled a bagel out of the fridge and popped it in the toaster. A smear of cream cheese and he was good to go until lunch. Twenty-five years on the force and the habit was ingrained. Never much for breakfast, Jack liked to hit the ground running.

He was going to wait until nine to call Cruz, but at quarter till, the four phones placed strategically around the loft trilled as one.

"Morning," Jack said into the receiver. His face broke into a tight grin. "C'mon up."

218

"So, you're not gonna believe this, or maybe you already had a hunch, but the Dirks never made it to San Francisco," Cruz said as he opened his computer on the dining table and booted up.

"Do tell," Jack said, pleased with how the day was starting. He handed Cruz a cup of coffee and came around to view the computer screen.

"It won't give you a minute-by-minute breakdown, but the GPS does give the time they logged on and started their trip." Cruz took a sip of coffee and waited for the program to boot up. "Okay, here it is. They left Malibu on Wednesday at five eighteen in the morning somewhere near Trancas, took Las Virgenes road to the 101 to the 405 and then north, to the 5. They took that route all the way to the outskirts of Sacramento. A state park in Rosemont. MapQuest puts the trip at five hours forty-three minutes. They could have reached their destination around eleven.

"At one thirty-seven they were on the I-5 again. That's when they reprogrammed the GPS system."

"Where were they headed?"

"To an address in Big Sur. And I guess they knew how to get home from there because there was no more activity until they were back in Santa Monica, and then it was to a downtown address in the garment district."

Jack's brown eyes narrowed and then his face slowly broke into a wolf's grin. "Toby lied about the time they left L.A. He said Tuesday night at seven, wanted to miss traffic. And Terrence and Toby both lied about their destination. Even if they stopped in San Francisco on their way down from Sacramento, they wouldn't have taken the 5 to get to Big Sur. Easier to shoot down the 101."

Both men took a sip of coffee, assessing that piece of information.

"If they left at five, that could've given them time to hijack the cartel's drugs and drive up north," Cruz said, looking to Jack for confirmation.

"You bet your ass. Send me the file. I want to check the address in Sacramento and see where that takes us."

Cruz couldn't mask his pleasure, knowing he'd hit it out of the park. He banged Send, ran his fingers through his spiky black hair, and Jack's computer dinged.

Jack input a Google search, and Rosemont Park turned out to be a suburban section of Rosemont, part of Sacramento County. Without an address there was nothing more of interest. Next, Jack tried Sacramento newspapers, to see if there were any items of interest on the day in question.

The first hit was a winner, a front-page headline in the *Sacramento Bee*. "Purple Haze Shattered with the Brutal Slaying of a Marijuana Entrepreneur."

"*Ricky J Blufeld, owner and operator of five Sacramento medical marijuana pharmacies, was found executed and buried on his property in Rosemont*." The article went on to say that no drugs were found on the property, and Ricky J's body hadn't been discovered until three days after his cold-blooded execution-style murder. The reporter of the article stated that it looked like a professional hit, and the body had been found secreted in a hole in his backyard, covered by a plastic garden shed. Neighbors were alerted to the crime scene by the incessant barking of the deceased man's dog, a small Boston terrier. Robbery was the suspected motive.

Jack forwarded the story to Nick Aprea and bcc'd Cruz, who immediately read it and let out an involuntary yelp.

Jack had that electric charge running down his spine again.

"Take the company credit card, and take yourself and a nice-looking friend out to dinner, Cruz."

"Way to go, Boss. You're in the hunt."

Jack grabbed his cell phone and keys, fist-bumped Cruz. "Let's get 'em." And he was out the door.

————

Jack was sitting in a booth at Philippe's, eating a French-dipped lamb sandwich with spicy mustard, talking to Nick Aprea. "Why would they make a trip to one of the biggest medical marijuana suppliers in the Sacramento area unless they were going to off-load the cartel's drugs? To cop a joint?"

Nick wasn't as convinced. "No drugs were found on the property. And you can't prove they visited the victim. They were in the area. And there's not enough to tie the two cases together. The Dirks, as of today, are not persons of interest in the cartel heist and murder, and not on the radar screen for the killing up north. The captain won't pay for a flight. If you can bring me a little more than a false itinerary, and a gut reaction to people you're predisposed to dislike, and who now have you on their shit list, I'll revisit it with the man."

Jack knifed some more spicy mustard onto his sandwich and took an eye-watering bite like he was snapping the head off a snake. "I'll fly up," he said. "Can you grease the wheels for me with the local gendarmes?"

Nick was willing to do that. "I know one old-timer up there. Name's Wald. Worked narcotics, Hollywood division, before he moved north. Good man. I'll reach out to him, get back to you."

Both men glanced at their empty plates.

"Can you do another?" Jack asked.

"You buying?"

"Beef?" Jack asked as he slid out of the booth.

Nick nodded, "And another brew."

Jack walked away, frustrated but filled with resolve.

———————

Eva was doing 70 on the San Diego Freeway, heading for home. The windows were down, her blonde hair whipping out the window of her baby-blue Beetle. Toby pulled alongside in his black Jeep, flashed a peace sign and a smile, before slamming pedal to the metal and jumping ahead toward the beach.

Meeting secretly was getting old, Eva thought, but then Toby had suggested a vacation, and the energy in her aunt's back bedroom lightened up some. They cracked open a bottle of wine and tossed out ideas. Eva recommended Santa Teresa, a beach town in Costa Rica she had seen on HGTV, and Toby immediately signed on. A perfect choice, he said. Sun, surfing, and . . . He never finished the sentence.

Their lovemaking was furious but reassuring. Eva didn't question why she was feeling so sensitive, why she would cry at the slightest provocation; something had been taken from her she could never get back. A little time away might help mend what was broken. Toby was sure of himself, and Eva wouldn't say no to change.

No, she told herself, life could be good again as she pulled her VW to the curb outside her mother's house.

Mr. Marks was standing by his fence, and his furrowed brow and pained expression gave her pause. Before she could ask what was wrong, three black-and-whites with lights flashing rocketed up the street from one direction, and three more came to screeching halts from the other.

Eva was roughly ordered out of the car and down onto the street, spread eagled. The blood drained from her face and she felt light-headed. Afraid she was going to faint, with the multiple gun barrels threatening, she slowly lowered herself to her hands and knees and tried to comply without touching the macadam road with her cheek.

The cops swarmed, ground her face into the pavement, and snapped on handcuffs. She was hauled to her feet as Lieutenant Gallina and Detective Tompkins exited an unmarked black Ford that had just slid to a stop behind the squad cars.

Gallina offered a curt greeting, and then announced that Eva Perez was under arrest for the murder of Dr. Charles Brimley.

Tompkins joined his partner and read Eva her rights while he led the trembling, silent woman into the backseat of a waiting patrol car.

Eva's frantic eyes locked on her neighbors. Mr. Marks stood frozen in place, grief stricken, cell phone outstretched, making a video record of the arrest.

The last thing Eva saw was an electronic battering ram being deployed to violate the front door of her home. "I had keys," she said quietly, eyes welling, her scraped face beginning to throb. "Why didn't they ask for my keys?" Her voice rose to a pitch of hysteria as the car jolted from the curb—throwing her back against the hard seat of the cruiser—and the only security she had ever felt in her life was left behind in the rearview mirror.

Twenty-seven

Jack followed Detective Kevin Wald up the cobblestone pathway to the police-tape wrapped, midcentury house owned by the recently deceased, Ricky J.

Wald, who had picked Jack up at Sacramento International Airport, wore a two-for-one rumpled brown suit that looked slept in. Gravity was getting the better of his heavily veined face; gray was taking over his thin, tousled brown hair. With his hound-dog jowls, bloodshot eyes, and prominent bags, the detective gave the impression of a man who had stayed too long at the party and was severely beyond retirement. Yet one look beyond the physical gave a clue to his innate intelligence. And Jack was a man who respected time in, as long as there was an exemplary record to back it up.

Wald swatted one side of the yellow tape off the door, took a last pull of his cigarette, and flicked it pinwheeling onto the manicured front lawn. Then he keyed the door and the two men entered the crime scene.

Wald stepped into a modern, spacious living room and turned to Jack. "Like I said, we already picked the scene clean, but go for it. I'm never opposed to another set of eyes when we're drawing a blank. Do you want to start in the house, or where the body was found?"

"Lemme do the interior, get a feel for the man, then look at the temporary grave site."

"Knock yourself out." Wald flopped into an overstuffed leather recliner. He hit a button that bounced his feet parallel to the burnished hardwood floor, exposing stretched black socks and oxblood loafers with leather heels that were severely worn on the outside edges. "Oh, I brought these for you to look at. I'll send off copies to your computer."

Jack opened the manila file and pulled out a newspaper article with pictures of Ricky J at one of his medical marijuana pharmacies, looking very serious and professional for the camera. Three color glossies showed Ricky J as the police found him. Dead, folded head to knees, and stuffed in the steamer trunk, buried in the rectangular hole. Two additional shots depicted Ricky J stretched out before they zipped up the body bag, one head-to-toe, and one close-up of his face.

The two neat holes, spaced an inch apart on his forehead, recalled the bullet grouping on Tomas Vegas's chest, the murder that started this case. ".22's," Jack stated.

"At close range," Wald shared. "No more than three feet. No powder burns, but the ME's certain of the distance. We're pretty sure he was standing in the doorway from the trajectory of the bullet. If so, the shooter was tall. Six-one or so."

"Pistol?" Jack said, not trying to lead the detective but getting that itch on the back of his neck. The Dirks were all over six feet tall.

"Could be, jury's out. Might be a ratter, but hard to say. One bullet went through and through, ended up pancaked in the kitchen wall. The second shot careened around his skull before lodging in his hip. It's a frag, and no good to anyone."

"Time of death?"

"Three days in the hole made it hard to pinpoint, but the coroner places it noonish on Wednesday."

Jack nodded and started walking through the house. That fit neatly into the Dirks' time line. What was shocking—even to Jack, who had experienced more than his share of violence—was the body count. As far as Jack could tell, four adults and one child had been murdered over a four-day crime spree.

Jack pushed aside his personal feelings and got back into cop mode. He stepped into the kitchen, walked over some crunchy residue—dry food for the dog. He looked from the bullet's entry site in the wall, down the hallway to the back door. Wald gave a running commentary with each room Jack entered.

"No electronic devices, cell phones, etcetera. Whoever shot Ricky J wiped the place clean. We're looking at phone records, but these guys are very savvy when it comes to communication. A high-tech security camera was in place, but an empty CD was in the breach. The system was turned off, leading us to believe that he knew the intruder."

"The man had money, lived clean," Jack said as he walked back into the living room.

"We found eight thousand dollars in the freezer, so money might not have been the motive. And the man had a record, was never off our radar screen. He had a partner, but he was in Provence, France, when the crime occurred. I called him. Guy seemed pretty shook up. Felt right. He's flying home for the funeral. I'll talk to him at length at that time. Said Ricky had no enemies that he was aware of, but the fierce competition inherent in the pot trade speaks for itself."

"Where'd Ricky do his time?"

"I'll check and get back to you on that. We interviewed the

employees who worked in his facilities. The man was well loved. He overpaid. The workers felt like they were on a mission."

"You ever think it would come to this when you were working narcotics? Risking your life for an ounce bag?" Jack asked.

"Fucking war on drugs, my ass. Should have legalized it twenty years ago. Rather come up against a guy smoking a joint than someone flying on vodka or PCP."

"Can't argue that. Let's see the backyard?"

Wald grunted as he cranked the recliner upright and hefted himself off.

"I saw the dog bed in his bedroom, and there's dry food scattered around the kitchen floor," Jack noted.

"Yeah, cute little pug or something. The interesting part, whoever shot Ricky J was a dog lover. Left a mountain of dry food and enough water for a week on the kitchen floor."

"Huh. Where's the dog now?"

"Next door neighbor's holding it until someone in the family comes forward to claim it. Parents on the East Coast are in transit. C'mon, I'll show you the grave."

The men stepped off the back porch and inhaled in unison, both relieved to be in the fresh air and out of the oppressive environment of the crime scene.

Wald immediately lit another cigarette.

"The hole was precut?" Jack asked.

"The steamer trunk was sunk into the hole, it was a perfect fit."

"Any trace of drugs?"

"No trace of anything. The killer made off with something, or else why did he go to the trouble of finding it? That rubber tool shed was covering the opening. Couldn't have been too easy to find, given the circumstances."

"Maybe he knew about it beforehand? Maybe Ricky J was branching out into cocaine?"

"Maybe, maybe, maybe. So tell me, make your case." Wald's eyes were sharp, his cop antenna focused on Jack, all business now.

Jack scanned the perimeter of the backyard, taking note of how private it was, and began: "Bullet pattern: same caliber weapon. Proximity: GPS records take my suspects to the vicinity of Rosemont Park around the time of the murder. Possible motive: if my guys ripped off the cartel's drugs, they'd have to have somewhere to unload them."

Wald's gaze turned inward as he worked through Jack's litany. He arced the butt of his cigarette out into the yard, lit another with an old Zippo, and faced Jack, his expression neutral. "You've got nothing, my friend. Don't get me wrong; I would've done the same thing as you. I'm big on the hunch leading to an arrest. Sorry. I'd like to fly to L.A. and interview your suspects, but I need more to go on.

"All you've got is proximity. Everything else is supposition. Won't fly. Not yet. Build me a case, and I'll come running."

"Fair enough," Jack said, disappointed but determined.

"You miss the badge?" Wald asked as he locked the back door and the two men walked through the kitchen toward the front of the house.

"It had its benefits. Politics was wearing thin toward the end. I became a manager, missed being out in the field. But if it wasn't for my bum back, I'd probably still be working it."

"Hell of a case you broke. That sex slavery thing. Nick was bragging on you."

That added a collegial note. "Yeah, worked out okay."

Jack stepped out the front door, stretched his back that was starting to spasm, and waited while Wald locked up and reattached the police tape.

"I'm hanging up on the damn dog," Jack admitted. "I can't read the psychology of the killers. They brutally murder a man, bury him in the backyard, and then feed the dog. Made sure it had enough to stay alive."

"We haven't bought into the *they* theory yet."

"If it's my brothers, and I know they're dirty as sin, then it fits as snug as the thousand-dollar suits they sell."

Wald remained neutral. "Keep working it from your side, I'm working it up here. We'll stay in touch."

The men got into Wald's government issue, and it took two turns of the key to fire up the tired eight cylinders.

Jack stared at Ricky J's house as the Crown Vic pulled away from the curb. The crime scene had the Dirks' stench all over it.

Terrence was walking a middle-aged male client wearing a kelly-green golf shirt and tan chinos to the door, while Toby straightened inventory on the racks. As the door was closing, a bartender from the Ale House, a few doors down, stuck his head in and said, "Hey. So last night, about one a.m., I was taking out a case of empties. As I tossed them into the Dumpster, I saw a kid scoping out your van. He was staring through the windshield and looked like he snapped a few photos with his cell phone. I asked him what's up, and he smiled and said everything was cool and wasn't it a cool ride and like he was thinking about getting one and converting it and driving across the country."

"Did he seem okay?" Terrence asked.

"A little too much information, a little too late at night, so I thought I'd run it by you."

"What did he look like?"

"Short, not a bad-looking dude, black spiky retro hair, clean cut, probably nothing but what the hell."

"Thanks, Jeff. Appreciated. I'll keep my eyes open."

Jeff took off for his shift at the Ale House and Terrence stood stone still as the door closed and the bell rang in the bartender's wake. The only movement was a vein pulsing in his temple.

Then the answer came to him. "That's the kid that works for Bertolino. Susan said he was a technical genius." Terrence swatted the hanging drapes open at the rear of the shop and exited the store into the alleyway. He walked up to the company van and peered through the windshield, Toby fast on his heels.

"What do you see? I don't see anything interesting enough to photograph," Toby said, standing shoulder to shoulder with his brother.

"Nothing. Really, nothing at all." And then, "Wait a sec, I can see the VIN number. It's prominent. That's about it." He walked around the van to see if there had been any attempt at entry. The vehicle was clean. Locks intact.

Back in the shop, Terrence was lost in thought until, "Fuck! Goddammit to hell."

"What?"

"You said you used the GPS when you were up north?"

Toby nodded, "To get to Ricky J's and then to Diskin's place in Big Sur."

"Did you input Ricky J's street address?!" Terrence asked, his tone rising in volume and intensity.

"Calm the fuck down. Of course not. We dialed in a park in the general area, and then Sean found the way from there. Why?"

"I'm not sure, but I'm pretty sure."

"What?!" Toby said, getting frustrated.

"That you might be able to hack into the van's GPS system if you've got the VIN number." Terrence became instantly decisive. "I want you to take it to our mechanic, now, Toby. I'll call him and bring him up to speed. Tell him we were hacked and I want him to clean out the hard drive in the van's computer system immediately."

Toby walked behind the cash register to grab the keys while Terrence checked his phone directory and hit Dial. He cupped the phone, lips pulled tight against his teeth. "Toby, get your ass over there now."

Toby hustled out the back, slammed the door behind him. Terrence feigned an easygoing tone and explained to their mechanic what he required, hoping the effort wasn't futile.

Jack was driving with the top down on his Mustang, being swept along in a sea of red brake lights and a solid stream of glaring white headlights passing south on the 405.

It was a comfortable seventy-two degrees. The sun was hovering over the horizon and the darkening blue of the sky hinted at a scattered star field as Jack pulled onto 90, the Marina Freeway, and home.

He left a voice mail for Captain Deak asking him to check for any boats registered to the Dirk brothers. He hadn't eaten a thing since breakfast and his stomach was growling. He planned on stopping home, washing up, and then running over to Hal's Bar and Grill for a quick dinner.

———

Cruz was still at the dining table when Jack walked into the loft. He made a beeline to the cabinet, grabbed his meds, and swallowed them with a gulp of tap water.

"That good?" Cruz said as Jack willed the pills to vanquish the pain shooting up his back.

"I was stuck between two drinkers on the flight who carried on a nonstop conversation over me. The flight was full or I would have paid a thousand bucks to upgrade. Why are you still here?"

"Couple of things came up. I wanted to bring you up to speed."

Jack poured a glass of wine, let out a long labored breath, took a sip, and chose to stand at the kitchen island. "Shoot."

"So, I put in a call to Forward Thinking, the design shop in San Francisco. I figured you were jamming and I'd try and get an answer for you."

"You were right, and thanks."

Cruz got right down to business. "So I spoke to a guy named Rob, he owns the shop. I pretended to be a client waiting on the order the Dirks said they picked up. Gave the date, said it never arrived, wondered when I could expect it.

"So, Rob looks at his books, and says he has an order for the date in question, and when I asked if he actually saw the Dirks on that date, he asked my name and started to get squirrely. Said he was on the run all day and might have missed them, then amended that and said they had stopped by, but he wasn't there, and asked my name again. I gave them your name, just kidding, I faked a name and said I'd take it up with the Dirks and hung up."

"Good work. Rob played it both ways, but if we subpoena his records, he'll probably spill, depending on the loyalty factor. What else?"

"This came over the Internet and I TiVo'd the four o'clock news." Cruz walked past Jack to the wall-mounted flat screen and hit Play. Jack put down his glass of wine and stepped closer as a Channel 7 News helicopter camera pushed in close on the take-down of Eva Perez in the San Fernando Valley. She'd been arrested for suspicion of murder in the shooting death of Dr. Charles Brimley, the reporter said as a booking photo of a distressed Eva showing cuts and bruises on her face and a glossy of the doctor were shown side by side.

"They haven't gone into a ton of specifics, but I thought you'd want to know."

"You did good," Jack said as he picked up his landline and pulled up Eva's number on the off chance she'd already made bail. The phone rang twice and was picked up on the third ring.

"Hello, who's this?"

"Who is this?" Jack asked. "Who am I speaking with?"

"Bertolino?"

"Gallina?"

"What the fuck, Bertolino. I want your ass down here post-haste!"

"Tomorrow is as hasty as I'm gonna make it. I've been on the run all day."

"Then explain something, big shot. Why do you have this number?"

"Overlapped with the Sanchez case."

"Christ, Bertolino. That case is closed. *Finito.*"

"Do you have a murder weapon?"

"We picked up a .22 pistol along with a Colt police issue .45 and a .38 café pistol. They're with ballistics as we speak."

"Don't crow until you get the ballistics report back."

"Or what?" Smug.

"Or you'll be scraping egg off your face, Lieutenant."

"Is that so? We've got hate mail sent from Eva Perez's phone, and death threats sent to the Doc from her computer. They're with the lab now. We had more than enough to compel the district attorney's office to issue a search warrant and an arrest order. I'm afraid it's you who's going to be served up some crow."

"Motive?"

"Get your ass down here at first light, and we'll trade information. If you're not here by eight sharp, I'm going to send a car and we'll do it the hard way, smart ass."

"You gonna charge me?"

"Accessory after the fact, withholding information on a capital murder investigation, obstruction of justice . . ."

"Stuff it, Lieutenant."

Gallina cackled and disconnected.

Jack could hear the dial tone as he placed the phone back on the receiver.

Cruz sat silently, waiting for Jack to speak.

Jack took another sip of wine, decided to hold off on calling Leslie until he had more information. He grabbed the phone again and pulled out his cell. He scrolled through the directory in his cell phone and tapped a number into the landline. "Erica Perez, Eva's mother," he shared with Cruz, who nodded.

The phone rang eight times before going to voice mail. Jack requested a call back from Erica as soon as she received the message. He offered to have his lawyer, Tommy Aronsohn, look into

Eva's case, but he couldn't proceed without her okay. He promised to do everything in his power to help and hung up.

"You think she'll respond?"

"She's a smart woman. I hope so."

"I tracked down the guy who lives at the cell phone address Kenny Ortega delivered. Frank Bigelow, the one who's been making the late-night calls? His apartment is only a few blocks away from Susan's rental. And get this. Frank Bigelow is Susan's cousin."

That shocker struck him like a blow. "Really?"

"Maybe that's why she's being tight-lipped. You think he's bleeding her?"

"He looks good for the twenty grand. Might be trying to dip his beak again." The tumblers in Jack's mind were revolving, trying to fit this new information into what they knew already. "Great work, Cruz."

"You gonna call DDA Sager?" Cruz asked, intuiting Jack's next move.

"I've been summoned down to headquarters in the morning. I'll stop by after my meeting. I generally do better with Ms. Sager face to face."

"He cut her up like a dog. Like he was spaying a dog." Toby was prowling the main room of their shop like a man possessed. His generally placid eyes were blazing with dark, ungodly hatred. "Sanctioned sterilization. Like a fucking Nazi. A total hysterectomy on a twenty-one-year-old woman. A perfect fucking woman. My woman."

"Take it easy," Terrence said gently as he turned the OPEN sign to CLOSED, locked the front door, and pulled the blinds. The store phone rang, and Terrence let the call go to voice mail.

Sean was sitting on the leather couch, drink in hand, face set in stone.

"You fucking take it easy. It was my baby. He killed my fucking baby. And Eva's getting night sweats already. Crying all the time. And there was nothing I could do to help. What the fuck would you have done? The man needed killing."

"And now she's in jail, and the trail brings us to light again."

"The trail ended with Ramirez!" Toby was shouting now. Red-faced fury, his voice a painful growl. "He can't prove he didn't shoot the prick from the grave."

"Bertolino tied you to Eva. He probably shared the information with the police. They'll be knocking on your door."

"Fuck 'em!" Toby went to the minifridge and grabbed a long neck, twisted off the cap, and drank half a bottle in one angry inhale.

Sean spoke for the first time. Quietly. The brothers had to stop all movement to hear him. "We got a call from Rob, up north. He fielded a call from someone in L.A. asking about the phantom furniture pickup. Young voice, he said. Wanted to know if Rob had actually seen us. Promised he covered for us, but you know Rob, he's the nervous type. The man won't go down with the ship."

"Nobody's going anywhere," Toby said with conviction.

Terrence walked over to the three-way mirror and hand-combed his long red hair. Blue eyes unblinking. Analytical. "It might make sense to put you on a plane. Get you out of town for a few weeks, maybe a few months, depending on how this all plays out."

"Eva and I were planning a trip to Costa Rica."

"That could work. But I want you to take the emotion out of the equation. You have to go alone. If she makes bail . . ."

"When she makes bail! She didn't kill the man. They won't be able to keep her inside for making death threats. And my guess is, she wasn't the only one. He butchered eighteen women over a two-year period. The guy was a fuckin' monster." Toby drained the rest of the Dos Equis and went for another.

"We've got to slow Bertolino down."

"Permanently?" Toby asked, hopeful.

Sean waited for the energy in the room to dissipate before he spoke. "No more bodies. No recriminations for what's already been done. There's blood on all of our hands. But I want you to hear this, Toby, we have to stay smart. And that means no more bodies. We're done. Out of the killing business. And I have to know that you're not going to choose Eva over family. I've got to know that. It's important, Toby. Make me believe you."

The room went still. All eyes were trained on Toby, looking for a reaction. Horns blared on Main Street and shadowed figures moved past the storefront.

Toby's face drained of color; his ears rang as he felt the heat of his brother's gaze. He fought to keep the bile from surging from his stomach into his mouth. His mind raced through all of the possible endgames if he didn't choose his words carefully.

"Or what?" he finally said, as quietly as Sean. Almost mocking. No one was smiling. It was the four-million-dollar question.

"Don't answer a question with a question, Toby. This is serious," Terrence said, trying to diffuse some of the testosterone spiking in the room. He walked over and poured himself a scotch. Drained it, and poured another.

Toby now knew that his two brothers were like-minded. They

had a plan in place in the event he went rogue. They couldn't turn him in or they'd all go down. There was only one move left on the game board. Toby knew he couldn't sleep on the answer, or he might not wake up. He took some deep breaths to slow his heart rate and went Zen on the situation.

Toby slowly crossed the room and poured Sean a scotch, refilled Terrence's glass, and grabbed another beer. He made direct eye contact with both brothers and held their gaze.

"Nothing . . ." he said and took a long beat for dramatic effect. "Nothing will ever come before family. I'll work it out with Eva when the smoke clears. I will not be the reason the Dirk Brothers fall."

Toby clinked his bottle against Sean's glass, eyes clear of doubt, studied innocence, and waited until Terrence walked over, huddled with his brothers, and joined the toast.

Susan walked out of her en suite bathroom wearing nothing but red cheeks from overzealous sex and Jack's five o'clock shadow. She slid perfectly under her Egyptian cotton sheets and rolled Jack on top of her. He nuzzled her lips, her neck, and her breast, before kissing the side of her ear, eliciting a moan.

"All that, and he cooks, too."

"The house smells like my loft the first time we made love."

"Sex, garlic, onions, and San Marzano tomatoes. I went to your deli and told Dominic I wanted to buy Jack Bertolino's normal supplies. Dominic packed an Italian care package and I took a selfie with him as a thank-you."

"I'm impressed. And I'm hungry. I'll get the water boiling and meet you downstairs." Jack jumped out of bed, shrugged into his black T-shirt, stepped into his jeans and running shoes, and headed for the kitchen. He had planned on getting the truth out of Susan before dinner, but Susan meeting him at the door wearing nothing but a smile altered Jack's plans.

Susan stepped behind Jack as he was dropping two nests of egg pappardelle into salted boiling water. She picked up a wooden spoon and stirred the pot of simmering sauce. Then she scooped some out, blew to cool it some, and slurped the entire spoonful.

"You've outdone yourself, Bertolino."

"I have my gifts," he said, checking the time on his watch for al dente, the only way he served or ate his pasta.

"I heard something out front as I was coming down the stairs. You?"

"No, I've been banging away in here," but he walked out of the kitchen through the living room and opened the front door to check.

A manila envelope had been wedged under the welcome mat. Jack pulled it out and carried it into the house, thinking it might be a call sheet from the studio, although the envelope was mighty thin. He noticed the flap hadn't been secured and his cop radar got the best of him. He opened the envelope and the contents: a single Polaroid, drifted to the hardwood floor.

"What was it?" Susan yelled from the kitchen.

Jack picked up the Polaroid and his stomach lurched. The photograph had turned sepia-brown with age, but the image was still powerful. A boy who couldn't have been more than nine was getting oral sex from a young girl with brown pixie-cut hair. Her bare back faced the camera, but with a sinking heart, Jack knew it was Susan. Seven? Eight? Gut wrenching.

Susan read Jack's expression as he entered the kitchen and stormed over to the kitchen table, still holding a wooden spoon.

"What is it, Jack?" she asked, her voice threatening. It was clear that she had some idea.

It was time to drop the bomb. "I think your cousin Frank Bigelow left his calling card," Jack said calmly.

"I don't have a fucking cousin, Jack!" When he didn't respond, she went on, "I don't know what the hell you're talking about, but I don't like your tone or the inference. Give me my mail and get the fuck out of my house! I don't know where you get off, looking at my private correspondence—"

Jack handed her the envelope. Susan savagely grabbed for it, ripping it wide open. The Polaroid fell face up on the table and Susan froze. She placed both of her hands on the table for support, eyed the photo with a shattered expression. She tried to rise up, but didn't have the strength. Instead she melted onto the chair beside her.

Jack walked over to the stove, shut off the burners, and brought two glasses of red back to table. He placed one in front of Susan, who was staring off into the distance. "Tell me," he said softly.

She finally turned her haunted gaze toward Jack.

"I grew up in New York City on Forty-fifth and Tenth. A shotgun apartment in Hell's Kitchen. My brother, Teddy, who was two years older than me, and my dad. Mom abandoned the family when we were kids. The old man was a stage father who pushed us into the business. He was a frustrated actor himself and managed our careers.

Susan took a sip of wine, steeled herself, and continued. "At age five, the molestation began. Both me and my brother. Dad was an equal-opportunity purve. And not just us, my cousin Frankie and anyone else he could get his hooks into with the promise of turning them into stars."

By now her face had turned ashen. "Frankie became part of the sex play. Dad would set the scene, we were the actors, and Frankie was in charge of shooting the Polaroids. Sometimes Frankie would join in, and Dad would be the director and the cameraman. Girl and boy, boy and boy, and sometimes a threesome. My father had quite the imagination."

Jack was so angry, he had to force himself to breathe. "And that's what Bigelow's been using as a weapon to extort money?"

Susan nodded despairingly. "He has pictures of me at eight, nine, ten having vaginal and oral sex with my brother and himself. He showed me a few of them, and they're damning." She reached out for Jack's hand and grabbed it tightly.

"I'm finally an overnight success after fifteen years of small parts and hard knocks. Frankie threatens to sell the pictures and destroy me if I cut off the money."

"Where's your family now?"

"Teddy killed himself with smack when he was sixteen, and Dad died of a massive coronary. Not young enough to satisfy me. I'd kill him myself if he was still alive," she said without any rancor, and Jack believed her.

"As soon as my career took off, my cousin was there with his hand out. It started with loans that were never repaid, and when I tried to blow him off, he threw down the gauntlet and got real. You found the twenty grand I paid him last year. That would've been enough for some people. Not my Frankie. He's demanding a big payday. A hundred fifty thousand, or the pictures go public."

"Will you help me, Jack?" Susan let go of his hand, and took another sip of wine, sucked in a breath, and nailed him with her killer eyes. "Will you help me out here? Help me stop him?"

Jack didn't like the direction the conversation was taking. He had nothing but sympathy for the abuse Susan had suffered, and understood her desperation, but his unease grew with every tick of the clock.

"Jail won't cut it, Jack. There's only one way to make sure he can't sell the pictures. They'll destroy me. Do you understand what I'm saying here?"

Jack was thrown. She hadn't spoken the words yet, but her intent was clear. If he were still wearing a badge, he'd be compelled to arrest Susan Blake for solicitation to commit murder. He took a healthy sip of red wine, trying to formulate a response.

"So, this is what it's been about from the beginning?" Jack asked, knowing the answer. "Between you and me. The sex. The flattery. The painting."

"I'm not that smart, Jack," but her words rang hollow.

"I used to think I understood women. I should have learned from my ex-wife, who told me I didn't have a clue. Sadly, she was right. But I'm clear on one thing."

"And what's that, Jack?" Susan asked, struggling for control.

"I'll take Frank Bigelow down because he's a scumbag. But I won't kill him. Because I'm not."

Jack got up from the table, splashed the remains of his red wine into the sink, and left the house.

———

Frank Bigelow pounded up the stairs to his one-bedroom rental unit above a garage. He slammed the door behind him, carefully placed his camera rig on a long wooden table, and snapped on the overhead light that cast long shadows over the modest studio apartment. The only sound: the squawking and squeal and tinny voice emanating from a police scanner.

Three white manikin heads sat in a neat row at the far end of his wooden worktable. One had a blond wig, one brunette, and both sported colorful striped bandannas. It was his signature among the paparazzi. When Frank ripped off his bandanna, his blond wig came with it, exposing a head that hadn't seen a lock of hair since his sixteenth birthday, when he was stricken with alopecia and his life, destroyed. He slammed the wig onto the third white head, securing it with straight pins.

Staring at himself in a wall mirror, Frank ran his hands over his shiny bald pate, like a man running his fingers through his hair. Then he started scratching, bringing up painful, manic welts. Wild eyed.

"That should shake things up some. Shake a few bucks loose from cuz. She doesn't really know who she's dealing with here. She's gonna learn."

Frank turned to the far wall. He had tacked five nude photographs of Susan Blake to the wooden slats. She was drying her hair in one, as if she had just stepped out of a shower. Another showed her putting on a lacy bra. It was Frank's favorite. He fantasized Susan getting dressed for him, and it was the one he sent to TMZ. Then there was a picture of Jack Bertolino stepping out of a limousine with Susan by his side. Jack's eyes had been slashed in the photograph.

His Inguity HD camera drone, shaped like a Darth Vader star-fighter, was docked on a stand on the kitchenette counter. Frank remembered how excited he was taking the photo. Standing in her backyard, feeling as if he was in the room with her again. Inside her pussy again. That was the plan. To have Susan Blake all to himself.

He had come close in New York City, and would've been successful if it hadn't been for that FBI agent who was dogging him. It was the only time in his life that his bald head had saved his skin.

Now all he had to deal with was that has-been PI. He could get around that. He'd do her. She would come over with the $150,000 and he'd take her right in this room.

Twenty-eight

Jack saw Erica Perez sitting on a bench outside the modern glass and stone structure that housed the Los Angeles Police Department. The woman appeared to have aged since the last time he'd spoken with her, Jack thought. Her thick body leaden, shoulders slouched forward like she was contemplating jumping off a cliff, putting herself out of her misery. Her smoky-brown eyes, swollen, red rimmed, and wet. Her voice quavered as she spoke.

"I sent the first email on Eva's computer," she offered like a supplicant in a confessional. "She was still in the hospital ward, still locked up, she couldn't have sent it. And here's my phone. It's what I used to send the texts. I erased them, but I've seen on television how they can get them back. We both have E's in our first name, and my phone is listed as E. Perez. The police made a mistake. I get her calls and she sometimes gets mine."

"When's the last time you texted the doctor?"

"After I saw you. On my lunch break. I was furious."

"I think the doctor was dead by then," Jack said. "That might

245

help your case. I mean, why would you send a death threat if you knew he was already dead?"

"You have to help my little girl, Mr. Bertolino. You said you could help. She can't deal with being locked up. It almost killed her the last time."

"Why did you wait to call?" Jack asked, running his hands through his unkempt hair. He hadn't shaved and his face was strained from lack of sleep.

"I was scared. If I get arrested, it'll be my third strike. I haven't had any arrests in close to fifteen years, but my sister put the fear of God in me, said they'd throw away the key and I'd never see my daughter again. I feel so ashamed." Erica started to keen, her shoulders shuddered, and the maternal pain she experienced cut Jack to the core.

"Tommy Aronsohn has agreed to help. He's on his way now. He'll talk to the district attorney and see what can be worked out. We'll do everything we can to get Eva's release. We're going to have to prove the weapons belonged to your husband or it could get dicey with Eva still being on parole. But Tommy's the best in the business. He'll know how to handle it." The downtrodden woman tried to smile, like she believed him.

"I've got to get inside and talk with Lieutenant Gallina. Stay strong, help's on the way." Jack walked toward police headquarters and entered the building through the glass doors.

"Is it personal, Jack? This need to fuck with me," Lieutenant Gallina said, playing up the drama.

"Arresting me for a murder I didn't commit is still on my short list of reasons why I might hold a grudge."

"Ancient history."

"But I'm not."

"What?"

"Holding a grudge."

Gallina looked at his partner Tompkins, threw up his hands, and said, "Why doesn't he understand the Vegas/Sanchez case is closed? I think it is, the mayor thinks it is, the chief of police is sold. We're all happy, Jack, it's a done deal. It was Ramirez's gun; Ramirez is dead, end of story."

Tompkins knew his partner's rant was rhetorical and took a sip of coffee from a stained mug that said WORLD'S BEST DAD. "Let's hear what he has to say."

A labored sigh from Gallina, who pushed his chair away from his gray metal desk. "Christ. Go ahead."

"Toby Dirk lied about his relationship with Eva. As did Eva and her mother, who's sitting outside, but we'll get to her connection later.

"It's a known fact they were an item before Eva's arrest. And I suspect still an item now. He had a motive to take down Vegas."

"Old news," Gallina said.

"Captain Deak just verified that the Dirks have a registered inflatable that could have taken them to Catalina and back the night the cartel boat was hijacked and the men murdered."

"Whoa! How the hell did you make that leap? That's crazy even for you, Bertolino. Where's the connection?"

Jack had known he would protest that. "Bear with me? The captain has his men going over the tapes of that night to see if their craft left the marina or returned within the time parameters.

"When I questioned Terrence the day after the hijacking, he

looked like shit, he looked guilty, and when I interviewed Toby later, both brothers told the same lie about Toby and Sean's schedule, driving up north. Both said they left the night before, hours before the hijacking, giving them an alibi.

"I have their GPS records that contradict their story. And a route that took them to an area outside Sacramento. Not San Francisco, where Terrence told me they had gone to pick up a furniture order."

"Do I dare ask how you came into the possession of their GPS record?"

Jack skipped lightly over that point. "Not germane. So, my associate put in a call to the vendor in San Francisco who waffled on whether he had actually seen the Dirks in the flesh on the day in question. All he has to corroborate their statement is a computer-generated invoice. I think he'll spill if questioned by the authorities," Jack said, seeing if they were staying with him. "Nick Aprea filled you in on the murder of Ricky J in Sacramento. I think the trail of bodies are all tied together."

"You're the only one, Jack."

"Toby has motive for killing Vegas, and then for setting up Ramirez to take the fall and get the cartel heat off his back. If the Dirks were the hijackers, it's a reasonable assumption that they were going to Ricky J's to offload the drugs. The man ran five marijuana clinics, and spent time in Lompoc with Sean Dirk. They were cellmates. And again, I have Sean and Toby in the vicinity of the crime the day he was murdered."

Gallina's face was still hard, but Jack could see that Tompkins was interested. "And here's the kicker. Eva, as you probably realize by now, wasn't the shooter of Dr. Brimley. What did ballistics come back with?"

"The guns hadn't been fired in months, maybe years," Tompkins said.

"And I have the mother, Erica Perez, waiting to make a statement claiming that she can prove she was the one who left the death threats and hate mail. E. Perez. Erica, not Eva Perez. It was a simple mistake, easily rectified."

Gallina never missed a chance for a glib eye-roll.

"Okay," Jack went on, "you know the good doctor's history. There are fifteen different lawsuits against the man for the illegal sterilization of incarcerated women.

"Brimley killed Eva's unborn child. And I think it's a good bet Toby was the father. That's enough motive and probable cause from my point of view to bring Toby in for questioning and apply for a warrant to search his house, the Dirk Brothers store, their boat, their company van, and personal vehicles."

"I'm not feeling the thread," Gallina announced grandly. "The connection. Too many holes, too many leaps of faith. You pasted together an interesting story, but it's supposition heavy. I don't think the DA would sign off on it even if I were inclined to get on board, which I am not."

Jack persisted. "We need a search warrant before the brothers clean house, if they haven't done so already. We'll find a connection."

Gallina went on as if Jack hadn't just made his final plea. "So, if I'm doing the math correctly, Toby and his brothers are responsible for the murders of . . ." Gallina started counting on his fingers.

Tompkins answered, "Five men and one child, in a four-day period."

"That's mighty prolific," Gallina stated skeptically. "The Dirk Brothers, retailers by day, the James Gang by night."

"And culpable/accessories after the fact for the murder of Ramirez and Playa, the Bull," Jack added, fighting for his case. "Say we could locate Ramirez's girlfriend Angel, and his running buddy Tito. With the heat the cartel is exerting, we might be able to loosen their tongues and prove Ramirez wasn't the hijacker."

Gallina splayed his hands out on his desk. "You're killing me here, Jack. Here's what went down. Joey Ramirez took Vegas out, and the kid was a fatal mistake. He and the other two bangers hijacked the cartel's boat; they were able to get over on the cartel's men, because they knew them. They killed the two men and tried to destroy the evidence. All in an attempt to move up the food chain. Greed, a story as old as organized crime. That's plenty of motive in my book and more than enough for the powers-that-be." He then added another fact to his case. "The DEA traced the drugs found buried in Ramirez's yard to the Sinaloa cartel and the hijacked weed. Each batch is color coded, and the wrapper matched the most recent shipments smuggled into Dallas, Chicago, Detroit, and New York.

"Here's something else," Gallina continued, pleased with himself. "I put in a call to Sacramento, talked to your friend, Detective Wald, who isn't buying into the theory that there was more than one shooter, and he hasn't found one shred of evidence to tie Ricky J's murder to L.A. There were no cartel drugs found at his home, and they did an inventory at all five shops and audited his books. Everything was jake. Need I say more?"

No, Jack had heard enough. The onus was on him, in other words. He turned to leave and added, "Eva's mother's a straight shooter."

"Bad choice of words, Bertolino, but if she comes in, I'll talk with her. I'm a reasonable man."

"Tommy Aronsohn is representing her."

"Good for her. And Jack, don't go over my head or try to pull an end run. I appreciate the fact that you've been working overtime on this, but let us take it from here. Spend a little more time with that actress you're connected at the hip with. Everyone around here is jealous." Then he reconsidered that statement, not one to end on a high note, "Except Susan Blake appears to be high maintenance and probably needs all the help she can get."

"Hollywood, go figure," Jack said as he nodded to Tompkins and walked out the door, heading for ADA Sager's office. So much for holding off on the end run.

———

A male African American orderly with salt-and-pepper hair pushed a metal cart of food down the concrete floor of the holding cells that housed the female prisoners waiting for a bail hearing, release, or a more permanent home dictated by the current federal and state laws.

He delivered a tray of food through a slot in the heavy metal door, exchanged a few friendly words with the female prisoner before moving down to cell 217A.

The orderly grabbed a second tray, peered through the door's square peephole, and paused. The cell looked empty. He checked again, craning his neck before placing the lunch tray back on his metal cart and grabbing up his delivery sheet. He looked into the cell again. Shaking his head, he reached for the master key that hung on the side of the cart and keyed the door. When he tried to push it open, though, he was met with resistance. He put his shoulder into the task and the door opened wide enough for the elderly gent to stick his head in.

Eva Perez, wearing only a bra and panties, was slumped against the door. The leg of her orange jump suit was tightly wrapped around her neck and tied to the door handle. Eva's beautiful face was a frightening shade of blue, her lips swollen, and her brown eyes that were once ringed in gold were opaque and sightless.

The stunned orderly stumbled against his cart as he backpedaled and wildly banged on an alarm on the cellblock wall. He glanced back at the door, horrified, and ran down the hallway for help.

————

Tommy Aronsohn and Erica Perez were already seated across from Leslie when Jack gave an air knock at the open doorway followed by, "Knock, knock."

Leslie smiled with her eyes, a move missed by Erica but picked up on by Tommy.

"Come in, Jack," Leslie said. "I'd offer you a chair but . . ." All the chairs were spoken for.

"Mrs. Perez has already brought me up to speed on the mix-up with the cell phones. It seems reasonable enough for me, and the dismissal will be a slam-dunk when her phone is tied to the doctor's. The guns might become an issue, but the fact that Eva lives in a granny suite behind the house and the weapons were confiscated from Mrs. Perez's bedroom closet should be sufficient—along with a sworn affidavit of ownership from Mrs. Perez—to drop all charges against her daughter. I'll still have to run it up the flagpole, but I feel confident we'll succeed."

"Gallina knows that she's in the building. Should I walk them over?" Jack asked.

"Let's wait until I talk with my boss. Gallina's on a star turn, full of himself. I think he's already shopping a book deal."

The men laughed, Tommy gave Erica a reassuring pat on the shoulder and the suffering woman let out a long breath as ADA Sager fielded a phone call.

Leslie shot up out of her chair and fought to control her demeanor. She abruptly excused herself and strode out of the room.

Jack knew something was profoundly wrong; he could read Leslie in a pitch-black room. He followed in her wake. When they were halfway down the hall, Leslie spun, her eyes wild with disbelief.

"This is bad, Jack. Something really bad has happened, and I don't . . . oh, that poor woman. This is going to kill her."

"Erica Perez?"

Leslie fought back tears she would never share with her boss. Never show weakness.

"Eva Perez was found dead in her jail cell. Twenty minutes ago. She hung herself."

"Jesus. Was she on suicide watch?" Anger colored his question.

"I don't know. Don't know. Sit tight, don't say a word until we figure out how to handle the . . . Oh God, Jack, could it be any worse?" And Leslie ran down the hallway and took the elevator to the twenty-first floor.

––––––––

Lieutenant Gallina, being the point man responsible for the arrest of Eva Perez, was chosen to deliver the shattering news. Two female officers followed him to Leslie's office. They remained outside, but stood by ready in case things got out of hand.

A somber, deflated Gallina closed the door behind him as he entered the room. Jack didn't envy the lieutenant's position. From personal experience he knew this was absolutely the worst part of the job.

Jack watched through the glass window as Gallina turned to face Tommy and Mrs. Perez, who sat ramrod straight.

The sound that bled through the closed door and reverberated through the second floor of the LAPD Administration Building touched everyone within earshot. Deep in their bones.

It was an excruciating primal wail.

Twenty-nine

Toby Dirk was sitting on his surfboard, shooting the shit in a calm sea with his buddy Dean, when he saw Terrence and Sean walking stiffly across the sand, long dark shadows trailing behind. Yesterday's growing sense of dread came on again like a thunderclap. Their meeting had taken some of the tension out of the family dynamic, but it came roaring back as he saw his brothers kicking up sand, stopping at the water's edge, standing shoulder to shoulder. Tall and thin like two Maasai warriors.

"What the hell's that all about?" Dean asked, reading the vibe.

"Can't be good," Toby said as he slid down on his board and paddled.

Toby hit the shoreline, unbuckled the ankle strap, and stowed his board on dry land. He and his brothers walked away from the sunbathers scattered on the white sand. When they were out of earshot, they stopped and huddled.

"What the fuck is going on? Talk to me," Toby demanded.

Terrence searched for the words. Sean's face was stoic, but his eyes uncharacteristically welled up.

"C'mon, you're freakin' me out. Who died? Are we busted?"

The brothers remained silent.

"You're starting to piss me off. Go fuck yourselves."

Toby spun on his heel, but Terrence spoke before he stepped away: "Eva's gone. She's dead, Toby. She died this afternoon."

Toby turned back, his face devoid of emotion. His eyes narrowed as if searching for something in the distance. A flock of gulls screeched overhead, but Toby remained mute.

Sean looked a question at Terrence, who remained silent, giving his younger brother time to process the information.

"How did it happen?" Toby asked, his face placid.

"They think she took her own life. They're doing an official investigation now. Erica called the shop, hysterical. She tried you on your cell."

An eerie buzz was whirring in his ear. "What time did she die?"

"What?"

"What time did she die?" Toby wanted to know what he was doing the exact moment Eva took her last breath.

"I'm not sure."

Sean swiped at his eyes, looking confused at his brother's lack of reaction.

Toby read them both and said, "Well, that must be a relief, huh?"

"What the fuck, Toby," Sean said. "Don't go there. It's not right."

He added bitterly to Terrence, "It's one problem out of the way. One piece on the chessboard you don't have to worry about controlling."

Terrence took the jab in stride, knowing his brother was in shock.

Sean started to unravel. "You're fucking nuts. Certifiable. We try to do the right thing by you—"

Toby swung from the depth of his soul and landed a punch to Sean's jaw that snapped his head back and drove him to the sand.

Terrence wisely took a step back.

Sean shook it off, took in a deep breath, dusted off the sand, and got to his feet. "I'll give you one, brother. The next one will be your last."

Terrence cut in, defusing the situation, "Sean, why don't you pick up Toby's board and drive the Jeep home? I'll take him with me."

Sean rubbed his swelling jaw with the back of his sandy hand, nodding his assent. He and Terrence started walking in opposite directions.

Toby hung back. Still. Confused.

Terrence walked back to his brother.

"My legs won't move," Toby said in a whisper.

Terrence put his arm around Toby's shoulder, took his weight, and started walking him across the sand and up the incline to the Pacific Coast Highway and the family truck.

Sean plucked Toby's favorite board out of the sand, grabbed his backpack, and followed his brothers at a distance, not quite sure what to make of what had just transpired.

Jack was sitting on a director's chair in the covered stern of his cabin cruiser when Captain Deak appeared in his brisling war chariot. He pulled to a stop at the end of Jack's dock. He jumped off, tied off in studied perfection, and walked with a military gait down Dock 23 to Jack's slip.

"You're living the dream, Jack. I'm going to do a study on being you."

Jack chuckled. "Yeah, I'm living the life."

"Don't be modest. Susan Blake, a sturdy craft, exciting cases . . ."

"I'd like you to meet Susan," Jack said as she stepped out of the cabin, wearing Katherine Hepburn sunglasses, a diaphanous white blouse, aqua-blue capris pants, and a broad smile. She was carrying two glasses of red wine. With Frank Bigelow getting more brazen, Jack couldn't leave Susan to her own devices. He was concerned she might take matters into her own hands.

"I apologize if I spoke out of turn," Deak said, turning schoolboy red in the face. "No offense meant."

"None taken, sailor. I heard you were the man who saved Jack's life."

The crimson spread to his ears and neck. "Right place, right time," Deak said, passing it off.

"Can I offer you a glass or are you still on the clock?"

"Still on the clock, ma'am, thanks for asking."

"I play my cards right, I'll remain a Ms. for many years to come."

"Right, sorry." Deak's smile was disarming.

"You want to come along for the ride?" Jack asked Susan.

"Tommy's on his way. I'll be fine," but her smile fell short of the mark, Jack thought.

He punched a number into his cell as he stepped on board the Coast Guard's war craft.

"Put your phone away, I'm here," Tommy said as he walked up to the chain-link gate and waited to be let in.

Jack had checked Susan into a suite in the Marina Ritz-Carlton Hotel, Tommy's home away from home. Too many surprises at the rental house the studio had provided.

Jack raised his hand toward his friend—as in message received—and then grabbed a railing as Captain Deak executed a power one-eighty and cruised away from Jack's dock doing the legal marina speed of 5 mph.

"So, we have nothing with the Zodiac leaving the night of the hijacking. A few shadows covered by larger craft during the hours in question. But at first light we have what looks to be the Dirk Brothers' inflatable returning to the marina. The image isn't clear enough for a definitive, but the man piloting is tall, thin . . ."

"Red hair?"

"Black hoodie. Not enough for a positive ID. But I'll show you their craft." Deak pulled back on the throttle and drifted perfectly snug to the nearest dock. Jack jumped off and tied the boat fore-and-aft. "I can't allow you to board their vessel until you have a warrant, but I can't stop you from taking a good hard look."

"Terrence told me he was doing inventory the night in question," Jack said as he walked from one side of the slip around the bow to the other and walked down to the tricked-out Zodiac's stern. "Do you think this craft could make it to Catalina and back?"

"No question. It's got a long-range tank."

"Stand up to the ski-boat?" Jack asked.

"Not likely," Deak said without any equivocation. "Not unless there were other boats in the equation."

"That's what I'm feeling. Gallina thinks the cartel scumbags knew their killers. He's sure Ramirez and his crew are good for the crime, but he's wrong about that, just as he was dead wrong about Eva Perez. And that's a mistake that will haunt him to the grave."

All the while Jack was studying the craft, walking slowly past it. He stopped short near the central instrument panel. "What's that look like to you?" he said, pointing at the backside of a tubular curved metal piece that held the steering wheel assembly in place. It had a chunk blown out of it. A torn, ragged piece of metal in an otherwise perfect stainless steel and fiberglass housing. "What could have done that?" Jack asked, knowing the answer.

"High caliber, maybe from an AK."

"That's what I'm thinking."

"Hmmm," Deak said. "Looks like someone got lucky. An inch farther to the right, and this puppy would've been on the bottom of the ocean next to the cartel's ski-boat."

"Seems that when the Dirks get lucky, people turn up dead," Jack growled. "I'm gonna do something about changing the equation."

Captain Deak thought about the case some. "You're close, but it might not be enough."

"Enough to tell me I'm on the right trail. And I'll ride that until I take them down."

The captain was equally stern. "You need backup, I'm a phone call away."

"I owe you more than I can repay, but push comes to shove, I'd be willing to double-up on the Vig."

Captain Deak grinned as he turned over the engine. Jack untied the craft and jumped on board as Deak pushed the throttle forward and their stealthy craft headed back toward Dock 23.

———

Terrence sat shirtless at the kitchen table with a first aid kit opened in front of him. Not an ounce of body fat on his thin, muscled frame. The bandage on his shoulder was leaking a reddish-brown discharge, and Sean struggled to open a new dressing.

Toby was in a near catatonic state, staring down the empty

hallway, knowing he'd never see Eva walking into this room or his life again.

The only sound was the coffee maker, spitting and steaming Starbucks Colombian dark roast, and an occasional passing car.

Three plates had been set on the table. Toby's plate stood empty. The other two had remnants of fried rice and Kung Pao chicken. Five opened cartons of takeout were scattered about haphazardly, and the room smelled of egg rolls and brewing coffee.

Sean ripped the bandage off Terrence's skin in one quick tear. Terrence never blinked. The wound looked infected and painful.

"You didn't kill her," Sean stated in even tones, with his back to Toby. "Eva is not on you." He used a cotton ball to apply Neosporin to the torn skin, and then put a small bead on the bandage before covering the shrapnel wound with the clean bandage and securing it with tape.

Terrence nodded his thanks, stood, and shrugged into a clean dress shirt that had been neatly hung on the empty chair. "It's a nightmare, Toby. I'm not saying I understand the depth of your pain, what you're experiencing, but Sean is right on target. It's a tragedy, but not your fault." He glanced at Toby's thousand-yard stare and poured himself a cup of coffee while Sean closed the first aid kit and tossed the soiled bandages into the trash bin.

"And as inopportune as this tragedy is," Terrence went on, "we, the family, have to contemplate our next move very carefully. There will be ramifications."

Toby remained unresponsive.

"We need you present, Toby; time is not our friend. You were talking about taking a trip to Costa Rica. It might be the right time to book you a flight. Get you out of harm's way. Give you time to heal."

Toby finally made eye contact with both of his brothers, trying to gauge the subtext. He wasn't sure if he trusted them, wasn't sure if he trusted himself. "Not until Eva is buried," he responded in a hoarse monotone. "If I'm not in the picture, it will create more questions than answers."

"Let's sleep on it."

"Not until she's buried!" erupted from Toby, on his feet now, red faced and wild eyed. The vein in his temple threatened to explode.

"Okay," Terrence said gently. "Okay?"

Toby tried to control his breathing as he sat back down.

"You make a good point," Terrence said. "Let me think on it."

"You do that," Toby said. But he was resolute.

"I've got to get to the store. I've got that seven o'clock consultation. I'll be late, but I'm on my cell if you need anything." Terrence walked out the back door, fired up the Ford F-350, and drove the big truck slowly down the driveway.

"If you've got plans," Toby said to Sean, "I'll be fine."

"No, I'm good for a while," Sean said, giving no thought to leaving his brother alone until he calmed down some. "Maybe later we can hike up to the Brigg, and toss a couple back?"

Toby nodded. "We'll see."

Thirty

Jack left the side door open in case a hasty retreat was in order and moved quickly through the darkness of the Dirk brothers' garage. With Toby's Jeep parked on one side, even with the main house in total darkness, he couldn't be sure it was an all clear.

Cruz had reported at least three people still moving around the shop on Main Street, but he couldn't see in, and couldn't go closer and be seen. Jack's orders.

Jack froze as light spill from a passing car played across the far wall. He clicked on a micro Maglite. It lit up two Hobie kayaks along with two surfboards stowed overhead on the wooden rafters. One of the kayaks had what looked like a recent patch job on the craft's upper edge. Add the Zodiac to the mix . . . ? These guys had to be talented to take down the cartel's boat, but it was doable. And the varied bullet pattern on the cartel's scuttled craft started to make sense.

Jack rifled through the workbench that dominated the second side of the garage and found nothing of interest but gun-cleaning supplies. Nothing illegal about that unless they could be tied to murder weapons.

———

A dark room, suddenly illuminated by a struck match. Toby Dirk put a small hash pipe into his mouth, lit the bowl, and filled his lungs with a healthy toke. He was sitting meditation style in front of a small altar. He lit a votive candle that illuminated Eva's face in a photograph taken before her arrest. A free spirit who embodied all that Toby loved.

Next to the photo was an automatic pistol, the newest addition to his depleted arsenal. Toby exhaled the fine smoke and palmed the gun, contemplating his next move. His reason for being was no more.

He felt the heft of the .38.

He placed the barrel against his temple but cocked his head instead of the weapon, turning toward an unfamiliar sound.

Toby leaned down and blew out the candle.

———

Jack walked over to Toby's Jeep, checked the rear quarter, the glove box, behind the sun visor, the side door panels—and came up empty. He carefully closed the door but silently cursed himself when the door clacked as it shut. That wasn't loud enough, he judged after the initial shock passed through him. He looked over the Jeep's simonized black hood toward the back wall of the garage and the neatly placed garden tools that had been professionally hung. He saw nothing out of the ordinary range of tools, and then he noticed an anomaly. A rake, the only tool that wasn't plumb on its hook.

Jack lifted the rake off and quietly placed it against the wood-paneled wall. With the Maglite in his mouth, he started feeling the boards behind and around the now empty space.

And he scored.

One section of board, about three feet long, pulled out, revealing a secret compartment. But the kicker that fueled the electric jolt running down Jack's spine was a faint but very specific stain on the back wall of the hidden space. It formed the dusty, oily outline of a small rifle. Just about the size of the .22 dug up in Ramirez's garden bed.

Jack's head turned as he heard something moving outside the garage. He quickly replaced the board, making sure it was flush with the wall. He had to move, fast.

The automatic garage doors started to roll up.

Jack rehung the rake.

The overhead light snapped on.

Jack spun in place, staring down the barrel of Toby Dirk's brand-new Python 38 and reflexively raised his hands.

"Adding car theft to your résumé, Bertolino? Not a classy move."

"Put the gun away, and we'll talk about it."

"You overstepped all boundaries the last time we talked. No badge, no talk, Jack."

Jack lowered his hands, palms up in submission. "You must be hurting?"

"What am I going to do with you, Bertolino?" Toby said, ignoring the comment.

"If I were Tomas Vegas, you'd leave my body in the gutter. Young Maria, dead on her living room rug."

Toby's lips pulled tight over his teeth. His eyes belied nothing.

"If I were the doc, dumped in a ravine. Sinaloa cartel, twenty leagues under the sea. Ricky J, a sad hole in his backyard. But the doc, the doc had your signature all over it."

Toby was curious despite his sneer. "How so?"

"The shot to the balls. One neat bullet hole to the forehead, one to the heart, and one to the crotch. It was a good touch, but a bad move. A crime of passion. I can relate to it because I'm a romantic myself."

"You're a lone wolf, Bertolino. Howling at the moon. Nobody's listening and nobody's buying your bullshit."

Jack rolled his shoulders as if he were considering Toby's case. "All right, maybe I'm wrong." And then in a sleight of hand, he drew his Glock from the belt line behind his back and squared off with Toby Dirk. "But now that we're on equal footing . . ."

A hiss of air made Jack snap his head around just as an aluminum baseball bat raked the side of his skull and slammed into his shoulder. His neurons exploded; hot-white light flashed, and instantly pixelated to black.

———

Cruz fed another four quarters into the parking meter on Main Street. He had parked with a good view of the Dirk Brothers store but was far enough down not to be noticed. As the last quarter dropped, the front door to the shop swung open, and two thirty-something beauties exited, followed by Terrence Dirk. Where the hell were Toby and Sean?

In the reflection of a jewelry store window he watched the trio walk up the block. As the group entered the Ale House, Cruz pulled the cell phone out of his pocket and hit Speed Dial. When it went to voice mail, he texted Jack, 999, which meant get the hell out of Dodge, jumped into his car, and sped toward Venice.

Two blocks from the Dirks, Cruz picked out Jack's car and slowed his pace, not wanting to call attention to himself. When he was a half block away, Toby's Jeep with Sean riding shotgun came barreling out of their driveway. They sped past him, heading toward the canals, almost forcing Cruz into the row of cars parked curbside.

Cruz cursed as he stared into the rearview mirror. He wasn't sure, but he thought he made out a tarp-wrapped bundle in the rear quarter of the Jeep. Cruz felt a ripple of fear he had never experienced before.

He executed a power U-turn and followed the Jeep, being mindful to drive at a safe distance without losing them. Jack had taught him the finer points of surveillance. Cruz could only pray he was up to the job and prayed the bundle wasn't his boss.

The Dirks made a left off Washington and then a quick right near a construction project that dead-ended at the canal. That wasn't a sign of good intentions. Cruz parked in a red zone on Washington and followed on foot, pulling out his phone, ready to call for help—or shoot a video.

He found the Jeep parked back-end facing the canal that fed into the marina proper. The brothers were struggling with the large parcel. "Is he breathing?" Toby whispered.

Sean shoved his hand into the parcel and checked for a pulse. "I don't think so. *Nada.*"

On a three count, the brothers heaved the contents into the brackish water. "Let's get the fuck outta here!" Sean hissed as they stowed the tarp, jumped into the Jeep, and tore off.

Cruz, hidden behind a large John Deere earthmover, kept the video running and grabbed a shot of the Jeep's license number as it roared past. When the brothers skidded around the corner, Cruz pounded toward the canal, praying Jack was alive. Praying he was up to the task at hand.

Jack was floating facedown in three feet of murky water. Cruz splashed in, relieved to find it was shallow. He spun his partner around, grabbed him under his arms, and dragged him onto shore. The side of his sodden head was bleeding down his ear and neck, his shirt a bloody mess. "Holy shit, Jack, what the hell did they do to you?"

Cruz ripped off his own T-shirt to support Jack's head. He applied compression to Jack's chest, administering CPR, and then checked for breath. The exhale was faint, but Jack Bertolino was alive.

Cruz dialed 911, reported their location, and said a silent prayer as an EMT ambulance rounded the corner, flooding the area with blinding red, blue, and white lights.

Thirty-one

The front of the Dirk brothers' Craftsman house looked unoccupied. The blinds were drawn and only a smattering of light bled through them.

The brothers were assembled in the kitchen. Terrence, whose rage was barely contained, held court.

"So, I leave you for five fucking hours and the two of you threaten to tear down the house!"

Sean and Toby sat at the dinner table, silent.

Terrence was just working up a head of steam. "Is he dead?"

"If Jack Bertolino isn't dead, he won't remember his mama," Sean said, barely audible.

Terrence, pacing the kitchen floor like a caged animal, directed the next question to Toby. "And what did he have to say before he was smacked down?"

"He's on to us big-time. And I think he knows more than he shared."

"What more could Jack Bertolino know that I'm not privy to? Who's holding back on me?!"

"I don't know how he's connecting the dots," Toby said, not

cowering. "He's on to us up north. Ricky J is enough to hurt us good. And we're all in on Ricky J."

Terrence looked incredulously from Sean to Toby. "Hurt us?" he said with simmering rage. "The rest of our lives in prison? Hurt us?"

Sean knocked back some scotch and Toby sat waiting for his brother's edict.

"If he's got us for Ricky J, then he's got your .22," he directed toward Toby. "Your time line crumbles and takes him all the way to Tomas Vegas and the little girl.

Dead silence.

"Any ideas?" Terrence asked, toning down the rhetoric.

Sean kept his head low, and Toby cleared his throat.

"I'll pack a bag and book a flight to Central America out of John Wayne to get them off my scent."

"It's too late for that. Jack is well connected. His people knew where he was headed. They're about to swarm us like the Republican Guard."

Sean finally weighed in. "We can hide out on the backside of Catalina for a week or two." To Terrence he pointed out, "You come out clean on Ricky J no matter what they've got on us. Worst case, you charter a boat or plane to fly us off the island and we'll go underground. With the money we've raised, we can buy our way clean. Five years down the road, we can meet up at our compound in Scotland."

Toby didn't raise an objection.

Terrence's heart was threatening to break. "Pack up! If he's not dead, they're rallying the troops. Take one kayak. I've gotta grab the doctored books at the shop and drop the Jeep at LAX. I'll take a cab and pick up the Ford."

Nobody moved or breathed for an instant. Life as they knew it had just come to an abrupt halt. All three brothers knew this was possibly the endgame. Their worst nightmare had come to pass in the guise of Jack Bertolino.

"Start packing! Now!"

———

The last time Jack had visited St. John's Health Center in Santa Monica, his son Chris was the patient, in the same ward, being treated by the same doctor. A killer driving a Cadillac Escalade had run him down.

Dr. Stein, never ego challenged, was checking the thick dressing on the side of Jack's head and admiring his handiwork. "So, it appears that Bertolino males enjoy challenging metal objects traveling at high rates of speed with their skulls. The good news is, it was a grazing blow, the bleeding, surface capillaries caused by the cut to the scalp, no permanent damage. Your head is as hard as your son's, probably no surprise to you."

Jack wasn't enjoying the comedy quite as much as the doctor. "You should take your act on the road."

Stein grinned. "It'll hurt for a few days. How many fingers do I have up?"

The doctor held up a fist.

"Just one, doc," and Jack flipped the good doctor off.

"Testy, it's a good sign. You've got a minor concussion. I want you to lay low for a few days, at least until the swelling goes down."

"I only use ten percent of my brain, I'll be fine."

The doctor's tone became more stern. "You get active too soon, all you'll be good for is selling pencils on Hollywood Boulevard."

"There's the bedside manner I was missing."

"How is the son?"

"Doing great, Doc. We have you to thank for that."

"Every once in a while we get it right."

Jack felt gingerly around his bandaged head. "Did you have to shave the side of my head?"

"Everyone's a critic. Forty stitches and we shoved as much of the excess brain matter back in as was feasible. You shouldn't miss the rest."

"Funny."

"I keep telling anyone who will listen. So, there are five people waiting in the hallway who all claim to be family. Two at a time, or the nurse will start pushing her weight around. Not a pretty sight, Jack."

"Thanks, Doc."

———

The Dirks were moving with purpose in the garage, stowing supplies into the kayak that had been secured onto the back of the F-350.

Toby's hair had been cut short and darkened. Sean's, just darkened. Terrence laid the brothers' false identities and passports—that had always been part of their worst-case-scenario escape plan—on the workbench. He pulled fifty grand in hundreds and twenties out of a leather briefcase and slid the money along with the doctored paperwork into a waterproof bag. He also handed both brothers clean phones and keys to the storage facility where the lion's share of the money was being stored.

"Just in case it doesn't go well for me here. Give it some time, sneak back across the border, and you'll be set for life." He patted the phones inside the bag. "Safe phones only, no devices that can be traced by their GPS signature. As soon as I can break free, I'll ferry over more supplies. You can't show your face in Avalon. You can't be seen, period.

"Mr. Diskin's in Europe until the end of next month. I'm thinking two, maybe three weeks max, and they'll get tired of watching me. I'll borrow his yacht, pick you up, and drop you across the border in Ensenada." Both brothers nodded in agreement, encouraged Terrence was planning ahead.

"I'll book separate rooms for you in separate safe houses and resorts, wire money as needed, and work out an itinerary that should keep you on the move, out of the public eye, and off the cop's radar screen. They'll be looking for two brothers. Travel alone, stay smart, and you'll stay ahead of the law."

He clapped his hands loudly. "Okay, let's do it."

Sean was strung tight as a drum. Toby remained silent as the three men mounted up. Terrence slid behind the wheel of the Jeep; Sean and Toby fired up the Ford. As the brothers powered down the driveway, the automatic garage doors rolled shut, leaving the house dark, empty, and cold.

———

Nick was alone with Jack in the hospital room while they waited on Leslie, who was fielding a call from Judge Charles Wainwright, hoping to talk him into signing off on an all-encompassing search warrant of the Dirks' properties that would include the house, the store, and all of the vehicles.

Jack was sitting up in bed, almost comfortable, his traumatized back dueling with his throbbing head, dreading the point at which his pain meds would start to fade.

"The gang squad's been dropping in on Tito's mother's crib periodically," Nick said, "hoping to catch the prodigal son. They found him this morning."

"What did he have to say?"

"Whatever his last words were he shared with the Sinaloa cartel boys. Hard to know. ME said they killed his mother first, probably with the son watching to loosen him up, and then started in on Tito. It's like that old Monty Python bit. They accuse you of being a witch and toss you in a barrel filled with water. If you float, you're found guilty and they kill you. If you drown, you're innocent. So, we'll never know."

Jack grunted at the harsh joke. "We already know, and we're going to have some answers if Wainwright comes through for us."

Leslie entered the room before Nick could respond. "The man of the hour," she said with genuine concern.

"Alive and well," Jack said.

"Well, alive. You are a piece of work, Bertolino." A phrase Jack had used with Leslie in better times and not lost on the patient.

"I'm happy to be living up to your expectations," he said.

"I'm happy you're alive."

"She's a sucker for the infirmed," Jack said to Nick.

Cruz popped his head into the room and then stepped in, clearly wired.

"The real man of the hour," Jack announced. "The EMT said if you hadn't dragged my sorry ass out of the canal, I wouldn't be sitting here tonight."

Cruz deadpanned, "Don't ever fucking do that to me again, Jack."

Nervous laughter from everyone in the room, except Nick, whose eyes narrowed, planning to exact some revenge on the Dirk brothers.

Leslie picked up the thread. "I talked with Judge Wainwright. He knows you, and trusts you. He's receiving a lifetime achievement award, as it turns out, but said he'll sign off on the search warrant as soon as he gets home, which should be in the next hour or so.

"He counseled you to stay out of it now, and stay alive. He had some very positive things to say about you that I won't share because if your head swelled any more, it would endanger your health."

"Great news." And then, "You might want to step out of the room for a moment. For your own good," Jack advised.

"I didn't know you still cared."

Leslie turned to leave, but her exit was blocked as Tommy Aronsohn and Susan Blake rushed in.

"You scared the hell out of us," Tommy scolded good-naturedly as he came forward.

Susan ran to Jack's side, oblivious to everyone else in the room. "We were worried sick. How do you feel?"

Before Jack could answer, the nurse, weighing in at 190 pounds, plowed through the crowd. "Okay, ladies and gents. You all know the rules and Dr. Stein's orders. Two family members, max. Now, who here is family?"

Cruz shouted, "He's my father."

Nick, "Brother."

Tommy, "Cousin."

Susan, "Bodyguard."

Leslie, "Father of my children."

Raised eyebrows from the entire room. Leslie, uncharacteristically, blushed like a teenager.

The nurse, going along with the love fest, said, "I'm going to take a ten-minute break and smoke a ciggy. When I come back, I expect all of you college graduates to decide who is family and who has to hit the pavement. Mr. Bertolino needs his beauty sleep."

The room emptied a few minutes after the nurse, leaving Nick and Cruz behind.

Jack filled them in on the hidden compartment with the outline of the rifle he had discovered in the Dirks' garage. He also divulged another clue that had been floating around his subconscious mind since his trip to Ricky J's house.

It had finally been dislodged with the crack of an aluminum bat.

Thirty-two

Lieutenant Gallina wasn't happy being awakened at two in the morning, but he was furious to be the last to know about the arrest warrant generated for Toby and Sean Dirk, along with the search warrants to be served on all of the family's properties and vehicles. He was the lead detective on the case and had lost all control before he had achieved REM sleep. And Gallina wasn't a go-with-the-flow kind of guy.

To make matters worse, he would have to depose Jack Bertolino about tonight's activities, and admit his own error in judgment for the second time in twenty-four hours.

At least Bertolino was still in the hospital, the lieutenant thought. He wouldn't have to suffer the ego-driven man's gloating until he had ingested a few cups of coffee into his system.

Gallina pulled his Crown Vic to the curb in front of the Dirk residence, snugged up against a local news van, looked up the driveway, and the red that slowly engulfed his face betrayed his fury.

Jack Bertolino was standing off to the side of the house, head bandaged, eyes glazed, talking with Nick Aprea, who seemed to be running the show.

Gallina slammed the car into park, slammed the door behind him, ignored the on-camera TV reporter who shouted a question in his direction, and strode up the driveway.

Nick saw the storm coming and jumped out to run interference. "Sorry it played out this way, Lieutenant, but it was a fluid situation, and we had to jump on the opportunity," he said with as much civility as he could muster in the middle of the night.

Gallina nodded, afraid if he spoke, he'd start yelling. And then to Jack, "How's the head? We'll have to get a statement when you're up to it."

"Whatever you need, Lieutenant."

"Is Terrence Dirk being interviewed?" he asked Nick.

"In the living room. Tompkins is doing the honors."

"How did he get here before me?" Gallina asked snarky, not expecting an answer. "And not to put too fine a point on it, but Jack should stay off the premises. Since he is the victim, we don't want any conflict of interest issues when we bring the case to trial."

"I'm leaving now, Cruz dropped me off to pick up my car." And to Nick, "I'm on my cell."

As Jack walked away, the local news hounds on scene snapped photos and videos of the bruised and bandaged private investigator. He was about to become an unwilling celebrity again.

———

Detective Tompkins was sitting in one of the stuffed armchairs in the Dirks' living room, interviewing Terrence, who sat rigidly on an austere Stickley couch. His face tightened each time he heard one of the cops bang open a drawer, or rifle through a closet.

"I don't know where the Jeep is. My guess, with my brothers. We are all independent contractors. Communication isn't one of the orders of the day, unless we're working a job."

"When was the last time you saw your brothers?"

"Around six thirty. I had a seven o'clock meeting at the shop, it ran late, and I came home to an empty house—well, except for you gentlemen. But, God knows, you'll be the first call I make when I hear from them."

"Do they often just take off, without keeping you in the loop?"

"They're adults, detective. As long as everyone gets their job done, we go our own ways. They might have gone back up north on a whim. They do that sometimes. Get a buzz on and drive. Could've gone to Palm Springs? Joshua Tree? Arrowhead? I'm sure I'll hear from them before too long, and again, you'll be the first to know. I'm sure there's been a mix-up of some sort."

Terrence was relaxed and controlled, trying to placate Tompkins, who scribbled into his dog-eared leather-bound notepad.

Tompkins, not buying his play, was getting ready to drop the hammer. The detective pocketed his notepad and made a big show of pulling out his cell phone. He tapped a few keys, and then handed the phone to Terrence. "Could you take a look at this and tell me what you see?"

Terrence's demeanor strained some as he looked at the video Cruz had shot earlier that night.

"It's a Jeep."

"Whose Jeep is it, and do you recognize the driver, or the man in the passenger seat?"

Gallina had entered the room by now, and he knew where his partner was going with the interrogation. He wisely chose to remain silent and give Terrence time to come up with the truth, or the expected lie.

"It's hard to say, the quality is—"

"I'm not asking for a definitive," Tompkins said smoothly. "Ballpark. Who do you know that drives a black Jeep?"

"My brother Toby."

"Does that look like Toby behind the wheel?"

"I can't say for sure."

"How about the passenger? Who does that tall, thin man remind you of?"

Terrence feigned confusion. "Put on a watch cap," he finally said, "it could be you. Again, it's a little too dark to speculate."

Gallina joined the interview. "Take a wild guess, Mr. Dirk. Two tall, thin men, about your size and height, driving the same car you already stated your brother owns."

"There are tons of black Jeeps in the area," Terrence said with attitude. "It could be my brother's, it's possible, but I'm not going to go on record making a statement until I'm sure of my facts."

"Fair enough. Detective Tomkins, could you pull up the next shot? It might help the cause."

Tompkins grabbed his phone and forwarded the video to the last few seconds, and hit Pause. He handed his phone back to Terrence, who viewed the still carefully.

"The photographer got lucky with this shot," Tompkins said,

staring into Terrence's unblinking eyes. "The Jeep drove under one of the construction lights as it exited the site. Do you recognize the license plate?"

"Not offhand," Terrence said, trying to work up some spit in his mouth, now cotton dry.

"Cut the shit, Dirk," Gallina barked, frustrated. "Enough with the games. It's your brother's Jeep, your brother's license plate, and you could damn well pick out your brother's body types at five hundred yards. Your family is, how do I say it, uniquely built. Now, do you want to continue this downtown, or are you going to get with the program and tell us where we can find your brothers?"

Terrence remained silent, clearly weighing his options.

"You could spend time behind bars for aiding and abetting. Your brothers, at this point in time, are good for attempted murder. Sweet guys. They brained Bertolino good with a baseball bat and left him floating facedown in a canal to die. But hey, that's just the beginning of our investigation. When we add murder one to the mix, the charges against you will triple, as will the time you'll spend in lockup."

Terrence remained stubbornly silent.

"A little quid pro quo will go a long way to reducing your culpability in this matter. Work with us, we'll work with you."

At last the eldest Dirk brother came to a decision. "Do you know what time it is, detective?"

"I'm a lieutenant. Call me Lieutenant."

"I think I'll call my lawyer instead. We're finished here, gentlemen."

Gallina took a step toward Terrence, dying to rearrange the

freckles on his smug face. His partner stopped him with a shake of his head.

"Stay out of my detectives' way while they're executing the warrant," Gallina said, "or I'll run you in for obstruction of justice. Let him make the call," he directed at Tompkins and stormed out of the room.

The night sky was a dark cobalt blue against the black sea. Without any light pollution the star field was bright, and with the full moon reflecting on the light chop like broken shards of mirror, Sean and Toby were able to pick out Sentinel Rock against the dark shoreline on the backside of Catalina Island.

"I caught a twenty-pound white sea bass right off the rock," Sean said. "Lived off it for the next two days. Started with sashimi, segued into ceviche, and grilled the cheeks and a few steaks the final night. Washed it down with a few chilled bottles of Grgich Hills Chardonnay. It was a successful trip."

Sean was unaware that his brother, in the forward of the kayak, was contemplating eating his gun before the campfire was lit. Dead is dead, he thought. What the fuck?

They approached Shark Harbor, their destination and Sean's camping site of choice. As they continued around the far bend, a cut in the rock face opened up, revealing an obscure sea cave with just enough room to pull his kayak into protective cover.

After his time in lockup, when Sean had taken his one-man adventures to get his head screwed on straight, this was where he landed. He'd discovered Little Springs Canyon by accident, and then it became his go-to destination. Desolate, off the beaten track, it offered plenty of privacy and cover. The herd of buffalo that roamed the plateau kept campers at a distance.

It was a perfect spot to wait out the heat on the mainland until Terrence could slip away and secret them across the border into Mexico.

Thirty-three

Day Eleven

Jack stepped off the elevator on the penthouse level of the Ritz-Carlton and walked into a world of hurt. Susan gave Jack a look that told him Tommy was in the dark about her relationship to the stalker, and her childhood abuse, and it should remain that way.

Tommy, wearing his usual blue pinstriped shirt, casual khakis, and cordovan penny loafers, was sucking down a black coffee in the living room of Susan's suite while she sat in an overstuffed chair, pissed.

Tommy gestured toward a manila envelope. Jack took in the energy in the room and pulled out a nude photograph of Susan about to clasp a lacy black bra over her bare breasts. He did a slow burn as Tommy explained.

"You know Margaret, in my New York office. She was surfing the net, did a Google search on Susan, because, you know, everything that's been going on, and found this on TMZ. She thought we should know."

Jack remembered the bra. He had gotten up-close and personal with it in the limousine the night of the art gallery opening.

And he knew who was standing behind the camera. "He used a drone. Your bedroom's on the second floor. It's the only way he could've gotten the shot."

"First New York, now L.A.," Susan said, starting to tear up. "I don't know if I can take it. If all of this is worth it."

Jack wondered if Susan was putting on the waterworks for Tommy and waited for her to continue.

"Oh God, who am I kidding?" The tears miraculously disappeared. "Of course it's worth it. Get the creep, Jack. And slap him around some before you arrest him."

Jack's face split into a tight grin.

"Better yet," Susan said, working up a head of steam. "Let me slap him around. Jerk!"

Susan blew her nose like a drunken sailor, then demurely folded the Kleenex and tossed it into the wicker basket by her feet.

"All right," Jack said, formulating a plan. "This is bad, but we know who's behind it. We'll get him, Susan. We'll get him and make him suffer."

Jack knew Terrence Dirk would be under twenty-four-hour surveillance until his brothers were found, and Nick promised to keep him in the loop. It would give him some time to handle Frank Bigelow, who was escalating out of control.

"Susan gave me the nod," Tommy said, "and I had my office file an injunction against TMZ, barring them from transmitting her image without a release. But you know how it plays; it's hard to put the genie back in the bottle once the image has been downloaded." And then to Susan, "But I'll sue *People*, *USA Today*, the *Post*, and any other rag that even thinks about printing your image without consent."

"Do me a favor, Tommy?" Book a lunch for two at Willie Jane, on Abbot Kinney for this afternoon. And have Margaret call TMZ and let them know, off the record, that Susan Blake's going to be the guest of honor." And then to Susan, "Lunch is on me, you're going to be fine." And Jack headed out the door, knowing Susan was in good hands.

"We've got nothing," Nick Aprea rasped into his cell phone. He was sitting on the Dirks' front stoop, balancing the phone, a bagel with a smear of cream cheese, and a cup of Starbucks. The man looked worse for the wear, and his voice was as rough as gravel.

"We got nothing. The outline of the rifle in that compartment in the garage? It's like the shroud of Turin. A debatable point even if it's a perfect match. You know how many squirrel guns they sell in the U.S.?"

Jack walked into his office with his cup of coffee and sat down behind his desk, rubbing his forehead even though it was the stitches on the side of his head that throbbed. "It's the dog, I'm telling you," he said. "You shoot Ricky J through the forehead, same signature, same grouping as Tomas Vegas, and then you fold him up like an accordion and stuff him in a hole. You're that stone-cold, but then you take the time to leave a pile of food and enough water to keep the dog alive for a month on the kitchen floor."

Then Jack popped the idea. "If you care that much about a fucking little dog you just met, you've got to touch the mutt. It's human nature. You touch the dog, or the dog rubs up against you for being a killer with a heart of gold."

"Ehhhh?"

"Do the Dirks have a clothes hamper? If they do, check out the sides even if the clothes have been dry-cleaned. And check the dryer. The lint catch."

Jack heard Nick's sigh and could've written his response.

"Jack," said a man who had been awake for too many hours, "the men are on it. They're good at their jobs. The house is as clean as it's ever been. They vacuumed the drains, the clothes, every fucking place. If there is dog hair to be found . . ."

"It's a black and white Boston terrier," Jack reminded him.

"Whatever. If it's there, they'll find it. Okay? We should know something by this afternoon."

"No word from the Dirks?"

"Terrence-the-Red lawyered up. His noncommittal statement of last night is as much as we're going to get. We've got an APB out on the Jeep, and we've got the airports, bus terminals, and Amtrak covered for Sean and Toby. We circulated their pictures to the local news channels that led with the story this morning. The boys are going to find it hard to stay gone.

"The team is finishing up here and then moving to the Main Street location. We're taking Red along to unlock the doors. I'm sure he'll be doing his Mick Jagger impersonation while we try to bust his ass. I'm sending you over the video that was shot around the house. Lemme know if you catch anything I missed."

"Will do. Thanks, Nick." Jack signed off and pulled up the e-mail Nick had forwarded onto his computer.

The tour started in the bedrooms, hit the closets, the bathrooms, living room, dining room, and all the cabinets and furniture pieces before checking the yard and ending up in the garage. It looked the same as when Jack paid his visit except the surfboards and a kayak were lying on the garage floor where Toby's Jeep used to be parked. The camera zoomed in close to the patchwork on the kayak and the outline of the .22 rifle in the hidden compartment.

Nick was right, Jack thought. The faded ghost of the rifle

might not hold up in court on its own, but with the preponder-ance of circumstantial evidence on the prosecution's side, it might be enough to tie the Dirks to the other murders.

Jack wanted to refill his coffee, but then he realized something was missing from the video coverage. He picked up the phone and tapped in a number.

Nick picked up on the first ring. "No dog hair yet! What?"

"Was the second kayak left up in the rafters?"

"There was only one kayak on the premises."

"There were two before I got brained. Unless it's a sleight of hand, the brothers might be making their escape by water. They could have dropped the kayak into the Pacific, anywhere along the coast."

"I'd head for Mexico," Nick said. "I knew a dude that used to traffic in pot in the late eighties out of San Diego. Used a kayak to go back and forth. Had a good business going. Easy to slip across the border and back cloaked in darkness without raising too many eyebrows."

"You might give Terrence another run with that piece of in-formation. Might shake something loose."

"It's worth a try. Good catch, pard. I'll spread the word and ring you up later."

Jack got Cruz on the phone, brought him up to speed on his plan to take down Frank Bigelow, and agreed to meet at the loft in a half hour. He was bringing one of their GPS trackers and they needed to act quickly while Terrence was otherwise occupied.

———

Yellow police tape was draped over the front door of the Dirk Brothers store on Main Street. Looky-loos who had seen the news reports prowled slowly past the locked front door with the CLOSED sign firmly in place, hoping to catch a glimpse of Terrence Dirk. Some posed for selfies in front of the now notorious shop.

Across the street, two dark-skinned men took special notice of the activities.

Both men wore mirrored sunglasses. One was of medium height and build, and the second man was noticeably short. Besides his diminutive stature, he had another distinguishing trait. A thick scar that ran across his throat, from ear to ear.

In the showroom, Gallina and Tompkins sat on the leather couch eating a takeout breakfast, while Terrence sat behind the cash register, giving them his studied deadeye. His lawyer was ambling among the suits on the racks, eyeing the prices. He felt confident this case was going to deliver a big paycheck.

Nick was giving the accounting books a cursory once-over while a tech team checked every square inch of the front and back rooms.

A separate unit worked the Mercedes van.

Six thousand dollars had been found in the large safe in the storeroom, not an unusually large amount for a successful Santa Monica business.

No drugs, nothing of note had been found, and the men were dead on their feet. Nick was getting more pissed off as morning turned to afternoon, and nothing of substance had been unearthed, except the missing kayak. But so far, no word of the brothers' whereabouts.

Ernie, one of the tech team, dressed in a white jumpsuit, stuck his head inside the back storeroom, pulled off his wire-rimmed bifocals, and signaled for Nick to follow him into the alley.

"What kind of dog were you asking about?" he said, keeping his voice low in case the suspect or his lawyer were in earshot.

Nick's bloodshot eyes came alive. "Uh, a pug—no, no, a Boston terrier, I think. Jack said the dog's hair was white and black."

"Huh," Ernie said, fighting a grin as he squeezed the bridge of his nose and slid his glasses back on. "Would black and white work for you? You know, 'Ebony and Ivory,' like the song?"

"Cut the shit, Ernie."

Ernie smiled as he pulled a small paper envelope out of his top pocket and revealed a piece of clear CSI lifting tape. Thick, wiry white and black hairs were stuck firmly in place.

"Son of a bitch," Nick said a little too loud, his heart pounding. "Jesus Christ," he said, his voice in control again. "You done good, Ernie. Where did you find it?"

"What?" Gallina shouted from inside.

"Nothing," Nick shouted back.

Ernie was on a roll. "It looks like the van was recently detailed. But whoever did the work forgot to vacuum the entire seat. One of our guys had hair on his shoes, or slacks, whatever, and rubbed it off on the curved underside of the seat cushion. It's a clean sample. And if it's a match . . ."

Nick was ecstatic, ready to start dancing in circles. "I love this fucking job sometimes. Sometimes. Damn, Ernie, good work, my friend." He put his hand on the other man's arm. "Let's keep quiet about this for the time being. Wait until we're sure it's a match. Save it for maximum effect and then nail Terrence the Red with checkmate."

"You know best, detective." Ernie slid the sample back into the envelope, gratified to have hit pay dirt at last. "I'll call Sacramento and get this in the works ASAP."

"I'm gonna make a call, bring Gallina and Tompkins up to speed and gloat a bit. Then you know what I'm gonna do? I'm going home to take a shit, a shower, and pour myself a stiff one."

During the long summer days, Abbot Kinney was part carnival, part street festival. The stores and restaurants were full, galleries, open to the public, booze flowing, the scent of marijuana and incense melding with the sound of pitched voices and live music. Tattooed, pierced, and artsy patrons of every age, gender, and ethnicity choked the sidewalks and spilled out onto the street, bringing traffic to a slow crawl. Wall-to-wall people queued up for exotic fair offered from color-splashed food trucks that crowded the parking lot of The Brigg and snaked down the street toward Santa Monica.

A small knot of paparazzi stood outside Willie Jane, a southern comfort restaurant, eyes trained on the front door, waiting for the lunch crowd to thin, and their money shot. A short female dressed entirely in red tapped a bandanna-wearing man on the shoulder and showed him a photo posted seconds ago on Instagram. It was a photo of a beautiful plate of fried chicken, next to a plate of grits, and a full, honey-colored glass of chardonnay. "I don't know how she keeps so trim, eating all that fry. I'd blow up like a balloon."

"She has a personal trainer," Frank Bigelow answered knowingly, pulling the blond hair out of his eyes to get a better look. "And once a month she does a liquid fast. She only has eighteen percent body fat. There's a good article about Susan Blake in *Cosmopolitan*."

"Oooh, looky here," the woman said, turning her iPhone screen toward Frank. "She's got a new boyfriend, and he's hot."

Disturbed, Frank grabbed the phone out of the woman's hand.

"Hey! Easy," she said, reaching for her phone.

Frank stared at the screen, holding the phone out of the petite woman's reach. His face turned a dangerous shade of red.

It was another Instagram photo.

Tommy Aronsohn sat at Susan Blake's table, wearing a thousand-dollar suit now, and a million-dollar smile.

"Gimme, you asshole! You'd think she was your girlfriend the way you act."

Frank pushed the phone into her hand, spun, and stormed off, leaving the young woman muttering expletives.

Cruz, who had been standing inside a gallery across the street from the restaurant, put a cell phone to his ear and followed in Frank's wake, obscured by the crowd.

Jack appeared on the opposite side of the street, matching their progression. When Frank turned left off the main drag, Cruz followed, staying a half block behind. Jack hoofed it to the next corner, darted across the street to honking horns, and disappeared from view.

The crowd thinned, the ruckus sound lessened, and soon Cruz found himself walking directly behind the blond man.

Frank spun unexpectedly on his heel; his blond hair whipped, as he strode back toward the main drag. He flew past Cruz, who jabbered into his phone like he was on a social call. Cruz made no eye contact, and received no visible response from the target.

Frank spun again, eyes blazing, and watched Cruz walk down the road, making a turn at the first cross street he came to.

He pulled off his wig and bandanna and slipped it into his camera bag. He turned a corner, walking with blind fury. He was about to head up the stairs to his apartment above the garage when Jack hoofed it across the street.

"Excuse me," Jack said, "can I have a word?"

Frank, caught off guard, stepped back down from the first step. He concealed his recognition of Jack, but wasn't sure how to play his next move.

All Jack saw was the sunlight, reflected off Frank's shiny bald head, his hawkish nose, and twisted eyes.

"What the fuck do you want?" Frank sneered, taking the offensive.

As Jack stepped forward, Frank pulled the wig out of the bag and took a threatening step toward Jack, who saw the flash of a six-inch blade secreted amid the blond hair.

Frank lunged, thrusting the knife toward Jack's chest.

Jack blocked his wrist with one hand while the other hammered the side of Frank's head. The whiplash took him down onto one knee. The next violent punch Jack delivered cracked the man's cheekbone and knocked him flat on his side unconscious.

"That's for Susan," Jack said harshly.

Cruz ran up. "What do we do? What do I do?" he asked, panicked.

"Cuff the bastard." Jack handed off a plastic tie while he caught his breath, and Cruz made short work of cuffing Frank's hands behind his back.

"Hand me his keys, give me fifteen minutes, and dial 911."

Cruz rifled through Frank's pockets, came up with the keys, and handed them to Jack. He ran up the wooden stairs, fit the key into the lock, and stepped inside the apartment. All he could hear was the squawk of the police scanner.

Jack pulled out his cell phone and snapped photos of the drone, the recent nude pictures of Susan, a picture of himself with his eyes gouged out, and the police scanner. He spied a computer on the kitchenette table. Jack slid in a flash drive and downloaded Frank's hard drive. Then he hit Delete and washed the hard drive clean.

Jack scoured through every cabinet and hiding place in the

small apartment, and found a thick bundle wrapped in brown bag paper secreted under the plastic liner in the garbage canister. Jack pulled off the thick rubber band and unfurled the paper. There was a stack of Polaroids. Enough to satisfy a pedophile's jones for a lifetime.

The police scanner squealed and reported a stabbing incident in Venice, moving Jack into high gear. He rifled through the stack of child pornography, grabbed the Polaroids where Susan could be clearly identified, and left the shots where Susan's face was obscured. The pile he left behind was more than enough smut to put Frankie away for years. Jack pocketed the damning photos, locked the door behind him, and took his place beside Cruz, as distant sirens grew louder.

Frank Bigelow remained cuffed and unconscious at their feet as two black-and-whites arrived, followed by an EMT unit.

———

Jack pulled his Cutwater 28 close enough to the dock where Terrence Dirk's Zodiac was moored. Now that Susan's case was closed, he could focus on the Dirk brothers and avenging Maria Sanchez's death.

Cruz jumped off, strutting high from the Bigelow bust, and boarded the craft like he owned it. He had already studied the specs of the rugged inflatable boat and knew exactly where to hide his GPS tracker.

By the time Jack had done a smooth one-eighty, Cruz was dockside. He leapt aboard the cabin cruiser as Jack powered back toward his own slip at the far end of the marina.

"Just keep your cell and laptop charged at all times, and you'll get an alarm beep as soon as the Zodiac starts to move," Cruz said.

"How much lead time can I give him?"

"As much as you need. As long as you're powered up, you'll know where he's headed and where he docks. The distance is your choice. We're bouncing off satellites, whatever's safe," he said with the emphasis on *safe*.

Jack's cell rang, "Yeah? Hey." He mouthed, "It's Nick." Jack's face broke into a grim smile as he was brought up to speed on the case. "I'm going to have to adopt that dog. Fantastic. Call me as soon as we get final word. Good work, Nick."

Jack clicked off and Cruz could hardly control his excitement. "We got them," Jack said. "They found dog hair in the van, and when the match comes in from Sacramento—and it will match—the warrant for the brothers' arrest will be bumped up from attempted to first-degree murder."

"Jesus, Jack. Good one. Really good, man."

Jack pushed the throttle forward a bit, pushing the speed limit. A sea lion broke the water's surface as a snowy-white gull squawked his approval and challenged the thermals. Jack felt the salt air whipping his hair back off his strong forehead, and the vibration of the boat, and a wash of relief that was indescribable.

"We got 'em, Cruz," Jack repeated. His intense brown eyes narrowed and the crescent-shaped scar on his cheek flattened. "Now we just have to find them."

Thirty-four

Jack dropped off Cruz at Dock 23 and powered his cabin cruiser over to the Coast Guard station. There was something about taking care of business by water and averting L.A. traffic that put Jack at ease and helped him focus. Coast Guard Captain Deak Montrose walked down the pier just as Jack finished tying off.

"It depends where they dropped the kayak into the surf," Captain Deak said as the men walked outside the Coast Guard building, watching the nautical activity up and down the channel. "Not to mention, they might have dropped it into a landfill or scuttled it, just to throw you off track."

"I'm open to all options," Jack admitted, "but let's say they were in a hell of a big hurry. They thought they'd killed me and were worried the law would follow. They had two or three hours max for Terrence to drop them off and get home, where the cops were waiting with the warrant. So that's reasonably an hour max in each direction. We haven't found their Jeep yet, and I'm voting against by land. So give me a quick tutorial about by sea."

"Okay, down south an hour . . . from Laguna, let's say, they could make San Diego and cross the border into Mexico, in a few hours. Off any beach north, from here to Ventura, Santa Catalina Island. A little farther up the coast toward Oxnard, you've got the Channel Islands . . . five islands in that group. Anacapa, Santa Cruz, Santa Rosa, San Miguel, and Santa Barbara. Out of the five, I'd pick Santa Cruz Island if I were on the run. Plenty of sea caves, fresh water springs, and deep canyons to hide out in. We caught some drug traffickers offloading panga boats on the northwest coastline last season."

"Catalina?" Jack said.

"Plenty of rugged cliffs, mountainous terrain, and secluded shoreline on the backside of the island. It's a definite maybe."

"Close to where they hijacked the cartel's drugs," Jack mused.

"Tell you what I'll do, Jack. And you're invited. Let's do a fly-over of the island, and I'll blast the brother's photos and that picture of their kayak to all my guys up and down the coast. They'll keep a sharp eye out."

"I'm all in," Jack said.

———

Toby and Sean were sitting up on a bluff staring out at the Pacific. Blue skies, dark-blue water capped in white. A cell phone on the rock between Sean's legs.

Toby looked out toward the horizon. "You think he'll show?"

"Not until things calm down. What, you don't think . . . ?"

"Would you?"

"Fuck, yeah. Why wouldn't he?" came out as an angry hiss. Sean had taken about all of Toby's bullshit he could handle.

Toby gazed at the thick cumulus clouds that raced past the horizon. "He's sitting pretty. Four mil, the store, the house, we're on the run on very specific charges."

Sean dismissed his younger brother's perspective. "We're family. We're blood."

"It's happened before, situations like this."

"Not to us, never to us." Sean's voice rose in volume.

"He hung up on you!" Toby shouted, matching his brother's intensity.

"The shop was swarming with cops. He's under a fucking microscope." And then, "You and that fucking dog!"

"Is that an answer to all our problems, mister non-fucking-sequitur?"

"They had nothing. Terrence said they can tie us to Ricky J through that fucking dog. Our faces will be plastered all over the news again, and guess who we'll have to deal with now?"

Toby sat tight-lipped.

"Guess! Goddamnit!" Sean balled up both fists and nailed Toby in the chest, knocking him on his back. Both men rolled to their feet, pistols drawn. "I told you to guess."

"LAPD, DEA," Toby said, breathing hard, thinking how sweet it would be to put a bullet into his brother's skull. Instead, "Jack fucking Bertolino, and oh yeah, we can probably throw the Sinaloa cartel into the mix." A thought came to him, and he added, "And Ricky J was on *you*, scumbag, or are you rewriting history?"

Sean listened to a wave crash on the rocks below before speaking. "What does it matter? We're dead men." And he lowered his weapon.

Toby went Zen, let Sean's negativity dissipate like the sweet smoke of a Macanudo on an ocean breeze. He stowed his weapon in his shoulder harness and turned back toward the Pacific.

A pod of pelicans flew in a tight V-formation under the

brother's cliff-side position, strong, confident, ready to feed if the opportunity presented itself.

"Lots of people disappear," Toby said, bringing an end to the rancor. "We can still make it happen."

The brothers heard a helicopter approaching in the distance. On the double they jumped under their camouflaged lean-to, disappearing seconds before Captain Deak's Coast Guard chopper thundered past doing a low flyover around the perimeter of Catalina Island.

"When the wind shifts, this place smells like cow shit," Toby said, peeking out of the lean-to watching as the helicopter grew small on the horizon.

His eyes drifted over the herd of buffalo that stood grazing in the field below the brothers' cliffside position.

The mountainous chaparral, boulders, and scrub trees that ran down the incline on the left side of their camp led to a natural bowl of grassy land that provided grazing and a windbreak for the herd.

Directly beyond the natural enclosure was a campground, bathroom/shower building, and a scattering of picnic tables. Empty in the early season.

Blocking the herd to the right, a series of rusting water tanks, boulders, and trees.

"Don't call them cows," Sean said, trying to lighten the mood. "They're very sensitive animals."

Toby nodded his head, but failed to muster a grin.

"And see that big guy, at the head of the herd? The one with the broken horn?"

A single bull stood a head taller than the rest. Snorting, pounding the hard ground. One horn had splintered, leaving a razor-sharp edge.

"Eight hundred pounds of scary?" Sean went on.

"Yeah?"

"Stay out of his way. He's a mean prick. I saw him charge a group of campers last summer just for the sport of it. Nearly killed a German who got too close, taking his picture. Stupid fool."

Sean stopped talking because it was clear his brother had stopped listening.

Toby lay back on the grass, recognized a shape in one of the thick cumulus clouds, and flashed on Eva, the only person in his life who had rendered him whole.

Toby made the instantaneous decision that he'd go down fighting, guns blazing if things went south on the family.

———

Jack was sitting in one of the rear seats of the Coast Guard helicopter. Captain Deak was seated in front next to the pilot. All three men wore headphones to communicate.

"Damn, I've never seen a herd of buffalos in the wild before," Jack said. "Only in movies."

"Back in the twenties, Zane Grey imported them for his western called *The Vanishing American*. The beasts never made it to the big screen, but they never left the island. They keep the herd to about one hundred fifty to two hundred. It's an ecologically sound number for a nonindigenous species."

"How do they pull that off?" Jack asked.

"Birth control."

"That's a hell of a job . . ."

Deak turned to face Jack.

" . . . sliding a rubber on a buffalo."

That got a howl from the pilot and a big smile from Deak as

the chopper banked up and around the south side of the island, heading for dry land.

———

The front door to the small bungalow exploded off its hinges. A cop wearing a helmet and carrying a riot shield was the first into the living room. Four startled gangbangers drew weapons from under couch cushions, holsters, and nearby tables, and as orders were shouted, and more cops streamed into the tight enclosed space, they started firing. The lead man with the shield and a vest was knocked to the floor by the sheer force of multiple rounds to his protective gear.

Susan Blake leapt over her officer, shouting, "Down on the ground! Now! Now!" She fired twice, taking out one of the gang-sters. As she turned her pistol toward a fifth gunman entering the room, her 9mm was knocked from her hands, and a tattooed forearm grabbed her in a throat lock. With his gun to her temple, he ordered the cops to drop. . . .

Susan elbowed the gunman in the throat, cutting off his voice and his threat. As he loosened his grip, she spun and kneed him in the groin. The gunman grunted in pain and fell to his knees. Down on all fours, struggling to breathe, he puked up a cheeseburger.

With one of the bangers bleeding out, and the second puking, the other three associates dropped their weapons and raised their hands before being swarmed, knocked to the ground, and cuffed.

"Cut! Cut! That was effing brilliant, Susan!"

The stuntman, who remained on his knees, red-faced, wiping puke from his mouth and ready to go ballistic, was patted on the back by Henry Lee, who assumed a crouched position and spoke in a hushed tones.

"Enrique, that was the best work you've ever done. Bar none. You just transitioned from stuntman to actor. And with award season coming up . . . you did it, my friend. It was real."

Enrique blinked twice, wiped his mouth, and said, "Gimme another take, Henry, I think I can do you one better."

"Moving on, folks!" Henry Lee shouted, jumping to his feet, so the gaffer and electricians could set lights for his star's close-up.

Dean stood perched next to his rusted 1988 Toyota Camry with the surfboard rack and his two faves tied off and covered. He had a bird's-eye view of Sunset Beach and could see his crew, bobbing on the water's surface, waiting to catch the next good set. The only man conspicuously missing that afternoon was Toby Dirk.

The orange sun was low on the horizon as Dean nervously ran his hand over his crew cut, from his tanned forehead all the way to the large blue-inked bar code that decorated the back of his neck. His mother had given up on her son the day he showed up with the tat. No way to hide it, she'd admonished. No one will hire you. You'll never amount to a hill of beans now. The jury's still out, Dean thought, unforgiving of his mom.

He was so caught up in his private moment that he was startled when a black Lincoln Town Car glided to a crunching stop over the sand and gravel curbside at Pacific Coast Highway, sending a cloud of dust billowing in Dean's direction.

A diminutive man with a thick scar that ran from one ear to the other got out first. His mirrored sunglasses hid frightening dark eyes. The driver slid out of the car as if he were on a sightseeing trip. He carried a brown bag under one arm. Both men gave off heat.

Dean nodded his greeting, because he was dry mouthed, unable to keep his eyes from drifting to the short man's throat.

"What are you staring at, ese?" was almost lost on the ocean breeze.

Dean swallowed hard. "What I have to look forward to if I'm not trading solid advice."

"Speak," the little man ordered.

"Okay, after he got out of the joint, Toby's brother Sean went a little crazy. He had anger issues. So occasionally he'd take off at midnight, alone, in a kayak, and paddle to Catalina Island to get straight. Toby's words. We all thought he was nuts. And he'd spend a few days camping out on the backside of the Island. Shark Harbor, Toby's words. Toby's words on many occasions."

Dean pulled a hand-drawn rendering of Catalina out of his pocket and handed it to the scarred man. Ballpoint-penned arrows directed the eye to Shark Harbor. Dean freaked when he saw his own reflection in the little man's mirrored sunglasses and picked up the pace.

"So, the way I see it, last-minute hideaway. Cops on their asses. That's where they'd go until things calmed down.

"The news stations said the cops tied them to the murder of the pot guy up in Sacramento. The only reason to go there in the first place was if they had product to sell. Your product."

"What about the oldest brother?" the short killer asked.

"You'll never get close to Terrence. He's got cops on him 24/7."

"*Puto*," the small man said.

"The fuck you call me?" came out reflexively—and with instant regret.

"You sell out your compadres."

"No friend lies to me. He used me as an alibi. Pulled me into their play and offered me nothing. Fuck 'em," Dean said with wavering bravado. Not sure if he'd come out of this transaction alive.

The driver, who was tall enough to look Dean straight in the eye, took a step forward. Dean backpedaled instinctively. The scarred man smirked. The taller man handed over a brown paper supermarket bag, folded neatly around a thick parcel.

"Nice heft," Dean said, feeling stupid before the words left his mouth. But he couldn't help taking a peek into the brown paper sack. By the time Dean pried his hungry eyes from the thick bundles of cash, the Lincoln tore away from the curb, spitting up a contrail of stones and sand, forcing Dean to dive clear.

"Mother fucker!" he shouted, dusting off the knees of his jeans. Dean was sweating, his hands shaking as he placed the bag in his trunk, hiding it under a beach towel. Scared shitless, he jumped behind the wheel and sped off down the PCH.

Dean did not plan on stopping until his two hundred thousand landed him on the north shore of Oahu.

Thirty-five

Day Twelve

Jack's four phones rang as one. He considered not picking up, until his digital phone system announced that George Litton was on the line.

"George?"

"Where the fuck is she?"

Jack hung up the phone, too tired to engage. He checked the time; it was eleven o'clock. He'd overslept. The phones rang again, and Jack picked up because his curiosity was piqued. "Who?" he asked.

"Susan, why do you think I'd call, you—the man sleeping with my star—and ask about anyone else. No games, Jack. She had an eight o'clock call time. It's costing me a hundred grand an hour to keep a crew standing around with their dicks in their hands."

"You've got a lot of women on the crew." Jack couldn't help messing with the man. He was an easy mark.

"Jack . . ."

"Okay, I'll call her at the hotel."

"She checked out yesterday. Moved back to the rental. Got tired of the hotel."

"I'll get back to you," Jack said on the move, trying to tamp down his anger for not being kept in the loop.

"Do that, Jack, please."

Jack hung up and dialed the house. It went to voice mail. He left a message for her to call. He called her cell, same deal. He dialed up Tommy, who answered on the first ring.

"Frank Bigelow made bail an hour ago," Tommy said, anger coloring his voice. "I just got the call."

"How the hell?"

"Nobody thought it possible. Bond was set at a million, and some old dowager showed up and put her Brentwood estate up as collateral."

"Have you heard from Susan?"

"She was going to be my next call. Listen, I'm at LAX, but I can grab a later flight."

"Catch your plane, I'm on it." Jack hung up, slid into clean jeans and a black T-shirt, and put on his shoulder rig as he ran out the door.

He dialed Susan's cell again as he raced to her rental home. Summer rain pounded the windshield, and the wipers were beating a rhythm that made Jack's gut churn.

The Mustang slid to a stop in Susan's driveway and he leapt out of the car, and banged on the front door. No answer. The rain was so heavy it obscured all other sounds. He dialed the cell again, and it went to voice mail.

Jack walked calmly back to his car, put it in reverse, and drove down the road.

Seconds later, in a crouched run back to her place, he hugged the privacy shrubs and disappeared around the side of the house.

Jack peered into the kitchen window. It was empty, but a blue light flickered down the hallway, in the living room. Someone was watching television.

Jack edged around the side of the house, and as he neared the living room window, he stopped in his tracks and dropped onto the wet grass.

Frank Bigelow walked by the window, bald-headed, bare-chested, glanced out, and then moved on.

Jack eased back up, his heart pounding. Bigelow should've remained incarcerated—fucking committed—not released by the courts. Jack had to compartmentalize his anger or Susan would be the one to pay.

Susan was sitting in a straight-back chair, wearing the sports gear she wore to the set. Her legs were tied to the legs of the chair and her arms secured with an electrical cord.

Frank Bigelow was nude, hairless, manic, and lost in conversation. He held a sharp knife to his lips, as though searching for the right words, and then swung the blade through the air like a conductor punctuating musical notes.

Off his rocker might be helpful, Jack thought as he moved quickly to the back door, slipped off his shoes and socks, and inserted his key into the dead bolt lock. He dialed Susan's number with one hand, and when the phone started to ring, he turned the key, unlocking the door.

He hung up, took a deep breath, and power-dialed the number again. As soon as the phone rang a second time, he eased the door open, stepped into the kitchen, closing it quickly behind, mindful of the storm's noise. Jack's nerves were taut as piano wire as he slipped deeper into the kitchen, out of view of the hallway.

"He's certainly persistent," Frank said, using his bedroom voice. He sounded like a man who had just had sex. The notion

made Jack sick. He had second thoughts about not taking the
man out when he had the chance.

———

"Look," Susan said, remarkably calm. "Any man willing to risk
his life to spend time with me is the kind of man I'm looking for.
Untie me, and let's get an early lunch at Hal's. Give your paparazzi
friends a little treat. Or you can take a selfie of our first date and
post it on Facebook."

Frank walked in a circle, unabashed in his nakedness; the
flat blade of the knife pushed against his pursed lips again and
stared at himself in the oversized gilded mirror. He touched the
fractured bone in his battered cheek and flinched with pain. His
attention then caught on the reflection of the television that was
muted, but set on HGTV's *Love It or List It*.

Susan kept talking. "I'll explain the situation to Jack, and my
guess is we can get him to drop all charges if he sees we're an item."

"Won't he be jealous?"

"He's Italian, what do you think? But I can control Jack."

That notion agitated Frank, who started pacing as Susan's cell,
set on the coffee table next to his blond wig, started ringing again.
Frank walked over and picked it up, looked at the incoming number. "It's him again. Fucker!" he shouted at the phone.

"So, untie me, Frank," Susan soothed, as if speaking to a lover.
"I'm getting sore sitting like this."

Frank spun, his crazed eyes drilling Susan. "Who do you
think I am? An idiot?!"

The phone rang again.

"Fucker! Stop calling!" And shouted at Susan, "You think I'm
a fool?"

The phone rang again.

"Mother fucker!! Mother fucker!!!"

Jack ran silently down the hallway and in blinding motion burst into the living room, charging straight for Frank Bigelow and his blade.

The knife slashed down as Jack moved in. He clenched Frank's wrist, stopped the blade an inch from his face. Muscling the knife to the side with one hand, Jack unleashed a right that exploded into Frank's shattered cheekbone.

Frank screeched in pain, and the knife skittered across the hardwood floor. Jack hammered a tight punch into the naked man's bony chest, knocking the wind out of his lungs and sending him to the floor gasping.

Jack pounced on his back and pinned the man's waist in place with his knee.

As Frank fought for breath, Jack roughly cuffed his hands behind his back and, using two plastic ties, bound his ankles. Jack muscled Frank up by his neck, with two hands, contemplated strangling the prick, and threw him into a chair.

Jack rushed to Susan, pulled out his Leatherman, and cut the electrical cord that bound her arms and legs.

Susan leapt out of the chair and into Jack's arms. "He was going to kill me." Susan started to unravel, shaking. "Rape me, and then kill me."

Hot, angry tears streamed down her face and drenched the collar of his T-shirt. Jack held her close, keeping one eye on Frank.

Abruptly, Susan pushed away. She sucked in her runny nose and walked deliberately over to Frank, who was still gasping for breath. "You were gonna kill me, Frankie?" Susan pulled back a fist and unleashed a punch with all of her fury. A clean shot to his hooked nose. "You fucker!" she screamed.

Susan stood tall looking down at her abuser, her breaths coming in fits and starts. She wiped her nose with the back of her sleeve as Frank's drool mixed with his own blood from the solid face shot she had delivered. Susan watched with satisfaction as the reality of his capture set in, and cousin Frankie started to whimper.

Disgusted by this whole pornographic parade, Jack tossed a throw pillow over the man's privates. "Cover yourself up, for crissakes."

"I did it," Susan said. "I did it, Jack."

"You did good. It's over, Susan." Jack dialed the LAPD and asked for Lieutenant Gallina, who picked up on the first ring.

"Whadda you want, Bertolino? You calling to gloat?"

"No, Lieutenant, to make your day. I thought you might want to take a run over to Susan's Blake's rental on Palms. In Venice. I've got her stalker here."

"What? I thought he was in county," Gallina said.

"He made bail. Don't ask me."

"Where is he?"

"In her house. Naked. Trussed up like a turkey and ready for delivery. You can nail him for, oh, kidnapping, attempted rape, child pornography, and extortion. Trust me, Lieutenant, he's not going anywhere this time."

Thirty-six

Susan Blake was afraid to spend the night alone, and Jack could hardly blame her. After making sure Susan was comfortable in his bed, Jack drifted off into a rocky, fitful sleep.

Somewhere between finding himself lost in an unfamiliar dreamscape and battling for his life, Jack's cell phone started dinging. He was dragged out of his paranoid dream directly into the eye of the storm.

It was 2:00 a.m.

Terrence Dirk was on the move, and so was Jack.

He slipped into a black T-shirt, black jeans, and black running shoes.

He texted Nick, and then Cruz, who would man the phones and call in the troops if things went wrong with their apprehension. Jack wanted to be the one to drop the net on the brothers, and he wanted to take them alive. Too many loose cannons could lose the war.

Across the bed Susan was out cold. She'd been through enough traumas in the past forty-eight hours; she didn't need to worry about him.

Jack strapped on his shoulder rig and grabbed three extra clips for his Glock. He checked the load on his throwaway gun and secured it to his ankle before lowering the cuff of his jeans.

He wolfed down two Excedrin and a Vicodin with tap water, grabbed his laptop, and was out the door in less than five minutes.

————

Nick Aprea kissed his young wife, Lynn, on the cheek and donned his black clothes and black leather boots, carefully laid out on a chair for just this eventuality.

He checked the load in his Colt, tucked four full clips into his black leather jacket, and headed out.

————

Cruz was sitting on a deck chair in the opened rear cockpit and sprang nervously to his feet when Jack and Nick came roaring into the parking lot. He was hyped, but ready to man up.

————

Jack handed Cruz the laptop while Nick untied the boat. He eyeballed the Colt Defender in Cruz's shoulder rig.

"I don't want you in the line of fire, Cruz."

"I'm good."

"If you hear gunplay, call in the troops. Captain Deak's standing by, ready to deploy if we need backup."

"Let's hope it doesn't go that far," Nick said grimly as he jumped on board, still a bit rocky from his nightly affair with Herradura.

Jack reversed out of the slip and into the channel that fed into the main body of the marina, heading for the breakwaters.

Cruz's eyes were glued to the computer, which sounded a regular beep as it tracked Terrence Dirk's Zodiac. "He's headed straight for Catalina."

Jack nodded as he hit the open sea and throttled forward, teasing the full twenty-eight knots out of the boat's capable engines. "Smooth as silk," he murmured, admiring the power of his new craft. They were a half hour behind Terrence, and Jack wasn't about to lose his prey.

————

"I hope he stopped at In-N-Out Burger like I asked," Toby said, shivering in the damp night air. His eyes were peeled on the shoreline, waiting for a glimpse of Terrence. The moon was a fat three-quarters and gave off enough light to navigate by. The plan was to offload a cache of supplies that should last the brothers a few weeks. At a later date, Terrence would "borrow" the Diskins' yacht, tow the kayak, and drop the two brothers safely south of the border. No one the wiser. That was when the brothers' real odyssey would begin.

"In-N-Out isn't open at two a.m.," Sean pointed out.

"Jack in the Box is."

"Why don't you shut up? We lucked out he could sneak away at all." In another moment his voice had reverted to nice and easy. "So, we know the park rangers check on the herd twice a day. We can use the shower in the campground after their first pass in the morning. One at a time. We'll both feel better."

"Maybe." And then, "I don't know how you developed a taste for this pouch food. Your survivalist shit."

"Quit bitching. It doesn't help."

"I could also do a double quarter pounder and some fries."

Sean refused to continue the conversation. What he was wait-ing on were a few bottles of Macallan.

———

Nick was going over a topographical map of Catalina while Cruz kept his eyes on the computer screen and Jack kept the boat on course.

"He's heading for the south side of the island," Nick said. "If I were in the boys' shoes, I'd be shored up somewhere on the back-side. Less traffic, less tourists, more mountainous terrain. The first stop that looks interesting is a small beach called Shark Har-bor. It looks like there's a way onto the island, with rocky cliffs on both sides."

"If Terrence is offloading supplies, our timing is perfect," Jack said, thinking about his head start. "If he's picking his brothers up and making a run for the border, it's going to be tight."

———

Terrence Dirk slowed the Zodiac to a crawl, and when he was sure the beachhead was empty, he hit the gas with enough force to slide up onto the sandy shore. He drew down on a sound he heard to his left, but pulled his weapon up when he saw Sean step out from behind some scrubs that hid a path up the hillside.

"Sight for sore eyes," Sean said, giving his brother a bear hug. "Let's do this and get you on your way. No sense poking the cops with a stick. We've got enough on our plate."

"I did the best I could with three cops following me around Whole Foods. I had to look like I was shopping for one. But with the dried meat, and fresh food in the cooler, and the extra canned goods I grabbed from the pantry, you should be fine."

Sean looked a question at his brother.

"Oh yeah, and scotch for you, and weed for Toby."

"Outstanding," Sean said as he picked up the first box and headed up the path to their camp.

———

The two cartel operatives pulled their black Town Car into long-term parking and exited the vehicle. The small man ran his hand over the thick scar on his neck as he waited for his partner to open the trunk. They grabbed two heavy knapsacks and walked toward Berth 95 in San Pedro Harbor. They passed Island Express toward Cat Excursions, which was headquartered at the far end of the dock where their Sinaloa handlers had set up transportation to Catalina.

It had been the cartel's idea for the men to travel in the middle of the night, ensuring the element of surprise. Too much time and resources had already been wasted on this family of thieves. The flight took an estimated fifteen minutes, but the paid assassins wanted to strike before daylight.

A tall, trim, blond California surfer type greeted them, standing next to his pride and joy. "Welcome, gentlemen. I'm Captain Rouche."

The modern helicopter was a burnished navy-blue, six-passenger, turbine-powered beauty. "I'll stow your bags in the rear of the craft and we'll make short work of the trip." He reached for the men's knapsacks—and almost lost a hand. "Okay, have it your way. The customer's always right in my business." The captain wisely never asked for his passengers' names, because this flight never happened.

He opened the door, and the two Mexicans were treated to

fine leather seating, bottled water, beer, and wine in a cooler. "Make yourselves comfortable, gentlemen, I'll do my final check and get us under way."

As Captain Rouche closed the door, his smile went cold. He pulled the chocks from under the wheels of the craft, jumped on board, and buckled up for the flight.

The beacon stopped exactly where Nick thought it might. Shark Harbor. As the men passed Sentinel Rock, Jack switched off the lights and throttled back. He stayed as close to the rocky shore as was reasonable, using the cliff face for cover. When he saw a green buoy just yards from the entrance to the cove, Jack used it to tie off his craft. The men sat in silence until their eyes adjusted to the moonlight.

Jack unclipped the inflatable attached to the roof of the cabin cruiser and made the first trip to shore with Nick. As they paddled around the bend, they saw Terrence's Zodiac beached on a tight strip of sand. Nick stepped onto the rocky shore and hurried into the sharp shadows created by the light of the moon, while Jack made the round trip and returned with Cruz. They pulled the inflatable up onto the shore. Using hand signals, Nick pointed out the boot prints in the sand, and then upward to where the Dirk brothers appeared to be hiding.

Keeping an eye out for any movement on the trail, Jack crawled over to the Zodiac. He pulled out the blade on his Leatherman and punctured both sides of the thick rubber float, rendering the craft useless.

Nick and Cruz ran at a crouch across the small sandy beach and flattened themselves against the cliff, followed by Jack. "When we get near the top, I want you to hang back," Jack whispered to Cruz, who nodded stiffly, hoping his nerves wouldn't get the better of him.

They tried to remain silent, but as the men worked their way up the ravine, Nick's boot slipped on a loose patch. He cursed under his breath at the sound of gravel sliding down the ravine. The climb was nearly vertical; the men moved in and out of shadow—the path was rocky but accessible. Nick stopped to catch his breath at the first switchback.

"We want them alive," Jack said. "I want both of you alive. Let's do this."

The men continued their ascent, and as they stepped around the second switchback, a bullet thwacked into the rock face ten feet above their location.

"Shit," Cruz yelped. "They fucking know we're here."

Jack held his finger up to his mouth, signaling his young charge to silence. "We're good."

Jack, Nick, and Cruz proceeded with more caution, hugging the cliff. All they could hear was the sound of the Pacific breaking against the rocky cliff face below.

"They blind-fired," Jack whispered. "They know we're here, but they don't know where we are." He leaned in toward Nick. "If they shoot again, lay down suppression rounds, and when I make it to the top, I'll cover you. If I make it to the top, clean, you'll know when to make an appearance." And then to Cruz, "It's time to call in the troops."

Jack unholstered his Glock 9mm and continued the climb.

Cruz pulled out his cell and sent a text of their coordinates to the LAPD, along with a 911 signal to Captain Deak. He could only pray the troops would arrive in a timely fashion, armed for bear.

———

"We are so fucked," Sean said to Terrence in a tight whisper. "Who do you think it is?"

"It's got Bertolino's stench all over it," Terrence said, eyes narrowed.

"Fuck him! He won't walk away this time," Sean rasped.

Toby ran to the cliff's end and sent a volley of bullets raining down on the crew. Toby jumped back wild-eyed when a bullet nicked his cheek and blood started to spill down his neck.

"Save your rounds," Terrence said in a thick whisper. "Let them think we're on the run. When they breach the summit, we unload with everything we've got."

The three brothers stood shoulder to shoulder like gunslingers. Their faces pale in the moonlight. Terrence in the middle, his red hair whipping in the breeze that rolled off the Pacific. Sean stood to his right, Toby to his left. Three pistols leveled at the summit.

Thirty-seven

A compact canyon oak had seeded itself near the summit of the cliff. Darkness was Jack's ally as he grabbed it and carefully worked his way to the left of the pathway, out of the expected line of fire, and crawled to the top. He peered over the edge at the Dirks' location. The herd of buffalo was in silhouette, bunched in an undulating, tightening group behind the Dirks. An eight-hundred-pound bull with a broken horn stomped the ground.

"Terrence, Sean, Toby . . . Bertolino here," he shouted over the grazing field. "It's over. You're on an island, your boat's scuttled; the LAPD is in the air. There's only one good choice and one way out."

"Son of a bitch," Terrence spit as he signaled his brothers to spread out, widening their circumference and shooting range.

Nick and Cruz used Jack's distraction to move rapidly up the path.

"How many are you?" Terrence shouted.

"You know me, Red, I'm a lone wolf. Drop your weapons and live to hire a good lawyer," Jack shouted back. "Terrence, you're fairly clean at this juncture. I guess the real question is whether your brothers will let you leave the island alive."

"Fuck you, Bertolino," Sean's voice echoed in the damp night.

"That you, Sean? A tougher road for you, but I think it's brother Toby who's going to take the major hit. But who knows? Do the right thing, get the right jury, you'll do time, but you're smart guys, you can play the system. Your call."

"Who do you have with you, Jack?" Terrence shouted, not buying the lone-wolf routine.

"Clock's ticking, Terrence. I need you to drop your weapons and come out with your hands raised. And I need your answer now."

"I got your answer right here, Jack," Toby snarled as he raised his pistol and fired a single shot that echoed in the night.

Terrence nodded, and the Dirk brothers took one step forward and attacked. Three automatic weapons spit fire, throwing flames into the darkness, chewing up the hillside in the direction of Jack's voice.

Jack dove for cover, flattened against the hillside, eating dirt as rounds divoted the rocky soil inches from his body.

———

The herd of buffalo, led by the broken-horned monster, started to shuffle, disjointed at first, spinning in place, and pawing, and then running slowly in a looping, circular pattern in the grazing field until the bull abruptly changed course and pounded down the rise, away from the intense firearm assault, in the direction of the campground followed by the herd, a hundred and fifty strong.

———

Jack glanced skyward. The sound of gunfire was obscured by a sudden calamitous windstorm kicked up by the massive rotors of a helicopter as it circled the area, looking for a landing site near the campground.

"That's not the Coast Guard," Jack shouted to his men.

The roar of the chopper and the spit of automatic weapons fire sent the buffalo into a frenzied, panicked stampede.

The monster with the ragged horn changed course. He pounded away from the thrumming rotors of the helicopter, followed by the herd, thundering straight back toward the Dirk brothers' position and Jack's team.

Jack rapid fired at the Dirks, laying down suppression rounds. He shouted to Nick and Cruz. "Separate their line of fire!" The men complied, dashing over the rise, finding safety behind trees, and boulders, and shadows, just below the ridgeline.

The Dirks were breathing hard as they slapped in fresh clips. They knew Jack had support, but were unsure of the number of men and guns. Bullets were pinging off rocks, dirt, and scrub from multiple directions now.

"If I had my fucking .22, we could sit tight and I'd pick them off," Toby said. "There's only one way in."

"We've got bigger problems," Terrance shouted, dreading the answer. "Who's in the chopper, and why are they here?"

Sean signaled down the slope. The brothers turned to see the herd pounding in their direction and ran for cover.

Captain Rouche yelled over the sound of the rotors, in the cabin of his navy-blue helicopter, "This is insane. There's no way I can set her down."

The tallest of the cartel's men shoved the barrel of an AK into the pilot's neck. "We go down," he shouted. "One way or the other."

With cold steel pressed against his neck, Rouche did a tight, dangerous spinning maneuver, and started to lower the chopper onto the middle of the campground. "You no move until we say," the short man screamed. The pilot tightened his jaw, and set the bird down.

The cartel operatives, brandishing their AK-47s, leapt out of the cabin and duckwalked until they cleared the spinning rotors. The short man trained his automatic weapon on the Dirks who were shadows on the move, and let loose with a series of short bursts. He strafed a buffalo and then a second. Both huge beasts thundered to the ground, dead on the spot.

The bull snorted and stomped the earth as the herd spooked, scattering in all directions. But the sound, and the whirling rotors of the navy-blue chopper, kicking up dust and grass, kept the giant beasts running in crazed patterns in the natural bowl of the grazing field, making it all but impossible for the cartel killers to get off a clean shot.

———

Jack watched as the melee of wild beasts and armed gunmen forced the Dirks to separate. The apprehension of the brothers was spinning out of control, but Jack took the moment to charge from his elevated position and reconnoiter with Nick and Cruz, who was white faced but alive. "They're shooting the fucking animals," Cruz cried.

"They are animals." Nick shouted from his position. "When were you going to tell me about the buffalo, Jack?" Nick asked, not expecting an answer.

"It looks like the cartel enforcers figured out the play," Jack shouted. "They're after the Dirks, but they'll kill anything that moves, so stay lively. Shoot first, ask questions later. I'll cut toward the water tanks. Cruz, you stay back by the path, make sure you're well covered, and only shoot if someone runs in your direction." And to Nick, "Flank on the left and try to work your way behind the brothers."

A second helicopter thundered overhead. "Captain Deak's here," Jack shouted and pointed skyward with his 9mm.

"Yes! Fuck!" Cruz shouted as a thousand-candle spotlight snapped on and crisscrossed the action, lighting the battlefield like a klieg light at a movie premier.

"Can you get him on the horn?" Jack asked. Cruz grabbed his cell, dialed, and handed it to Jack. "It's a cluster fuck down here, Deak. Some cartel scumbags arrived on scene, gunning for the Dirks who stole their drugs. Automatic weapons, AKs, watch your approach."

Jack gave the cell phone back to Cruz. "Let's take 'em down, boys," and the men split off running.

———

The scarred commando raised his AK and rapid-fired metal-piercing rounds into the air trying to down the Coast Guard bird that, already alerted, veered up and out of harm's way.

But then the little man saw that the rotors of his own chopper had started whipping again, gaining velocity, ready to lift and escape, leaving him and his partner without an exit strategy.

He dodged a charging bull, screamed, "*Chinga tu madres pendejo!*" and unloaded his banana clip of high-velocity AK rounds in a lethal spray across the body of the navy-blue craft, piercing the polished metal and finding the chopper's turbine engine.

Captain Rouche, the chopper pilot, fought to steady his craft. He grimaced as the high-velocity rounds pierced the skin of his chopper and his cabin filled with smoke. The stick shook violently in his hand as he lifted the helicopter off the ground, leaking fuel and smoke. Rouche could see the buffalos stampeding below and the Coast Guard helicopter above. He uttered a silent prayer as his chopper vibrated violently, reversed direction, and went into an uncontrollable death spin.

The small cartel gunman ran for his life.

The concussive explosion tore Rouche and the chopper to pieces, dropping shards of metal and liquid fire to the ground, revealing the battlefield in its lurid light.

Thirty-eight

The mushroom cloud billowed thick white smoke against the black night sky.

Captain Deak's chopper, caught in the shock wave, wobbled violently, and then pulled up and circled away.

Jack could feel the heat of the flaming fuel on his face. Shrapnel rained down on the war zone. Smoke melding with dust choked the combatants and beasts as the men ducked for cover. Jack took off running. A man on the hunt.

———

Sean ran to cover Terrence, who was exchanging rounds with Nick, but was forced behind a boulder as five buffalo pounded in his direction, horns lowered, and then veered off at the last second, leaving him spitting dust. Sean was unaware that a cartel killer was close on his trail.

Toby saw the small gunman stalking Sean, but was too far away, and the killer, too close to his brother to stop the inevitable. "Nooooo!" he screamed on the run. "Sean!" Sean's head snapped in the direction of his brother's voice as the cartel assassin sprang from shadow, and in one violent slash, pulled a serrated knife across Sean's neck, nearly severing his head.

Sean dropped to his knees, bleeding out. He clutched his neck as blood streamed through his fingers. The short killer grunted as he spun and plunged his knife into Sean's stomach, ready to slice him from his gut to his heart.

Toby closed the distance and emptied his 9mm into the cartel enforcer's body. Tears flooded Toby's vision as his bullets tore the small man apart.

Terrence heard the commotion, fired at Nick, and ran from cover. He sucked in a ragged breath when he saw Sean's desecrated body. He fired two rounds into the assassin's face, and then Toby stripped the AK off the dead man.

Terrence grabbed Toby around the shoulder and pulled him tight. "I love you, brother." His blue eyes blazed. "We split up, we stay alive. I love you, Toby. To the grave."

Toby nodded, slammed home a fresh clip into his Python, and slid the strap of the AK-47 around his neck.

One of Nick's bullets ricocheted against a granite boulder sending shards flying. Terrence moved toward the water tanks, Toby ran deeper into the chaparral.

A black and silver LAPD chopper joined the Coast Guard bird in the night sky. Its high-intensity light joined the Coast Guard's, raking the battlefield. Its powerful speaker squealed to life. A disembodied voice boomed, "Drop your weapons. Drop to the ground with your hands behind your head. This is the LAPD. Drop your weapons, and drop to the ground, hands behind your head."

Undaunted by the ghastly scene, the LAPD pilot set the police chopper down next to the burning hulk, its door swung opened, and its SWAT team deployed.

Jack caught sight of Terrence leapfrogging from one shadow to the next, making his way toward the rusted water tanks, and followed, staying in cover.

Terrence planned to make his exit beyond the tanks, on the far side of the cliff, where a tight trail led back down to the narrow beachhead. He'd hijack the boat Jack arrived in and make his escape.

Jack's attention shifted as he saw the second cartel enforcer tracking Terrence from behind. Jack knew he had to take the killer out. The wild card was making his apprehension impossible.

The gunman raised his automatic weapon.

Jack stepped from cover, aimed his 9mm in Terrence's direction, and fired twice.

Terrence thought the bullets were meant for him until he turned to see two dark patches blossom on the cartel soldier's chest. The killer staggered back, losing consciousness, wildly squeezing off a full clip of high-intensity rounds. The AK spit flames and the bullets arced across the rusted water tower, sending a spray of water onto Terrence. The cartel hit man toppled to the ground.

Terrence spun in place and fired his 9mm at Jack, who had just saved his life. Jack dove for cover as Terrence's weapon dry-clicked. He ejected the magazine and grabbed a full clip from his pocket. He was about to slam it home when Jack, hell-bent on ending the carnage, charged.

Jack closed the distance in a heartbeat and bulldogged his shoulder into Terrence Dirk's abdomen, slamming him against the water tank. As the tall, thin redhead blanched, and spouts of water streamed from the tank drenching them both, Jack pulled back a fist and smashed him in the face. Terrence's head bounced and echoed off the metal tank, but the concussive blow didn't stop him from throwing a sizzling uppercut, which rocked Jack on his heels and into the path of the stampeding herd.

Jack dodged one charging buffalo, brushing against the flank of another beast that threatened to knock him down. He caught his balance and stepped clear of the onslaught, straight into Terrence's fist. Jack shook off the blow and countered with a lethal punch of his own. His fist hammered the side of Terrence's neck, staggering him and sending him down onto one knee. The main body of the herd was closing in fast. Jack dove out of the way of the massive hooves and rolled heavily on the hard pack.

Terrence tried to rise to his feet, but Jack grabbed him by the back of his shirt and whipped him back down, followed by a fist that flattened Terrence's nose. Blood splattered his pale face.

———

Nick was stalking Toby, exchanging shots on the move. "LAPD! Drop your weapon, Toby, and you can walk out of here alive," he shouted. A bullet twanged past Nick's head and he return-fired multiple rounds, forcing Toby to take cover.

Nick slammed in a full clip.

Toby stepped from behind a tree, calmed his breath, and fired his last bullet.

Nick took a solid punishing round to the shoulder that knocked him back against a rock facing. "Fuck! I'm hit!" he yelled alerting

Cruz, wincing in pain, but he didn't go down. Nick pushed away from the granite and charged Toby, who raised the AK, flashed an ugly grin, and fired. The automatic weapon jammed.

Cruz stepped from behind a boulder, his 9mm pointed at Toby, prepared to take him down, but couldn't get off a clean shot without hitting Nick.

Nick lowered his good shoulder, and slammed into Toby like a defensive linebacker before falling to the ground himself.

Toby stumbled backward on the uneven rocky soil, his arms flailing as he tried to maintain his footing. The AK went flying.

The eight-hundred-pound bull with the jagged horn, spooked by the thunderous downwash of the LAPD chopper, was determined to make somebody pay. He charged like a locomotive and smashed into Toby's back.

Toby went airborne and slammed down hard onto the ground unconscious.

The bull lowered its splintered horn, snorted, bucked, and charged again, going for the kill.

Nick knew he was vulnerable and summoned the strength to one-arm drag himself out of harm's way.

Cruz, freaked, ran from cover, grabbed Toby by the scruff of his collar, and dragged him out of the path of the beast's deadly horns and hooves, saving him by seconds.

The bull reared its massive head, spittle flying, ground thumping, and then turned and thundered back down the hill followed by his wild herd.

Cruz rolled Toby over and plastic-cuffed his wrists, and then his ankles. He pulled out his phone and speed-dialed the Coast Guard chopper, shouting, "Man down! LAPD detective Nick Aprea has sustained a bullet wound. Police officer down!"

Cruz dropped to his knees beside Nick. "Shit, man, how bad is it?"

"I got hit good," Nick said, his face devoid of color.

"Man down! Man down!" Cruz shouted across the battle-field to anyone in earshot, praying for help as the sun crested the horizon.

———

Jack and Terrence were lost in a pitched mano a mano battle.

The LAPD had arrived on scene and ordered the men to hold up, but the combatants weren't listening. The SWAT team stepped back and let the drama play out.

Both men, bloodied and fatigued, continued to throw punches.

Jack hammered a hard right into Terrence's face for the trail of bodies the Dirk brothers had left behind in their greedy wake.

He pounded one of Terrence's eyes shut and hammered his nose again. Jack's own blood streamed down his cheek from an open gash on his forehead, blinding him in one eye.

Terrence was in a primal battle for his life. He saw an opening and threw a haymaker, hitting Jack on the side of his bandaged head, staggering him, and then he swung and nailed him again.

Jack refused to go down. He gasped for air and rocketed a punch from his heels, connecting with Red's jaw.

Terrence's head whiplashed back. The tall, thin man reeled, swayed, and then crumbled to the ground.

Jack, staggered over, reached down, and yanked Terrence up by his bloody, wet, matted red hair. He pulled his face close and growled, "They told me you were the brains of the operation. Go figure."

Jack shoved Terrence Dirk toward a young SWAT officer who spun him around and snapped on the cuffs.

Captain Deak's chopper set down next to the LAPD's. For a moment, all the men could hear were the sounds of receding hooves pounding down the grassy plains in the distance, as the massive rotors whipped to a stop. The sun had breached the horizon, and the black sky was melding with steaks of orange and blue.

The calm was soon joined by the muffled screams of Toby Dirk, who started struggling with two members of the SWAT team. Jack watched as they dragged Toby, his legs still bound, toward their chopper. He took some joy when Toby tried to head butt one of the cops, and they dropped him facedown on the hard pack.

Jack heard Cruz's cry and ran across the grazing field. When he realized Nick had suffered a gunshot wound, he ripped off his T-shirt, bunched it up, and compressed the ragged bullet hole in Nick's shoulder. Nick had lost a lot of blood and was in danger of going into shock.

"When's the last time you washed that dirty rag?" Nick mustered in an angry rasp.

"Eighty-nine. It's a collector's item." And then to Cruz, "You just suffered a trial by fire."

"No shit," he said irreverently.

"You passed the test."

"Fuck. Him," Nick croaked. "I'm the one who's shot."

Two Coast Guard medics ran from Deak's chopper carrying a military evacuation stretcher and a satchel of first aid gear.

"Yeowww," Nick groaned as one of the medics cut off his shirt and staunched the flow of blood, while his partner started a field IV drip.

"Go easy," Jack cautioned. "That's a police officer in your care."

Once Nick was stabilized, the two men lifted the field stretcher.

"Hasta la bye bye," Nick said before letting his head drop heavily down on the stretcher.

"We'll meet you at the hospital," Jack said, running with Cruz, alongside, as the medics hoofed it back toward their helicopter. Plans had been made for Captain Deak to fly the wounded detective to St. John's, where the emergency room had been alerted of his imminent arrival and doctors were standing by.

––––––

Jack and Cruz stepped away from the Coast Guard chopper as Nick's stretcher was secured, the doors closed, and the bird lifted off.

They surveyed the carnage. Dead bodies, dead animals, the smoldering carcass of the destroyed chopper. They knew it would take days to fully assess the damage.

"We did okay," Jack said to Cruz. And then, "I've got to call Nick's wife."

Cruz handed him his cell. "Oh, boss," he said, and Jack turned back, "your head's bleeding like a stuck pig."

Jack looked resigned as he touched the side of his stitched head and came up with a handful of blood. He wiped it on his jeans.

A young cop handed Jack an LAPD T-shirt. He thanked him, shrugged into it as he stepped away, dialed, and got Nick's wife on the line.

"Hi, Lynn, no, he's okay. He's been shot, but Lynn, the EMTs said he wasn't in danger. . . . I know, if he wasn't in danger, he wouldn't have gotten shot. . . . Shoulder. They're flying him to St. John's. Alive and snarky as hell . . . I'm sure . . . I'll see you there when he's out of surgery."

Jack clicked off and watched as Terrence was walked, and Toby, bleeding and in shock, dragged, across the killing field to the waiting LAPD helicopter and their short flight to the mainland and incarceration. Jack was weary, disgusted, and angry as he contemplated the Dirk brothers. Entitled young men who could stand shoulder to shoulder with upper-crust society and murder six people in a four-day killing spree. They were responsible for another four deaths after the fact, and had to bury one of their own. And for what?

Greed and retribution.

Epilogue

Jack was keeping the tone light for Nick's sake, but he was worried. Nick was propped up in a hospital bed at St. John's. His left shoulder and arm were set in a solid plaster cast. Only his fingers were exposed, and they were swollen and stained orange.

Cruz stood off to the side, haggard, in shocked silence. The battle with the Dirks, and the cartel enforcers, was more than he had signed on for, and he was having second thoughts about his career path.

Three IV drips hung from metal contraptions and emitted beeps at odd times. A monitor tracking Nick's heartbeat sent a green neon line oscillating across a screen.

His face was pale, his eyes glazed, and as good as the pain medication was, the big man was clearly hurting.

Jack stood bedside, wearing a fresh T-shirt and jeans. He'd showered on the boat, cleaned his wounds as best as he could, and ran to the hospital as soon as he'd moored.

"Doc Stein said I should find another line of work. He restitched my head, put in eight over my eye, checked my prostate, and I'm good to go," he said.

The zaftig nurse who'd attended to Jack a few days earlier

barked a laugh. She unplugged an empty bag that was emitting a solid tone now, switched it out for a full bag of antibiotics, and reset the timer. The IV started beeping again.

She looked from Jack to Nick and clucked, shaking her head. "You both need to find something new to do with your lives," and then to Jack and Cruz, "Don't stay too long. My next ex-husband needs his beauty sleep." And she was out the door.

Nick wasn't amused. Jack handed him a cup of ice chips to keep him hydrated. Nick grabbed it with his one good hand. "Now what?" he grumbled.

Jack grabbed the cup and placed a few chips into his friend's mouth. "The good news, it's your left shoulder."

Nick sucked on the ice chips and nodded his head; Jack placed a few more in. Finally, "But it's attached to my left hand."

"Yeah?"

"So I do a lot of *things*, primarily with my left hand."

"Hold a gun?"

"No."

"Write?"

"No."

"Eat?"

"No. Just think about it," Nick said. His eyes blinked closed and then opened again with a start.

"So," Jack said, "Detective Wald called to check on you. Sent his best, owes you one for making him look good."

"It's the fucking dog he should be thanking. Oh, and possibly you."

Jack deflected, "Sacramento is filing paperwork for the Dirk brothers. Said Ricky J is a first-degree murder case, it's in their jurisdiction, and the boys belong to them."

"DA's probably up for reelection," Nick said, drifting again. His eyes snapped back open. "Thanks for calling Lynn. I made her take the baby home."

"No problem."

"She blames you."

Jack had to laugh. It made Nick chuckle and the pain made his face grimace, but the light moment was worth it. "Captain stopped by, they're bumping me up a pay grade. They think I keep solving these high-profile cases. Thank you for that." Nick's eyes flickered.

"Hey," Jack said, "how come you took a bullet, and you look better than me?"

Nick tried to come up with a pithy comeback and fell asleep.

Jack placed the cup of ice chips back on the metal tray, nodded to Cruz, and winked at the nurse as they walked out of the ward.

Hospitals are for the sick, Jack thought as he and Cruz jumped into his Mustang and drove away.

———

Jack was standing in the men's room at Hal's Bar and Grill, trying to freshen up. A wave of nausea and dizziness rolled over him like a storm cloud, threatening to take him down. Jack grabbed both sides of the sink until the feeling passed. He appraised himself in the bathroom mirror and hardly recognized the face staring back.

The butterfly suture protecting the stitches over his eyebrow couldn't hide the swelling. Jack's eye had gone from a yellowish green to a dark purple. The new stiches in the side of his head were itching, but his head had survived the trauma of the fistfight. All and all, Jack thought, he looked, and felt, like hell.

He walked carefully down the stairs and slid into the comfort of his favorite booth with its unobstructed view of the entire room.

Arsinio, the sage waiter he was, placed a Stoli on the rocks in front of his friend, and Jack nodded in approval. His bruised knuckles hurt as he picked up the glass, and the vodka burned some going down, but the burn turned to warmth, and the warmth would jack up the Vicodin and stanch some of his physical pain.

Jack had placed a call to Chris, wanting to give him a heads-up before his son witnessed the carnage on the local news. Jack told him not to worry, and Chris told him to find a new line of work. He also shared how proud he was that his dad had put away the killers. Jack got a bit sloppy on the phone. His son's stamp of approval meant the world to him.

Jeannine and Jeremy had arrived at Stanford acting like teenage lovers, but they were working very hard not to impose on Chris's personal life. Jack wondered how long that would last. At least Jeremy's claiming back his woman meant that the trip to Palo Alto was only a visit.

Jack promised to drive up north when the dust had settled.

He had an early date with Susan, but was anticipating some kind of emotional fallout. Jack wasn't too adept at reading women, but he felt it in his bones. And his bones were sensitive after the abuse they'd suffered the past few weeks.

As if on cue, Susan Blake walked through the front door. She waved to the bartenders, making their nights, and turned heads as she glided through the room. She buzzed Jack's cheek and slid into the booth sitting opposite. Arsinio arrived on the spot and placed a glass of Benziger in front of his favorite client.

"Why, thank you, Arsinio. That's very thoughtful."

"We're all just glad you're okay, Susan."

"We both know who we have to thank for that."

Arsinio looked at Jack, his eyes a little moist, and made himself scarce.

"Hah, you're on the heavy sauce?" Susan took a hearty drink of her red wine.

"It's been that kind of week."

"You look better than expected."

"Huh. I'll take that as a compliment."

Susan smiled. "How's Nick doing?"

"He lost a lot of blood. The bullet splintered his clavicle and tore up his muscle. The Doc says three to six months of physical therapy and he should be back on his game. Real violence . . . very different from Hollywood's version."

Susan, caught in a rare loss for words, clinked her glass against Jack's, took a controlled sip, and nailed him with her gray-blue eyes. His heart skipped a beat somewhere in that sequence of events, and when she finger-combed her chestnut hair behind one ear, she looked ravishing to Jack. And he didn't know if he'd ever used the word.

"So," Susan said, "I had a conversation with Tommy about getting me out of my contract for *Blond Cargo*."

"You're going back to New York?" A statement, not a question.

Susan smiled, nodded knowingly. "After the shoot. After we wrap *Done Deal*. I'd never leave George high and dry. But it's all been . . . way too much, Jack. I realized that I couldn't move forward without letting go of my past. And that's going to take some honest, intensive work."

Jack nodded in agreement. "It's time to take care of you now," he said thoughtfully. "You've had all these bastards exploiting you. I like what I'm hearing, Susan. It's time to do some healing. What did Tommy have to say?"

"He recused himself." Susan's eyes crinkled into a smile. "Said it might cost you your back end money, and he'd never do that to a friend."

Jack wasn't engaged in a one-up contest, but had to admit it felt good his old friend had his back. "What did you say?"

"I fired him." Susan scrunched up her face like a child. "It's nothing personal, Jack, but I didn't get where I am playing second banana. I'll save that for my fifties, thank you very much."

"I don't think second banana is in your DNA."

"You're a lover, Jack." Susan took another sip of wine. "So, what do you think? You want to go home and get crazy tonight?"

Jack gave that question the thought it deserved, but already knew the answer. "You're putting it on me?" he said wryly.

Susan raised her eyebrows and smiled, cutting him to the quick.

Jack matched her, smile for smile. "You knew I wouldn't say yes."

"I did, Jack. No hard feelings. I owe you my life. I literally owe you my life. And I will be your friend forever." Her eyes got wet, and she dabbed them with the cloth napkin.

Jack finished his cocktail and said, "That's good enough for me."

Susan took a deep breath and they shared an intimate moment. Then she finished off the wine in one tilt of her beautiful head, wiped her mouth with the back of her hand, leaned across the table, and kissed him square on the lips.

"You are the man, Jack Bertolino."

Susan Blake slid out of the booth, walked slowly through the dining room and out the front door without ever looking back.

Arsinio arrived at the table and dropped off a fresh Stoli rocks and a dish of fried calamari with spicy tartar sauce, then made himself scarce.

Jack thought about show business, and the capricious nature of Hollywood. The jury was still out. His mind drifted to Leslie Sager and he felt some melancholy, but wasn't sure what that was all about. Suddenly, Jack smiled and raised his Stoli in a silent toast.

Through Hal's front windows, Jack watched as George Litton's stretch limo pulled away from the curb and disappeared into the night.

Acknowledgments

I want to thank Karen Hunter for opening the door to this great adventure, and Brigitte Smith and the entire team at Simon & Schuster for all of their support. Editor extraordinaire, John Paine, you did it again. Many thanks to Leslie Abell, my friend and lawyer. And heartfelt thanks to Gordon Dawson, Bob Marinaccio, Diane Lansing, Deb Schwab, and Annie George, for taking the time out of their busy schedules to read my work and share their thoughts. I'm grateful.